Spore Press

TAPE
RUNNERS

TAPE RUNNERS

By

Pierre Leveque

SPORE PRESS LLC
LITTLE ROCK

TAPE
RUNNERS

TAPE RUNNERS
Pierre Leveque
Copyright Pierre Leveque 2013
Published by Spore Press

All rights reserved.

ISBN: 978-0-6159211-4-3

SPORE PRESS LLC
6916 Incas Drive, North Little Rock, AR 72116, USA

PRINTING HISTORY
Spore Press eBook/ December 2013
Spore Press Paperback / December 2013

For information, address: Spore Press Marketing
6916 Incas Drive, North Little Rock, AR 72116.

http://www.sporepress.com

Spore Press Books are published by Spore Press LLC
SPORE PRESS and the "Spore" design are trademarks of
Spore Press

Dedication

This book is dedicated to my father - Christian Leveque - a true adventurer who passed away shortly before the completion of this novel.

1

The car—a tweaked up Nissan 350Z with chrome Barracuda rims and glowing blue LED underlights—came to a stop outside the sliding doors of a Citibank, in an obscure cookie-cutter industrial grit-city in West Germany. The car stood there, its sports exhaust trembling, the 30 mm lowered suspension making it fearful of the curb. A full minute went by, the tinted windows slick with rain and vibrating with sonic pulses.

The front passenger door swung open and a scene kid, hair dyed black, layered and streaked with neon highlights, wearing tight-fitting pants and a fur-lined jacket with colored patches on it, got out and stood on the curb looking up and down the empty street. He walked over to the bank, inserted a credit card in the slot and the sliding doors opened. He went inside, to the first cash distributor, and withdrew €500 from a student savings account.

He returned to the Nissan, climbing in the front passenger seat, and a blonde girl, wearing horn-rimmed glasses with pink frames and a yellow scarf around her neck, tousled his hair as he got in.

"Fick dich!" The boy shoved her away.

She laughed, then said, "Did you get the money?"

"I got the money. Now shut up and drive."

From the backseat, an albino-black kid with shortly

cropped wooly white hair and white eyebrows leaned forward and said, "You make a right here, under the bridge."

The girl nodded her head, her hands tensed on the air-leather grips of the sports steering wheel. They drove under a heavy rail overpass and turned onto a tree-lined residential street, and came upon a series of concrete blocks with walled gardens and shelf balconies.

"Pull over here," said the albino, and the girl parked the Nissan in front of a green recycling dumpster, at the foot of one of the apartment blocks.

They were in a working-class neighborhood, as could be told by the graffiti-tagged vans and lower walls. GISMO. BASE. SCHLOSS. A group of hoodies were idling by a bus stop, clinging beer bottles and chatting loudly. They clocked the car, too posh a ride to be from the neighborhood, and one of the lot—a thin, bronzed foreigner, in a black Adidas vest and sporting a white cap—spat on the ground and walked up to them.

"Hey Toby, what's up?"

He gave a lazy handslap to the albino. "Who are they?" he asked, motioning to the other two.

"Just some friends," shrugged Toby. "Have you seen Lucky Luke?"

"Not since Friday," said the hoodie. He spat again on the ground and rubbed the spittle in with his trainers. "What are you all up to?"

"I got to see Lukas—"said Toby. "He isn't home and he won't answer his handy. He owes me money."

"Naja. Lukas owes everybody something. He's always in debt, man."

"Look, you see him around, you tell him I came by, right?"

The foreigner shrugged, *sure*.

"Watch the car, right? We're going inside."

The hoodie shrugged again and headed back to his posse. Toby motioned to the two kids to follow him. He went to the entrance of the first block and rang the buzzer. There was a moment's silence, and then a voice came tinny over the intercom.

"Ja, who is it?"

"Janko man, it's Toby, open up."

The buzzer sounded and Toby pushed the door open. The posh bird was looking anxiously at her car. The scene boy was rubbing his hands together with excitement.

"Come on," said Toby, stepping inside.

They went up to the third floor, and on the landing stood a young man with dark, curly hair and a sunbed tan. He was in his late twenties. He went back into the apartment, without saying a word, and Toby and the two others followed him inside.

Toby clicked the door shut, and the guy pointed to an imitation leather sofa and told them to sit down. His apartment was sparsely furnished as if he had just moved in. There were cardboard boxes and cartons of take-out food everywhere. Toby sat down and kicked his feet up on a rickety glass-and-metal coffee table. He patted the sofa and the boy sat down beside him and the girl sat next to the boy, her arms wrapped around him and her chin resting on his shoulder.

Janko was wearing a red soccer jersey with PANTELIC 9 written across the back. A flat screen TV was perched on a low table, tuned in to Formula 1 racing. The sound was muted.

"Well don't be so fucking shy," said Janko pleasantly. "Tell me your names."

"Uh… I'm Matthias," said the boy.

"Heike," mumbled the girl.

"And I'm the famous Janko," Janko said, with a broad grin. He clapped his hands together. "Who wants a drink or two?"

Toby interrupted him, "I can't stay long, man. I've got to find Lukas."

"OK, just one drink then," smiled Janko. "Red vodka?" He stared at his visitors and they nodded in confirmation, and he went into the kitchen and they heard him tinkering around in the cupboards and fridge. He returned with a bottle and three glasses. He filled them up and held them out, one by one.

"Show them the stuff," said Toby.

"Ah, you want the stuff…" Janko set the bottle down on the glass coffee table. He lifted a finger and said, "I'll be right back."

He padded over to another room and returned with a black portable jewelry case with a combination lock. He set the safe down on the coffee table and kneeled on the carpet next to it. He spun it around so the combo was facing him. He turned the dial and the case clicked open.

Janko reached into the case and withdrew a 60 mm glass petri dish, closed the case and placed the dish gently on top.

Matthias and Heike leaned forward and saw what looked like a dozen or so colored, wafer-thin blotters.

"So lemme see… we've got red, green, and blue." He indicated the distinctive colors. "Red is *Titanic*. Green is for *Triassic Park*. Blue is *Hydroworla*."

"How poetic," murmured Toby.

"Thanks. So… they are going for 250 a piece, yes? You give me the money, and you can choose one each."

Heike whispered something in Matthias' ear and he said, "No fucking way…"

"What was that?" Janko asked the girl. "It's all right. You can ask."

"You… wouldn't have Dirty Dancing?" the girl inquired.

Toby burst out laughing, spitting up a mouthful of vodka. Janko shook his head, "No," he said simply. "This is already a very good selection. In two to three weeks I get some Tarantino, and then maybe some Clint Eastwood—Dirty Harry or a Western, I don't know—but to answer your question again, no, I have nothing with Patrick Swayze. I am sorry, but I think your boyfriend will be relieved."

Toby guffawed and slapped his knee.

"So—what's it going to be?" Janko asked them.

Matthias looked at his girlfriend. "Please, not *Titanic*."

He saw her face drop. She removed her glasses. "What's Hydroworld?"

"Big adventure production—with Kevin Costner," Toby explained patiently. "Kind of a *Mad Max* on water, if you will."

"Is it any good?"

"Of course," said Janko, looking a bit insulted. "They are all good, or I wouldn't be selling them. But, if you want to try the same one, I suggest you take something you both know. Or, if you like you can watch the original film beforehand and get familiar with it. It helps. Of course you can also go in with no prior knowledge, but this tends to be very confusing for my clients."

"Not *Titanic*," Matthias pleaded.

The girl bit her lip then said, "You want to go for *Triassic Park*?"

"Spielberg is always a good choice," counseled Janko.

"Wait just a minute," cut in Matthias. "What the hell kind of cheap sweatshop imitations are you trying to pawn off on us? Shouldn't this be *Jurassic Park*? And what's the story with this Hydro-shit? Don't you mean *Waterworld*?"

Janko glanced uneasily at Toby, cleared his throat and said, "Look—this is kind of an alternate version. The lab that makes these, they do this with all the tapes…"

"What for?"

Janko shrugged, "I believe it was initially intended as a means to evade copyright issues with the film studios. See, these tapes were developed by a major entertainment corporation, but the project was swept under the rug after some, hehe, setbacks with the product testing protocol."

"What setbacks?" Matthias asked suspiciously. "What's wrong with them?"

"Nothing. Jesus God, you're a curious little fucker," grumbled Janko. "You kids are getting more and more picky. If you aren't interested don't waste my time—I'm a very busy man."

"OK, OK," Matthias relented. "They aren't dangerous are they?"

"Healthy as tapwater," Janko swiftly reassured him.

Matthias nodded slowly. "Well, if they're as good as Toby says, I wouldn't want to miss out on the thrill. Let's go for it."

"That's the spirit," said Toby, beaming.

Janko held his hands out, waiting, a satisfied grin on his greedy face.

"Two for *Triassic Park* then," said Matthias. He fished out his wallet and withdrew a wad of crisp bills. He handed them over to Janko who counted them and put them in his pocket. He took a second, smaller empty petri dish from the case and with a pair of tweezers he selected two green blotters. He put them in the dish and then he took an eyedropper and squeezed a pinch of lubricating fluid over them. He closed the lid on the dish and handed it to the boy.

"To use within the next 24 hours. You can keep it in the fridge if you have to wait… but no longer than three days."

"And how do we take it?" Heike asked.

Janko gave her a long stare, and then he stuck his tongue out and tapped the tip of it with his finger.

"Right here—it will dissolve on its own."

"Just like a kiss," said Toby.

"Yes," Janko nodded, snapping the case shut. "Like a magic cinema kiss."

"Here she comes!" said Lukas, elbowing his brother Mikail and pointing to a young woman in a red dress running up the stairs of the steamliner from the well deck, heading toward the stern of the ship.

"Now remember, loverboy Jack is going to be lying on a bench, smoking, and staring at the stars with that romantic mug of his when he sees Corset Kate run by. I'm going to intercept him and get him out of the way and you coax her back off that railing before she jumps. You'll be the hero that wins her heart."

"But what about Leo... I mean Jack?"

"Screw him. He doesn't belong with her anyway. He's a third-class passenger. OK, go quickly!"

He patted Mikail on the back for luck and Mikail sprinted off after the running girl. He ran up the deck, past the benches and deck chairs and great looming smokestacks, and he smelled the salty spray of the ocean as waves crashed against the side of the ship. He saw her clinging against the base of the stern flagpole, panting.

She hitched her dress and climbed onto the gunwale. She had her back to him and the flag was flapping above her, and her red hair was blowing in the wind. She was looking down at the dark roiling water beneath the ship, preparing to jump.

"NEIN!" Mikail called out. "Ich meine—don't do it!"

The girl whipped her head around. Had he spoken in German? She saw a skinny, teenage boy with spiked black hair, dressed very inappropriately for a sea cruise, in what looked to be some sort of eccentric fashion. "Stay back! Don't come any closer!" she shouted.

From where he stood, Mikail could see her pale face was moist with tears. That Kate Winslet was some actress.

He held out his hand, "Come on… I'll help you get back in."

"No! Stay where you are! I mean it. I'll let go!" she warned. Her eyes were wide with fright.

"I don't think you will," Mikail said, confidently.

"What do you mean, no I won't? Don't presume to tell me what I will and will not do. You don't know me!" she snapped in a posh, arrogant voice.

"Come on—give me your hand!"

She refused. "You're distracting me. Go away."

"Holy crap. Corset Kate…" Mikail was floundering for words. "Look, the water's fucking freezing and I don't want to have to dive in after you."

She gasped in shock at his crude language. "W… Who are you?"

"George Clooney. Now shut the fuck up and give me your hand. I'm freezing my fucking balls out here," he snapped impatiently.

She looked at him, stunned. Then slowly she extended the palm of her hand. He took it. She shifted her footing to face the ship, then her foot caught on her dress and she slipped and plunged toward the water.

And Mikail, who had forgotten she would slip, was taken totally by surprise and he yelled out as she slid from his grip and fell 60 feet through the air, shrieking one last time and crashed into the waves below and disappeared beneath them.

"Oh shit! Fucking hell!" Mikail bent over the railing, squinting in the dark and trying to catch a glimpse of her. All he could see were bubbles of white froth. Rose had sunk before the ship.

He turned back around, guiltily, and saw the quartermaster sliding down the ladder from the docking bridge and running toward him.

"Here! What's all this?"

"What's what?" Mikail gulped.

The bearded quartermaster regarded him sternly. "I heard a noise."

"What noise?"

"It sounded like someone screaming. Like a girl."

"Well… you must be mistaken, because as you can see, there's no one here." Mikail motioned around him at the empty deck. The quartermaster eyed him suspiciously and then he grunted something and headed back across the fantail to his post. Mikail breathed a heavy sigh of relief.

As he was heading back along the promenade, he was accosted by Lukas, who held up his hands and said, "Hey bro, that Jack is so goddamn clingy… I had to tell him they had a poker game going on with Fabrizio in the third class general room…" He paused, mid-sentence, his voice trailing off.

"And uh… where is she?"

Mikail gave him a goofy grin. "It didn't go exactly as planned."

"Why? What do you mean?" Lukas' eyes narrowed.

"I mean I did everything like you said… but like she slipped and I tried to catch her but she was just too fucking heavy, man. So she went overboard."

"She went overboard."

"Yes."

"You've got to be fucking kidding me. Mickey!" Lukas threw his hands up angrily. "Great! That's just great! Like twenty minutes into the picture and you've managed to kill off the leading lady."

"She was going to jump anyway," Mikail said, holding his hands up defensively.

"Yes—ergo you were supposed to catch her. I mean—fuck. What the hell do we do now? We're stuck on a steamliner, in the middle of the fucking Atlantic Ocean, and you get rid of the main character; the girl with the one nude scene in this goddamn picture!"

"I'm sorry—"

"Yeah well sorry won't bring her back to life now will it? And we've got like two and a half fucking hours until this thing hits the iceberg. And what are we supposed to do now? Go to the damn dining saloon and eat caviar with that dumb cow Molly Brown and that stuffy Cal. And do you realize when he finds his fiancée is missing what a stir that's going to create?"

"There weren't any witnesses," mumbled Mikail. "Besides, there are plenty of other things to do on this ship. We can go play cards and mess with Jack. Or we can go to the reception, drink vodka and Red Bull and chat up those first class passenger bitches."

Lukas rapped his younger brother on the head with his knuckles. Knock-knock. "Hello, you dimwit, it's 1912… there is no Red Bull and there certainly aren't any bitches."

He walked away back down the plank deck toward the cabins, swearing to himself, his brother hurrying after him like a lost puppy.

"Unbelievable. Twenty goddamn minutes into the picture and he manages to kill off Rose. Un-fucking-believable."

When he woke up, some thirty minutes later, Lukas' head was pounding as if he were experiencing a hangover. He gingerly got up from the couch and headed to the bathroom to puke. He swallowed some paracetamol with tap water and brushed his teeth. When he came back to the living room Mikail was also sitting up and groaning. He held his head in his hands.

"Holy shit, my head is killing me!"

"It's the liquid silk membrane does that," said Lukas. "You don't feel it when you're inside the picture—only when you wake up. But it will go away in about twenty to thirty minutes." He went over to the fridge and took a bottle of Coca Light and drained a third of it in one long swallow. He passed the bottle to his brother, who drank from it thirstily.

"That was so… epic!" Mikail said, as the grogginess was clearing and his memories were returning to him. "I'm sorry I screwed up—"

Lukas waved him away. "Nevermind. It was your first time—you weren't prepared. It's my fault."

"Were you scared when we struck the iceberg?"

Lukas shrugged. "Not really. But I knew what it was going to be like."

Mikail said, "I was scared shitless. I had no idea it would be that loud! And the people—they were really in a panic. One lady tore my Adidas windbreaker to shreds as we were fighting over a lifeboat. It was a good thing you had already reserved a boat—with champagne and caviar no less. It would have been quite pleasant sitting under the stars, watching the ship go under, except that it was so fucking freezing. I couldn't even feel my hands. Even under the blankets. And all those people screaming and thrashing about in the water—I almost would have felt bad for them, if I hadn't known it was all a movie."

"Yes. You must always keep that distinction in mind," explained Lukas. "Otherwise you won't know how to react properly. See if I had panicked, we might have spent the last half hour in the water, clinging to a raft of floating debris, and that would have been most unpleasant."

Mikail shuddered at the thought. "We'll have to do it

again—when can you get some more?"

"I already owe Toby for this one."

"How much?"

"500."

Mikail let out a long whistle. "That much!"

"Hey, this isn't some cheap hallucinogenic trick. These are state-of-the-art organic biochips with millions of micropatterned variables and potentials. Add to that, they're not exactly legal. I mean, they aren't technically illegal either. But it won't take long for the European Parliament to wake up to their circulation and implement some bullshit precautionary control policy."

"Where do they come from?"

"Clandestine biotech labs in Holland... maybe America, and Japan too from what I've heard... look here Mickey," Lukas said, his tone becoming serious. "You mustn't go around telling everybody what you just experienced. Not if you want to keep on *taping*. Toby insists on keeping things low key. He'd rather his circle of clients be people he knew and trusts, which is why I've got to pay him back before he blacklists me. Now come on, get up and help me get my BMX and skis from the storage room. I've got to assess their value."

Mikail sat up suddenly, "You're selling off your bike?"

"And my computer."

"Are you crazy? You'll soon have nothing left."

Lukas gripped his brother by the shoulders and stared at him intensely. "I don't need them," he said. "Don't you get it? I don't need anything anymore."

3

RURAL FRANCE, 300 KILOMETERS EAST OF PARIS...

Marie Venet was washing dishes in the kitchen sink when the doorbell rang. She dried her hands off on a towel and turned down the radio. When she answered the door there were two men in dark blue suits standing on the doorsteps. One of them was tall and thin, the other short and rotund, carrying a black attaché case. There was a silvery Audi 6 parked on the gravel driveway behind them. She thought they were salesmen.

"Madame Venet?" the taller one asked. He was wearing dark sunglasses and he had long sideburns and a peculiar accent she couldn't quite place.

"Yes," she said, "What is it?"

"I'm First Officer Perrin. And this is my colleague, Liaison Officer Lambert."

"I'm sorry—are you from the police?"

The man removed his shades. His eyes were light green and had crow's feet. He opened his wallet and showed her a laminated blue badge with a circle of yellow stars. "Not exactly. We're from Europol. We'd like to speak with you about Christopher Venet."

At the mention of this name Marie felt a queer sense of panic and relief. Perhaps finally there would be someone to explain what had happened.

"Come inside," she said, stepping aside and letting them in. She led the way to the living room and offered them a seat. She offered them coffee but they declined. Marie sat down, in an armchair, feeling tired and tense.

"We understand your son is at the CHU, in a Type II coma," said Perrin.

Marie nodded her head. "Since two weeks ago," she admitted.

"Can you explain to us what happened—in your own words?" Officer Lambert asked. His accent betrayed him as a Belgian.

Marie couldn't for the life of her understand what her son's condition had to do with a law enforcement organization. Had he been involved in criminal activity? Drugs? No, that was ridiculous. Christopher was a perfectly well-behaved, quiet boy. His only addiction was his computer and video games. Or was this in regard to online piracy? No, that seemed too far-fetched as well. She would have to wait to find out.

She drew a deep breath, fidgeting nervously. "I come home from work one evening—around 7 I.M., I work the production chain, for Wella cosmetics, and I call out to Chris to help me carry some groceries from the car. He doesn't answer. I think he must be upstairs, on his computer or listening to music, and I go to his room and he's lying there on the bed, perfectly still, like a statue, and his hands are folded across his chest. I think he is asleep. I call his name, but he doesn't wake up. I touch him on the shoulder, but he doesn't move. Then I shake him, and there's no reaction—nothing at all… so I run to the phone and I call the SAMU…" She faltered, trying to find her words.

"It's all right. Take your time," Perrin said.

Marie bit her lip. "They… asked me what was wrong with him. I didn't know what to say. He was breathing when they got him into the ambulance. At the hospital they ran all kinds of tests. They couldn't find any physical trauma. They did a CT scan. They did blood work. A spinal tap. Everything seemed normal. The doctors, they had no explanation for his condition. How could they say that a seventeen year old boy, in perfect health, could just go to sleep and never wake up?"

The two men exchanged significant looks. Officer Lambert cleared his throat and said, "Madame Venet, prior to this incident, had you noticed anything odd in your son's behavior? Any changes to his personal habits? Maybe coming home at late hours. Bringing strange friends to the house. Cutting classes…"

She was shaking her head. "No. Nothing out of the ordinary."

"Did he ask you for money? Steal from you? Was he stealing at school…"

"No. My son is no thief," Marie said, now feeling indignant.

Officer Perrin raised his hand to calm her and asked, "How about his belongings? Was he losing things? Valuables…"

"No he—" She paused, thinking, and then said, "Actually yes. About a month ago he complained that somebody at school had stolen his BlackBerry. It was a new one, quite expensive. I scolded him, because he wasn't supposed to take it to school. He'd already forgotten his Lacoste sweater on the bus the week before, and so I was quite upset... but what is this all about? Is Christopher in some kind of legal trouble? My boy is not a criminal I can assure you—"

"We're not implying that," said Lambert.

"Then what are you here for?" Marie could feel her tension mounting. She wanted to yell at them—officers of the law or not: WHAT HAPPENED TO HIM?! TELL ME. TELL ME IF YOU KNOW SO MUCH! But she kept her frustration and anger in check.

"We think that he may have been a victim," said Perrin cautiously, weighing his words. He was careful not to divulge too much.

Marie's eyes widened. "A victim? Of what?"

"That's what we're still trying to find out," said Officer Lambert. "See, there's been an alarming number of similar cases—and not just in France, but throughout many different countries in the Union. Too many in too short a time for it to be a medical coincidence. Type II comas hitting healthy teenagers and young adults. All between sixteen to thirty years of age. And none of the usual symptoms or causes. No substance abuse, trauma, stroke, epilepsy..."

"Madame Venet," Officer Perrin cut in, "it would be the greatest service to us, to get to the truth of this matter, if you were to allow us permission to take your son's computer with us back to The Hague, so that our informatics experts can examine the hard drive. Now, technically you are in your right to refuse, as we have no reason to suspect any wrongful behavior on Christopher's part. However, I must insist that you think carefully about this. I believe that the only way your son will have a chance of being cured, is if we are able to find the cause of his affliction."

"By searching his computer? For what? Downloads? Chat messages?"

Officer Perrin looked at his superior and then said, "I'm afraid I can't comment further, I can only stress that it is vital to our ongoing investigation. You want to know what happened to your son…"

Marie nodded. "Yes, of course."

"Then help us—help you."

Marie didn't want to betray her son's privacy. But at the same time she desperately wanted to get at the truth. What if her son had been involved in something illicit? Was there incriminating evidence on his computer that could get him in trouble? If she didn't cooperate, and they contacted the judicial police and obtained a letter rogatory—would that make the situation worse? What did she stand to lose by cooperating? All she cared about was seeing her son recover. She drew a deep breath.

"What must I do?" she asked them.

Officer Lambert clicked open the attaché case and withdrew a sheaf of glossy papers. He selected two copies and passed them to her to read over.

"You must sign your name and write 'Read and

approved' at the bottom of each," he said, passing her a ballpoint pen. Marie scanned the papers, which were marked AUTHORISATION FOR SEIZURE OF PERSONAL PROPERTY. She read the clauses carefully and signed her name and copied the text on both documents. Then she put the pen down, her hands trembling.

"One copy is for you," said Officer Lambert, gathering the other one and putting it in his case. Noting her distress he added, "Everything will be fine. It's not your son that we're after."

"Where is his computer?" asked Officer Perrin.

"Upstairs in his room," said Marie, getting up from the armchair. Her legs felt heavy. "I'll show you."

She led them to Christopher's bedroom, which was unusually tidy for that of a teenage boy. There was a wood closet with a large mirror on it and below it, a set of barbells on the floor. Beside the closet stood a CD storage tower, the discs arranged in alphabetic order, and next to that, a bed made with quasi-military neatness. Lambert took stock of the movie posters on the wall above the bed. There was one depicting a woman lying on her belly on a bed, ankles crossed, handgun in front of her, cigarette in one hand, and magazine spread open under the other. Another showed three Italian-Americans in dark suits, hovering over the 1960s streets of Brooklyn. LES AFFRANCHIS. A cadaver was lying on the ground beneath them.

Marie saw the officer staring at the posters and said, "He's a real film buff... he wanted to enroll at ESEC—the private cinema school in Paris—when he graduated. I told him we couldn't afford it, but he wouldn't take no for an answer."

Officer Lambert gave her a grim, forced smile and moved toward the desk, near the window, where there was an Inspiron 580 desktop, the screen dark. Beside it lay a thick hardcover book titled: 50 ANS DU CINEMA AMERICAIN. He unplugged the computer case and carried it down the stairs.

As he was departing, Perrin said, "Don't worry. You should have it back within a couple of weeks. Now, if your son should regain consciousness—or there should be any improvement in his condition—I want you to contact us straightaway." He gave her his card. "Call the number at the bottom. It's my private line. Also, if anybody shows up here… looking for Christopher… please keep us informed at once."

Marie took the card and stared at him, perplexed. "I … don't quite understand what you mean, Monsieur l'Agent. If you're talking about his friends—"

He waved her off. "No, no. I'm talking about somebody you wouldn't associate with him at all. Somebody whom you've never seen before."

"Should I be concerned?"

"No. But it is important that if such a person does show up, you contact us. Try to give a detailed physical description. If there is a name to go with the face, all the better, but names mean less to us than physiognomy. I promise you, that when we are able to shed more light on the matter, you will be notified."

He gave her a rather old-fashioned salute, "Good day,

Madame Venet."

She followed him outside and watched him walk to the Audi. He opened the passenger door and paused, fingers suspended in the air and he said, "Oh and one last thing—"

"Yes?"

"I implore you to keep the purpose of our visit confidential. I know it's a difficult thing to ask, but it would make our work all the easier. Should you feel the need to talk with someone about this, call the number of our home office? I sincerely hope that whatever the cause, your son will make a full and speedy recovery."

"Je vous remercie."

He got into the car and slammed the door. The driver gunned the engine. She watched the Audi back out of the driveway and exit the village. Her house was the last one on a long strip of renovated farmhouses, most of them retaining the same rectangular shape with the large arched barn door, common in the region. She watched two neighborhood children ride by on their bicycles, pedaling hard and hollering excitedly. One of the kids waved at her as he passed. Marie waved back and then she went into the house which was empty now that both her husband and only son were gone.

The strange, unexpected visit did nothing to alleviate her fears. But her curiosity was roused and provided a welcome distraction to her plight. She was oddly relieved too that someone had taken an interest in her son's case and was working to elucidate the mysterious circumstances. Nothing was worse than not knowing why.

Where are you, Christopher? She wanted to ask. *Ou es tu, mon petit?*

(TRIASSIC PARK TAPEWORLD)

Heike's legs were itching after a long march through the tall pampas grass and ferns. The steam plumes rising from the volcanic fields of the island increased the already unbearable humidity in the air. She had taken off her yellow scarf and had tied it around her waist and was just beginning to realize how inappropriately dressed she was for such an outing—with her Mango pencil skirt and her pink, checkered slip-on Vans. Her boyfriend, Matthias, was looking also thoroughly uncomfortable, the humidity ruining his carefully layered hairdo. He had abandoned his fur lined jacket and flung it over a liana somewhere in the jungle, and he was itching from a million mosquito and bug bites and slapping at his face and grimacing as he marched through the open meadow.

"Look," he tugged her at the arm, pointing up ahead. They saw two green and yellow Ford Explorer Land Cruisers and a red-striped Jeep parked next to what looked like a bloated rhino lying in the tall grass. Surrounding the animal were six people: three men, a woman, and a boy and girl.

"The man in the blue shirt wearing the hat is Dr. Graham—he's like a cheaper version of Harrison Ford in Indiana Jones—and the woman in the shorts is Dr. Ella Stapler—she's a paleobotanist... like a prehistoric florist,"

Matthias said to her, indicating Sam Neil and Laura Dern. "That animal is a triceratops."

"Is it dangerous?" Heike was frightened. They knew the raptors and T-rex were yet to come, but the walk through the jungle, filled with its guttural sounds and shifting foliage, had made her very edgy.

"It's sick—it's eaten some poisonous berries," Matthias said. "Come on—let's go say hello."

As they approached the clearing they saw the group gathering around the triceratops, laying their hands on its horns and armor plates. A veterinarian in khaki uniform and safari cap was pacing back and forth, his arms crossed.

"Oh Ella, she was my favorite when I was a kid and now I think she's the most beautiful thing I ever saw," Sam Neil said.

Laura Dern was bent over, inspecting the tongue of the creature, when the vet spotted Heike and Matthias coming toward them and said, "Hey! Hey what's going on?"

The five others looked up, startled by his voice and distracted from the whinnying triceratops.

The shifty looking lawyer, Genco, squinted and held up his hands in confusion. Dr. Graham and his colleague Ella came forward. The blonde woman put her hands on her hips and said, "Who are you?"

The Chief vet said, "You're intruding on private property! This island belongs to the Genzyme Corporation—"

Dr. Graham held up his hand, interrupting him, "How did you get here? The only way in is by boat or helicopter..."

"I'm confused," said Genco, tugging at his tie. "Are you related to Mr. John Parker?"

"No way!" said the girl, Lex. "She's definitely *not* part of the family."

The boy named Tim was holding a book on dinosaurs in his hand. He was staring at Matthias.

"Why is your hair that funny color?"

"Shush, Tim," Lex said.

"We're tourists," smiled Heike and she removed her pink-framed sunglasses.

"Tourists?" repeated Dr. Graham, stunned. "On this island?"

"This is all very confusing," stammered Genco. "I'm going to call John right away. This is a serious examination on the behalf of the investors, not a goddamn Sunday picnic!"

"The dinosaurs are breeding!" Matthias blurted out. Heike suppressed a burp of laughter. He wasn't supposed to give away the plot so soon.

"What?" Dr. Graham scratched his head. "Say that again."

"Yes. The engineers used fragments of West African frog DNA to fill in the gaps in the dino DNA strands. And you know how some frogs spontaneously mutate their sex? Well the same thing is happening here…"

"What are you talking about?" Ella's mouth hung open.

"OK, everybody get in the cars," said Genco, clapping his hands. "We're going straight back to the visitor center. The tour's ended."

"But I want to see the other dinos—" Tim whined.

Dr. Graham's eyebrow furrowed, he was thinking hard. "What about them?" he asked. "We can't leave them out here—it's not safe."

"Maybe they should come with us," ventured Dr. Stapler. "What are your names?"

"I'm Matthias—and this is Heike."

"We're German," Heike said, pleasantly.

Genco slapped his hand to his forehead. "Jeez… German tourists on the island. What's that crazy old geezer going to surprise us with next? This is all highly unorthodox."

"This is what Milestone was talking about," Dr. Stapler said. "The uncertainty principle or whatever…"

"Oh please, don't start with him!" Dr. Graham snapped.

The group moved back to the Land Cruisers, all of them griping and arguing. The girl in the purple baseball cap, Lex, came skipping up besides Heike.

"I like your sunglasses," she said.

"Here," said Heike, taking them off and handing them to her. "You try them on."

"Really?"

"Sure."

"Wow. Neat." She put them on and struck a pose. Behind her Tim made a screwy face. She caught him mimicking out of the corner of her eye and flashed her tongue at him. They came to the Land Cruisers and Genco went to the radio and called the control room.

There was a hiss of static and then a voice came over it. "Hello—who is this?"

"Arnold, this is Genco. Is John Parker there?"

Then another voice replied, this one with a Scottish brogue. "Yessh. What is it Genco?"

"We've got a problem. There are two unauthorized visitors on the island."

There was a click and then they heard other people talking in the background.

"...*what is he talking about?*"

"Now you see the problem with your park John—" Jan Milestone, the consulting mathematician, radioed from the rear Land Cruiser. His voice sounded uncannily like Jeff Goldblum's.

"Don't give me any more of your chaos theory bullshit," Parkerd snarled. "Genco—are you there?"

"Yes, I'm listening John."

"Who are these people?"

"A boy and a girl—teenagers. They say they're German tourists."

He heard the owner of the site John Parker mutter something inaudible and then he spoke, his voice stern and commanding.

"Have Dr. Hardy bring them to the control room immediately. I want to know exactly what's going on."

"Copy."

He signed out, as Ella and Dr. Graham got back into the front Land Cruiser where Genco had replaced the radio on the console.

"That was John," said Genco. "I'm going to tell Dr. Hardy to take those two… whatever-their-names-are… back to control."

A splash of rain hit the windshield. There was a low rumble of thunder in the distance. He looked up at the darkening skies.

"Looks like there's a storm coming, all right. Don't worry—I'm sure they'll find a way to reroute the tour vehicles," he said. "I'll stay with Dr. Milestone."

Lex and Tim climbed into the back of the Land Cruiser as it started to rain. Genco ran back to the other vehicle. He could see the Jeep driving off in the opposite direction, back across the meadow.

"They looked so weird, those two," giggled Lex.

"You're weird," said Tim.

"Shut up!"

"OK, kids, that's enough," snapped Dr. Graham.

Ella gave him a concerned look. *What is going on here?* She mouthed.

Dr. Graham exhaled softly. "I don't know. Honest to God, I don't know.

4

MONCHENGLADBACH, GERMANY

Polizeihauptmeister Horst Hellmann and his commanding officer, Polizeikommissar Oberfeld, of the "Kripo" Branch, from the Landeskriminalamt Nordrhein-Westfalen, were waiting on the platform of the Hauptbahnhof for the Regional Express from Venlo, which was due in five minutes. They were both in plainclothes. Horst was reading a copy of Spiegel; his partner was eating a currywurst and fries and studying the timetable. They had been tailing the boy for the past three weeks. He came always on the RE from the Netherlands—on the weekends—a stupid thing to do, if you were a drug runner. But this boy was not the usual fare. He'd been stopped once, by a border canine brigade, who had searched him from head to toe, before dismissing him as clean.

The Bundeskriminalamt had a covert operation underway that had been commissioned by the Federal Ministry of the Interior, in partnership with Europol and Interpol, and coordinating with the LKA of six different states as well as the Dutch KLPD. They were gathering information on a possible chain of traffickers operating between Germany and Holland, France, and more recently Belgium. They suspected a new designer drug—some yet unlisted molecule, in the form of a pill or blotter. But they had yet to apprehend anyone transporting it. They had tracked mules carrying large amounts of cash into Rotterdam and Amsterdam, Kerkrade and Venlo, and returning seemingly empty handed. Cars had been stopped by the border police and searched, without results. Suspects had been arrested and questioned by customs investigators. In every case the suspects had been released within 48 hours, with no further detention on remand. And yet Europol was convinced the drug existed, and that it was wreaking havoc. But the sales didn't seem to take place in the usual places. No nightclubs, bars, train stations, red light districts... the traffickers shunned these places. They passed through the towns like shadows, lingering briefly in one place, and then leaving for somewhere else—never establishing a definitive territory, making the police work all the more difficult. And yet in whichever town or city they were known to pass through, there would be reports of teenagers and young adults falling prey to comas, or retrograde amnesia... and still the investigators had nothing.

"Here she comes," said Hellmann, as the train appeared at the far end of the tracks. Komissar Oberfeld dumped the remains of his snack in a trash bin and wiped his hands on a paper napkin.

The train came to halt with a hiss of the air-brakes. The sliding doors opened and two dozen passengers dismounted. Hellmann scanned the crowd rapidly, distinguishing older couples in double-denim, a swarm of girl students chattering vibrantly, a punk with red hair and checkered pants... a male and female emo, both wearing mascara and dressed identical.

And then they saw him.

Emerging from the last wagon—a boy, early to mid-twenties, wearing a black varsity jacket with imitation leather sleeves and a white cap on his head, the inscription of which they had both committed to memory.

123 KLAN. French graffiti crew, working for an up-and-coming Serbian streetwear label.

He was carrying a rucksack this time. He walked right toward them, utterly composed, not a hint of anxiety on his face.

He had almost entered the station hall when Oberfeld blocked him, flashing a bronze, nameless badge. "Dejan Vidic?"

The boy stared at him, uncomprehendingly. Then he responded slowly, "Ja. Was gibt's?"

"Kriminalpolizei, we'd like to ask you a few questions?"

"I don't understand? What is going on?"

"Come with us," said Hauptmeister Hellmann. "To the car."

"But I haven't done anything—" he protested.

"We're not asking you," snapped Oberfeld. "Now come on."

They led him through the station hall, past the kiosks and newsagents and ticket machines and to the parking where there was an unmarked Mazdaspeed6 next to a row of bicycles-for-rent.

They shoved him in the backseat and Hellmann got in beside him. Oberfeld put the car into gear and steered them away from the station and down a wide street past a line of hotels and pubs.

"Where are you taking me?" Vidic asked. Oberfeld didn't reply, he was staring at him through the rear-view mirror, dark circles under his eyes. He drummed his fingers ominously on the steering wheel.

"May I ask where you are coming from?" Hellmann inquired.

Vidic smoothed out his rucksack. "Holland, Alter."

"Where in Holland?"

"Venlo," he replied, without a trace of hesitation.

"What were you doing there?"

"I was shopping around the Markt. You never go there?" He patted his rucksack, then passed it to Hellmann, saying, "Only clothes. Go ahead and look."

The two men exchanged glances—it was impossible that the kid was transporting any illegal substance. He was too confident. Anything they were after wasn't in that bag, and they weren't after the kid anyway.

"Who's Janko?" Hellmann asked suddenly.

Vidic turned his face to the window, his hand moved just slightly. "I don't know who you mean," he said.

"That's funny," said Kommissar Oberfeld. "Because we've seen you at his squat in Düsseldorf."

Vidic gave a snort and tugged at his cap. "I've never been to Düsseldorf in my life… Klar?"

"You called him twice from a telephone booth in the city," said Hellmann.

"This is ridiculous…"

"Janko Konjovic. 29 years old. Former B-grade soccer player with ties to the Zemun clan. Now owns a café and Internet call shop in Oberbilk. A place you were spotted less than a month ago."

Hellmann reached into his vest and pulled out a pack of Dunhills and a gold-plated Zippo. He offered one to Vidic who declined. Hellmann fired up and blew a thick cloud of smoke to the car roof.

"Don't play games with us," Hellmann warned. "If you're doing business with Janko, better come clean right now—save yourself the trouble. Whatever he's paying you—it isn't worth it."

"You're making a mistake," Vidic insisted. "Whoever this Janko character is, I've got nothing to do with him."

"Do you know what a Readmission agreement is?" Oberfeld asked. "150,000 of your people, living illegally in the EU are going to be repatriated. Ten thousand of them will be deported from Germany this coming year." The figure was closer to two thousand but Oberfeld had purposely exaggerated it for effect.

Vidic was silent.

"We know there is a certain Milinka Trajkovic residing at your apartment. She's a Kosovo-Albanian refugee, am I right? A few calls to the right place, and maybe she makes the list for repatriation…"

"Is that a threat?"

"Give us a name. Somebody living in Venlo. And get

yourself out of all this before it is too late..." advised Hellmann.

"I don't know anybody in Venlo," said Vidic. "You're wasting your time."

Hellmann sighed and opened his wallet. He clicked a ballpoint pen and wrote down a number on the back of a supermarket loyalty card. He handed this to Vidic. Oberfeld brought the car to a stop, on the curb, across from the Rheydt shopping gallery. Hellmann opened the door and indicated to Vidic to get out of the car. He stood on the pavement, clutching his rucksack. Hellmann got back in front and leaned out the passenger window.

"If you get smart and change your mind, you call that number. All we want is a name, and you are clear. If not—" he hunched his shoulders as if to say too bad for you.

He flicked his cigarette butt out the window. It landed at Vidic's feet.

As they drove off, sending a flock of pigeons scuttling into flight, Hellmann said, "You think it will work?"

"Let him digest the situation for a bit," said Oberfeld. "He's a bottom-feeder. He's in it for the easy money—not for loyalty."

"Maybe he's afraid of Janko," said Hellmann.

Oberfeld laughed and shook his head. "Janko's a bottom-feeder as well. They're all replaceable. Only one thing isn't: that's the product."

VILLAGE OF BERGAMACHT, 25 KM EAST OF ROTTERDAM

A small, thatched-roof nineteenth century farm house, overlooking a narrow canal of running water and a meadow of grazing cows. Johannes van der Vlugt came in through the back garden and leaned his bicycle against the picket fence. He went up to the screen door which was locked and rang the bell.

He was carrying a plastic bag in one hand, containing a six pack of Dr. Pepper, a few packs of Marlboro Lights and four borrowed DVDs. He waited for a moment and then somebody called out behind the screen.

"Wie is het?"

"It's me—" Johannes said.

The latch on the door clicked open and a cute, 26-year-old Vietnamese girl peered out and said, "What took you so long?"

"I punctured a tire on my bike—I had to walk part of the way," Johannes explained, moving past her into the house. "Did you finish the tape?" he asked.

The girl, Kim Nguyen, was an organic chemist who had earned her Ph.D. at Can Tho University, and then been lured away from a high-paying job at a biopharmaceutical company by a shadowy, charismatic entrepreneur who said he was putting together a team of electro-physiologists and biological and computer engineers to create something that no one else was doing. Two years later and Kim had found herself sharing a countryside house with eight other people, working night and day on the most thrilling line of projects she could have imagined—and being paid handsomely for it (albeit on some rather dubious offshore accounts).

Johannes was not technically part of the production team. His job was as gopher. He took care of their errands and requests, as the work was very complicated and oftentimes required their full attention for hours on end. Johannes did the shopping and the cleaning, and in his more inspired moments, the cooking (his fish and seafood waterzooi being a house favorite). The rest of the team were generally holed up in the barn, bleary-eyed, on a nicotine-caffeine-sugar rush, hunched over electron microscopes, DNA sequencers, membrane potential amplifiers... and the roomfuls of other gizmos and ultra-sensitive equipment that were needed to create the finished product: a 20-micron-thick dissolvable film containing 100 million modified sensory neurons and microelectrode arrays.

"Yeah, it's almost done," Kim now said, leading the way through living room and kitchen to the barn. "We had a little problem at the last minute with the Uma Thurman character. There was a glitch in the hippocampal neuron culture. Some debris collection and we had to rectify it before sealing the well... and some of the olfactive stimuli are off. Xander's working on it."

"Bummer," said Johannes, having no idea what she was talking about. "I'd sure like to try it when it's done."

"I don't think that's a good idea. Dr. Yin says that prolonged use may have adverse effects."

Johannes giggled. Kim gave him a sour puss look.

"What's so funny?"

"When you say Dr. Yin... I mean the guy's younger than me..."

"And only a hundred times as smart," said Kim. "Show some respect." She gave him a playful slap on the shoulder.

"Ouch."

They entered the barn which had been adequately soundproofed with a blend of sheetrock and state-of-the-art acoustic foam and contained eight laboratory bench tops illuminated by direct and indirect lighting fixtures, where the rest of the team were gathered at work.

The lab's prize asset was a hybrid computing platform capable of one petaflop (1,000 trillion calculations per second) of performance within a single cabinet. The supercomputer, nicknamed Betty, or Betty Boop as they liked to call it, had been provided to the team by their recruiter, the man everyone called De Schaduw, for his uncanny ability to appear exactly when they needed him, and then disappear. The head computer engineer of the team was Richard Mitchell—or "Rick"—a self-proclaimed pseudo-geek (meaning he'd actually had a girlfriend) from Silicon Valley. He claimed that Betty had been assembled from off-the-shelf parts, but that she wasn't from any known computer producer. His guess was that she had been made in China, and supplied by the Chinese government. A supercomputer of that thinking power and size was, in his mind, worth well over 100 million dollars. How De Schaduw and the Chinese planned to recuperate this investment, Rick couldn't tell. He reasoned that the films they were making were perhaps only a test step toward something bigger and even more lucrative.

Now Rick looked up from his readings on four aligned 22 inch flexible OLED monitors. He spotted Johannes and Kim and said, "JoJo where did you come, by way of Australia?" and laughed hard at his wit.

Johannes managed a brief chortle. Pseudo-geek humor was beyond him. Rick looked over from one of his comp screens to Xander Philippe, a fat neuropsychopharmacological genius (also a Silicon Valley "Techie") who was standing in front of a dissecting microscope conducting an air-phase electroolfactogram recording. This was for the "scent reproduction" stimuli of the tape.

"Are the electrodes set?" Rick asked.

"Yeah, dude. Just one secondo…" Philippe hummed. He turned the knobs on an amplifier connected to a digitizer and said, "Okay, we're ready to record the signal."

"It's about time," said Rick, tapping a series of commands on his keyboard.

Johannes came up behind Philippe and patted him on the back. "Hey Xander…"

Xander spun around, knocking into the micromanipulators. A bottle of sodium chloride solution crashed onto the floor, rousing the rest of the research team who had been so involved with their individual tasks they hadn't noticed him enter the room.

"Shit, we've got to start over!" Xander cussed. Some of the other members of the team applauded his clumsiness.

"Way to go Triple X!" a French scientist—Laeticia Lejeun—remarked snidely. She was in charge of the "Baths," which were special sterilized recording chambers for the neural cultures, maintained at 37 °C like the human body and under a humidified airflow of 10 percent carbon dioxide. These living cultures were bred and modified to latch onto brain cells and interfere with the signals, providing alternate sensory information for a determined period of time. Additional stimulus was provided by the microelectrodes. They were encapsulated in macromolecule-size protein coats (the carriers) and layered on a pullulan strip (the Tape) that would dissolve when in contact with the enzymes in saliva, allowing the product to enter the bloodstream and find its way to the brain.

"Stilte austublieft!" Dr. Yin held up his hand. He was the captain of the team, despite being the second youngest member. He was 27. "Come on people, let's stay serious. We're almost done. JoJo, how many times must I tell you... please stay out of the lab while we are recording."

"I hate it when you call me that," Johannes moaned. His cheeks were flushed red and his flaxen hair hung limp across his scalp, lending a defeated air to his lank, boyish figure.

"Make yourself useful and put some champagne in the cooler," said Dr. Yin. "In a short while *Plump Friction* will be complete."

"If I can get this damn reference electrode back into place!" grunted Xander. "No thanks to you JoJo! By the way Kimmy, I'm using the 50-fold dilution you prepared—is that right?"

"What?" Kim, the chemist, looked up. "You should be using the 100-fold bottle for the five-dollar milkshake scene. I told you that a hundred times."

"Oh shit, I've got to replace the bottle," said Xander. "One sec…"

From the OLED monitors Rick whistled in exasperation.

"I'll be in the house if you need me," said Johannes. He put the bag with the DVDs, frisdrank and cigarettes down on Rick's desk. Rick peeked inside, reading the titles out loud.

"*Casino*… nice choice… *2001: A Space Odyssey*? Jesus, there goes our next three weekends! *The Silence of the Lambs*… What the hell are we going to call that?"

"How about *The Violence of the Rams*," suggested Kim. "In keeping with the whole sheep theme."

"You guys are nuts…" Johannes snickered.

Rick looked at the last DVD, "*Basic Instinct*. Verhoeven! I totally recall this one. I just knew we'd get around to something Dutch-made, you cheeky bastard."

"Just keeping it real. I'll be in the house if you need me," said Johannes. As he was leaving he could hear Xander whistling and singing "Kimmy Kimmy Kimmy can't you see, sometimes ya style just hypnotize me…"

Geeks, geniuses, pseudo-geeks, they were all the same, thought Johannes. Only Kim was anything worth saving.

Johannes was sitting on the couch, with a bag of chips and a mayonnaise jar in his lap. He had the TV on and was watching a show on Humor TV 24, the national comedy channel. He was dipping the chips in the mayonnaise and reciting the famous lines from *Pulp Fiction*.

"Do you know what they put on French fries in Holland instead of ketchup?"

He was literally pissing himself with laughter as he stuffed his gobbler. "Mayonnaise!"

Forty-five minutes later he'd just about fallen asleep when he was roused by Dr. Yin's distinctive twang. "Uncork the bubbly... *Plump Friction* is a wrap."

"Nice title by the way," coughed Xander. "Sounds like a cheap porno—"

"Where's our dinner?" Dr. Yin demanded.

Johannes jumped to his feet. "Oh, shit... I forgot."

The other members of the team were piling into the living room, rubbing their hands together, rubbing their eyes and yawning, looking more strung out and wasted than excited.

"He forgot the champagne," Dr. Yin apologized to the team, who looked as if they couldn't care less. Most of them just wanted a hot shower and to get some shuteye. "What have you been doing for the past hour you lazy boy? Waardeloos!" he shouted, moved to insult him in his native tongue. "We are all working, like buffalos—up to our eye sockets! And you are taking a nap and forget about the champagne and what about dinner?"

"I'll make some stew—"

"You'll make, you'll make... only empty promises,"

lectured Dr. Yin. "Up! Off that couch and prepare us something nice and warm for tonight—some Hutspot—or I tell De Schaduw to replace your worthless ass!"

"I'm irreplaceable!" snapped Johannes, springing up from the couch. "And besides, I know too much. De Schaduw could never fire me, so there—"

"Maybe he found a way to make you disappear, eh?" Dr. Yin suggested playfully.

"That's not funny—"

"Guys. Guys! Cut it out!" Kim intervened. "We should be celebrating, not fighting. This is our finest work yet. Tarantino would be proud."

"Rubbish! He would take us to court and sue us," Bart, a former biotech researcher from Crucell said. He was the only other Dutch member of the "House."

"Screw Tarantino! What we have done far surpasses the meager accomplishments of motion picture history—" said Dr. Yin. "This is a quantum leap in terms of visionary entertainment. People—the world over—experiencing a movie from the inside!—becoming part of it!" and his eyes took on the hazy, faraway look of the dreamer or utopist.

"Let me try it!" Johannes begged.

"Never. Do you know what this tape cost to produce?"

"Just one, please. I'll give you a first-rate critique."

Dr. Yin was shaking his head. "It's too dangerous. You've had enough tapes already. We want to preserve what few working neurons remain in that numbskull of yours!"

Johannes was about to reply with something sharp-tongued, when Kim cut in. "He's right," she said. "We have no idea what kind of effect repeat use of the tapes could inflict on the brain. I think it would be wise to refrain from overuse. It's for your own good."

Finding no argument to counter her gentle remonstrance, Johannes headed toward the kitchen and began rummaging in the cupboards and drawers. The rest of the team was heading up the stairs to their bedrooms. They would catch up on sleep while Johannes prepared supper. Then tomorrow would begin the laborious process of copying the tape over 12,000 times onto a pullalan strip. The end product would be a reel no larger than the film canister of a throwaway camera which would be delivered to their distributor in Rotterdam and sold for somewhere between 750,000 to a million euro. The sales and distribution was not their department. That would be handled by De Schaduw's "accountants," who ironically enough, never looked like the kind of men for whom math was a strong point. Each master tape produced got them €10,000 in cash each, and at the rate of two master tapes a month that was a quarter million a year—more than they could have hoped for starting off in a legitimate business. And the money wasn't the only incentive. De Schaduw knew that for a scientist the project was as important, if not more so than the pay. And where else could they find projects as stimulating and exciting as those of his design?

KATENDRECHT PENINSULA, SOUTH ROTTERDAM

The Autobedrijf Maas was a used car dealership situated along the Brede Hilledijk Avenue, with a view of the Maashaven docks across from a busy construction site. It was Sunday and the showroom and repair shop were closed, but there were a few visiting cars parked near the service entrance… posh cars bearing foreign license plates. There was a Nissan 4x4 and a sleek BMW from Belgium. A Mercedes Class S from Germany and Range Rover Sport from France—both armored—had also recently arrived.

Inside the repair shop, a handful of men were standing in separate corners, awaiting their turn to meet with De Schaduw in his office. There were two Moroccans, with close cropped hair, shaved on the sides of the head, wearing dark leather jackets over Jezequel polos. There was a group of four heavily tattooed Chinese idling near the coffee distributor. Two muscular ex-KCT officers stood in front of the door to the office, where De Schaduw and his two accountants were bartering with a pair of Turks.

One of them was older, in his fifties, balding, with a gray mustache and a gold watch and gold caps on his teeth. The other was perhaps thirty, with a full head of hair that had been slicked back. The two men were wearing Italian designer suits and arguing amongst themselves. The younger one carried a silver-toned metal briefcase. He spoke good English and served as translator.

The older man scratched his head, at a loss over the explanation. "What is this tape—this thing called *Pink*

Fiction?"

The younger one rolled his eyes in exasperation, squeezing his fingertips together and gesticulating emphatically. "Baba... Bu *Plump Friction* denir! P-L-U-M-P."

The older man flashed an uneasy gold-and-chrome smile at De Schaduw who was waiting patiently for them to reach an agreement.

"Let me handle this," the younger one said. He straightened his tie and cleared his throat. "How much for three hundred copies?"

The older man's eyes fairly popped out of his head. "Üç yüz!"

"Baba!"

De Schaduw's lean, weathered face was an impassive mask of Dutch patience and diplomacy. "I can give you three hundred copies for 30,000," he said. "600 for 50,000."

After some more passionate arguing, the two men agreed on 400 tapes. De Schaduw nodded at one of his accountants who measured out the tape and cut off the required amount at a film cutting station. He wound the tape on a plastic spool and clicked it into place in a disposable Kodak.

The younger man opened his briefcase and counted out eight bundles of cash held together with elastic bands. He placed them on the desk in front of De Schaduw. The accountant came over and took the bundles and fed them one by one into a bill discriminator. When he was satisfied with their authenticity and the amount, he handed over the camera, saying, "You must put this in a warm saline solution before sale, to activate the neurochip. Once activated it must be used within 24 hours… or kept in a cool place for up to three days. Afterwards, the quality will degrade. The characters will fade. There will be holes in the scenario, blank spaces in the Tapeworld."

The Turk nodded, while his father looked on uncomprehendingly. The old baron knew all there was to know about guns and organ trafficking, drug-running, honor killing, bath-houses, prostitutes and metal kebab skewers. His knowledge of cinema was slightly more limited, centering mainly on John Wayne and 1970s pornography. Still, his son had assured him that this was the next big thing—and he didn't want to appear old-fashioned.

His son put the Kodak into the briefcase, alongside a few additional money rolls. De Schaduw stood up and shook hands with the two men, and then he opened the door to his office and nodded at his watchdogs. One of them activated a switch on the wall and the roller door rose.

The guard stood at the entrance to the repair shop, arms crossed, and watched the Turks carry their booty to the Audi. When they had driven off he looked over to the two Moroccans, snapped his fingers and made a gesture indicating they were next.

The Moroccans came from Anderlecht, Brussels. They were part of a newly formed crime syndicate who were looking to expand their operations beyond the narrow confines of the immigrant neighborhoods of their city. The racketeers, the loverboys, the gun-running from Czech Republic and Poland, and the football and taxi mafia, those were activities well known to the police and rife with competition. But this was an entirely new and undeveloped sector. They had already sold 200 tapes in their home city. Today they would buy double. If all went well they would contact their associates in Namur and Charleroi and begin the construction of an empire. The profit margins were simply phenomenal: €100 on each tape. Ten thousand today, perhaps a million tomorrow. The tapes had the additional advantage of attracting people who were not interested in the usual vices. The playing field was much larger. And, for the time being anyway, they were indecipherable to the police. It was as easy as trafficking air. No hassle no worries... just a disposable camera sitting inconspicuously on the dashboard.

(TRIASSIC PARK TAPEWORLD)

Rain drummed loudly on the roof of the Jeep as Dr. Hardy steered them across the bumpy terrain, the windshield wipers flogging back and forth and the radio hissing static. They were driving along a high ridge, overlooking a Mesozoic jungle river, passing through the *Dilophosaurus* territory—land of the frill-necked poison-spitting dino that was going to kill off the fat, slovenly computer maintenance engineer turned traitor before the end of the night.

From the back of the vehicle Heike tapped Matthias on

the shoulder and whispered to him, "Ich gehe züruck."

Matthias eyes widened "Are you mad?" he hissed back at her. "We've been in this picture for nearly an hour. The *Tyrannosaur* could pop up anytime now!"

Dr. Hardy looked over, annoyed. "Hey! What's with all the secretive whispering? Speak English, goddamit!"

"It's nothing—she's just telling me she's hungry," said Matthias, shifting tensely in his seat and looking out the windshield. All he saw was pouring rain, the dark outlines of strange, prehistoric trees and dense jungle shrubbery and in the distance the high-rise electrified fencing which he knew was going to give out very soon.

"I bet you damn kids don't realize the kind of trouble you could be in," grumbled Dr. Hardy. "Trespassing on private property. Mr. Hammond's going to be pissed as hell. He's got this phobia of industrial spies—"

"We're not spies," objected Matthias. "We're tourists."

Dr. Hardy snorted. "Yeah, right."

As they were speaking, suddenly and without warning, Heike flung the back door to the Jeep open and jumped out. Dr. Hardy gave a surprised yell and slammed on the brakes. The Jeep fishtailed on the muddy road. He got out in time to see the girl running away, back across the dark fields, her yellow scarf shining in the night. He waved his arms, shouting furiously.

"Get back here! Hey you!"

Matthias got out of the Jeep, cupping his hands round his mouth and calling out, "Heike! Komm züruck, bitte." He made to go after her, but Dr. Hardy grabbed him by the collar of his band shirt and held him fast.

"You stay right here!"

"I have to go with her—" Matthias pleaded.

"Oh no you don't. You're coming right back to the control room, with me. You've got a lot of explaining to do—"

"But she's putting herself in a lot of danger going back there… the T-rex, he's going to escape from his enclosure… "

Dr. Hardy's jaw bunched. "Who told you we had a *Tyrannosaur* on this island? Who are you working for?"

"I'm not working for anybody. But I know that one of your computer engineers—Donald Neri—shut down some of the perimeter systems, so he could get across the secured areas of the park to bring stolen dinosaur embryos to the dock."

The vet's eyes narrowed at this news. His face was glistening with the downpour. Lightning flashed and streaked across the sky, illuminating the rain-drenched jungle to their right, and the winding maintenance road on which they had been driving. Matthias saw the silhouettes of reptilian animals scurrying furtively through the foliage. He heard the uncanny, otherworldly guttural sounds of prehistoric creatures: possibly *Dilophosaurus* or maybe compys. Part of him knew that these hisses and squawks were recording effects… a clever mix of ordinary birds and mammals. But it was quite hard to sustain the illusion of this being mere entertainment, when you could feel and hear and smell everything around as real as anything you had ever known. Matthias was suddenly frightened.

"Come on, back in the Jeep," ordered Dr. Hardy,

pushing him forward.

"But my girlfriend—"

"We'll send someone after her. Muller is in charge of security. He'll know what to do. We can't stay out here any longer. If half of what you've told me is true, they'll need to know immediately. Now get in the car."

As Dr. Hardy was speaking they heard a series of twittering peeps and saw a flock of dark green animals with clawed forelimbs and slender snouts, maybe a foot tall, moving across the brush illuminated by the Jeep's headlights.

"Compys!" Dr. Hardy and Matthias both said in unison.

Dr. Hardy gave Matthias a hard stare. "They don't usually move at night—they must be scavenging…"

The compys moved with a peculiar bobbing gait, like chickens; their tails protruded stiffly behind them. A few of them came close to the Jeep. Matthias was moved by curiosity to look closer, and he bent over one, marveling at the ripples of muscle beneath the leathery green skin, the nostrils that flared, the beady eyes that blinked as it cocked its head to one side and opened its miniature jaws revealing rows of pointed teeth and squeaked pitifully.

"Don't get too close—" Dr. Hardy started.

Too late! The compy sprung at Matthias, its jaw snapping. He jumped back but not fast enough to prevent the animal from sinking its Wilkinson-sharp teeth into his hand. He kicked at it, and the compy scurried off after the rest of the flock.

"Ouch... it bit me," he whined. "The ugly gangrene chicken bit me!"

"What did you expect?" Dr. Hardy said in a reproving tone. "These are hostile critters. Not dairy-farm pets."

Matthias felt a throbbing pain in his finger, and then the pain was replaced by a sort of numbing warmth as the anesthetic poison worked its effect. He held his finger to the headlights and saw a trickle of blood.

Blood! He was bleeding! He hadn't expected to bleed in a Tapeworld.

"That'll teach you to respect a NO TRESPASSING sign," grumbled Dr. Hardy as they got back into the Jeep and he shifted gears. Matthias squeezed his wound to stop the bleeding.

"There's a pack of bandages in the glove compartment," murmured Dr. Hardy. "Better put some antiseptic on it as well. Compys ain't the cleanest creatures."

Matthias opened the glove compartment and found a first aid kit. He popped the lid, and saw there was a card taped to the inside of the box. It read:

DEAR TAPER, WHOEVER YOU MAY BE... IF YOU CAN MAKE IT ALIVE TO THE TYRANNOSAUR LAGOON THERE IS A SURPRISE BONUS WAITING FOR YOU.

HOPE YOU ARE HAVING FUN
GOOD LUCK FROM YOUR PROGRAMMING

TEAM! XXX

P.S. If you are reading this we suppose you have been hurt to some extent. Try and be more careful in the future. Triassic Park is a dangerous place to be. Lol.

Matthias closed the kit, debating whether to show Dr. Hardy the note. Would he understand what it was? Could a character in a tapeworld possess the intelligence to comprehend he was in a Tapeworld, or a movie for that matter?

"*You're not real!*" Matthias wanted to scream. "*You're an actor, for crying out loud. You're a DVD on my shelf. You came out in the cinema before I was born. How can you talk as if you were a person? As if any of this was real?*"

Then Matthias was stricken by the terrifying notion that there were no rules here. Not like in a game. And unlike a movie, where things happened in a neatly defined and chronological order, and one knew the way events unfolded, anything and everything could happen here.

Indeed, his presence in the picture had already spawned a chain of events that would render the whole storyline obsolete. Nothing was a given anymore. And if people died in Triassic Park, then who was to say that he and Heike were not to be victims—slashed to pieces by raptors, or chomped up by a hungry T-rex with a penchant for German sausages that ran and screamed.

With a terrifying shiver he realized that he had entered a world with far more genuine risk than he had anticipated.

His life in the tapeworld was suddenly monumentally important. He could feel anxiety, he could feel pain... if he could feel that, than he could be hurt... quite possibly even killed.

What happened if you died here? Maybe you couldn't get out...

He felt a sudden rising rush of panic.

"Dr. Hardy! Sir!" He reopened the first aid kit, fingers shaking and peeled off the card. "Look at this, please... "

The vet drummed his fingers on the steering wheel and squinted out the windshield. His weathered face was unreadable. The outline of the park visitor complex was visible in the distance.

"Doctor Hardy!" Matthias called out, louder.

"Jeez. What is it now?"

He held out the card. "Can you read this?"

The vet glanced at him, perplexed. "Read what, son?"

"What I'm holding in my hand."

"That's a flashlight," said the vet. "Why do you want me to read a flashlight? Put it back."

And Matthias turned the card over in his hand and saw that now there was a new message written on it—two very simple words that gave him a sinking feeling in his stomach, and the jeepers-creepers.

NO CHEATING

5

Duisburg

(The usual assortment of Marilyn Manson successors, white hip-hoppers, scene kids, glue-sniffers, suicidal emos, and *I-only-drop-E-on-the-weekends* kids which compose a healthy German high school...)

Lukas caught up with his younger brother as he was exiting the red-brick Gymnasium, running up the concrete steps, his schoolbag slung lazily over his shoulder, texting on his iPhone. Lukas looked at the throngs of students idling around, waiting on the school bus, waiting on friends, waiting to grow up and get on with their lives, and he felt a strange pinch of nostalgia. High school was the best and worst time. There was that sense of restless excitement, of wanting to leave the prison of education and explore the real world. But when you grew older, you realized that the excitement, and the anticipation, those were the best things in life. There wasn't much beyond the Great Expectations. Not the dregs that usually followed... being crushed under a merciless wheel of work, so-called responsibility, a career, and the mind-numbing boredom of stability.

Lukas had felt himself suffocating... living in a tiny, one-bedroom flat in a neighborhood overrun by foreigners. No steady girlfriend. Working at a deadbeat job for a miserly pay to make ends meet. He had felt his life going steadily nowhere, settling into the slaughter of consumer mediocrity. But now… everything was different. Now he had found a way out. An escape. Anytime he wanted, night or day, he could leave the boredom and futility of his life behind, and enter worlds of fascinating characters and tantalizing possibilities; worlds where nothing was stale or ordinary—where everything was fresh and vibrant, alive and magical.

Mikail spotted Lucas standing near the bus stop, cuffed hands with a few of his friends and then came jogging over.

"Hey, what's up? What are you doing here?"

"I got some new ones—" Lukas whispered.

"You got tapes?" Mikail's face lit up with anticipation. "Which one?"

"*Plump Friction*. Just in fresh from the Netherlands."

"Shit, that's my all-time favorite flick. Let's go to your place and try it."

"Yeah… but I don't have the tapes on me," explained Lukas. "Toby has them. He called me half an hour ago. I got two hundred left over in cash, after I settled my debt. But that's not enough for even one copy, let alone two… "

"Sheisse… and I'm fucking broke. How much more do you need?"

"Toby says he can do 2 for 450, because I'm a regular. But the copies are selling like crazy. He says he can't guarantee there will be any left by the end of the weekend."

"Well can't he give you credit?"

Lukas negatived. "Toby says he don't do credit no more. Says everybody is asking for credit, and it would fuck him over."

"So just ask him to reserve two copies—"

"Yeah, that's what I told him, but he says everybody wants a piece and it's first-come first-serve and that he isn't in the business for love."

"That damn Drecksneger!" Mikail cursed. A pair of Manga-eyed scene girls sporting two million colored bracelets each and rainbow hairdos heard the ethnic slur and tittered.

"Keep your voice down," chided Lukas. "Look you want a tape, find 250 by tonight, OK?"

"How the fuck am I supposed to do that?" Mikail wailed. "I'm broke. What do you want me to do, snatch a purse?"

Lukas shrugged noncommittally. Mikail blinked in stupefaction. "Are you serious? You want me to steal the money?"

"Look … I don't know. We need to come up with 250, that's all I'm saying. Think smart. Think Lola Rennt… twenty minutes and she managed to pick up 100,000 in cash. We can do a meager 250 in four hours."

"News flash: that was a fucking movie, Lukas. A movie. This is real life."

"No it's not." Lukas grabbed his brother's shoulders and looked him fiercely in the eye. "It's all fiction," he said. "We can play this world like a movie. It don't matter, see. Nothing can happen to us here. Anytime we want we can escape—slip over to the other side. Don't you get it? With this technology we're untouchable. THE UNTOUCHABLES, ha-ha. Nobody and nothing can get to us…"

"You're talking nonsense. What's gotten into you?"

"No!" Lukas insisted. "Jesus, Mickey you're seventeen years old, you don't have a clue. Wake the fuck up and look around you. What the fuck is so great about this world? We can have ten, twenty… a hundred times more in a Tapeworld. Anything we want is there for the taking. What's a measly couple of hundred between us and the thrill of a lifetime?"

The Stadtbus arrived and the students loitering around the bus stop began milling toward it, pushing and shoving and laughing as they boarded it. Geeks up front. Rowdies in the back. Girls in the middle. The predictable teenage social stratification.

Mikail moved toward the line at the front of the bus. "I'll think of something," he said. "Why don't you come by the house tonight? Mom says you should come over for dinner."

"No way—I don't want to see that asshole she's living with."

"He's all right," Mikail said, unconvincingly.

Lukas snorted in contempt. "Right. And Bill Kaulitz isn't a buftie boy. Look—if you can get the money—be at my place at nine, OK? I got to go. I'm supposed to meet Veronika at the Kaufhof."

Mikail cast his brother a bewildered look. "You're not honestly seeing her again—"

"Why not?"

"She took you for an arsch once with that footballer—
"

"Hey that was a long fucking time ago. Things change."

The driver, a beefy and bald Pole who looked like Bruce Willis on steroids, honked the horn at Mikail. He held out his broad-knuckled hands.

"Is your Majesty waiting for his horse and carriage?"

Mikail took the hint and got on the bus. "See you tonight," he waved at Lukas who was already heading off in the other direction, toward the city center. He and his brother had always been close, but when his mom remarried, only a year after their father's death, Lukas moved away from home and although he lived in the same city he might as well have been on the other side of the world. Lukas had never been one to apply himself at anything. He'd always been a sort of easygoing drifter, moving around from sensation to sensation. He'd spent his youth chasing pills, booze and girls, bouncing from bar to nightclub to scene, never really fitting in anywhere—just a typical westernized fuckup with too much time on his hands—living in a blank soulless era. A Greg Parys—"Why Don't We Just Fuck?"/"Sunglasses-at-night" type of club washout. Twenty-six years old and nothing to look forward to but the same goofball existence he'd always had.

"You need to grow up," his stepfather had told him. That was after he'd nearly been trampled to death at the Duisburg Love Parade. "You're no bloody teenager anymore."

Lukas had taken him at his word and left home. But nothing had changed. He was still the same hollow and fractured millennial kid caught in the special syndrome of delayed adulthood that was the plague of the age. From thirteen to thirty it was all a gray zone. And when you got kicked out of the scene, what the mature adults liked to call moving on, it invariably turned out to be nothing but an exile from youthful indulgent pleasures without recompense.

Then Toby had entered his life, with the magic ticket to Neverland, and he was instantly hooked, and knew that nothing would ever be the same again.

Dejan Vidic had one hundred copies of *Plump Friction* sitting in a film canister in his fridge. He was supposed to hold them for Janko, who had new buyers coming in to MG from four different towns around Düsseldorf for test samples. But Janko didn't show up at the appointed time, and Dejan began to worry. His run in with the police investigators had made him very wary. Of course they couldn't know what they were after. They had him clocked as a drug-runner, and that made his job all the easier. So long as the police pursued that line of reasoning, they would never be able to put their finger on anything. But Janko should have brought the buyers in on Thursday, and it was already Friday afternoon. He thought about bringing the tapes up to Düsseldorf, but Janko had given him explicit instructions not to meet him in that city. Dejan figured he had his reasons. The guy had a respectable criminal record, and had even served time at Willich prison on a burglary charge. He'd shared a cell with Yasar Bayrak aka Hans Lang—the prisoner notorious for orchestrating his escape by hiding in a cardboard box in the laundry room and being carried out with the mail. It was Yasar who'd told him about the existence of the tapes, back in 2009. He'd given Janko the name of a cousin in Holland who formerly ran drugs along the expressways around Venlo. Now he ran tapes.

That was the story Dejan had been told. Dejan knew Janko from a retro disco-bar at a hotel in Belgrade, where he'd been visiting with family last summer. Serbian mobsters loved 80s disco-dancing (the Scarface complex), and after rocking out to the sounds of Frankie Goes to Hollywood and The Trammps they had struck up an acquaintance. They were both soccer fanatics and over several shots of Jagermeister and some chit-chat on different Bundesligaclubs, Janko had offered Dejan a position in his new business venture. He was setting up distribution houses, all around the Nordrhein-Westfalen state, and he needed people he could trust. Good old-fashioned homeboys to help him in his venture. Dejan had never been particularly allured by crime, but Janko's plan had sounded clean. There was no mention of guns, or narcotics, or any crossborder sleaze—just simple, straightforward distribution and sales of a very remarkable new product.

His girlfriend Milinka—sensing he was troubled— came in to the tiny kitchen from the bedroom and put her slender arms around his waist. She had the tan-olive skin and the narrow, sparkling eyes and thickly stenciled eyebrows of an Albanian. Her naturally dark curly hair had been bleached and ironed out according to fashion.

"What's the matter Dede?"

"Gar nichts—" he said dismissively, wondering if he should call Toby. He was Janko's distributor in Duisburg. A black albino whose look was so peculiar that it lent him an air of mystery that served him well in the business. Toby spent his days building and maintaining his obscure client list. There were eight other Tobys to Vidic's knowledge, in and around Düsseldorf. Toby was an alias, given to the distributors by Janko. He insisted upon not using real names when dealing with clients. Dejan didn't have to use an alias, because he only did transport, and had no contact with any of the tapers. The problem with the business they had set up was that it was doing well—too well for its own good. The news of the tapes existence was spreading like wildfire all over West Germany. And every new client heightened the risk of discovery or betrayal. But they couldn't stop. The money was coming in too much, too fast, and too easy.

"Where the hell is he?" Dejan suddenly muttered out loud. And Milinka pulled back from him and said, "I know something is wrong… is it that Janko you are always talking about?"

He didn't answer her. He stood up and paced over to the window and looked out from the fourth floor of their tenement at the empty street below. The neighborhood was caught in that quiet spell of an early weekend evening, disrupted only by the occasional sound of a passing car or delivery van. He watched a Taxi stop on the curb in front of the building, thinking it might be him. But no, an old woman got out, complete with a cane and shopping bags.

"You've been sitting in this apartment for two days straight," Milinka now said. "Why don't you just call him?"

"It's none of your business—" Dejan snapped hastily. Then he said, "I'm not supposed to call him, unless there is an emergency."

"Then what are you worrying about—silly goose," Milinka stretched her arms over her head and yawned, her gym top lifting to expose a slim well-toned navel with a slight Caesarean scar. She went to the fridge and took out a bottle of Isostar. She looked at the black and yellow (Big Up for Wiz Khalifa!) Kodacolor 200 canister that contained the merchandise.

"I can't believe people really are going crazy over this," she said. "What's so great about it anyway? You can watch any movie on your home computer."

"It's not at all the same," said Dejan. "The difference is night and day."

Milinka pouted. She picked up the canister and removed the plastic cap. Vidic leapt to his feet and wrenched it from her hands, shoving her violently against the wall. She slapped him on the head, sending his 123 KLAN cap flying.

"Eat flies, kopil!"

"Don't touch them, I'm warning you—" He recapped the canister and shook it in her face. "This is worth the price of a new car. And it doesn't belong to me. It's been bought with Janko and his partners' money."

"His partners? Ha, you think you are such tough boys," Milinka sneered. "Playing your little games. I don't care about your stupid tapes. I'm bored to death of sitting here molding away in this stinking flat because you are too paranoid to pick up your handy and call that fake mobster with the long hair. I want to go out tonight. I want to go drinking. I want to go dancing… if you don't take me I call my girlfriends."

"Do whatever you like," Dejan waved her off impatiently, picking up his cap and putting it back on. "Don't forget who pays the bills around here. Who pays your gym membership? Who pays for your handy and all those late night calls to that gypsy family of yours—"

Milinka gave him her most withering glare. "Komisch. And I suppose you think you get to fuck me for free." She slammed her Isostar bottle on the IKEA table so hard it shook. Then she went to the bathroom and began primping in front of the mirror, applying perfume, lip gloss, a quick brushing. Milinka primped like a boy, all done haphazardly and in five minutes. *Owing to her gypsy upbringing no doubt*, Dejan thought. Still, she looked fabulous.

"Where are you going?"

"Out. I can't stand being cooped up for one more minute in this rinky-dink hovel of yours. If you are making so much money you should be able to afford a better place. You decide you had enough of sitting around you can find me at the Sahara."

"I don't want you down there," Dejan moped, as she pushed past him and went to the entrance to unhook her coat. She flung it on.

"You hear me? I don't want you hanging around with

all those rubbish Kurds."

"They are not Kurds—they are Turks," she said. "And look who is talking. You go see them every week."

"That's not the same. That's for business."

Milinka gave a short, crisp laugh. "It's all business, Dede. You, of all people, should know that."

And then she stormed out, slamming the door behind her. He could hear her heels clicking on the stairs. He debated whether to go after her, but Janko could come by with the buyers any minute. He had to stay in the apartment. There would be plenty of time to party when the transaction had been completed. And in a week's time he would return for the next order: 200 copies of *Fatal Impulse*, which was already in the works. The one tape that Dejan was truly tempted to try. Janko had warned him very clearly and early on to never confuse business with pleasure. And Dejan had followed his advice and not succumbed to temptation.

And it was true, he was making enough money to afford a higher living standard. But that would simply arouse additional and unwanted suspicion. Already they were having difficulty handling the cash flow. Janko's Internet and Call Shop was part of a chain of Serbian-owned cafés that had been set up for money laundering purposes. But at the rate things were developing the shops alone wouldn't be enough to cover the inflow. They would have to appeal to his contacts to include the steakhouses, nightclubs, night shops and Spielhallen—all to camouflage their skyrocketing profits.

He must find out what was going on, what was

delaying Janko.

He decided he would call Albino Toby from the Sahara Shisha Lounge and get the low-down. It would also provide an opportunity to keep an eye on his girlfriend, who it seemed to him was getting too familiar with the Turks.

Dejan threw his varsity jacket on and headed for the door.

The thick fruity scent of hookah tobacco stung his nostrils as he entered the Sahara, which was already crowded at 8:30 in the evening. All the booths and low, wall-to-wall couches, were occupied by young and trendy students, rastas, phony German hip-hoppers, local Ausländers, and noisy pre-clubbers. There was a small mixing table set up in one corner, where a resident DJ wearing an annoyingly showy screen printed glow-in-the-dark tee was mixing French Rai and Turkish pop.

Dejan spotted Milanka at a curtained corner booth, just beneath the DJ box. She was sitting on a cushioned bench on a pile of embroidered pillows and sharing a pipe with three other people: two German girls with bland, plump Natalie-Horler looks, and a lean, dark-skinned man with hairy forearms. Possibly Turk or Arab. The whole table was riot with laughter, and Dejan felt a pinch of jealousy seeing his girlfriend enjoy herself without him.

She hadn't noticed him come in. He went up to the bar, where there was a cute, doe-eyed barwitch wearing some traditional headdress with silver coins dangling from it. She had a sexy, short halter top on, bust spilling out, and glitter on her cheeks and neckline.

"Abend. I'm Amal. What can I get you?" she asked him.

"A Flying Hirsh," he said.

"We don't serve alcohol here."

"What kind of fucking bar is this? Kein alcohol ist auch kein losung, weist Du?" he added, paraphrasing the famous drinker's witticism.

"It's not a bar—it's a hookah lounge."

"Give me a coffee then… a normal coffee. None of that Turk slop."

The barwitch rolled her eyes to the ceiling-fan, already annoyed, when Dejan asked her, "You got a phone here?"

"Yeah. But it's for private use."

He reached into his varsity jacket, pulled out a thick wad of banknotes held together by a silver clip. He peeled off two crisp bills and slammed them on the chrome counter.

The barwitch with the glitter-tits gave him a blank stare and then she took the bills and picked up a cordless phone from behind the bar. She handed it to him. He squeezed into a corner, sticking a finger in one ear so he could hear. He dialed Toby's number.

It rang and rang, and there was no answer. Dejan hung up and then he dialed it again.

This time Toby picked up. "Hallo?"

"Toby?"

"Hallo?"

"Toby, it's Dejan… here in MG. I got a problem—"

"Dejan? What's going on?"

"Do you know where Janko is?" There was a rustle on the other end. "Hello? Can you hear me—"

"I don't know who you're talking about," Toby said.

"Come on, don't fuck around. Just tell me—"

"Where are you?"

"I'm in a fucking bar, OK. Now what's happening?"

A methodic pause. "He's with the bulls."

"Was?"

"They nabbed him on some trumped up credit card scam from the last fucking century. Scare tactic. But it don't matter now, because he's out of the picture... the clan wants in."

"The clan wants in," Dejan repeated.

"The clan wants in," Toby affirmed. "I can't talk more. Come to the H-town market, tonight."

"I got *Plump Frictions*," said Dejan. "A whole fucking reel that's gonna spoil."

"Bring the movie."

"All of it?"

"Yeah. Bring it. I'm almost out of stock."

"Right—see you in an hour," Dejan said and hung up. He went back to the bar and forked over the cordless to glitter-tits. He spied Milinka at the back of the lounge, grooving sensually to an R'n'B/zouk mix, shaking her rump with that randy Ausländer moving in on her, and she allowing it! Dejan decided it was time to intervene. He pushed his way through a crowd of dimpled, charisma-deficient, curly-haired students in pastel-colored shirts, and he grabbed Milinka by the arm as she was dancing, yanking her away from her entourage.

"Aie! Let go!" she hissed.

"Come with me—"

"No!" She wrenched herself free from his grip. Then, as if realizing it was him, "Dede! What are you doing here?"

"Go back home," he said.

"No. I'm staying—"

"Fine," he grunted. "I'm out of here."

He brushed her off and pushed his way out of the lounge, leaving his coffee to steam on the counter. She called something after him, but he didn't turn round. He walked briskly from the Altstadt back home where he called for a Taxi to take him to Duisburg. The fare would be expensive: a couple hundred euro. But it didn't matter. He had a fair 20,000 worth in his jacket pocket and he would demand a reimbursement from Toby.

It was raining hard when the cab pulled up at the Ladenstadt, just below the SPD Bauwerk of Hochheide, the high-rise projects where Toby lived. What the wannabe badboys liked to call H-Town. It seemed that every city in Germany now wanted to have its own ghetto. The German kids were so desperate to rival the Americans that they even went so far as to invent ghettos where they didn't exist. Rival rappers started feuds on television and brawls outside concert halls for no apparent reason other than because it was expected of them. There was the occasional knifing, and even shooting, but it was still a far cry from any US gangland drive-by. To the German hip-hoppers, the merchandise, the style, the attitude, the baggies and the Apple Bottoms and the horny ass girls still came before the violence, which was generally staged. But lately it seemed more and more that the feuds were turning serious, perhaps out of some last-ditch attempt to lend authenticity to a scene that had always seemed a parody of the American one.

For a German youth, being street was a careful study of emerging trends, of lingo and aesthetic, of poise. It wasn't about a Glock 9 mm or selling crack over at Kotti. It was all about style over substance—about the need to define yourself as a teen idol in the information-saturated Internet age.

Because they had too much to preserve, the Germans could never be true gangsta.

But alone in your room, with your boyish fantasies of power and control running wild, the virus of the street plaguing your mind, standing in front of the mirror after pumping iron, arms flexed, pretending a baseball bat was a shotgun, *Scarface* poster on the wall behind you, *Knallhart* playing on Blue-Ray DVD, the image of a black siren in club-wear bent over the hood of a luxury Audi S8, thrusting her prominent oiled booty at you, allowing your mind to wander, you dreamt of having it all.

The marketplace was normally a hangout for all the juvenile gangs by night. But oddly, tonight, the scene looked empty. Dejan paid the fare and took shelter beneath the Kaufland arcades. He had barely waited two minutes when a black Audi A5 Sportback, with blue neons cruised by and then rolled up to Dejan. He could hear harsh Srpski rep blaring over the sound-system, causing the tinted windows to vibrate.

The front passenger window slid down. The volume dropped. Dejan saw the two men sitting in the front and he felt a chill come over him. They were hard-looking, older men. The driver had a shaved head, and a dark scowl and blue ink creeping up his neck. He was wearing a shiny Nike tracksuit. His colleague was a thin man with sunken cheeks, a crooked nose and a neatly trimmed goatee. Hair pulled back tight in a small ponytail. He had on a tight red shirt, collar turned up and a large gold chain with a heavy gold Orthodox cross dangling from his neck. The Zemun were not masters of understatement.

The co-pilot made a gesture for Dejan to come over. When he saw that Dejan was suspicious, he spoke to him in his native tongue.

"You're Toby's colleague, no?"

"Who are you?" Dejan asked. "Where's Toby?"

The man scratched his cheek. He had a lazy eye. He looked behind him and nodded his head at their passenger. The back door opened and Toby got out, his eyes red pinpoints in the dark. He looked jumpy.

"What's going on here?" Dejan asked him.

"It's OK," said Toby, "They're Janko's family."

"His family?"

The driver muttered something to his colleague and the guy turned to Dejan. "You got the tape?"

"It belongs to Janko," Dejan said.

"Well good, I'm Janko's cousin," said the man with the Gold Cross. "He's temporarily unavailable. Let me see the tape."

Dejan hesitated. "Go on, give it to him," urged Toby. He sounded scared.

"It's not mine—" Dejan protested, looking down the arcade alley, over the pavement slick with rain. He knew it would be useless to try and make a run for it.

The driver in the Nike tracksuit reached beneath his seat and pulled out a stubby, black Skorpion machine-pistol. He trained it at Dejan, who froze, feeling his guts clench.

"Give him the tape," he said softly. His eyes were void of any emotion. Like a dead fish.

Dejan reached into his pocket, fingers numb, and handed over the film canister. The driver put down the Skorpion.

Janko's cousin signaled for Dejan to come closer and when he did he held out an unmarked manila envelope.

"What's this?"

"Your cut. Go on—take it."

Dejan cautiously accepted the envelope, and took a quick peek inside. It was packed thick with €100 bills. He estimated a good two or three thousand in there.

"From now on—you work for us," said Janko's cousin. He cocked his head, like a bull terrier. "Understood?"

"Sure. But what do I have to do?"

"Same as now," the guy with the gold cross said. He scratched his crooked nose, and then he reached in the glove compartment and pulled out a cell phone. "Take this," he said. "You keep it on you all the time, OK? You got to text someone, press the C key first. When we call you—you come."

"Where?"

"It doesn't matter where. If I say Düsseldorf—you go there. If I say I want you in fucking Hamburg, you go to fucking Hamburg, understood—*brate*?"

Dejan nodded slowly.

"Can you drive?"

"What?"

"Auto." Mr. Gold Cross mimicked steering. "I see you come in taxi."

"I don't have a license."

"I didn't ask you about license. I ask if you can drive."

"Yeah. I can drive. Sure."

"OK—so what kind of car you want? You like Alfa Romeo? You want Audi, what?"

"I like all kinds of cars."

The two men looked at each other and broke into coarse laughter.

"Give me your ID."

"What?"

"Your Ausweise. Komm schon."

Dejan glanced in Toby's direction. He felt as though he were being held up. It was an unpleasant feeling. Grudgingly he reached for his wallet and handed over the credit-card size ID. The man flapped the laminated card against his palm.

"We'll find you something. No more fucking taxi," said Mr. Gold Cross. "No public transport, you got that, brate? You kids have been fucking around long enough. Jumping all over the place—like lice. You lucky you not transporting *gudra*, or you'd all be in fucking jail by now the way you run things. Now we're taking command of the operation. We gonna tighten things up a bit, see—watch out for you… now go on home to your girl. I call you in a bit."

The tinted window slid up and the driver gunned the engine and backed out of the arcade. They watched the departing Sportback and Dejan spat on the ground and said, "Thanks Toby. That was a class act, all the way. Next time I want a gun pointed in my face by Mr. Fucking Hostel I'll be sure to let you know."

"Hey man, I had no choice. They just showed up, like. It was you who called me, remember. You got your cut, so just chill."

"You are some fucking piece of work, you know that?"

Toby's handy came to life with that screwy Armand Van Helden "Duck Sauce" collaboration. Electro-house for the easy-jet set. He turned away from Dejan and began pacing. Toby belonged to that breed of people who simply had to pace back and forth when on their handy.

After a few rapid exchanges he snapped it shut and said, "I got some buyers coming by the house. Why don't you come with me? You can crash at my place, I got a spare room."

"Yeah, sure. It's the least you could do." Dejan looked at the handy he had been given, figuring it was pre-paid with possibly inbuilt encryption software for texting and some modification to make the IMEI and IMSI untraceable. He decided to put it to use and went ahead and texted in an SMS to Milinka.

DaD HDMDL GNK (Translation: Ich denke an dich. Hab dich mega doll lieb. Gute nacht kuss.)

21st century schizoid romance.

(PLUMP FRICTION TAPEWORLD)

"How did you get the gun?" Lukas asked his brother. They were standing on a junction of West Sunset Boulevard, Los Angeles, watching cars and campers zip along the wide, palm-lined street. The sky was postcard blue; the temperature a perfect seventy degrees,, with a light breeze from the Hollywood Hills, to the North, and the white-painted universally recognized Hollywood sign just barely visible over the city smogline. There was a large all-week garage on the left, and across from them a giant billboard advertising the 2004 summer hit movie *Kill Bill Volume II*.

"In the mailbox. Jesus, don't you ever play video games?" Mikail said, tucking the 9 mm Star Model B into the waistband of his striped Abercrombie-and-Fitch shorts.

"Yeah but how did you know it was in there?"

"The number, dummy, 666. It's the same combination as on the briefcase. A dead giveaway. When you see a clue like that, you know you're supposed to look inside.

"So we're supposed to go where?"

"1525 North Van Ness Avenue," Mikail recited. That was the location of the apartment where Brandon and his buddies were camping out with the mysterious briefcase belonging to crime boss Mosley Horace. The plan was to steal the MacGuffin before hitmen Joel Winston and Vinz Vegas showed up. They had exactly 8 minutes and 24 seconds to intercept it, or they'd be the ones in the line of fire.

"OK—so I guess we go up here then," Lukas said, reading the number on a Denny's coffee shop. "How much time have we got?"

"6 minutes and counting down," Mikail looked at his Casio, glad he'd taken his stopwatch with him into the picture. It was only his second time in a tapeworld, but he was already mastering the ropes quicker and better than his older brother. See, Mikail had guessed correctly that a tapeworld was a programmed environment, and so followed the same sort of parameters as on, say, a video game. He had noticed that one entered a tapeworld wearing the same clothes and with the same accessories that one had on before taking the tape. (He was dressed casual: colored shorts, Hawaiian shirt, sandals. Lukas had chosen a dark gray suit, offset by an ironed white shirt and thin black tie. Just like the killers). Additionally, the timeframe moved at the same speed as in the original movie. No matter where you went or what you did, an event in the original picture occurred in the tapeworld at exactly the same time (unless you intervened to disrupt it). Mikail had set his timer to 8 minutes and 24 seconds before entering *Plump Friction*, so that it would countdown from that timeframe the moment they entered the picture. At the end of the countdown the killers would show up.

"It's right there," said Mikail, pointing to a low-level hacienda-style apartment block, painted in cheery pastel tones.

The courtyard was lined with dark green shrubbery. They passed through the main entrance and entered the reception area, which was a carpeted lobby with square white columns and red-cushioned furniture—just like in the picture.

They went to the elevator and Lukas hit the "up" switch on the outer control panel.

"I don't get it," he confessed to his brother.

"What?"

"You saw that billboard, across from the garage. *Kill Bill 2.*"

"Yeah."

"That came out ten years afterPulp Fiction. Isn't that just wrong?"

"Naja. Think, Lukas. Whoever programmed this tape copied all the sets from the original as perfectly as possible, right?"

"Right…"

The lift doors opened. They got inside. Mikail pressed the button for the fourth floor. Brandon's apartment was number 416. It helped to be well versed in movie trivia.

"…but to fill in the surroundings they must have used some sort of virtual mapping system. I mean, this building we're in doesn't exist anymore in the real world. Even the diner that Jackson and Travolta are sitting in right now, having breakfast and arguing about pigs vs. dogs, it was torn down in 1999."

Lukas began humming the heavily reverberated surfer rock theme song of the picture, Misirlou. "Da da da dum dum da da…"

"Cut it out —"

Lukas tapped him on the shoulder. "Let me have the gun."

"No."

"Come on—I paid for this tape."

"With whose money? Veronika's?"

"None of your goddamn business. I paid for the tape. You did fuck all…"

"I told you I was broke."

"I bailed your ass out. I should be the one carrying the gun."

The lift doors opened with a soft *bing!* and Mikail strode out into the hallway. He checked his stopwatch. "Four and a half minutes. Quickly!" He hurried through the narrow corridors, taking a left, then a right, rapidly scanning the numbers on the doors as they passed.

"This is it—" he whispered, stopping in front of one. "Look here, you take the gun…"

"Are you sure?"

"Yeah. I mean, after all you did pay for it." He handed the Spanish pistol to his older brother, who turned it around in his hand, marveling at its weight, at the rugged texture of the grip. The programmers had really thought of every detail.

"Geil!" Lukas spoke in an excited whisper. "What's his name again?"

"Who?"

"The guy who's gonna answer the door…"

"I believe he's called Marvin... the guy at the table is Brandon. The kid lying on the couch is Roger. I mean, he doesn't have a name in the movie, but that's his name on the script. I looked it up. Don't forget there's a fourth guy hiding in the bathroom... he's armed."

"Right."

"Three minutes. Hurry!"

Lukas rapped on the door with the barrel of his gun. They heard footsteps approaching, and then the bolt clicked and it opened.

A thin black kid peered out, his expression changing from anticipation to bewilderment. He hadn't been expecting them.

"Can I help you?"

Lukas thrust the barrel of his 9 mm Spanish pistol in his face and cocked the hammer. "Help yourself and step aside, Marv." The boy's face went white, he cowered against the wall. Lukas and Mikail strode into the room, with the cocky assuredness they had visualized and rehearsed.

Brandon was sitting at a small, round table in a dumpy room. In front of him, on a pile of grease-stained wrapping paper was a Big Aloha burger, fries and a Sprite. The other boy, Roger, with the Flock of Seagulls haircut, was lying on a checkered couch near the window looking as dopey and off-guard as in the original cut.

"Do you know who we are?" Lukas asked. The boys shook their heads. No.

"Well let me refresh your memory then. We're

associates of your old business partner—Mr. Mosley Horace. You remember him don't you?" Lukas pointed the Spanish pistol toward the preppy kid with the neatly combed hair, sitting at the round table.

"You must be Brandon, am I right?"

The kid gulped and nodded affirmatively.

"Seems like we caught you at breakfast. What are you having?"

Brandon swallowed hard, "H… Hamburgers."

"What kind of hamburgers? Wendy's? Jack-in-the-box?" Lukas was struggling to keep a straight face, but a sort of snicker escaped him and Mikail said, "Two and a half minutes—we don't have time for these charades…"

"All right. I'm gonna make this quick. We're here for the briefcase. The one that belongs to Mosley Horace. So nobody move and nobody gets killed… and that includes your friend hiding in the bathroom." Lukas spoke loudly enough for the fourth guy to hear. Mikail went straight over to the kitchen and rummaged in the cupboards beneath the sink. He found the case and flipped it on the counter. He turned the combination to 666 and opened it. An orangey glow lit up his face. Lukas, still training the gun on Brandon said, "What's in it? Mickey… what's in it?"

Mikail smiled. In the case was nothing but three illuminated flashlights and a note that read:

"Dear taper, whoever you may be… congratulations. You've got the case. As a reward there's a green 1974 chevy nova waiting for you outside the building. The keys are in the ignition. Hope you are having fun—your programming team.

"P.S. Get out now!!!"

Mikail snapped the briefcase shut. Lukas glowered at Brandon in his best Samuel L. Jackson impersonation—which was only about half as frightening. He was lacking the Afro and sideburns. And his babyish, milchbubi complexion didn't quite work in his favor. Still, he was trying.

"Do you read the bible, Brandon? There's this passage I got memorized. Ezekiel 25: 17… The path of the righteous man is beset on all sides by the… the… tyranny…" He blinked, trying to remember the rest of the verse.

"Come on let's get out of here. We got to move! We've got no time for impersonations." Mikail cut him off, moving to the door.

Lukas cursed, "Fukushima! Forget it. You're a lucky sonofabitch—" He tucked the gununder his belt and made after his brother, then stopped and ran back into the apartment and grabbed the juicy Big Aloha burger from the table and took it with him.

They sprinted down the corridor. They came to a junction and Mikail checked his watch. "Forty-five seconds," he said. "Shit, do we take a right or keep on going straight?"

"I don't know. I can't remember where we came from… everything looks the same."

"What the fuck is that?" Mikail pointed to the greasy Big Aloha that Lukas had clenched in his hand.

"I couldn't resist—" Lukas said, sheepishly. "It's really good. Wanna try?"

"Quit fucking around. They're gonna be here any second... quick..."

"Look there are the elevators!" Lukas motioned to the end of the corridor.

"Not the lift. They're coming by the lift. The stairs—" Mikail pulled him in the opposite direction. They ran down a flight of red-carpeted steps, just as the elevator doors opened in the hall above them and John Travolta and Samuel L. Jackson, aka Joel Winston and Vinz Vegas, stepped out with their trademark confident swagger. Lukas peered around the landing and heard them talking to each other.

"I still hafta say, you play with matches you get burned—"

"What do you mean?"

"You don't be givin' Mosley Horace's new bride a foot massage..."

They ran down four flights of stairs, and burst out of the apartment complex and into the bright L.A. sun. Just across the street was the prize Chevy, parked between a rusty trailer and a bright red Pontiac Firebird. Its polished rooftop and chrome fenders glinted in the sunlight.

Mikail ran to the car.

"Where are you going?" Lukas hurried after him.

"It's our ride—" Mikail swung the passenger door open and tossed the case in the backseat. "You're going to have to drive. I don't know how."

Lukas got in the drivers seat. There was a set of keys dangling from the ignition. The Chevy smelled of warm leather and hairspray. There was a gun-toting semi-nude Pam Grier sticker on the dashboard.

"What's in the case?"

"A note. It said to take this car."

Lukas turned the ignition. The engine whirred and choked. He floored the pedal. The motor chugged but wouldn't start.

"Shit—it's not working…"

"Keep on trying—" Mikail felt a lump of anxiety forming in his throat. Was this a trap? Lukas grimaced and twisted the key again… he pounded the accelerator repeatedly.

"Be careful. Don't flood it!" Mikail started… Then he saw the two hitmen dash out onto the street as if chasing someone. They froze, looking up the avenue, in the opposite direction. The black man scratched his Afro.

"Oh shit!" Mikail shouted. "They're right in front of us! Start the fucking car! Lukas!"

Lukas twisted the key a third time and the engine roared to life. The two killers in the dark suits pivoted around. The John Travolta character cocked his head. His earring glinted. Samuel L. Jackson's eyes went white with fury. He whipped out his own Star model B.

"Hey! Hey, that's my ride, motherfucker!"

Vinz Vegas pursed his lips and trained his Colt .45 at the windshield, preparing to fire.

"Lukas!" Mikail screamed.

Lukas kicked the gear into reverse and spun the wheel. He floored the gas and the Chevy screeched out into traffic. Vinz fired and a side-view mirror exploded into splinters.

"Fuck!" Lucas screamed, ducking his head. He backed the car off as Jules fired two other rounds and the windshield exploded, and another bullet whizzed past his ear. He accelerated in reverse and the Chevy swung out into a crossroad and smashed into the bumper of an incoming vehicle. The force of the collision sent them spinning around, as in a centrifuge.

The two hitmen were running toward them, guns brandished. They heard the Jackson character yell, "Oh you dead as fuckin' fried chicken!" and a series of bullets slammed into the trunk. POW! POW! POW!

"I'm trying!" Lukas shifted gears, spun the wheel and turned in the opposite direction, gunning the 5.7 liter V8 motor for all it was worth. The Chevy lurched up the avenue; Lukas twisted the wheel and swerved to avoid a car backing out of a garage. He dared a glance in the rear-view mirror and saw the killers still running after them, but receding into the distance as they gained momentum. Up ahead was roadwork, lined by traffic cones. He swerved to the right, burning a red light and barely made it in front of an approaching transit bus, which honked loudly.

They cruised down West Sunset Boulevard, past the shimmering blue Metropolitan hotel tower. Lukas saw a strange eclectic mix of Asian shops, Googie-stylebars and grillshacks, fast-food outlets, gaudy motels and budget inns.

They passed the gateways of massive film and recording studios.

"Have we lost them?" Mikail asked, still cowering in a ball beneath the dashboard, his hands cupped protectively over his head.

"Yeah, it's all right," Lukas said. Mikail lifted his head back up and saw that the windshield of the Chevy was splintered and there was a finger-size hole in the glass directly in front of him.

"Fucking hell, I could have been killed," he gasped. Then he said, "Where are we?"

"I haven't got a clue."

"This city can't go on forever. It would be impossible to program that much..." said Mikail. He was thinking carefully and then he said. "It must be a parametric design."

"What do you mean?"

"Look at the hills. They're behind us—right?"

Lukas glanced in the rear-view mirror and saw the peaks of the Hollywood Hills looming in the background.

"OK, now take the next hard right, up by the Starbucks there... "

"What are you trying to prove?"

"Just do it."

Lukas turned 90 degrees onto an adjacent avenue, and Mikail said. "The mountains should be on our right side now."

"Yeah," said Lukas. "So?"

Mikail tapped the rear-view mirror. "They're still behind us," he said. "It's a closed loop universe. We're driving in circles, no matter which way you turn."

"Then how come we haven't passed the same building twice?"

"Because the order they appear in is scrambled, I guess. It's following a repeating pattern—but it's much too complicated for us to comprehend."

"And the people? Are they repeats too?"

"I don't know. I'm not going to start counting them, if that's what you want to hear."

"What's the time?"

Mikail glanced at his watch. It had stopped at the 00:00 mark. "We must be about twenty minutes into the picture," he said.

"What's happening now?"

"Now?... Now I would imagine Mosley Horace is sitting in a topless bar talking to the boxer—the Bruce Willis character..."

"Right, right..." Lukas nodded. "So then they bring him the briefcase. Only—they won't show up... because we got the briefcase. Which means Vinz isn't going to take Tia Horace to Whack Babbit Jim's. He'll be too busy looking for us, trying to get it back. He won't dare go to Mosley empty-handed... which also means that Tia will probably be at Whack Babbit Jim's alone."

"Are you thinking what I'm thinking?"

"Disco!" exclaimed Lukas. "But... where is Whack Babbit Jim's?"

"Well, it was never a real diner. It was built in a

Miramax studio warehouse in Culver City… so I guess we got to look for that."

"And how do we get there?"

"Ask one of these tape-people. I don't have a map in my bloody head."

They stopped in front of a line of colorful discount stores and bazaars advertising clothes and jewelry at under $5.

A funny looking little guy came strolling by, dressed in a dapper suit. He stopped in front of a thrift shop advertising vinyl jazz 45s and began rifling through a collection. Lukas got out of the Chevy and went up to him.

"Excuse me—"

The little guy spun around, and Lukas experienced a shock of recognition. He'd seen his face before: those bulging eyes, that shaggy receding hairline… a face that was filled with a sort of sneaky, creepy desperation. He was a character actor. Lukas was sure he had seen him in a film. A heist thriller. What was the title? *Wilde Hunde? Reservoir* something… What was he doing on the street in a tapeworld?

"Do you live around here?" Lukas asked. The moment he'd said it he felt silly. But the man seemed to take him seriously.

"In the city? Yeah, sure… I mean um… I came out to Hollywood because um… I originally wanted to be a uh screenwriter. But eh like things got complicated… and now I'm just tryin' to get two pennies to rub together so… ah, well uh yeah I live just round the corner… why?"

"We're trying to find this place—it's like a 1950s icon-themed restaurant in Culver City—"

"You mean Whack Babbit Jim's?"

"You know the place?"

"Are you kidding me? I work there. I'm a uh—a waiter."

"No shit. It's a small world. Can you tell us how we can get there?"

The guy looked past Lukas, at his brother sitting in the Chevy and scratched his head. His drooping eyelids twitched. "No problemo… you just uh… take the next right, go down to the end of the Boulevard and you'll uh see it on your left. But it ain't open. The uh place… the joint opens in the uh… evening."

"That's fine," said Lukas. "Thanks a lot." He ran back to the car. The little guy made as if to say something and then turned back to browsing the records. He whistled at a hippie-chic girl in jeans shorts who came roller-blading by. She pirouetted around and promptly gave him the finger.

"So what did he say?" Mikail asked.

"He says that Whack Babbit Jim's is just down the next street. But it don't open until the evening."

"Which means it's going to open in the next five to ten minutes," said Mikail. "About a half hour into the picture—tapeworld time."

"Shit, we better hurry—" Lukas put the car into gear and drove off from the strip and cut into traffic.

"That guy looked so familiar—I could have sworn I'd seen him in a movie," he said.

"This is a movie."

"No I mean a different one than this… I don't recognize him from this picture."

"That's odd—" Mikail reached behind him and took the briefcase on his lap. He opened it and the gimmick lit up with that gold-orange flashlight glow. Inside was a silvery Smith and Wesson 659 and two loaded magazine clips. There was a new note, taped to the interior lining of the case that read:

"A little gift from Mr. Pink"

"You wanna know who you were talking to back there?" Mikail said, a sly smile creeping across his face. "Steve Buscemi—"

"Of course!" Lukas slapped his head. "*Reservoir Dogs*. What's he doing here?"

"He must have a cameo."

They heard a heavy sputter as a blond, pale-face biker rode on the lane alongside them, sitting on a gleaming, customized Harley-Davidson FXR. He had a blue shirt with a silver star on it and leather boots with spurs. He glanced once in their direction and then sideswiped in front of the Chevy and veered left.

Mikail turned on the AM/FM radio—a big clumsy contraption—and twisted the knob. He hit on a jazz station, then static… then the sharp twang of heavy reverb electric guitar and saxophone… he turned the dial further and a radio announcer's voice came blaring over the stereo…

"You're listening to KFWB-AM live, Breaking News.

This just in—an armed robbery has occurred at the
Hawthorne Grill, on 137th street and South
Hawthorne Boulevard. According to eyewitness reports
a young, casually dressed couple—man and woman—
held up the eatery and made off with the contents of
the register as well as the wallets and valuables of the
customers. The suspects are currently being sought by
the LAPD, who have launched a bulletin and a
request for the public to assist them in capturing these
armed and dangerous criminals…
"… The man is reported to be about five-foot seven…
Caucasian, blond hair, green eyes, middle-aged with
a slight British accent…"

"Oh mein Gott," said Lukas. "We're really wrecking
things now. Munchkin and Honey Buns have held up the
diner… we've got Mosley's briefcase and Joel's car. And Joel and
Vinz are after us. I wonder what's going to happen next."

"Just don't stop at any pawn shop," counseled Mikail.
"I don't want to run into Maynard and Zed."

"Zed's dead, baby," Lukas said.

"Not in this film, he isn't…"

As Lukas steered them toward the Miramax warehouse
they passed a shutdown lap-dancing club. There was a neon
sign on the side of the building, the lamps switched off—the
letters spelled "Sully-Lee-Royce."

A few seconds after they driven past it, a well-built
bruiser (Bruce Willis) in a marine haircut, wearing a brown

suede leather jacket and faded blue jeans exited the backdoor of the club. He paused to light an unfiltered cigarette and then walked across the empty parking lot toward a white Honda Civic. In one hand he clutched a brown paper envelope and in his coat pocket was a pack of Red Apple cigarettes.

7

At the Centre Hospitalier Universitaire, Marie Venet sat by her son's hospital bed, holding his hand, which was limp as a rag. There were wires attached to his scalp, electrodes fixed above and below his eyes, and to his chin and collar bone. He had an oximeter clipped to his finger, acanularunning in his nose and an elastic belt around his chest, all connected to an HP monitor.In the upper-corner of the ceiling was a newly-installed infrared camera, silenty recording and monitoring Christopher. It was not a standard procedure with coma victims, but Marie was not aware of this. She looked at the bouquets of flowers and get-well cards that had been placed by his bedside and she felt an overpowering surge of emotion and got up and walked over to the window, feeling as though she were about to cry.

"Madame Venet," a nurse inquired softly. Marie blinked and turned around slowly.

"Yes?"

"Dr. Sameer would like to see you in his office, if you have the time."

Dr. Sameer was the head physician in charge of the Department of Neurophysiology. Marie had only met him once before, when Christopher had been admitted. He appeared to her like all the doctors she had known: courteous, neat, professional, and aloof.

The nurse led her to his bureau, which was at the end of the service ward, and knocked on the door.

"Come in," he called back. The nurse pushed open the door and ushered Marie into the room.

Dr. Sameer was seated behind his desk, studying a computer monitor. He was wearing a white jacketwith a blue shirt and blue silk tie underneath. He looked up as she entered the room and gave her a terse smile. Marie looked around. The office was brightly lit and neatly equipped. There was a row of colored binders on a shelf behind him. A three-line IP telephone and fax machine sat comfortably alongside an LCD screen. In one corner was a potted *Dracaena*: the stereotypical green-leafed office plant that brightened up bureaucratic settings the world over.

The nurse left.

"Sit down, please." He motioned to a hardback plastic chair opposite him.

Marie sat down and Dr. Sameer pushed back his ergonomic chair and folded his hands across his chest, drumming his thumbs. Then he leaned across the table and said, "First of all, I would like to make it abundantly clear, we are still in the dark concerning the cause of your son's condition. However, further testing has led us to conclude that the original diagnosis—that of a comatose state—may be incorrect."

Marie shifted in her seat. "Incorrect? How?"

Dr. Sameer sucked through his even, white teeth. He showed her a printed page of wiggly lines with a series of reference numbers. It looked like the printout of a lie detector machine.

"This is part of a prolonged EEG reading, which we conducted two days ago," said Dr. Sameer. "It's a device that measures brain activity. On this page we see predominant delta activity. This is what you would normally find during a state of slow-wave or deep sleep. Now we find prolonged bursts of delta activity in patients with intracranial or head injuries, usually accompanied by increased muscular activity and attempts to communicate. This however, is obviously not the case with your son, who is in perfect physical condition. Furthermore, we have charted recurring periods of EEG desynchronisation. This is characteristic of a state more closely resembling wakefulness…"

"What are you implying, doctor? That my son is conscious? That he is paralyzed?"

Dr. Sameer held up his hand. "I'm not saying that. But the fast, low-voltage activity recorded, especially these saw-tooth waves that you see here…" He showed her a second printout. "These are characteristic of what we call REM sleep. A stage of sleep we classify through three features: rapid eye movement, muscle atonia, and EEG desynchronization. Now Christopher lacks the saccades that are a fundamental feature of REM sleep, so we cannot qualify it as that. But this cyclic shifting between dominant delta activity and EEG desynchronization is not characteristic of someone who is comatose. In fact, it is quite impossible for someone who is comatose. To put it simply, none of it makes any sense."

There was a long, uncomfortable pause.

"What happens during REM sleep?" Marie asked.

"We dream," Dr. Sameer said.

Dejan returned to MG on Sunday night. The flat was dark. He let himself in and turned on the light. He saw that everything had been cleaned and neatly arranged. Even the water in the fish aquarium had been changed, and the carpet vacuumed. Every surface had been dusted, down to the remote control on the TV. He knew right away that Milinka was upset.

He pinned his varsity jacket on the wall and went straight to the bedroom.

The lights were also off, but from the faint moonlight filtering through the curtains he could distinguish her slender form, curled up in a fetal position beneath the sheets. He undressed in the dark and got into bed beside her. He put his hand on her bare shoulder. There was no movement, but he could tell by her breathing that she was awake.

After awhile she said, "What are you hiding from me?"

"What do you mean?"

"Are you seeing someone else?"

"No."

"Where were you?"

"I went to see Toby."

"Liar. I don't believe you."

"Then don't," he snarled, rolling over away from her. After a minute had passed he felt her turn over and snuggle against him, her breasts bare against his back.

"I worry about you—" she said. She traced a pattern along his neck with her fingertip. He felt a shudder of gooseflesh.

"You shouldn't—"

"If I don't who will? Are you in some kind of trouble?"

"No."

"Would you tell me if you were?"

"Probably not."

"Is it the police?"

"Ha!" he snorted contemptuously. "I can walk right through a police station with perfect immunity anytime I want. They have nothing."

"Then why are you afraid?"

"I'm not afraid—"

"Yes, you are. Something is bothering you."

"Go to sleep—" he told her. She got up and left the bedroom. A few moments later he heard the sound of the TV being turned on, and then the door to the living room being shut.

(*Triassic Park* Tapeworld)

Heike followed the guide rail across the *Dilophosaurus* territory to the crest of a hill, where in the dark she could see the taillights of the first Ford Explorer, which had stopped near the electrified fencing of the *Tyrannosaur* paddock. She was breathless after her mad dash through the ferns and foliage, and her bare legs were caked in mud, her socks soaked through and her normally ironed-blonde hair clung in matted clumps to her face.

She banged on the rear window of the first vehicle and the two men inside jumped.

"Jesus, it's that crazy girl!" Genco, the cowardly lawyer, said.

"Lass mich rein!" Heike called out.

"Open the door," said Jeff Goldblum, aka Jan Milestone. He pointed to the backdoor of the Explorer. Heike swung it open and got in. The two men craned their necks to look at her. Jan Milestone was dressed entirely in black and smelt of chewing gum. He regarded her with an air of curious amusement. Genco—sitting beside him—was not so amused. He was a thin, prematurely balding and nervous man. He looked very out of place for a jungle expedition.

"What the hell are you doing here?" he snapped. "You were supposed to go back to the visitors' center with Dr. Hardy…"

"I wanted to see the *Tyrannosaur*," Heike grinned.

"Jesus God, kids today. They just can't wait in line for a ticket like everyone else…"

Jan Milestone held up two fingers, indicating for Genco to be quiet. He stared at Heike through his tinted, horn-rim glasses. "And uh… how do you uh… know we'll see a T-rex?"

"Because the electric fences are down, all over the island. And it's been a long time since he's fed. And one goat isn't going to do it."

"How do you…" Genco's gaze fell on the loose chain, where a goat had been tethered for the animal's feeding. The goat was no longer there. He started to say something and then stopped and stared at her, baffled. The girl knew everything that was going on. She had some sort of preternatural awareness that was making him uneasy. He tugged at his tie and swallowed hard.

"Listen kid, I don't know where you're getting this information from, but this park has been put together by highly skilled professionals. It's not your average *Pirates of the Caribbean* tour—"

"If they're so skilled then why aren't the cars moving?" Malcolm asked. He pulled out a flask of bourbon from his leather blazer and took a sip. He offered it to Genco who declined. Heike giggled. He was the same obnoxious smartass as in the movie.

"You were great in *The Fly*," she said.

"Who are you talking to? Me?"

"Yeah you. Jeff Goldblum."

"What's she talking about?" Genco questioned. "What fly? What golden plum?"

"I don't know. She's rambling. Maybe she's got a fever…"

"I don't have a fever, I'm not delirious," said Heike. "The kind of control you're attempting here is impossible. If there's one thing that evolution has taught us it's that life cannot be contained… it breaks free…"

"She's right—she's right!" Jan Milestone excitedly

agreed.

Genco rubbed his eyes, "Oh, please…"

"It expands to new territories. It crashes through barriers. Painfully, maybe even dangerously, but it finds a way," Heike concluded.

"That's what I said to Mr. Hammond in the Hatchery… those were my exact words to him!" Malcolm said, stunned.

Genco scowled at Heike. "What are you? Some kind of psychic?"

They saw Dr. Graham get out of the front vehicle and run toward them. He held a water canteen in one hand. Jan Milestone opened his door and Dr. Graham peered in the car, his fedora dripping with the rain.

"Is your radio out as well?" He spied Heike sitting in the backseat and asked "What's she doing here?"

"She uh… invited herself along," Malcolm explained. "Says she wants to see the T-rex up close…"

"What have you got—a death wish?" asked Dr. Graham.

They heard a low rumble in the distance. Then another. And another. There were two plastic cups of water in a recess on the dashboard. Heike leaned over and saw the famous concentric rings. The Spielberg touch.

"What was that? Thunder?" Genco asked, squinting out the windshield.

"You wish," said Heike. "Those are impact tremors."

"Impact tremors!" Grant repeated.

"He's coming—" said Heike gleefully.

Genco could contain himself no longer, he whirled around angrily. "Listen kid, for the last time I'm warning you!"

They heard a dull thud as the goat's dismembered leg fell on the Plexiglas sunroof of the lead Land Explorer.

"Jesus God!" Dr. Graham spun around. "Ella!"

The *Tyrannosaur* appeared just behind the electric fencing. It threw back its huge, pebbled Elephant-man head, and downed the remains of the goat in one luxurious swallow. They could hear its raspy breath and its guttural groaning. The air smelled like a zoo.

There was a whipping sound as one by one the electric cables were torn from their connection bolts. A bright red DANGER sign came crashing down. The T-rex moved through the opening of the ruined fence, its powerful hind limbs flexing, flanks rippling, its massive tail rose in the air as it lowered its head and ROARED! Revealing rows of robust, yellowing, tusk-shaped teeth.

"Boy do I hate being right all the time," Malcolm said.

"Me too—" said Heike.

All three men stared at her. Gobsmacked.

"Everybody keep absolutely still!" whispered Dr. Graham, as the T-rex lumbered around. Heike rolled her eyes. We've heard this one before.

From the rear of the front Explorer they saw a blue spray of light. Someone was activating a Maxabeam. The *Tyrannosaur* stood right beside them, grunting and snuffling. Its clawed forelimbs hung daintily in front of it, as it spotted the light flashing from the other vehicle.

"Turn the light off!" Dr. Graham hissed under his breath. "Turn it off!"

The *Tyrannosaur* lumbered toward the light, its tail dipped and swung like a crane. Heike jumped out of the car and ran after it.

"Where's that lunatic going?" Genco asked shakily.

"I d…don't believe it" Dr. Graham gasped. "She's charging the T-rex!"

Heike ran straight to the *Tyrannosaur*, waving her arms wildly and shouting.

"Hey you stupid beast! Over here! Komm schon!"

The *Tyrannosaur* lowered its bulky head and nudged the vehicle with its snout. They heard a series of piercing screams. They saw her run right up to the T-rex and deliver a sharp and savvy kick to its hind leg.

The *Tyrannosaur* roared and whipped around. Its leathery snout moved from side to side, as if trying to locate Heike, who stood, perfectly still in front of it. Its eyes were pale yellow in the moonlight.

"Don't move… don't move…" Dr. Graham chanted under his breath. The three men were tense and poised. They could scarcely breathe. The crazy girl was going mano-à-mano with the most ferocious carnivore of all evolution.

"What is this girl?" Genco whispered in terror.

"She's uh… German," said Malcolm, as if this summed it all up.

They saw her clutching something behind her back. A

stone. She was holding a rock.

"Jesus Christ is she going to do what I think—" Dr. Graham started.

Heike hurled the stone at the *Tyrannosaur* with all her might. It struck a flap of tender skin, just below the creature's right eye. The T-rex let loose a shattering bellow that blew Heike to the ground. She scrambled to her feet and sprinted toward their car. The *Tyrannosaur* ducked its head and lurched forward.

"Holy shit she's bringing it here!" Dr. Graham yelled. "Nobody move!"

"Move! Move! For the love of God, move!" Jan Milestone sprung from the right side of the car—Genco dived out the left. Heike crashed into Dr. Graham, sending him toppling behind the Explorer. The *Tyrannosaur* smacked its leathery snout against the grill of the Explorer and the vehicle did a somersault, landing on its roof. It tore a tire straight off the axle and shredded it like a Hershey bar. The T-Rex's massivejaw muscles bunched as it chewed and they caught a whiff of rank, rotting breath.

The three men and the girl were crouched behind the upended Explorer, cowering for their lives.

"What have you done!" Genco hissed.

"Quiet!" snapped Grant.

"I'm going to die a genius," said Malcolm with an air of weary resignation.

Heike shook her head disdainfully. "Oh, come on, there are four of us. We can take it…"

Genco's eyes shot out of his head. "Are you plotzing! What planet are you from?"

"It's just a big lizard," said Heike.

Dr. Graham stared at her, stupefied. He looked at Jan Milestone who held up his hands as if to say *She's not my problem*.

They saw Ella Sattler emerge from the first car. She was waving a lit flare in her hand and shouting. The *Tyrannosaur* turned in the direction of the noise. It moved toward her.

"Ella no!" Dr. Graham yelled.

The two kids—Lex and Tim—ran screaming from the other side. The *Tyrannosaur* darted its head in confusion. Genco sprung to his feet and backed away. Jan Milestone stood up in a noble effort to distract it from the screaming children.

"Over here!" he yelled.

"Nobody move!" Dr. Graham called out. And in a moment of terrible lucidity he was struck by the absolute absurdity of the situation. The *Tyrannosaur* was surrounded by seven people, all dashing wildly in different directions, like players on a baseball pitch: Ella waving a flare, Lex brandishing a Maxabeam, Tim screaming bloody murder... three men shouting and gesticulating behind it and a nasty German girl who threw rocks. The situation seemed to be confusing the poor creature who by the uncertain way it was thrashing about seemed to have expected a less complicated dinner.

"Now we're all going to die," Malcolm pithily remarked.

An idea suddenly surfaced in Heike's mind. She ran

back to the upended Ford Explorer and crawled underneath it. She rummaged in the crumpled interior and found a metal roadside emergency kit. She opened it and a pile of road flares fell out.

She grabbed one in her hand and uncapped it.

The *Tyrannosaur* charged at Ella who tossed her flare into the brush near a wooden outhouse. The T-rex crashed through the outhouse smashing it to pieces, sending planks and splinters flying.

Heike struck a new flare against the coarse striking surface of the cap. It lit up with a wash of radiant sparks.

She ran straight to the concrete barrier of the T-rex pen. She stood atop it, waving the lighted flare. Behind her was a sixty-foot drop to the *Tyrannosaur* pen. It was a an erroneous gimmick put in the movie, a blooper, because scene-greedy Spielberg had wanted to film the car falling off that side and crashing into the trees below, even if the drop to the enclosure didn't make sense. Now, she would put it to even better use.

"Komm schon du blödes Schwein!" Heike hurled another rock at its flank and the *Tyrannosaur* swung around and saw her standing on the slick edge of the precipice, waving the flare like a dog biscuit.

All eyes were now on her and the T-rex. Still holding the flare aloft, Heike reached behind her and grabbed hold of one of the cables from the destroyed fence. With a last deafening roar it charged. Its mighty clawed feet hammered and the earth shook. Its massive jaws opened and its hot stinking breath flew in her face. She threw herself off the precipice and the *Tyrannosaur* sprung after her.

And the group saw its claws skid briefly on the surface of the concrete barrier and then its tail flick once as the T-rex tumbled over the edge and crashed into the ferns sixty feet below with a low whimper.

And that was it.

They stood there, all six of them, speechless in the pouring rain. Then they heard Heike's voice.

"A little help, please?"

Dr. Graham and Jan Milestone ran to the edge of the barrier and they saw her dangling from the cable, with the *Tyrannosaur* lying in a crumpled heap at the bottom of the precipice, near a drain pipe.

They grabbed her by the arms and hoisted her back up. The rest of the group gathered around her, with the look of Idaho corn farmers discovering a UFO landing site.

Heike crackled her knuckles and she panned over the row of dumbstruck faces.

"No more naughty T-rex," she said.

The Renault van stopped in front of the farmhouse gate and the driver got out, leaving the engine running. On the side of the van was marked *A&A Loodgieter Rotterdam.* The driver looked like your average Joe the Plumber, with his blue workman's outfit with the company logo on the back. He was carrying a toolbox in one hand, the contents of which had traveled a considerable distance, all the way from a lonely village in Moldova and into Holland via Istanbul.

He rang the bell at the back door. A rickety bicycle leaned against the wall, near a mottled greenhouse, the plants in it long dead. He watched a weathervane spin atop the thatched roof. In the distance a dog uttered a series of hoarse barks.

After a few moments the screen door unlocked and a lanky, strawberry-blond thirty year old appeared in the opening.

"What's this? You were supposed to be here four days ago."

The plumber grimaced. "Move bitch—get out the way," he snarled, in a thick, foreign accent. His face was heavily creased and lined. He smelt of cheap cigarettes and aftershave.

Johannes let the man into the living room. The place was drab and tidy, with a wood stove, framed paintings on the walls, a heavy-duty cabinet with a vase on it—no photographs—and an open kitchen where the remnants of breakfast were visible on a harlequin plastic tablecloth. Two large windows, devoid of drapes, allowed for a view on the grassy plains, where in the distance, a tractor was circling.

"Where is eferybody?" asked the plumber.

"They're working—" said Johannes. "You can leave the goods with me." He reached for the handle and the man brutally slapped his hand away.

"Get me the Chinaman," he said, gruffly.

Johannes resentfully did as told. He hated dealing with De Schaduw's men—especially the delivery boys. They gave him the willies; always same, with their unhealthy faces and indecipherable accents. They were never content to just deliver the product. They always had to make a damn spectacle out of everything.

He went to the barn and called Dr. Yin, who was orchestrating the production of the *Fatal Impulse* mastertape. They were about a third of the way through, somewhere in the Ronnie Roz nightclub scene. When he opened the door to the lab the sound of an acid-house track could be heard, squelching and pumping away. They were programming the audio and olfactive cultures.

Johannes returned with Dr. Yin, who was wearing a lab coat, knee-length, and who looked as if he hadn't slept in days. There were dark circles under his eyes. And his cheeks were puffy.

"You're late—" were his first words to the man.

"The organ train doesn't run on time," said the

plumber, and then chuckled at his wit, revealing his lack of dental insurance. He opened the toolbox and drew out a cylindrical portable incubation chamber containing two dozen 400-micron-thick brain slices that were kept in oxygenated artificial cerebrospinal fluid, maintained at a temperature of 28 °C by means of a battery heating system and LED temperature monitor.

"These are young samples, yes?" Dr. Yin inquired. "The last ones you delivered showed signs of protein degradation... barely acceptable."

"Not to worry, young and healthy," the plumber grinned hideously, tapping the plastic shell of the incubation chamber.

"We'll see about that," said Dr. Yin. "I'll need double the amount, next delivery."

The plumber regarded him through glassy eyes. He sniffed and said, "Double will take more time. A munt... maybe two munts."

Dr. Yin was shaking his head. "No. No, that's no good! Two weeks from now, I want fifty samples. You have a problem with that you talk to my employer, ok? We're starting a particularly complicated piece next week—Kubrick—need lots and lots of stem cells –"

The plumber glared uncomprehendingly at Johannes. "What is Cubri?"

"*A Space Odyssey*," said Johannes sassily. "Don't they have cinemas in Bratislava?"

The plumber's face reddened and a vein throbbed in his

temple. "How would you like to make 2000 dollar the hard way?"

"What way is that?" Johannes thrust his face angrily forward.

"JoJo, please!" Dr. Yin stepped between them.

"Hey. I put you on ice!" the plumber snarled, stabbing two fingers emphatically in the direction of his kidneys.

Dr. Yin, even with the considerable weight of De Schaduw's protection, felt it would be wiser not to provoke such a dismally seedy character. He ushered the plumber gently aside and said, "Fifty samples… in three weeks?"

The plumber shrugged noncommittally. "I see what I can do." He looked over Dr. Yin's shoulder at Johannes who was standing defiantly, arms crossed, a fresh smirk across his face.

"I put this Ned Flanders boy on ICE!" the plumber barked. He grabbed back his toolbox and stormed past them. They heard the screen door slam and the van screech off.

"Ned Flanders?" Johannes scratched his head, trying to fathom *The Simpsons* reference and work out if it came to an insult.

Dr. Yin spun around and slapped Johannes across the head. He winced—*Ow!* "Stupid boy! Waardeloos! You have a mouth like a whore's snatch. Always open. You are going to cause us big trouble someday."

"Don't tell me you're afraid of that Slovenian prick. He's a nobody," said Johannes. "He's just a fucking prune acting out his *Hostel* routine. He's nothing more than a glorified postman."

"I still don't see the need for provocation." Dr. Yin grumbled. He headed back to the lab, taking the portable incubation chamber with him. Johannes followed him into the barn, where the members of the team heard them come in and looked up from their bench-tops.

"We're out of coffee, JoJo," Xander, his rotund face stuck in the EOG, pointed to an empty decanter near the stainless-steel washing area.

Kim handed Johannes the decanter. She was at the sink, sterilizing dressing and bayonet forceps and stainless steel spatulas with a bottle of isopropyl alcohol. She loaded a row of borosilicate beakers into an autoclave for sterilization before use.

"What are you doing?" Johannes asked her.

Kim smiled and flipped the START switch for the autoclave cycle.

"The dishes," she said.

Laeticia LeJeun looked up from her station, underneath a laminar flow hood: an air filter system which kept the air over her working surface bacteria-free. She took the tissue samples from Dr. Yin and said, "If he's going to keep coming in and out like that we're going to need an airlock. The baths are too sensitive—"

"JoJo! For the final, umpteenth, and last time: stay out of the lab!" Dr. Yin shouted. "You are polluting our air!"

Johannes stomped off, grumbling a string of anti-geek protests.

Across the workspace, Rick, who was seated at his OLED monitors said, "OK Xander, go ahead with the hypnotic poison input." On one of his screens there was a revolving CGI-mesh image of Sharon Stone. Nude.

"The face of Dior!" Kim, the chemist said.

"Isn't that perfume endorsed by Monica Bellucci?" Bart objected from the back of the lab.

"Who cares? Nobody knows what *Fatal Impulse* smells like," Rick waved him away irritably.

"Bellucci sucks—" Laeticia casually reflected. "Vincent Cassel deserves better."

"Do I detect a hint of jealousy?" Xander muttered.

"Shut up Triple X."

Dr. Yin came up beside Rick and looked at the computer screens. On the third screen was a large, 3D image of a four story Victorian house set atop a steep hill. It was painted a pale ocean blue, with boxed and circular bay windows jutting out from the upper floor corners of the building and a white-columned entrance, lending it a gothic and distinctly Hitchcockien air. Above the building reproduction was a title card that read:

Nick's Apartment: 1158 Montgomery Street, San Francisco

Nicky Curry was the obsessive and unstable San Francisco cop—portrayed by Michael Douglas—in Paul Verhoeven's 1992 wank fantasy/thriller *Fatal Impulse*. The next sequence would involve reproducing his neighborhood and tying that in a loop with the other outdoor areas of the movie. Since most of the film had been shot in San Francisco and neighboring counties (except for the LA studio work), this was not too big a hassle. The major difficulty encountered when creating the tapes was that they had to give the impression of freedom of movement, while at the same time guiding the tapers toward crucial scenes of the movie.

"So we're going to include Chinatown and part of the North Beach area," Rick explained to Dr. Yin. "Give the tape some character and flair. A good local feel. You know what I mean…"

"You want to do all of the Italian and Chinese neighborhoods?"

"Yeah, why not?"

Dr. Yin hemmed. "I just don't want us to bite off more than we can chew. I mean, you've got the cafés, delicatessens, bars, strip clubs, jazz lounges, restaurants… then the tourists… lotsa people… multiple languages to consider. It just seems like a lot of complicated background, for this one particular spot."

"Yeah but it's important for the authenticity. This is the flat she sleeps with him in… it's also the place where he may or may not be murdered by her at the end of the picture. That's where we want to insert the bonus: the ticket to the interrogation room scene, which, let's face it, is what everyone is after. The rest of the indoor sets are pretty spare."

"OK. Let's do the whole of the North Beach area and then up to the Embarcadero, but just one or two waterfront piers maximum and we'll tie that in with the Tosca Café bit just after he drops her off at her town house following the interrogation. The two places are only a couple of blocks away. It's perfect. But that's as far as we go for the inner city."

Dr. Yin pointed to an online map and continued. "We'll have this section of the Embarcadero join in to this stretch of the Shoreline Highway, between Mill Valley and Muir beach. That's the first chase. Have a landmark, like a tunnel, inserted to separate this part from the rest of the city. Any taper with an ounce of intelligence is going to want to participate in that first car chase sequence up in the mountains, so we've got to make sure that anyone who comes by the beach house a half hour into the picture can see her leave and follow her."

"Right. And we can match up the other end with the Pacific Heights and Ronnie Roz's mansion in the beginning. So that anyone who wants to be a witness to his murder can see it happen and choose to help Detective Curry or blackmail Kathleen or whatever… it provides a perfect point of entry into the picture."

"Yeah I think that's where the taper should be when it starts."

"Dr. Yin?" Laeticia queried.

"What is it my little braniac?" he replied fondly.

"I've been wondering… why is it we base all our tapes on existing movies? Wouldn't it be more exciting and original if we created a new piece of fiction… entirely from scratch?"

Rick blinked rapidly behind his coke-bottle glasses,

seeming thoroughly uncomfortable with the idea. "What the hell would we want to do that for?"

Laeticia shrugged. "I don't know. I guess it would just make us feel more like… genuine artists… as opposed to a bunch of talentless hacks shamelessly exploiting other people's intellectual property for our own financial gain."

"That's a fine moral point," Dr. Yin said. Rick rolled his eyes and yawned, making a wanking gesture with his hand.

Dr. Yin continued, addressing the rest of the team. "And I swear once we've exhausted every blockbuster out there and we're down to copying Chevy Chase and Pauly Shore movies… you'll write us an original screenplay…"

"Oh really!" Laeticia clapped her hands together in excitement.

"But until then we're sticking to the programme. So concentrate on *Fatal Impulse*… before your artistic impulses prove to be fatal! Hehe…" He patted her benevolently on the shoulder and urged her back to her station. "Aw!" Laeticia moaned, as she returned to the cell cultures.

"Perfume on Kathleen Kastel is done—" Xander called out, from his station. "What's next?"

"Next we do the Foxy character," said Dr. Yin. He went over to Ursula Well's station. She was an introverted Swiss girl who hardly spoke, but was the most indispensable asset of the production team.

Ursula had a master's degree in Bioelectronics and was in charge of the "GRID." The polypyrrole-coated CNF nanoelectrode arrays so small they could penetrate the membrane of a neural cell and lock onto the axon, thus interfering with the signal.

"We're going to spice this one up a bit," said Dr. Yin to his team. "Rick, let's increase the jealousy factor on the motivation unit of Foxy's AP."

"Are you sure? It's already way up there," said Rick. He tapped the screen to his left where a databank of junk-DNA personalities was available. Three units controlled a wide variety of "states," ranging from physiological to psychological.

The emotions were divided into categories: primary, secondary and tertiary. For background and lesser-important tape characters, only primary emotions were used. These were fear, love, joy, sadness, anger and surprise. But on more complex characters, like Foxy, each primary emotion was linked to a list of secondary emotions.

And on even more complex characters like Kathleen Kastel, each secondary emotion was related to tertiary emotions, creating a labyrinth of behavioral possibilities. Love, for example was one of the six basic primary emotions. An emotion-tree related to love might read like this:

—Desire—Arousal—Lust
—Passion—Obsession

(LOVE—Longing—

—Adoration
—Attraction

—Affection—Caring
—Sentimentality

Of course even characters possessing only primary emotions had still the potential to create more complex emotional states by blending two or three primaries. In fact, the more one interacted with any character in a tapeworld, the more that character developed with regard to personality. The programmed characters' personalities and motivations shifted when interacting with the taper, just as they would in real life. Cause and effect.

"If we make her any more jealous she's likely to kill everybody in the club," Rick posited.

"I'll take the risk," said Dr. Yin. "I want her so obsessed that maybe she goes after Kathleen..."

Rick adjusted his Coke-bottle glasses on the bridge of his nose. "Your wish is my command." He altered the settings on a control bar, humming under his breath. "Welcome to Psychoville."

Kim Nguyen peeled off her gloves and changed her lab shoes for a pair of soft slippers and went into the house.

Johannes was sitting at the kitchen table, brooding as usual. There was a full decanter of coffee on the warmer near the sink. She poured herself a cup and sat opposite him.

"It must be hard being cooped up here by yourself all day," she said.

"I'm not cooped up. I can go out..."

"You know what I mean... anyway... Dr. Yin says that

when this tape is finished, we should all take a two-day break. Get this out of our system. We'll each take turns because we can't abandon the lab."

"Kind of like a shore leave, huh?"

She giggled. "You're silly."

"Not as silly as Captain Yin-Yang."

"Why don't you come with me?"

Johannes looked up in surprise. "Where?"

"I'll be going home—to Paris—to see my family. I'd like you to come along. That is, unless you have other plans."

"I've got plenty of other plans, except none of them are any good. Why me?"

Kim flicked back her smooth, dark hair and said, "Because I'm tired of seeing geeks and nerds. And who else do you want me to hang with?"

"Don't you have a boyfriend?"

"I don't have time. I'm not Tila Tequila."

"Who's she?"

"Reality TV bimbo. Vietnamese. We have the same last name. She did this dating game show called Tila Celib et Bi, and all my witty friends bombarded me on Facebook with the name. It stuck and I'm still trying to wash it off."

"I don't use Facebook."

"Lucky you." She sipped her coffee then said, "They made a movie about that, you know, about the Harvard student, who created the network."

"Maybe you'll make a tape based on the movie."

"I think we're sticking to the classics," Kim said. "At

least for the time being, anyway."

Johannes was silent for a while. He studied his fingernails and then asked, "Kim…"

"Yes?"

"What happens if you… die in a tapeworld?"

She set her cup down and her expression was suddenly strait-laced and pensive. "You wake up before the end of the session… that's the way it's supposed to work."

"Yes, but what if you don't wake up?"

"What do you mean?"

"I overheard Dr. Yin talking to De Schaduw. He said something about prolonged sleep paralysis."

"You shouldn't concern yourself with that," Kim said, and her tone was grave. "We manufacture the tapes, period. Whatever happens beyond their production is not our responsibility. Of course there are risks associated with their utilization, as there are with any untested technology. But if we eliminated all the risks in the world, we wouldn't have a world at all. You can't play safe and live. But think Johannes, a tapeworld is more than just entertainment. It's a gateway to that other place: the world that men have been trying to access since the beginning of time; a spiritual plane of existence, where all the laws of physics are broken down… where you can experience even death, without actually having to die. What we're making here, right now, this is just the tip of the iceberg. We're making entertainment… sophisticated games. But the technology, it allows for far more than that. It could be the beginning of a new human revolution."

"What do you mean?"

"I mean that the tapes already communicate among themselves—within a certain proximity—so users can share the experience, right? Now imagine what would happen if we were to master a blank tape, and people were to take that blank tape and create a network with it; a social network, just like Facebook. We'd supply an empty world, with just raw materials: seeds for planting and tools for building, etc. The users, they could create their own tapeworld. And if there were enough users sharing this world, why over time it would grow to become an actual parallel universe. Once the shared tapeworld became as complex as our own, however long that took, there would be a fully functioning society, with cities, traffic, landscapes… governing and educational systems. The tapeworld would continue to evolve and progress until it could create its own medium into another mental universe. A mise-en-abyme… like a Matryoshka doll."

"A tapeworld within a tapeworld."

"Yes."

"But if you came back out—which you would inevitably have to do in order to stay alive—the entire tapeworld would disappear. You could never keep on pursuing its progression and development."

If one person came out, that person's tapeworld would disappear, yes… But the implication of a social network is that the shared universe can be sustained by the remaining users. They would trade off, alternating trips between our physical world and the tapeworld in order to keep it alive and functional. Think of those massive, role-playing computer games. You can remove one character, but the system remains intact so long as there are others playing."

"But that's not going to happen... it's just a game. Right? Kimmy, tell me it's not going to happen."

Kim looked behind her, her eyes scanned over the empty room and then she lowered her voice and said, "I believe it already has."

"What do you mean?" Johannes' eyes widened and he leaned closer.

"I mean that what we're doing here... it's just the tip of the iceberg. I think we're being used to test the system and to fund further research with the marketing of our movie tapes. We're laying the groundwork, and preparing a foundational web of users worldwide. And we're not the only lab doing this..."

"How do you know that?"

"Because the design for the tape was *given* to us to reproduce. There are other forces at work, bigger and more powerful than De Schaduw."

"Who?"

"Governments, I suspect..."

"You're crazy," he scoffed. "Why would they be interested?"

"The building of a shared, parallel universe might be the only way to escape."

"Escape from what?"

Kim stared out the windows of the kitchen, at the

outdoor ditches and gentle pastures, and the shimmering postcard-blue sky hovering above. Blue. An S cone signal transmitted along a P cell pathway.

"Maybe the eventual destruction of our world."

9

At 9:15 on Monday morning, Dejan received a text-message on his encrypted handy. It read:

Autoteile A&B 117 Ellerstrasse, Dusseldorf.
12h00. Sei Da

He was alone in the flat. Milinka had already gone to one of her haunts: the Powerhouse Gym, or the Tante Maja café. Milinka was unemployed, but she wasn't eligible for welfare, because she was supposed to be living in a Manheim—a refugee center—subsisting in a cramped room on food packages and a €40.90 a month allowance. She hadn't lasted long at the Manheim. She preferred to work on the black, and eke out an existence in the foreign bars and Albanian-run discos that were proliferating all over Germany.

She'd worked at such places from Berlin to Hamburg, and even in Düsseldorf, slopping out Mixery Gelb and shots of Absolut for the ecstasy-bedazzled kandi-clubber crowd back in 2003, before all the mad Edam-brained ravers had been replaced by the depressive emos, who, realizing self-pity was less attractive than cuteness, soon adopted the Hello Kitty look, donned a pair of big dorky glasses, Twittered, and became "Scene "Kids.

And soon to be tapers…

She'd had an eclectic string of boyfriends. Everything from club owners and promoters to bouncers, busboys, drug dealers, DJs—and even a Duisburg rapper who after one fight had replaced her with a Nammer chick (think Asian, designer jeans, anorexic, ironed bleached hair likes to hang out with thugz) who ate up his bankroll even quicker than the dope could.

And then Milinka and Dejan had met. Out of all the men she had known, he was the only one she had stayed with for over a year. She told him he was the Good.

"*Good? As in what?*"

"*As in the Good, the Bad, and the Fucking Ugly,*" she'd said.

When she'd met Dejan he had just returned from a vacation in Belgrade. He had his own squat, a little cash. But most importantly, he had papers. He was legit. He had been working at the Kino, of all places. How ironic, that he went from selling tickets to movies, to transporting imitations of movies.

Still, if this was the ticket to a better life, he was determined to use it. His plan was to make a shitload of money, then invest it in something legit and spend the second half of his life in a trouble-free leisure zone. If he had to rub elbows with cops and gun-toting, Zlato-flashing fiends to fulfill his ambitions, those were just necessary inconveniences. Once he had his bundle, he'd get out. Knowing when to move onwas what distinguished the smart, entrepreneurial types from the deadbeats and the lockups. It was like playing the slot machines at the Spielhalle. You just had to know when to quit and you were OK. Timing was everything.

He showered quickly and dressed, then he took a quick breakfast at the Tchibo on the street corner and crossed the next street to the station where he took the first available bus to Düsseldorf, arriving a half hour early so he could take the S38 tramline to Oberbilk and be at the place in advance, so as not to piss off Mr. Fucking Zlato on their first day of business.

He didn't need to ask for directions. He knew the A&B Autoteile. It was just a block from Janko's Internet Call Shop. He'd never suspected the two businesses were related. But it was the beauty of the German foreign-built underworld. You never realized that if you jerked the rug out from under a Call Shop, you brought down a tanning salon, Spielhalle, night shop, kebab joint, Trinkhalle and some FKK swingers club out of town.

Six sides to the same fucking dice.

And now he was walking that familiar street, past the Lebensmittel with the fruit and vegetable stand on display, and the cheap franchised mini-marts, down past the rows of parked cars and hokey electronics repair shops and travel agencies, wondering why every city in Germany had to be so standardized and boring. They were a people of mindless, comforting repetition. The only color or flavor you got was ethnic. Everything German-made was as dry and tasteless as a bone.

He got to the A&B which had a big sign on the window

advertising 20 and 30% reduction. There was a sleek black BMW parked in front, which he hoped was the car he had been promised.

He entered the shop which was empty, and looked around at the shabby plastic packages of spare parts and the yellow-framed shelf displays of motor oil and car batteries.

"Ist jemand da?" Dejan called out.

He heard a toilet flush and a gray-haired man with a lousy face and a gray mustache emerged from the rear office and came up to the parts counter. He had on a polyester mechanic shirt with the Michelin Man depicted on it. There was a raggedy magazine roll stuffed in the back pockets of his pants.

"We're closed—" the retailer said.

"This is the A&B?"

"Says so on the door."

"I was told to come here."

The retailer scrutinized Dejan from head to toe. "Who sent you?"

"A guy… I don't know his name," Dejan explained. "Said to be here at twelve."

The retailer pointed to the door. "Outside."

"But you don't understand—"

"Outside," the man repeated. Dejan stood on the curb while the man drew a ring of keys from his shirt pocket and locked up. He took out a yellow pack of Jin Ling cigarettes, the Surgeon General warning on it written in Russian. *Baltic contrabanda*, thought Dejan, *moved from Russia to Germany via*

Poland or some other more circuitous route. He knew he was at the right place.

The man began smoking. He looked down the end of the street, not meeting Dejan's gaze.

"What am I supposed to do?" began Dejan.

"Quiet," said the man. "Wait."

He finished his cigarette and stomped it out. Minutes went by: 1, 2, 3... 10... A delivery van pulled up alongside the Stehcafé and kiosk across the road and began unloading crates of soft drinks and junk food.

A trim guy exited the kiosk, wearing a red Nike tracksuit with black warm-up pants. He spotted Dejan and the retailer and moved toward them, and Dejan realized it was Mr. Zlato. He wore a relaxed, almost friendly expression, which contrasted starkly with the grim, harsh-tongued, sub-machinegun toting hood that he had been at the Duisburg Markt. He now looked like just your regular Ausländer-neighborhood type.

"You are punctual... a good sign," Mr. Gold Cross said. He looked at the retailer and snapped his fingers. "OK, let's go."

They led him around the corner to an old brown-brick apartment block, the façade obscured by climbing plants. They went into the inner courtyard and the retailer flipped his keys and unlocked an up-and-over garage door and drove out a shiny green Daewoo Matiz.

"What the fuck is that?" Dejan spurted. The ghastly, bubble-shaped city car looked like something only a philosophy student fuckup or a 50-year-old ALDI-haunting spinster would drive. It instantly crushed his romantic notions of cruising around in a luxury, Yakuzamobile.

"That's your sled," said Mr. Gold Cross, the corners of his mouth turning upwards to form a seedy grin. "What do you think?"

"Are you serious? It's… it's a fucking Daewoo!"

"Ja, und?"

"So… I'm going to look like a fucking *dziber*. Like a clown."

"What did you think you were going to get? The Bembara?" Mr. Gold Cross looked at the retailer and the two men snickered. Dejan felt hot under the collar.

"Look," said Mr. Zlato. And his smile disappeared, his face darkening like a storm cloud. "This kind of car, it's like a magic cloak. Like Harry Potter. You drive this and no *murija* in his right mind is going to stop you. OK? It's your magical Harry Potter sled. Now see here—"

He opened the trunk and pointed to a Foot Locker duffel bag stuffed in the corner alongside an accumulation of other junk. He patted the bag, but didn't bother opening it.

"50,000," he said. "That's for *Fatal Impulse*. 500 copies… hey," he snapped his fingers, "You listening?"

"Yeah."

Dejan wondered how the guy could have known the type of tape that was coming out, not to mention the price tag. Probably through Toby. His guy in Venlo always knew the next tapes to be delivered, which meant that whoever manufactured them was working off a prefabricated list.

"Okay okay," said Mr. Zlato. "I want it divided in two. 250 and 250 equally. You bring half the merchandise to him—" He slapped the retailer on the shoulder. "The other half you keep at your place until further notice."

"Why don't I just bring it all in one go?"

"Hey. Ruhe. Too many fucking questions. We're setting up a gallery at a Hochbunker in Duisburg. Satisfied? So you go to the Turk and you do as instructed. I don't want anybody moving in on the source... okay okay? You're my source in the Netherlands. You keep mouth shut, you keep moving for me, and maybe you get the Bembara in some time. Okay okay?"

"OK," said Dejan.

"Okie-dokie. Give him the papers," Mr. Zlato said to the man sitting in the Daewoo. The retailer fished into his back pocket and opened his wallet. He handed Dejan his Ausweise and a drivers' license. The photo and signature on both cards were identical. The license looked authentic. It had even a slightly aged appearance. Dejan was, after all, 24 years old.

"Registration is here—" said the retailer, tapping the sun visor. He got out of the Matiz, leaving the keys in the ignition.

"All right, get out of here." Mr. Zlato told Dejan. "On your way..."

"Now?"

"What? You want to stay for lunch?"

The two men laughed like it was the funniest thing they'd heard all morning. Dejan got in the Daewoo, grumbling silently, already mentally baptizing it with a name: Scheisse-Schlitter. The shit-sled. Here he was, transporting €50,000 in a fucking economy-class vehicle made in Uzbekistan.

Still, Gold Cross was right about one thing, he thought as he drove off. No cop in his right mind would bother searching this ride.

(*Plump Friction* tapeworld)

"Jesus Maria, it really looks like the American 1950s," Lukas marveled as he parked the Chevy in front of the doo-wop diner where a gang of bikers and greasers in black leather jackets and newsboy caps were chewing the fat and horsing around in front of the entrance, creating an overall ruckus with their choppers.

"No, I'd say it looks like the 1990s imitating the American 50s," Mikail corrected him.

A waitress in a poofy-skirted housedress with high-heels and a white-and-red polka dot apron was smoking by the door, her cigarette stuck in a jade quellazaire. She had a perfectly groomed waved coif that sat like a duck atop her head and she was wearing black leather house gloves.

One of the greasers called out to her, "Hey Donna, howsabout you and me take a ride down by the docks…"

"Even if I wasn't working the answer would still be *No!*" she shot back.

There were cheers and cat-calls from the motorcycle crew. Undeterred, the greaser pulled a comb out the back pocket of his jeans and began restyling his ducktail. "I thought you was off tonight, baby."

"Jane's sick—I'm filling in—and I still ain't your baby."

She flicked her cigarette out in a standing chrome ashtray and reentered the joint. They heard a rock-and-roll number being played inside. Someone strumming a folk guitar with a lot of verve… and a rich, crooning, voice:

I been waitin' in school all day long
Waitin' on the bell to ring so I can go home…

"Check this out," said Lukas, pointing to the sky. "It's dark. It was daytime just five minutes ago."

"Because this is a nighttime scene," said Mikail. "Come on, I'm hungry. Let's go inside." He reached for the door handle. Lukas stopped him.

"What if he's here?"

"Who?"

"John Travolta… uh… I mean Vinz Vegas."

"He won't be."

"How can you be sure?"

"I can't. It's just a hunch. We've set off a chain of events that have annulled the classic way this flick runs… so it's highly improbable that anything will be as we expect."

"Yes, but what if he is?"

"Hey, don't be a—" Mikail traced the outline of a square in the air, and gasped as the dotted lines became visible, hanging briefly in the air, suspended on a cloud of movie magic, before they vanished with a sparkle.

"Wow, I wasn't expecting that to happen!"

Lukas tried it too. He traced a square in the air with his fingers, but nothing happened. He tried again. Still, nothing.

"How come it worked for you and not for me?"

"Try saying the line first."

Lukas said, "Don't be a——" and he repeated the gesture. This time the outline of a dotted square appeared in midair. "I get it. It's like a trigger phrase…"

A car hop waitress in a cute black and white poodle skirt zipped by on a pair of tacky roller-skates, balancing a serving tray with four bottles of Vanilla Coke, the tray upheld on three delicate fingers. She twirled around and blew a kiss in their direction with her free hand. A pair of bright-red cartoon lips fluttered through the air and landed with a SPLAT!—like a junebug crashing on the windshield.

Mikail tucked his Smith and Wesson into the waistband of his beach shorts. Lukas slipped his under his belt. They swung open the doors to the Chevy and Mikail grabbed the briefcase with him.

"What are you taking that for?"

"Just to see what happens. That's the whole point, isn't it?"

It was, of course, the point. You didn't enter a tapeworld to sit in a corner twiddling your thumbs. You wanted to get down and dirty. To be a part of the action. To see your favorite stars up close and personal. To provoke senseless and absurd reactions from them. To fuck up the plot. To get the swing and the feel of it.

They strode across the lot, feeling iconic, larger-than-life. Two, middle-class German kids from 2010 thrown into a 1994 American crime picture and a cinematic slice of jaded, L.A. jungle.

And entered Whack Babbit Jim's.

The first thing that struck Lucas upon entering was just how noisy the joint was. It wasn't like watching a movie, where the background sound was filtered and toned down to allow you to follow the dialogue. Here you heard loudest whatever was nearest to you. You were immersed in a cacophony of chatter and a pandemonium of bright lights. You felt the heat from the ventilators. You felt people brush against you as they passed. And there was a lot of stuff going on. The colors shot out at you, from all four corners of the restaurant. They were gaudy and aggressive and brilliant; stark, primary colors. Red and blue neon signs over the bar and on the faux stone paneled walls advertised ICE CREAM and COCKTAILS. A group of young hipsters gathered around a six-lane slot racing track, watching the electric cars whiz round. The atmosphere smelt of fries and burgers, hairspray and cigarettes.

Lukas scanned the car-booths and tables around the tachometer dance-floor. There was no sign of Vinz or Tia, for that matter. He wondered what was going on.

The maître d' stopped them as they were passing his podium. He wore a charcoal gray flannel suit, had deep bags around his eyes, and moved with the grace of the Tinman from *Wizard of Oz*. He was supposed to be Ed Sullivan, the famous television host whose long-running show had schmoozedwith every talent from the Beatles to Richard Pryor and the Jackson 5.

"Good Evening, gentlemen. How may I help you?"

"Have you got a reservation under the name of Wallace... er Horace" Mikail asked.

The maître d' scanned the register. "Ah yes... Horace... it's a uh... car booth for two."

"Perfect," said Mikail. "That's us."

The maître d' stared at them suspiciously for a moment and then he summoned over a midget in a short-jacketed bellhop outfit, saying, "Johnny, will you show these two to the Chrysler. Number four."

"Sure thing. Follow me," the midget said. As he led them to the car-booth, the Ricky Nelson impersonator descended from the stage to rounds of enthusiastic applause and Mikail asked the midget, "Who are you supposed to be?"

"Johnny Roventini. Who do you think?"

"Who's he?" Lukas asked.

"America's most famous bellboy. He was the mascot for Philip Morris. Jeez you folks from out of town or what?"

We're not American, if that's what you mean," said Mikail as Johnny the Midget opened the door to their car-booth and ushered them inside. They sat down, across from each-other. Lukas was sitting in Mia's spot and his brother was sitting where Vinz Vegas should have been. It was simultaneously thrilling and at the same time more than a bit sleazy.

Johnny slammed the door shut and leaned over the recycled convertible's side and said, "Where are you boys from?"

"From Europe," said Lukas.

"European!" The midget flicked his fingers."That explains it."

"I don't get this—" Lukas confessed, as the midget took off. "What's the point of eating in a car?"

"This is America, things don't have to make sense. It's part of the charm."

Mikail shook the table, which was a laminate countertop fixed to a steel post bolted directly into the car floor.

"Pretty sturdy," he said. He looked at the menus. They were big and glossy and had the bunny motorcyclist caricature on the cover. He flipped open the pages and looked at the list of hamburgers, sandwiches, side orders and fountain drinks.

"Hi I'm Buddy, what can I getcha?" A waiter, all dolled up in a prim white polyester suit and black horn-rims, appeared at their booth. He whipped out a notepad from his pocket and then did a double-take.

"Hey it's you fellas… from Santa Monica, right?"

"Yes."

"Well hey! Fancy seeing you here tonight. How did you get a reservation so quick? It's usually impossible to get a same-day booking here on weekends."

"We had a bit of luck."

"You sure got that right. So what'll you boys be havin'?"

Mikail looked down at the menu. "I'll have a Jim's Famous Speedburger…"

Buddy Holly scribbled this down. "And you?" he asked Lukas.

"The uh… Douglas Kirby steak."

"And to drink?"

"Five-dollar shake," they both said in unison.

"What kind?"

"Amos and Andy!" said Mikail.

"Martin and Lewis!" said Lukas.

Buddy scribbled this down then paused and raised an eyebrow, "And you tell me it's your first time here?"

"We heard a lot about the place."

"It gets good reviews on Google," said Mikail and Lukas snickered and kicked his shin under the table.

The waiter regarded them as if they were a rare and fascinating breed of insect. "I'll uh… be right back with your orders," he mumbled and wandered off toward the kitchen.

"Sweet Jesus! Check out the hooters on Marilyn," Lukas ogled the waitress serving the tables behind him. "So… Mia made a reservation here, but then she didn't show up. How come?"

"Because Vinz isn't around to take her out. Obviously."

Lukas gawked at the beach blondes and L.A executives up by the cocktail bar and he said, "I can't fucking believe we're actually in *Plump Friction*. You know when you're watching TV as a kid, and you see a movie and you see some character doing something stupid and you think man, if I was only there I'd be doing something else… and here we are, actually *in* a movie free to do what we please, but I just can't get my head around it. It feels so weird, because I'm expecting the frame to jump, or a scene to switch every two to three seconds, and it doesn't… we're just sitting here, like two regular clients."

Buddy, the waiter, reappeared with their five-dollar shakes. He set the chocolate one in front of Mikail and the vanilla shake in front of Lukas. He put two silvery canisters with the remains of the mixes down on the table.

Lukas and Mikail rushed on their straws at the same time and guzzled their milkshakes down.

"Oh shit!" Mikail dropped his straw.

"Ah! That's incredible!" Lukas smacked his lips. He picked up the cherry swirling atop the creamy surface of his drink.

"Oh shit…" Mikail repeated.

"Fucking brilliant—" Lukas said, popping the cherry into his mouth.

"Oh fucking shit," Mikail said again. And Lukas realized that he wasn't commenting on the milkshake. Something was wrong.

"What? What is it?"

"Don't turn around, but guess who just walked in?"

Lukas' head veered just a fraction to the right. "Who? Uma Thurman?"

"Yes… and her husband. Mr. Mosley Horace." Mikail felt his insides turning as he saw Uma Thurman and Ving

Rhames speaking to the maître d'.

"You idiot, we're at their table…" Lukas hissed. "Refresh my memory and correct me if I'm wrong but isn't Mosley Horace supposed to be like the ultimate badass? Makes Mike Tyson look like a choirboy?"

"Yes."

"Voice like James Earl Jones? Body of a thug. Band-Aid on the back of his head to cover the spot where the Devil sucked out his soul?"

"Yes."

"And he'd kill anyone to get his briefcase back… the one we have?"

"Uh-huh. And he's uh… coming this way."

Both of them instinctively flipped the menu cards open and held them in front of their face. Like a Japanese fan. They heard the maître d' speaking an apologetic tone:

"I'm very sorry for the mix-up Mr.Horace. We'll have this settled immediately."

They heard footsteps approaching and then stop. And a voice spoke. A voice as gravely as Louis Armstrong's; as grand and terrifying as that of a warlord or medieval King.

"Step aside, Ed."

Lukas peeked over his menu card and straight into the glare of Ving Rhames, his mug about as friendly as that of a bull mastiff, and his body a massive slab of obsidian, barely fitting into his tailored gray suit.

"I believe you're in my seat." Mosley Horace thundered.

Beside him Tia Horace rolled her eyes, looking the

perfect heroin chic in her white button-down shirt and black ankle pants. Her nails manicured and painted with Chanel's Vamp. Lukas dropped his menu and stammered, "There m... must be some mistake."

"You damn right about that!" Mosley crooned.

Uma Thurman droned atonally, "I'm going to go powder my nose."

"Baby, we gonna order our appetizers first," Mosley Horace's voice went from stentorian to smooth as honey. "Just as soon as these two fools leave our spot."

"We'll seat you in Zorro's section—" said the maître d'. He turned to Ving Rhames, "Again, I'm very sorry for the inconvenience..."

"We're not leaving," said Mikail. Lukas' eyes fairly shot out of his head at this reckless affront. He mouthed: *What are you doing?*

"*The briefcase!*" Mikail mouthed back, hinting under the table.

"I don't believe you understood me correctly" Mosley began. "Or maybe you don't know just who I am and what I do?"

"Oh we know who you are all right," Mikail cut him off. "You're Mosley Horace. Everybody's boss. Paid off prize-fighter Dutch Coolbridge to go down in the fifth round only earlier today at Sully-Lee-Royce's club. You had Tony Rocky Horror thrown out of a fourth floor balcony because he gave your coke-sniffing bride here a foot massage... am I right so far?"

Mosley Horace's jaw dropped like a pair of forty-year-old tits. He felt like a stooge.

"Oh and Tia... you were great in the Fox Force Five pilot. The network should have never canceled the show."

Mosley glowered at Tia and then at Mikail. "Fox Force Five? Babydoll, do you know this drugstore cowboy motherfucker?"

"N... No!" she stammered. "I've never seen him before in my life. I swear."

"Then how does he know you were in that pilot? Baby, nobody watched the damn show! Not even the producers."

"I'm telling you... I don't know the dweeb," she insisted, lighting up a cigarette.

"Excuse me. What is dweeb?" Lukas cut in. His knowledge of pulp jargon was limited and he was hoping to extend his vocabulary.

"It means sap." Tia blew a thin stream of smoke out the corner of her mouth. She struck a foot-popping pose and Mosley said in a tone both menacing and grandiloquent, "Sugar, please, this is between Me, Myself, and Mr. Soon-to-be-relinquishing-his-fucking-seat-peckerwood-motherfucker..."

The two of them stared each other down, so long and so hard that Lukas felt like whistling an Enrico Morricone tune.

POP! POP! POP!

A series of loud gunshots suddenly rang out, followed by screams and panicked commotion. There was the sound of a tray falling and plates shattering. A stage light came crashing down onto the dancefloor, as the cantilevered valence above the stage fell. Mosley and his wife, Lukas and Mikail, were distracted from their showdown by the sound of a man calling out in a cool, professional voice:

"EVERYBODY BE COOL. THIS IS A HOLD-UP!"

And then followed by a woman's high-pitched threat, screeching like nails on a blackboard:

"ANY OF YOU DICKLESS PRICKS MOVE AN INCH AND I'LL BUST A CAP ON EVERY LAST MOTHERFUCKER IN THE ROOM!"

"Shit," said Mikail. "Munchkin and Honey Buns are here. The plot thickens."

10

When Marie Venet returned home from her visit to the hospital she saw an apple-green Kawasaki parked on the gravel driveway in front of her house. Somebody in a black-and-silver one piece racing suit was standing on the terrace peeking in through the lower floor window. The biker spun around upon hearing her car roll in, flipped down the visor on the helmet and ran across the lawn, knocking over a garden chair. The biker jumped onto the Kawasaki and kicked up the side stand.

Marie sprang from her car as the biker unlocked the steering column and gunned the engine.

"Hey! What's going on here?"

The Kawasaki lurched forwards and she leaped in front of it, blocking the biker's escape.

"Turn it off!" Marie yelled. The biker hesitated, then realizing there was no possible escape without running her over, cut the engine.

"What's the idea? What do you want?"

The biker mumbled an inarticulate response.

"Take off your helmet. I can't hear you," she said.

Slowly, the visor was lifted. Marie saw a young boy, eighteen or twenty, with nervous, flighty blue eyes. She didn't recognize him. She knew all the kids from the village by sight. On the front of his helmet was the Monster energy drink logo with the famous green, three striped claw-mark.

"Where's Chris?" the boy asked.

"First tell me who you are—"

"I'm Toby," he said. "This is where he lives, no?"

Marie felt her heart beat fast in her chest. She remembered what the Europol agent had warned her of. *An unidentified visitor, asking for Christopher*. Try and gather a detailed physical description. All she saw was a scared kid on his motorbike. There was another sticker on the fork guard of the bike. Red with a black strip in the center decorated with three white crosses. She committed it to memory.

"Take off your helmet," she said.

The biker shook his head. "Where is he?" he asked.

"He's sick—" she replied. And felt that queasy, twisted feeling in her guts. "How do you know Christopher?"

The biker didn't reply. She moved closer to him, when suddenly, without warning, he flicked the starter and throttled the engine. She grabbed at his arm and he veered to the side, bowling her over and wheeled out of the driveway. She sprinted after him but he sped off down the street at breakneck speed and disappeared around the curve. She heard the recessive whine of the 650 cc engine as he fled the village.

She ran to the house, fumbling in her handbag for the card the Europol agent had left her. She found it and called the number inscribed at the bottom.

The phone rang three times and then an automatic operator picked up.

"Hello. You have reached the head office of the new synthetic substances unit—to speak with the head of unit press 1—to speak with the first officer press 2—to speak with alternate members of staff…"

Marie pressed 2 and waited. There was a click and then somebody picked up.

"Nicolas Perrin here—"
"This is Marie Venet speaking. I have something to report."
"Go ahead. I'm listening…"

After she had recounted the incident, she opened her laptop, and Googled the emblem that she had seen on the motorbike guard.

It took her barely two minutes of scanning web pages to find what she was looking for.

The emblem, with the three white crosses, was nothing else but the city flag of Amsterdam.

Dejan was off to see Nasr, Nasr the Turk—the Wonderful Nasr of Venlo, or N-67, as he was sometimes called. He lived in the center of town, in a large, renovated post-war urban block which, ironically enough, housed a police station on the ground floor. Nasr liked to joke that it was proof that cops and dealers could coexist peacefully. He even knew a few of the constables by name. It was another one of those Dutch peculiarities that Dejan couldn't quite fathom: a criminal and a policeman exchanging courteous greetings.

But Nasr was the careful type. Even in his hard-drug dealing days, he'd always eschewed the city center, preferring to conduct his business on the neighboring expressways, and rest-stops. And although he had a minor record, owing to some juvenile recklessness, he'd never actually done time. And it had been many years since his last arrest.

Now Nasr had all but abandoned his shady past for a venture that, in his opinion, presented far less risk. He sold tapes to just three other regular buyers, besides Dejan. There was no need to seek out more. Every time they came back, the demand was stronger. And Nasr was discreet. He knew that so long as the tape dealers were a small ring, they could operate peaceably. What Nasr feared was not so much the law, for the tapes did not even exist in the legal sense, but it was the problems that would arise once rival dealers and the organized-criminal networks caught on to this new phenomenon. He had already heard rumors of massive tape-galleries being set up in various German cities. Underworld markets. There were stories of tapes circulating in underground clubs in Switzerland and Austria. And other rumors of tapes being shared in skins parties in France. The skinners—always on the lookout for the next sensation—were quick to catch on to the hype.

Dejan parked in the underground lot below the square and took the duffel bag from the trunk. A quick peek inside revealed a pile of sports clothes and two pairs of Nike socks stuffed with thick rolls of €100 and €500 bills. The entire amount looked much less, as it always did.

Saskia answered the door, looking like a stripper on her day off. She had the curly dark hair and the thick, voluptuous lips of a mulatto, although her complexion was pale as a chard stem. She was wearing stretch jeggings and a studded tee by Bebe. She was barefoot. An ankle chain and toe ring glinted silver.

"Dede! Come on in... but take off your shoes, I just had the floor waxed," Saskia invited, her voice a raspy slur. She always looked high on something, even if there wasn't any evidence of dope in her flat.

"Is Nasr here?" he asked her, removing his trainers.

"He'll be back in five. Go on, make yourself comfortable." She indicated an elegant white leather sofa. The flat was in her name, but all the expensive designer furniture had been bought with Nasr's money. Dejan sat down as she picked up a ferret that had been slinking around a metal box-table and took it into her lap and began stroking it, making cooing noises.

His attention was diverted by some weird latticed structure fashioned of aluminum planks that had been installed against the corner of the wall, near the window overlooking the town square. It hadn't been there last week.

"What the hell is that?"

"It's a bookshelf, silly boy—" Saskia purred, stroking the ferret.

"Why aren't there any books on it?"

She giggled. Her teeth were large and gleamed white. The front two incisors curved slightly inwards. Dejan felt uneasy being alone with Saskia. She was exactly the sort of girl he instinctively didn't trust. Not like Milinka who always said everything she thought, who laid all the cards out on the table. Saskia was all Cheshire smiles and backhanded scheming.

"You want something to drink? Coffee?"

"Nah."

"Diet Coke with Jack Daniels then? You can't say no to that."

"It's fucking three in the afternoon—" Dejan looked at his watch. "What's Nasr up to?"

"Relax. I said he'd be here… what's in the bag?"

"Take a wild guess."

Saskia flashed him that sickly sweet vamp smile and she put down the ferret on the rug. It scampered off toward the bathroom and slinked in through a gap in the doorway. She stood up, arched her back and walked slowly over to the American kitchen and drew a bottle of whiskey from one of the cabinets. She took an ice tray from the freezer and knocked out a few cubes.

"You sure you won't have anything?"

"Nah, I'm fine."

He heard the clink of ice in a glass tumbler, and whiskey being poured, then the fizz of a soda-bottle being opened. She stirred the drink with her finger and licked it.

"MMM… so… things are going good between you and Nasr, you might say," she declared, moving back over near the sofa, and sitting on a woolen poof so ugly that Dejan knew it was by some contemporary designer, and probably cost a small fortune.

"You're making a lot of money, with those tapes of yours," Saskia continued. "I don't know how much, but it must be quite a bit, no?"

"I do all right," said Dejan. He looked around the spacious apartment, estimating the rent at well over 2,000 a month. "You seem to be doing fine yourself."

"Oh, we get by," said Saskia. She stretched out her long legs and crossed her feet. Her ankle-chain jingled. "Still... I'm missing that little thing, that extra, I don't know how you call this..."

"Greed?"

She tossed her curls and laughed dryly. "You're funny. Nasr trusts you, you know, even if you are a chetnik... not to be offensive. You're different, Dede. Smart. Not like all those clowns and pushers he used to deal with. You should think about making a change and moving up. A busboy is good for a summer job... but a busboy will always be just that, a busboy."

"What are you trying to say?"

She sipped her whiskey-soda, smacked her plump lips. "I know this guy—in Amsterdam-West—he's got loads of money, always looking to invest. Maybe you two like to meet?"

Dejan surveyed her coldly. "I don't burn bridges, Saskia. You try and fly too quickly, you crash. I got people to answer to back home. I got a girl to think about—"

"There's always a girl," Saskia tittered. "A pretty face

with a sad story. You know a lot about women, Dede?"

"I know there are all kinds."

"No there aren't. Only two," she said, matter-of-factly. "The kind that help you get where you want to go, and the kind that keep you from it."

There was a click at the door and in Nasr came: a small but powerfully built man in his mid-thirties. He was all Lonsdale and pitbull charm. Another man followed him into the flat—a tall, clean-shaven character in an Italian suit, carrying a silver-toned metal briefcase. Expensive watch. Well groomed and tan. Polite demeanor, not an enforcer, probably an accountant or banker. Nasr didn't introduce him.

He snapped his fingers at Saskia and told her to take a walk.

"I'm not dressed for going out—" she started, but his gremlin gaze silenced her. She went to the bedroom and closed the door. Nasr waited until she re-emerged, dressed more appropriately. She left the apartment without a word and he indicated to his guest to sit down.

Dejan opened the duffel bag and undid the money rolls from their wrappings. He laid them out on the low table.

"50,000," he said. "I need 500 copies."

Nasr's eyes flickered at the money. It was the first time Dejan had come in with such a large amount. The other man sat unfazed.

"Now you see my problem—" Nasr said, to his guest. "A guy comes in with this big bundle—wants to buy tapes. Most of this gets kicked back to my guy in Rotterdam. I'm left with five percent. I don't complain, but everybody's moving in on Rotterdam now. It's like the coop. You have to wait in fucking line, and every time they up the price. 100 today. 150 tomorrow. Who knows what's next. The supply is smaller than the demand. What can I do? I take what I can grab. But the bundles keep getting bigger and everybody is moving in. All over the fucking place. I get nervous with so much hustle… I got enough to worry about with the selling. That's what I'm good at, the selling. Not fighting for space with the sharks."

"And him?" The guest spoke softly, indicating Dejan.

"What about him? He's no brother but he's cool. We go back."

"Who is he with?"

"Nobody. He's a free agent."

"Everybody is with somebody," said the guest, with a world-weary tone. "See this," he picked up one of the money rolls. "A street-peddler he gathers cash in mixed bills. Fivers… tenners… fifty if he's lucky. This leads to big amounts very tricky to transport or to hide. You wouldn't believe how hard it is to manage. Money stacked on sofas, in cabinets, stuffed in cupboards like cereal boxes. And here this boy shows up with neatly ordered Bin Ladens. He didn't change this at a bank. He's a runner for somebody. We have runners of our own."

"But loyalties aside, your runners don't know this market. They don't have the right distributors, not like we do. This isn't brown we're talking about here. The kids we sell to, they don't move in those neighborhoods. They're clean kids. Middle-class on up. Playboys and huppelkutten. No junkie got

250 to spend on one trip. You hand this to the street peddlers and in five minutes you'll have every cowboy from here to Eindhoven knocking on your door. Turf wars, gang battles, who knows what's next. We got us a nice clean network. Nobody got a record on the street. They're invisible. No old-generation grudges to worry about."

"I'm going to speak to you in Turkish now, no offense to your friend, but what I have to say is between us."

Dejan nodded and they pursued their conversation in a regional dialect, indecipherable to him. He knew what was going on with Nasr: two things. Firstly, he had the same problems as Janko did controlling and integrating the cash flow, and he needed somebody like this man, who was most likely a hawalader and part of an underground banking system, old as the world. Secondly, the tape-market was developing in such a way that it might soon be necessary to have enforcement. You had to be backed by somebody when you rubbed elbows with the big boys, or they'd pick your bones clean first chance they got. Nasr was looking for an associate with muscle, for protection.

After a few minutes of rapid-fire verbal exchanges the two men shook hands. The guest opened his metal briefcase and drew out a sleek, front-loading battery-operated mini bill counter that looked like a small electronic printer or portable radio. There was an LCD screen on top of it. He undid the money rolls and fed them into the machine. Twice the machine beeped and "EE2" flashed. He removed two bills from the stash. He took the rest and put them in his package aluminum case along with the counter.

"49,000," he said.

"I need 500 tapes," Dejan informed him. "Divided in half."

"You owe me a G," Nasr said, shoving the counterfeit bills across the table. He went to the kitchen and took a film canister from the fridge. He brought these to the bedroom where he had a cutter set-up to slice the tape. The strip was numbered on the underside and dyed purple. He marked off the required amounts and sliced them. He packed the two reels in separate canisters. He gave them to Dejan who asked, "What's next?"

"*2001: A Space Odyssey.*"

"OK, when?"

"Two weeks."

They stood up and cuffed hands. Dejan picked up the rejected bills and took them with him. Nasr led him to the door and as he was putting on his shoes he asked, "You still work for Janko?"

"Yes," Dejan lied. "Why?"

"Haven't heard from him in a long time."

"He's lying low. Got some unsettled history with the cowboys, nothing to do with us."

"Okay, you watch out for yourself, right?"

"Sure."

Nasr watched him leave and then resumed his discussion concerning the details of his placement with the hawalader.

Milinka pounced on him as soon as he got home. "You have to stop this, Dede."

"What are you talking about?" He pushed past her, opening the fridge and placing a canister on the shelf bin. "I got to go. I'll be back around seven tonight..." He tried to give her a kiss but she deflected his embrace.

"Some men came to the gym today," she said. "They wanted to talk to me."

"And?" He was in the bathroom now, rifling through the medical cabinet for paracetamol. His head was nipping. He tore through the packages of pills and ointments, finding beauty creams, nutricosmetics, contact lens fluid—everything but what he fucking needed. Milinka was behind him, leaning in the doorway, her slender and tan arms crossed.

"They were asking questions about you—" she said.

He stopped his futile searching and slammed the cabinet shut. He saw her face reflected in the mirror. She looked scared.

"What kind of questions?"

"How long I've known you. Who your friends are. If I know Janko Konjovic..."

"And what did you tell them?"

"I said I didn't know anything, but they didn't believe me. They said you could be in a lot of trouble if you were running cross-border business for Janko, and that I could too, if I knew about it and I was lying to cover you. They said they'd find out sooner or later and that it was best to come clean."

Dejan started laughing. "Milinka—"

"You think this is funny?"

"Milinka, it's just smoke." He pressed his hands on her shoulders and looked her deep into her eyes. "Nothing's going to happen. I promise. Things are working out fine. I'm taking care of everything, OK?"

He cupped her chin and she wrenched her face away. When he tried to plant a kiss on her mouth, she squeezed her eyes shut and her lips were closed tight. He kissed her nose instead and gave another derisive snort of laughter.

"You worry too much, baby."

She didn't open her eyes until she heard the door slam shut. A minute afterward she peeked over the balcony of their flat and saw him emerge from the complex and walk over to the Daewoo. He got in and drove off, with no license, in a vehicle he hadn't purchased—like it was totally normal, like he hadn't nearly killed that kid in a drunken driving accident three years ago.

11

(TRIASSIC PARK TAPEWORLD)

"Way to go, Heike!" Matthias applauded wildly as the report came in over the radio of her having single-handedly slaughtered the *Tyrannosaur*.

He was in the control room, surrounded by a bunch of outdated 1990s computers. An IRIS Indigo and IRIS Crimson sat in the background, feeding 3D information to the computer screens. There was also a CM-5 supercomputer with its large panels of red blinking LEDs, which had been placed arbitrarily in the picture for visual dramatic effect. With the perimeter power out, all the images from the remote video surveillance monitors were black.

Ray Arnold (Samuel L. Jackson in the tapeworld), the chief engineer, was sitting at a Silicon Graphics workstation, chain-smoking and bitching as he tried to correct the bug that Donald Neri had placed in the system and restore control of the site.

"I beg your pardon!" John Parker roared, swinging his cane in Matthias' direction. He hobbled over, his bearded, grandfatherly face red and fuming. "Your girlfriend is responsible for the death of our most prized asset. And you have the audacity to cheer her on!"

"It could be worse, John," Arnold said. "A lot worse."

"He's right," said chief-of-security Robert Muller, a big-game hunter from Africa who had been brought on as a warden. "Your grandchildren are out there."

"Don't remind me of what I already know!" John Parker growled. "This is an utter fiasco! We're only a few weeks from opening this park to the public and our main attraction is laying dead in a storm gutter. It's like King Kong Island with no gorilla! I thought you had this all under control, Ray…"

"Look at this… he's right! The bastard turned off the Keycheck system so the computer didn't file his keystrokes. I have no way of knowing what he did unless I search the lines of code one by one," Samuel L. Jackson mumbled, sitting at Neri's messy terminal.

"It's not over. There are raptors loose in the park," Matthias butted in. "We'll need to take care of them as well. Tranquilizer darts won't do. We need massive firepower! Rocket-propelled grenades… we've got to go blitzkrieg on those suckers!… Ow! Take it easy!"

He winced as John Parker rapped him on the head with the amber-end of his cane, striking him with the brittle gemstone that held captive one of the fossilized blood-sucking prehistoric mosquitoes from which they had extracted the dinosaur DNA.

"Haven't you done enough damage already? You come waltzing in here like you own the damn place… killing off my creations. Do you know how much money we spent to engineer these animals?"

"Relax. You'll get it back at the box office."

"At the box office? Muller, are you hearing this?" John Parker wheeled around, furiously seeking an explanation from his staff. The park engineers and the chief of security were as mystified as he by Matthias' intrusion into their command center.

"You say that my dinosaurs are breeding... you tell Dr. Hardy that one of our computer engineers has disappeared with stolen embryos." Hammond's face was now flushed purple. He looked on the verge of a possible stroke or a heart attack. He was spitting mad.

"How the bloody hell did you get here? We're 120 miles from the nearest coast... and just what on God's-good-earth is that atrocious picture on your shirt?"

Matthias looked down at the image of four screaming teenagers wearing fluorescent clothes and Japanese hairstyles. One was brandishing a can of spray paint like a firearm.

"*Brokencyde*. They're a crunkcore band. You wouldn't understand."

The eccentric billionaire blinked a few times, feeling faint. He leaned heavier on his cane.

"Take this individual and lock him up somewhere."

"Where?"

"Frankly I don't give a damn. In the Cretaceous Café or the kitchen. Do what you want but get him out of my sight!"

The game warden put his broad-knuckled hand on Matthias arm. "Come on, son..."

"No wait!" Matthias protested. "You can't do this! The whole complex is going to be under attack very soon. We've got to formulate a plan of defense."

"My plan is to get you out of my damn way, so I can get things back on schedule…" Parker roared. A garbled transmission over the radio interrupted him from his wrathful pontifications.

"Yesh. What is it?"

They heard Jan Milestone's voice, slick with sarcasm. "We're uh… still out here John. Did the brochure specify an outdoor camping facility?"

"Drat!" Parker snapped off the radio. "Get the other gas-powered Saharas from the garage. Bring them back here at once! Put everybody in the dining area."

Robert Muller led Matthias through the vast, domed rotunda of the main hall. It was night and the place was dark, illuminated only by the blue glare of Muller's searchlight. Matthias felt a shiver of excitement, walking through that very space where the climax of the film occurred. Everything had been recreated down to the minutest detail. The air had that tangy scent of varnish and paint of a new building. The marble flooring was veined and polished and slippery, just like in a museum. There was the spiralwooden staircase, leading to the interior balcony, which was still under construction. They passed underneath the mock skeletons of dinosaurs set in a fighting pose, dangling from a mesh of wiry cables. There was the famous banner that read "*When Dinosaurs Ruled The Earth*," itself a sly reference to a 1970s low-budget motion picture. A set of suspended scaffolding stages led downward from the ceiling, hovering just above the replicas. Additional mobile scaffolds were parked beneath the bottom-floor windows, where square patches of moonlight cast a spell over industrial crates and lit up the engraved fossils on the broad, carved double doors of the entrance.

A draft rustled a transparent plastic tarp, shielding a limestone alcove. Matthias realized with a shudder that the building was not hermetically sealed.

"Over here—" Muller called at him. He pointed his searchlight up ahead and Matthias' heart skipped a beat and he nearly screamed with fright as he saw the shadow of a velociraptor, poised to strike. Then, when the creature didn't move, he realized that he was looking at a convex, panoramic mural depicting a prehistoric rainforest setting.

Muller led him to a side door and to the other side of the mural where the park cafeteria was situated.

They walked through the dining area which was arranged with round, wooden tables covered in white linens, surrounded by bamboo chairs. On each table a candle was burning. Additional candles flickered from holders near a timbered window wall with a view of an outdoor vegetated terrace through French windows. Ceiling fans spun lazily, generating a light breeze.

"All right you, stay put." Muller ordered. "You don't leave this cafeteria until I return. And don't touch the buffet!"

"And what am I supposed to do if one of those predators comes here?"

"Go to the kitchen and lock yourself in the pantry,"

Muller said.

"Is that a joke?"

"Last we checked the fences to the raptor pen are still functional."

"So long as they don't shut down the whole system to wipe out the bug. If they reboot they'll chew right through them."

He watched the game warden walk away, across the empty dining room and he knew he had to do something. If he was left here alone he would have no chance. He'd be defending himself against six-foot-tall, sickle-clawed prehistoric carnivores with a dinner fork or some other cutlery.

"You said it yourself, they should all be destroyed!" he yelled out.

Muller stopped in his tracks, he turned slowly around and his expression was grim and methodic.

"Take me with you," Matthias said.

12

When Dejan returned from Düsseldorf it was 7:30 I.M. He entered the flat and hung his jacket up. He took out the envelope of cash that was his cut: two-thousand five hundred. He kicked off his shoes and went to the bedroom where Milinka was lying asleep, one arm raised, finger pointed at the bedstead, her face tucked in the pillow.

He stashed his cash in the bottom dresser drawer, underneath Milinka's lingerie. He was amassing a fair amount and he had started placing it. He had rented a safety deposit box, at a local bank and put away a considerable amount in gold—and he was set up to meet with a guy Toby knew in Duisburg who ran a saunaclub anddodgy massage parlor, who was looking for partners to expand his business. Dejan knew that the key was to spread his assets around, investing in many different things, at the same time living discreetly, like he did now.

He closed the drawer and went over to the bed. He sat down beside his sleeping girlfriend and started playing with her hair, expecting her to roll over as she always did. Milinka was a light sleeper, easily woken.

She didn't.

"Are you still mad at me?" he whispered, brushing his fingers along her bare arm.

She wouldn't answer him.

He shook her lightly, "Milinka… don't be like that."

But she didn't respond, and when he shook her harder she still didn't move and Dejan rolled her over and her eyes were open, but they were staring right past him, to the ceiling.

"Milinka! What's going on? Wake up!"

He snapped his fingers in front of her. She gave no signs of consciousness. Her body was rigid… stiff as a board.

Frantically, he pressed his ear to her chest. Her heart was beating normally. He could feel the flare of her respiration as she exhaled. But she was completely unresponsive.

And then he spied a pair of scissors, lying haphazardly on the night table and he understood what was wrong.

He ran straight to the fridge and opened it. He took the canister from the shelf, uncapped it, dumped out the purple film reel, unwound it and checked the numbering on the underside. There was a slightly uneven cut on one end. The strip read up to E-98. Two copies were missing!

"Oh shit, Milinka, what have you done…"

TRANSMISSION TO WIRELESS NETWORK
SCAN FOR CONTROL CHANNELS
TRANSFER TO CELL
ORIGINATION MESSAGE AND CHANNEL
ASSIGNMENT
ANALOG TO DIGITAL CONVERSION
COMPRESSION OF VOICE STREAM
DIGITAL TO ANALOG CONVERSION…

"Hallo?"

"Toby… its Dede. I have a problem."

Forty-five minutes later Toby arrived, clutching his motorcycle helmet in one hand. Dejan ushered him to the bedroom, where Milinka was still lying in the same catatonic pose. Toby moved quickly toward the bed, knelt over her and closed her eyelids.

"How long has she been like this?"

"I don't know. At least an hour before I called you. So, two hours minimum."

Toby grimaced. "A tape session shouldn't last over thirty minutes. This isn't good."

"I can't leave her like this. She'll go into dehydration… she'll die!"

"Call an ambulance…"

Dejan gripped his arm, "Are you crazy? That's out of the question. I'm Michael Manned…"

"What's that mean?"

"I got enough heat on me as it is!"

"You got heat?"

"What if we put her under the shower and turn on the cold water. A thermal shock might wake her up."

Toby shook his head. "This isn't an OD, Dede and you know it. What did she take?"

"*Fatal Impulse*… two copies."

"What?" Toby's albino eyes flashed crimson in the dark bedroom. "She took two tapes at the same time?"

"I think so. She activated them using the fluid for her

contact lenses. I might have told her about the saline activation technique, I don't remember." Dejan paused, his lips pursed, and began pacing back and forth. "Oh Jesus, what do we do now?" He tore at his hair and then stopped pacing, "Wait a minute. The tapes can communicate, right? I mean within close proximity…"

"Sure," said Toby.

"So if I were to take one, I could enter her tapeworld. It wouldn't have to be synchronized. It would still log on, right?"

"Yes. In theory it would work. But—"

"I'm going in," said Dejan.

He moved back to the kitchen and took out the reel. He measured off a cut. Toby followed him, "I don't think this is a good idea."

"She's stuck in the tapeworld for some reason. I have to find out why." He grabbed a bottle of Bausch + Lomb fluid from the mirror cabinet in the bathroom and squeezed a few milliliters into a spoon. "You got a lighter?"

Toby passed him a Zippo and he heated up the underside of the spoon. Then he put the spoon down and dropped the tape into it. It swelled up slightly, like a cotton wad; like a user preparing his fix.

"Before you take that, hear me out," Toby cautioned. "She's stuck in the tapeworld, richtig? Now think Dede… she took two copies, so we're faced with one of two possibilities. Either the tape session is prolonged, which means that when it is over she will wake up and to follow her inside is unnecessary... or..."

Dejan watched the pullalan strip activate with a light phosphorous glow. "Or what?"

"Or the tapeworlds are superimposed," Toby said. "Which could be the reason she can't get out. If you go in there, you might not be able to either."

"I have to take the risk."

"What do you know about *Fatal Impulse*?"

"Not much... I saw it a long time ago, when I was twelve. I remember Sharon Stone's legs mostly," Dejan suppressed a burp of laughter. "It's not funny, I know."

"You need to watch it first," Toby said. "It's a dangerous film. If anything happens to you in there... if you get hurt, or killed, you'll lose all hope of finding her. If you go in, you've got to know what you're getting into. You've never taken a tape before, have you?"

"No," Dejan confessed. "But I'm a fast learner."

In the living room Dejan had switched on his laptop and found a free streaming of *Fatal Impulse* on the web. He knew the basic plot: *a former rock star named Ronnie Roz is found murdered in his San Francisco mansion. The prime suspect is Kathleen Kastel: a beautiful, best-selling novelist and lover of Ronnie Roz. The detective assigned to the case, Nicky Curry, enters into a lusty mind-game with the manipulative writer, becoming increasingly unhinged in the process, to the point where he is convinced of her innocence even though all the evidence hints to the contrary.*

They watched the film until its ambiguous finale and then Toby sketched out a diagram on a sheet of parchment paper with a black marker and a list of characters.

Kathleen Kastel: famous writer and (possible) murderer (Sharon Stone)

Nicky Curry: Homicide Detective (Michael Douglas)

Gus Moron: Nick's partner (George Dzundza)

Foxy: Kathleen Kastel's lesbian lover (Leilani Sarelle)

Dr. Becky Gardner: Police station psychiatrist, Nick's ex lover

(Jeanne Tripplehorn)

Etc etc…

"The way it works is like this," Toby showed him a drawing resembling a Formula 1 racing track. He had marked a series of checkpoints and drawn boxes with an arrow at each. The boxes ran all around the track, in a circular loop.

"Let's say that this circuit is the *Fatal Impulse* tapeworld, OK? And each of these boxes represents a scene, or a set from the movie. Now the tape begins with you at the first set: the opening reel. And it progresses in the same order like in the movie, right?"

"Yeah."

"But here's the catch. You're free to move where you want. Between each set is a programmed space for movement and interaction. We're talking lots of space."

"How much?"

"Could be anything from the size of a small town, to a large city. It could be the Grand Canyon or an entire volcano island. It depends on the movie milieu. There are things going on in this no-man's land that are not directly related to the plot. They're there for background effect, to give you the impression of reality… but if you keep on going in one direction you'll always end up bumping into another set, or another scene from the movie, get it?"

"Uh-huh…"

"Except that events in the tapeworld unfold in the timeframe of the movie they mimic. Let's say that ten minutes into the original movie an airplane explodes. That means that ten minutes from the beginning of the tape session, that airplane will blow up regardless of where you are. You could be at the airport, or you could be in another city, listening to a report on the radio, or watching it on TV."

"You can watch TV in a tapeworld?"

"It's just an example."

"That's twisted."

"I'm just trying to get you to understand," Toby said. "Now because you can interact with any character, and I mean literally *anybody* in a tapeworld—this could be the film star, or it could be the guy selling hot-dogs in front of the newsstand—whatever you do has an effect on the way the rest of the movie plays out and dramatically alters the plot, so when you get to another scene, it might be very different from what you would have expected."

"It sounds very complicated," said Dejan. "I thought it

was just like… a ride."

"In some ways it is, but in other ways it's very different. The main issue here is influence. You exert an influence on what happens through your actions and your decisions. Always remember that when you are in a tapeworld, you're not just a spectator. You are a physical component. And there's one more thing…"

"What?"

"The actors, they are complete embodiments of their characters. Never forget that the tapeworld is completely real to them. Sharon Stone is Kathleen Kastel in *Fatal Impulse*. She will toy with you wantonly and she will kill you if she gets the chance."

"So she doesn't know she's Sharon Stone?"

"Of course not. Because she isn't. To her she's Kathleen, flesh and blood. Don't underestimate her or anybody else, Dede. The characters in a tapeworld are not robots. They aren't Second Life avatars. They have as much intelligence and personality as anyone you could encounter in real life. If a character in the original movie is smart, trust me that they are just as smart in the engineered tapeworld. If the character is dangerous in the movie, they are equally dangerous here, if not more."

"Thanks for the warning."

"Don't mention it. Now are you still sure you want to go ahead with this?"

Dejan bit his lip. "In a worst case scenario, if the tapes are superimposed, what can I expect?"

Toby thought about this for a long time. "Anything and everything," he finally replied.

"If I don't come out, wait one hour and then leave. Take the rest of the tapes with you and call for an ambulance, OK?"

Dejan licked the tape off the spoon, and he lay down beside Milinka. While it dissolved and entered his bloodstream he saw Toby standing in the doorway, his skin ghost-white like an apparition: guardian angel of cybernetic sleep.

"Don't worry Mili," he said, grasping her limp hand and squeezing it tight. "Wherever you are, I'll find you."

SAN FRANCISCO, 1991 (*FATAL IMPULSE* TAPEWORLD)

Dejan blinked, accustoming himself to the bright light. He had no recollection of arriving here. He couldn't remember drifting off to sleep. It was like undergoing general anesthesia and being transferred from the operating table to the recovery room. One instant you were in one location, and then you found yourself somewhere else, with no recollection of time having gone by, trying to make sense of where you were... and just where was he?

He was standing on a residential street, in a lush and scenic part of the city; an upper-class neighborhood, judging by the ornate townhouses and Queen Anne style manors that lined the block.

In front of him was a towering and elaborately decorated Italianate villa, with wide, overhanging eaves and narrow, arched windows. A small belvedere sat atop the house's flat roof. There was a spearhead gate in front of the property, and wrapped around the gate and the whole front garden was a band of yellow crime scene tape.

"POLICE LINE DO NOT CROSS"

And then he realized where he was. He was standing smack in front of Ronnie Roz's Pacific Heights mansion, but this wasn't the beginning of the movie. It was daytime. By the looks of things the guy had already been murdered, and the police forensics had already visited the crime scene.

An old lady was walking her Shar Pei puppy down the sidewalk when she spotted Dejan staring at the house with interest.

"Are you with a network?" she asked.

Dejan spun around. The woman looked like a wealthy eccentric. She flaunted a wide-brim straw hat with a velvet ribbon around it and a pair of tacky color-framed sunglasses. She had on some horribly flowery frock and an enormous gaudy bead necklace that came down to her waist.

"No. I was just passing by… do you know what happened here?" he asked her.

"Why I should like to think so," said the old lady. "I live right next-door. The owner of that house was stabbed to death in his bedroom."

"When did this happen? Last night?"

"Oh Lord no. It's been three days now," the old lady

said. "But there's still a lot of talk going round. A buncha reporters have been popping their noses up here. The victim was a minor celebrity. Made the Bay headlines."

Three days, thought Dejan. Something was definitely askew. He'd just landed in the tapeworld, but a significant amount of time had already elapsed.

"Do you know where I can find the police department?" he asked her. "The one in charge of this case."

The old woman stepped closer. She removed her shades. One of her eyes had a star cataract that gave Dejan the creeps. She reeked of some retro cantaloupe-flavored perfume.

"I thought you were just passing by," she said, eyeing Dejan suspiciously. "But if you have anything to say, go to the central police station. Down Broadway, til' you come to Chinatown."

"Who found the body?" Dejan inquired. It was the house maid in the original film. He was testing to see what had changed in this version.

"Don't you read the papers?" the old lady replied, putting her sunglasses back on. "The cops already nabbed the murderer. She gave herself up, actually. Walked right into the police station and confessed to everything. The girl was clearly insane."

This was wrong. How could Kathleen have turned herself in? It was completely against her nature. It didn't make any sense.

"Who was she?"

"Funny, but I can't quite recall her name…"

"Was it Kathleen by any chance?"

"Lord no," the old lady grimaced, struggling to remember. "Something strange and foreign-sounding. Russian, maybe. Mili-something... Milinka, yes that's it!"

She saw the look of astonishment and confusion that crossed Dejan's face and she said, "The girl was a nobody, a vagrant. No ID on her person, no home. Just a transient, we've got loads of 'em in Frisco... social charity cases... hey!"

She called after him, but Dejan was already sprinting away, in a mad dash to the police station.

The SFPD lobby was brightly lit, sparsely furnished, and had the gleam and polish one associated with Sunday TV serials. It was located inside an old Spanish Colonial-style newspaper building with tiled domes on each corner and towers flanking the entrance.

Dejan addressed himself to the cop sitting at the counter desk behind a bulletproof Plexiglas shield. In the background he could see various law enforcement officers speaking on the phone or reviewing case files on clunky desktops. He didn't see anybody recognizable.

"Yes, what can I do for you?" the reception officer asked. He was a big, surly-looking cop in a dark blue shirt with gold buttons on it. He had a Freddy Mercury mustache-thing going.

"I need to speak with Homicide Inspector Nicky Curry," Dejan said.

"In regards to what?"

"The murder of Ronnie Roz."

The officer looked Dejan over from head to toe. "Are you from the media?"

"No, I'm not."

"Let's see some identification."

Dejan pulled out his wallet and withdrew his ID. He handed it over through the sliding tray. The reception officer studied it carefully and then he said, "You're German—"

"Yeah."

"Says here you were born in 1986. That'd make you about six years old. Nice try."

"It's complicated," Dejan winced. He hadn't expected a cop to be able to read that amount of detail in a tapeworld.

"Are you aware that it's against the law to carry a fake ID?" the cop now grumbled. He was getting all worked up, probably figuring Dejan to be some sleazy tabloid gonzo journalist. "Please, I must speak with Detective Curry or his partner, Gus. They've arrested the wrong person. Milinka Trajkovic didn't kill that man. Kathleen Kastel did!"

At the mention of this name the officer was suddenly alert, and his demeanor changed. He said, "Wait right here—" and left his counter.

After five minutes the officer returned with Michael Douglas in person. He had the slicked-back hair and the dimple chin, so real that Dejan wanted to pinch his cheeks. His eyes were piercing green and there were slight gray touches above his ears. But he wasn't smiling. He looked slightly pissed off, to tell the truth. He was attired in a handsome gray wool suit by Nino Cerreti (a movie wardrober who had dressed everyone from Clint Eastwood to Tom Hanks), far too lavish for a $45,000 a year salary.

"Mr. Vidic, I'm Detective Curry. I understand you would like to make a statement concerning the murder of Ronnie Roz."

Dejan nodded.

"We'll go upstairs to my office," the detective said.

As they rode the elevator to the second floor of the station, fifty-thousand things were flashing through Dejan's mind at once. *Why Milinka? Where was she? What in the hell was going on... I'm taller than Michael Douglas. He doesn't know he's Michael Douglas. He smells terrific. That's a cool tie. I'm still taller than him...*

The doors to the lift opened and they entered a busy workroom, where inspectors and secretaries sat at cluttered desks in front of piles of papers and ceaselessly ringing telephones, surrounded by metal filing cabinets and shoeboxes crammed with dossiers, hacking away at decrepit 1990s IBM keyboards. There was a glass-enclosed private office at one end of the room with Lt. PHILIP WALKER stenciled on the glass.

Detective Curry sat down at his workstation and pointed to a chair set opposite his desk. He flipped a desk lamp on and opened a folder marked CONFIDENTIAL and began reading through it.

"First off, I'd like to know what your interest is in this case. Are you related to the suspect, Milinka Trajkovic?"

What should he say? That she was his real world girlfriend? …that she was stuck in a goddamn movie and he was here to try and get her out? none of it would make sense to them. It would just complicate matters further for him. Dejan tried to put himself in the detective's place. The guy probably thought he was an investigative reporter, out to make a name for himself covering a trashy murder story, or at best that he was some do-gooder lawyer working *pro bono.*

"No relation," Dejan said. "But I know she didn't kill Ronnie Roz."

"Well, thanks for the sympathy note. I'm sure she'll find it most reassuring when she is sentenced," Detective Curry spoke in that annoyingly nasal Michael Douglas tone. "The desk sergeant downstairs said you mentioned a name… Kathleen Kastel, the best-selling crime novelist."

"Yes, she's the one that killed him."

Curry gave a snort of uneasy laughter. "And what makes you think that?"

"She was the last person seen with Ronnie Roz, wasn't she? She was at his club down in the Fillmore, on the night of his murder. She was a suspect until you coerced a bogus confession out of Milinka Trajkovic."

"Let's get this straight," Curry's voice rose a notch. "Milinka gave herself up. She walked right in here, twenty-four hours after the murder and she signed a six-page voluntary confession with no interrogation involved."

She gave herself up? This was even harder to believe. What kind of game was Milinka playing?

"People confess for all kinds of reasons. You must get false voluntary confessions all the time. Wack jobs... people lying to cover-up for someone else... to provide an alibi..."

"Yes and it's our job to distinguish between the true and false. Listen, she knew things about this case—inside things that haven't been made public."

"Like what? That the victim was stabbed exactly thirty-one times with a K-mart ice pick? That his hands were tied to the bedposts using a white Hermes scarf? That there were traces of high-grade cocaine found on a cosmetic mirror on the night table as well as multiple come stains on the sheets... I know all this too. Does this make me a murderer?"

Curry's face went from flabbergasted to smug as he struggled by gradual degrees to regain his composure and project an image of cool and professional aloofness. He tugged at his navy tie and said, "All that proves is that you paid someone in this department handsomely for this information."

"Then tell me this. What possible motive could she have for having killed him?"

"My guess is she was a sex worker," Detective Curry postulated. "Probably a drug addict as well. These people lead dangerous lives. They're highly unstable. She most likely thought that by killing a rock star she'd get her fifteen minutes of fame."

"Ex rock star..."

"Whatever. Look, Mr. Vidic, if that is really your name.

I don't know what you're trying to prove here. The bottom line is the girl confessed. On all counts. The case has been closed. If you're looking for a juicy story to make tomorrow's headlines, you're barking up the wrong tree. I've got no reason to discuss this case further with you. And I'd advise you to be careful using Kathleen Kastel's name. She'd sue you for defamation first chance she got, and hell I wouldn't blame her."

"Did you question her?"

Detective Curry glanced toward the office of his superior lieutenant, who was busy on the phone with the mayor.

"I'm not at liberty to answer that—" he said. But his beady eyes and shifty posture betrayed him.

"You had a hunch it was her," Dejan said. "When you first visited the scene. You even went up to her beach house in Stinson to talk to her. She answered a few of your questions, toyed with you for a bit and then she gave you the cold shoulder... isn't that right, Hoss?"

Detective Curry's face twitched and went pale. A lump formed in his throat and he swallowed hard. He gave Dejan his trademark, Michael-Douglas-white-male-paranoia look. Nobody but his longtime partner Gus called him Hoss.

"I think this interview is over," he said, coolly.

"You like to read? Why don't you look up a paperback by Kathleen Kastel... penned under the name Kathleen Woolfe. In it she describes the murder of a retired rock and roll star by his girlfriend. Read page 67... she does him in bed, with an ice pick, his hands tied with a white silk scarf."

The door to the lieutenant's office opened and his superior peered out. "Hey Curry, we got a 187 in the Bay area. The bodies are still warm…" He spied Dejan and he said, "Are ya busy?"

"No, we're through," Nicky Curry said, standing up. The lieutenant slammed his door shut. "You'll have to leave now," he said to Dejan.

"But she's innocent!"

"I'm not the one you should be talking to. You got something to say, tell it to her public defender. She'll need all the help she can get when this goes to trial."

"Where is Milinka?"

"She's been transferred to the county jail, awaiting prosecution. It's on 7th street, at the Hall of Justice."

"Thanks."

"Don't be thanking me. You best hurry or you ain't gonna make it. County closes at 1 P.M. Hope you got some genuine ID," Nicky Curry said, and he winked at Dejan. On the wall behind him was the station clock.

12:31. He had exactly twenty-nine minutes to find the jailhouse.

As he was leaving the station the reception officer called after him. "Hey! Hey Mister! You forgot something."

Dejan saw the cop waving a card at him. He walked briskly back to the Plexiglas booth. The cop placed the card in the sliding tray and pushed it over.

"Even a fake might come in handy," he said.

Dejan took the card and turned it over in his hand. On the back of it was a note, in simple block print:

"Dear taper, whoever you may be, you like games and so do we… here's a riddle for you to solve in exchange for a valid ID:

> I come before fighter
> And after mean
> There are four of me to a room
> I was played by Charlie Sheen
> Good luck from your programming team…

"P.S. Use your fatal impulse,' lol"

"Scheisse," Dejan cursed. "I don't have time for this pseudo-geek movie trivia crap!"

He exited the station, still twiddling the card in his hand, trying to make sense of what it meant. He passed in-between the parked black-and-white station wagons and patrol cars, wondering just how in the hell he was going to get to the county jail in time.

He walked down the street and looked around him and all he saw were Chinese restaurants, Mahjong parlors, and Dim Sum teahouses with pagoda roofs decorated with overhanging jade lanterns. Every sign was written in ideograms. Every other passer-by seemed to be wearing a bandana or baseball cap. The streets were congested with honking cars and chattering pedestrians. An unmarked truck was unloading crates of fortune cookies in front of a tea shop. He was in the middle of fucking Chinatown. He struggled to blot out the exterior nuisances. If the card had been given to him, that meant it was important. He had to solve the riddle and get to that jailhouse. It was obviously something to do with a movie… something involving Charlie Sheen. Wasn't that actor dead? Or in rehab? What did he have to do with *Fatal Impulse*? He wished he had been more of a film buff.

The first two lines didn't make any sense to him. He concentrated on the last two.

"There are four of me to a room"

Easy. It had to be a wall.

"I was played by Charlie Sheen"

Some movie character and something to do with four corners or a wall.

And then it struck him. *Hadn't Charlie Sheen and Michael Douglas played in the same movie? Some old 1980s flick about corporate greed and corruption. What was the title? Argh… some yuppie shit.*

A big yellow taxi came cruising by and parked on the curb, just behind the cookie truck. An old lady got out, carrying a bunch of Bloomingdale's shopping bags. Dejan realized with a shock that she was the old woman he had spoken to outside of Ronnie Roz's mansion. She hobbled off into one of the tea-houses and Dejan ran to the cab.

He knocked on the window. The driver looked like Mr. Miyagi, only younger. He pointed to the backseat. Dejan jumped inside, and he saw the bulletproof glass that divided driver and passenger and he remembered he was in America.

"Ryan Gosling!" he shouted out—his nerves frayed from the excitement.

"What?"

"Drive!"

"Where to, buddy?" the cabbie said. He was listening to some pounding, godawful Chinese trance music on his stereo. It made Goa trance sound like classical music.

Dejan was still going over the riddle in his head. He was mumbling to himself, when the cabbie, turned around in annoyance and said, "Hey, wassup dude, I said where to?"

"Wall Street!" Dejan yelled out. The cab driver stared at him like he was some crazy tourist. "There ain't no Wall Street in Frisco. Wall Street in New York, buddy. You in the wrong town." And he began to chuckle.

"No, I mean the Hall of Justice," said Dejan. "Sorry."

The cabbie shook his head and started the meter. "Sure, dude."

I'm right, thought Dejan with exhilaration. *Wall Street, with Michael Douglas and Charlie Sheen.*

Street-fighter
Mean-streets

Four walls to a room—that had to be it! He looked down at his hand and saw that he was holding a small, velvety black booklet. On its cover was the American seal and the title "Diplomatic Passport." He opened it and inside was his photo and a corrected birthplace and date of birth. There was also an attorney bar card from the state of California, with his name on it.

"Listen, man, I've got to be there in twenty minutes. Can you step on it?"

"Cost you extra—" the cabbie shrugged. He slammed on the pedal and the cab shot forward, screeching through traffic.

Fifteen minutes (plus two-near collisions with a cable car, one run-over dog, a partially run-over cat, and nine car jumps) later and the cab came to a halt outside the large, undulating jailhouse. There were a few patrol cars stationed in front, and an armored van parked near the entrance, where two deputies were wrestling a barrel-chested, shackled convict toward the intake center.

"This is it," said the cabbie.

"How much do I owe you?"

He tapped the meter. "45.60. We'll round it off to $45."

Dejan opened his wallet and pulled out a €100 bill and

stuck it in the change dish.

The driver picked it up and turned the banknote over in his hand. "Dude. What the fuck is this?"

"Keep the change," said Dejan, swinging open the cab door.

"Hey! Hey! hold on. I never seen this kinda money before."

"That's 100 euro."

"Euro? What the hell is euro?"

"A big financial and political mistake."

"Man, I don't know nothin' about that. We pay American dollars here."

Dejan's gaze oscillated desperately between the cab driver and the Hall of Justice. The building was surrounded by cops, deputies, bounty hunters, bail bondsmen—he couldn't make a run for it. If the cabbie made a scene he'd be tied up with hell to explain. He read the drivers ID taped to the glass partition. The name was Izzy Bao Ming.

Leaning closer to the glass, he lowered his voice to a confidential whisper. "Listen, I'm going to level with you, Izzy. I'm not from here—"

"Oh I know you're not from here, Mr. Monopoly."

"No, what I mean is… I'm really from the outside world. Out there…" He pointed through the windshield. The Shintok cab driver looked up at the sky, as if expecting the Roswell UFO to fly by.

"It's hard to explain," Dejan continued, "but this here—everything you see around you—it isn't for real. This is a tapeworld. Capiche? It's a reproduction of a cinema world that's been programmed on a neurochip to create an artificial reality. Now my girlfriend is in that jail because she's been convicted for a crime she didn't commit…"

Ming's expression went from doubtful to wary. "Look mister, if you need help you're talking to the wrong dude. I ain't no damn shrink—"

"You've got to believe me," Dejan pleaded. "Look at the date on that money. What does it say?"

"Says printed in 2006."

"How is that possible?"

"Because some banana republic counterfeiter made a mistake setting the printer," Ming said. "That don't prove nothing."

"You still don't believe me… ask yourself this: how come you never been out of this city?"

Ming snorted in exasperation. "Man, you crazy. I've been plenty of places outside Frisco."

"Like where?"

The driver's hand began to tremble. Dejan sensed a structural flaw in the artificial personality. He pressed on.

"Who are your parents?"

"I was born an orphan—"

"Where were you born?"

"Man, stop it—" Ming's whole body was starting to quiver. His hands were shaking real hard now.

"What kind of engine does this car run on?"

"I said give it up!" The suspension began to creak, and

the volume on the stereo shot up. Dejan looked again at the operator's license taped to the glass partition.

"That name's not Chinese..."

"So I took an American surname. Lotsa dudes do it."

"It's really an acronym isn't it?"

The whole cab began to shake violently now, the trunk popped open... the stereo was blatting white noise. The horn blared. Dejan saw that the driver's face was terrified.

"Izzy Bao Ming. What it really means is I-B-M."

"STOP IT!" Ming screamed and there was a terrible POP! Like a gun going off, as something struck the windshield and it splintered. Some cops exiting the building heard the noise and directed themselves toward the cab.

"Get the hell out of my taxi," Ming hollered. Dejan exited the vehicle and the cops changed direction and began heading toward their patrol car. He slammed the back door shut and the cab sped off. The LED reflector on the roof lit up as it sailed away.

At the visitation desk the corrections officer entered Dejan's name into a logbook. He checked his passport and said, "You got to register here in advance for a time slot. What's your relation to the inmate?"

"I'm her lawyer," Dejan said, producing his bar card.

The officer scrutinized the card and then he pointed to a stack of papers. "You'll have to fill out one of those forms there."

Afterward a female guard came and passed a metal detector wand under his arms and sides and made him empty his pockets. Dejan was taken through the Sally Port and by lift to one of the upper floors and down a brightly lit hallway marked by blue steel doors. She brought him to a tiny cubicle, hardly bigger than a broom closet, and told him to wait inside for his client.

There was a metal stool, bolted to the floor, and a telephone box bolted into the wall. In front of him was a plexiglass and latticed metal screen with a small slot for passing papers through. The room had a video surveillance camera in the ceiling corner. There was a steel counter fixed into the wall, waist-level, set underneath the security window, the paint on it chipped and scratched. There were tag marks and pen scratches on the walls of the booth.

"Xander was here"

And underneath a tiny scrawl:

"I fucked a booth bunny in San Jose"

While he was trying to make sense of this last inscription Milinka entered the other side of the visiting room and Dejan stood up and had to fight to keep from laughing at the utter absurdity of seeing his girlfriend in a neon-orange sweatsuit with a numbered armband, her hair disheveled like she'd slept in the street. She rushed to the glass and started jabbering and gesticulating wildly. Dejan pointed to the phone and she got the message and picked up her receiver.

"Dejan! They let you go! You're alive!" She splayed her fingers against the screen.

"What happened to you?"

"Oh Dede it's been so awful here. I was so worried about you."

"About me? You're the one in the slammer. What's going on? Baby, I know you didn't kill that man."

"She made me do it! That evil bitch," she shrieked, on the verge of hysteria and tears.

"Calm down. Come on, get a grip. Who are you talking about?"

"Dede, you've got to get me out of here! I can't stand it in here… the conditions are atrocious!"

"Baby, calm down. Sit down and we'll talk this out… you've got to explain things to me so I can help you."

Milinka was chewing her fingernails, obviously distraught. She looked peaked and at nerves end.

"The lawyer who came to see me, he said that because I signed that confession the prosecutor could put me away for life, if I was lucky and didn't go to skid row… but she made me do it. Dejan you must believe me. I'm innocent!" And by the way she was worked up Dejan gathered that she had forgotten this was only a tapeworld.

"Relax babycakes," he spoke soothingly. "You're only in a movie. Nobody's dead. Nobody's going to get a life sentence. You took the tapes at home, remember? When I was away? You took two copies of *Fatal Impulse*."

Slowly she regained her composure, as the reality (or

hyperreality) of where she was began to sink in.

"So… I'm not really in jail?"

"Of course not. You're back at the apartment, with me. You're sleeping in bed. You've been in a catatonic state for hours. If I don't get you out of here, Toby is going to call the medics. I don't want that to happen. Now, I've got to know exactly what went on. Tell me from the beginning, and in as much detail as you can remember. Start with your arrival in the tapeworld."

She nodded slowly. When she removed her hand from the glass it left a moist palm print.

"I remember it was nighttime…" Milinka reminisced, her eyes staring fixedly at him, as if she were entering a trance. "I'm standing on the sidewalk on this street corner, and I don't know where I am. It's pouring rain, and it's cold and windy. I don't recognize any of the buildings. I'm looking for a landmark, something to tell me where I am and I see this skyscraper in the distance and all these strange foreign cars driving by. Some bum is drinking out of a brown paper bag. Right across the street is this glowing café sign… so I go to it, thinking maybe I can find somebody who can explain to me where this is…" she paused, as if struggling to recollect.

"Take your time," Dejan said, and waited patiently as she closed her eyes, concentrating.

"OK, so I go inside and it's this bistro… well, more like an Italian café. Very rustic. Brass and red-cushioned. Old artsy photographs on the walls. It's quite crowded. Lots of people smoking and drinking. Looks like a midweek business crowd.

I'm soaking wet and my hair is dripping. Everybody is chattering away and I see an empty spot up at the bar. The barman asks me what I want to drink, and I ask him what city this is. He looks at me all funny. He asks me if I'm sober. I tell him I can't remember how I got here and he says 'Don't worry—ya probably won't remember how ya leave either.' And he starts laughing. Then he straightens up and says 'Well ya gotta make up your mind, are ya drinking or not?' And I say, I'll have just a coffee then while I wait. He goes serves somebody else down the other end of the bar. This woman comes in then, she's also wet, and she's shaking off her umbrella…"

"What did she look like?"

"I don't know really. Late 20s… brown hair, kind of a short, wavy cut. Prairie chipmunk face. She had on this trench-coat. She calls the barman over, asks him for a club soda. They make some small talk and she calls him by name. Charley… or Chuckie. I can't remember exactly. While she's waiting on her drink she sees me sitting there alone and she kind of smiles at me, and when she does I think to myself, I've seen this woman before somewhere. I know that face. I ask her if she's a model or an actress, and she laughs and says she wishes she were. That she'd be making more money and dating better men. She says she's a doctor. A psychiatrist—"

"Dr. Becky Garter," said Dejan.

"She didn't tell me her name."

"It's all right. Go on."

Milinka licked her lips, "Then the barman comes over

to me and he asks if my name is Milinka. I say yes, why? He says there's a call for me and he hands me this phone over the bar. There's this sudden commotion at the back of the café, so I can't hear properly at first… some men are getting in a row and the woman I was talking to she runs over to break it up. I turn away so I can hear better… and it was you."

"What do you mean me?"

"You, Dede. It was *you* on the phone. You said, 'Milinka, it's Dejan. I need you to listen very carefully. You must meet me at Ronnie Roz's nightclub. It's in the Fillmore district. Go to the main bar near the vestibule, and ask for a martini. I'll explain everything when you get there…' There was a long pause and then you said, 'I love you.' And I felt strange, because it didn't sound natural. Afterward you hung up."

"It wasn't me, Milinka."

"Just listen. You asked me to tell you, so I'm telling it like it was. It was your voice I heard. I know your voice out of a million. I leave the café and I walk back out in the rain. I ask around and after wandering for five or six blocks I eventually find the place… it's this big Gothic church all lit up with Technobeam lights. The rose window above the entrance portal is illuminated from within, shining like some weird hallucinatory beacon. There's a velvet roped entrance and a long queue waiting. Everybody is dressed like acid house ravers, but real old school… there are also some more conventional-looking people. The bouncers are all in leather and they're ushering some inside, and refusing others, and I get to the front of the line and they take one look at me and wave me in like I'm a regular, even though I'm wearing my gym top and cargo pants.

"Inside the club it's all flashing lights and smoke. There are these neon lit arches and stained glass windows everywhere. Above the dance floor is a truss in the shape of a cross. The busboys circulating are all dressed like altar boys. The music is pounding, real classic acid stuff. I find the bar and the bartender is done up like a priest. I order my drink and when he serves me I find I don't have any money to pay. I'm looking through my pockets, I can't find anything and the bartender is getting impatient and then this girl comes up to me and she offers to pay my drink."

"What did she look like?"

"Brunette. Maybe 25 years old."

"Come on be more specific. Was she attractive?"

"What does it matter?"

"It's important—"

"Yes, all right. She was a showstopper. Beautiful, in a glacial kind of way. Kind of gave me the creeps, to be honest. She asks me my name, and I tell her…"

"Did she give you hers?"

"No."

"What then?"

"She asks me if I know a guy named Dejan Vidic. And I'm surprised at first, and I tell her yes, that's my boyfriend. I'm supposed to meet him here. Then she tells me she has an important message for me from you. She asks me to come with her. I follow her through the crowd, behind a side altar and to the sacristy, which has been converted into a mensroom. Inside there are loads of party-goers doing coke and poppers and getting wild. I ask her what she wants from me. She points to this toilet cubicle and tells me to go inside. I tell her I'm not here for sex or drugs. She says that what she has to tell me is private.

She closes the door, locks it, people are laughing and hooting in the restroom. There are traces of coke on the toilet paper holder... a couple or a trio are making out in the cubicle next to ours. She's got this white satin blouse on and she reaches inside, and I'm thinking fuck, this lesbo is giving me the come-on... but she pulls out this photograph instead and she asks, 'Is this your boyfriend?'

"I look at it, and I see you Dede."

"Me?"

"You're in a room somewhere, spread-eagled on a bed, and your hands and legs are tied to each corner post. You've been gagged and stripped down to your underpants. There's a blonde woman in the photo, kneeling beside you, and she's holding a knife, or a sharp instrument up, above your naked chest, like she's going to stab you! Her back is turned to the camera, so I don't see her face.

"I ask her, 'What's this all about! What have you done to him?' And I jump at her, I want to smash her face in, but she pins me back against the wall with this tremendous force, and slaps me and tells me to shut up and listen. She says that you've been kidnapped. You're being held someplace nobody knows about. And that woman in the picture is a pure bred psychopath and she's going to kill you unless I go straight to the central police station and I turn myself in. She tells me I'm to confess to the murder of a man named Ronnie Roz. To say that he picked me up outside this same club the night before, at a midweekparty, and that he brought me home with him and that we had sex and I tied him to the bed and then stabbed him thirty-one times with an ice pick. She said if I didn't do exactly as I was told, that if I went to the police with any other story or intention, you'd be dead as New York disco."

"And you believed her?"

"Obviously... I mean, Nespresso, what else? I saw you on the picture, Dede. She knew your name. She knew my name, how long we'd been together... what was I supposed to do? I was scared."

Dejan shut his eyes and rubbed his temples.

"It was a bluff, Milinka. I don't know how they did it, but they tricked you."

"Who are they, Dede? Who was that awful girl?"

"I suspect that the one who spoke to you was Foxy... and the one in the photograph was Kathleen. They're lovers, see. Now I need you to think carefully, Mili, when you were in that club... did you see Sharon Stone on the dancefloor with Michael Douglas?"

"You know I don't watch movies, Dede."

"You read fashion magazines, Mili. You know what Sharon Stone looks like. She would be hard to miss, in a sequined gold dress. Did you see her, or anyone that looked like her, on the floor with an older man in a green V-neck sweater? Kind of out of place, not a hipster… looked maybe like the cop that took your confession?"

"No. No one like that. What does it matter?"

"It matters," said Dejan. "Believe me."

"What's going on here, Dede?"

"I think I'm beginning to understand… Toby said it could be this way. That because you took more than one copy, the tapes are superimposed, meaning there are two of them playing at the same time, one of which is feeding off the other. You entered this movie at the wrong time: a day after the murder had occurred. That wouldn't be possible unless the tapeworld is repeating itself… and I came today, two days after your incarceration."

"But how did they know who you were? How could they have photographed you if you weren't here? That girl, Foxy, she knew your name. She knew my name. It doesn't make any sense!"

"That's what I'm trying to figure out. See the fight that almost broke out in the Italian café—where the psychiatrist she intervenes—that's a scene from the original movie. That occurs *after* the police have interrogated Kathleen. What I don't understand is that you went to the police the very first night you got here. So that scene should have been playing *after* your arrest. You should have never seen it. But you did. You were there. How could that be possible? Unless… well unless the tapes really are superimposed and the two tapeworlds are sharing the same space. The original, primary one that is the source, and the superimposed copy that we're in… if Toby is right, then there might be a way to get you out of here."

"How?"

"By killing Kathleen. The blonde in the photo."

"What? You're going to kill her? You can't be serious!"

Dejan pressed a finger to his lips and glanced over his shoulder, at the surveillance camera, wondering if it was recording their exchange. The guard downstairs had said that it was only recording images—a safety precaution—that anything they said in that room was confidential. But Dejan lowered his voice to a whisper all the same.

"Hear me out—she's the reason you're in this jail in the first place. She's the one who murdered that man, Ronnie Roz. Now if I kill her in a scene from the primary tapeworld, then she'll be dead in this secondary copy that we're trapped in, right? The murder will have never occurred, because she won't exist. And you'll be out of here."

"That's crazy, Dejan. That doesn't make any sense."

"In a tapeworld it makes perfect sense. I'm going to give it a try."

Milinka's pulse was quickening, and her mouth was dry. He was really going to do it. Tapeworld or not, the idea of killing someone brought a chill to her.

"Don't—"

"I've got to."

They stared at each other, silently. She pressed her fingers to the security glass, and he kissed his and touched them to the grill. Then he hung up the phone and quickly exited the booth without looking back. He was going to corner Kathleen alone. He'd get his hands on a weapon, and he'd kill her where she was most vulnerable: at her luxurious beach house retreat in Stinson. If he was wrong, then he'd be a fugitive murderer. But if he was right, killing her would be the only way to implode the secondary tapeworld and free Milinka and himself.

There was no alternative.

First off, if he wanted to catch Kathleen alone, Dejan knew he would need a car. Kathleen Kastel owned two luxurious properties: one was a stately town house, only a block or two from Nicky Curry's apartment. The other, was a $6-million Cliffside mansion, in the Carmel Highlands (Stinson in the movie), 120 miles south of San Francisco (although the tapeworld itinerary would most likely be shorter). He opted for the second place, as Kathleen did not appear in the town house in the original movie, and he needed to off her in the primary tape, in order to annul her existence in the secondary one. He was grateful now for the information that Toby had given him, and forced him to review prior to entering the tapeworld. Milinka had been in the secondary tapeworld for three and a half days. The movie had a running time of just under two hours, credits not included. In order to remain synchronized, the primary tape had been repeating itself, Dejan assumed. At least forty times so far. This was an advantage, because if Dejan wanted to cut into a scene from the original movie, all he had to do was wait. If the scenes really were repeating themselves over and over, it would eventually come around again, even if he missed it the first time.

He was already formulating a scheme in his head to steal a car. Toby had told him that the key to manipulating a tapeworld was in the details; the little things that most movie-goers missed. Now Dejan was thinking of the incident his girlfriend had told him about—the brawl in the Tosca Café—which, unbeknownst to her had been between Nicky Curry and a jealous Internal Affairs investigator seeking to rile him up. The psychiatrist that Milinka had spoken to—Dr. Becky Garter—she was the detective's ex-girlfriend. In the movie she bailed him out and went home with him to her apartment. There they engaged in animalistic sex. But it wasn't the sex that now stimulated Dejan's interest. It was a casual detail he remembered from watching the movie. Upon entering her home, before removing her coat, the shrink dumps a keychain on the dresser near the door. He remembered it, because of the Bart Simpson figurine attached to it.

Her keychain.

There were a few keys on that one ring. It was highly probable one of them was the key to her car.

All he had to do was slip in while Michael Douglas and his shrink were fucking and take it and he'd have himself a ride. The apartment would be unlocked. Movie characters never locked their doors.

Outside on the street Dejan ambled through the downtown area, wondering how he was going to put his plan to action. In his wallet he had a list of addresses that Toby had noted down, to help him find his way through the movie labyrinth.

1158 Montgomery street: Nicky Curry's apartment
1402 Seadrift, Stinson (157 Spindrift Road in real life): Kathleen's beach mansion
162 Divisadero (2930 Vallejo Street in real life): Kathleen's town house
147 Queenston Drive, Salinas: Dr. Becky Garter's former home

Dejan grimaced. He had no way of knowing where Beth's current apartment was. The address in his hand was her old home, taken from a movie still of her driver's license, dating back to when she had been married. It was no use to him. If he wanted to steal her car keys, he needed to know where she lived now.

He kept on walking until he came to the foot of the Transamerica Pyramid: the white, quartz tower that his girlfriend had seen upon arriving. Ahead of him the street rose up to the top of a steep hill, bordered by slender, flat-fronted houses with circular Bay windows and lush, scenic stairway gardens. That was Telegraph Hill, Detective Nicky Curry's neighborhood.

Shit, how am I going to find her place, Dejan thought. *I can't very well go knocking on doors one by one through this whole fucking city.* A sense of desperation began to overtake him.

He hadn't imagined it would be so complicated. Of course other tapers never entered the tapeworld with an agenda. And here he was, faced with not one, but two parallel tapeworlds playing side by side.

Where the hell does she live?

He could try following her home, when she exited the Tosca Café with Michael Douglas… but she might not be on foot. He was still faced with the same problem: how to get his hands on her car. He wished he knew how to hot-wire one.

Where the fuck do you live? Dr. Becky Garter—

And suddenly the solution came to him, so easy he felt stupid for not having thought of it sooner.

You know her name. Look in a phone book.

13

NEW CIVIL HOSPITAL, STRASBOURG

The nurses wheeled Christopher's special, non-ferrous gurney into the MRI scanning room. They adjusted the height and shifted him onto the patient table and then left the suite. The operating radiographer attached a band around his head with a motion-tracking sensor, and positioned a quadrature Siemens channel array coil over his head and secured it with foam padding. Christopher was an easy patient, still as a waxwork. She raised the table with a foot pedal, so that it was at the proper height to enter the bore, where once inside, he would be subject to an electromagnetic field 30,000 times as strong as the Earth's.

She slid the table into the bore, and went over to the copper-shielded console room, where she started the pilot scan to locate his exact position within the scanner.

As the Saggital T1 scan began, the machine issued a series of tap-tapping sounds, and the first of the radio images began to appear on her computer screen. She was looking at a cross section of Christopher's brain showing the cortex, white and gray matter and the frontal sinuses.

The first scan block came to an end and she returned to the magnet room to give him an injection of gadolinium, the special dye that would help the contrast on the next series of scans.

She slid out the table. Christopher's prone body resembled an entombed Crusader. She placed a tourniquet around his arm and used a butterfly needle to inject twenty milliliters of dye into his vein. As the needle went in, one of his toes curled ever so slightly, but she did not see this.

The radiographer slid him back into the ring-shaped scanning machine and returned to the console room.

She sat at her desk and launched a new series of scans. The machine glowed and issued a series of clicking noises.

CLICK... CLICK... CLICK... the first of the new incoming images began to align on her screen.

CLICK... CLICK... BANG!

The noise startled her. It was not in the usual repertoire. She peered through the observation glass, where Christopher's feet were visible, protruding from the scanner.

BANG! THUMP THUMP! POW!

The noise was coming from inside the machine! Suddenly she saw his feet twitch and then his legs shake. She flung open the door and raced into the magnet room, and suppressed a cry of shock. His whole body was writhing in the center of the bore, arms and legs flailing in spasms, his head smashing the coil against the interior walls. She saw what looked like white froth streaming from his lips, followed by a trickle of blood.

She pulled at the table, but it wouldn't budge. She saw his hands gripping the borders of the borehole as he smashed the coil cage repeatedly.

Frantically she rushed to the wall of the magnet room, near the door, where there was a Plexiglas cage with a red button marked "Emergency Magnet Rundown." She heard him issue a scream. Yes! A terrible high-pitched cry, and she unhinged the cage and slammed the button down, quenching the magnet.

There was a loud thunderclap and then a hissing as the liquid helium coolant boiled and escaped the machine into a ceiling vent. The room too was clouded with plumes of thick, white smoke. She heard his maniacal banging as she moved through the vapor, and she pulled at the patient table again. This time it slid out with no resistance, and she bent over him and unclipped the head coil, and saw through the frosty smoke his eyes wide open, black pools with red flecks in them, and his lips were moving as if he were trying to speak. There were bubbles of saliva forming at the corners of his mouth.

"Ready when you are, Sergeant Pembry," she heard him say. And suddenly his hands shot up and gripped her by the hair, pulling her to him, and his lips parted as he bared his teeth and she had just enough time to utter one shrill shriek before he sunk his teeth into her face, snarling—blood gushing freely now as he dislocated her jaw in a few vicious tugs and proceeded to gnaw off her tongue.

(PLUMP FRICTION TAPEWORLD)

"ANY OF YOU DICKLESS PRICKS MOVE AN INCH AND I'LL BUST A CAP ON EVERY LAST

MOTHERFUCKER IN THE ROOM."

Amanda Plummer's shrill, psychotic voice brought the dinner conversation at Whack Babbit Jim's to a dead halt. Ed Sullivan pissed his pants. Johnny the Midget shrunk even further into his bellhop uniform. Marilyn Monroe passed out in her section and had to be revived by Zorro. The executives, the black hipsters and smutty blondes up at the cocktail bar all froze.

Mikail and Lucas watched Tim Roth, aka Munchkin, as he made his way round the dancefloor, his Smith and Wesson revolver easily separating the crowd, like Moses parting the Red Sea.

Honey Buns, dressed in an awful, shapeless purple frock with her orange sunset hairdo moved behind him, waving her pistol maniacally. In her hand was a black plastic garbage bag.

"All right people," Munchkin said, "Wallets out. All of you! Everything goes in that bag she's got. Cell phones. Jewelry. Nobody play the fucking hero, OK? And nobody gets killed. I want every fucking thing you've got in that bag. I don't care if it's a motherfucking nipple piercing…"

The terrified customers reached shakily for their wallets, while Mosley Horace glowered at the gangster couple, as if their interruption were more of an inconvenience than a threat.

"This is such a drag, Daddy-O," moaned Tia Horace, still clinging to her Mac's massive arm.

Mikail, ever a fervent admirer of Tim Roth… who had

seen all his work from *Made In Britain* to *Rob Roy*, was waiting for him to come closer, so he could get a look at the tattoos on his right arm up close. He was even dressed the same as him, with the same putzy Hawaiian beach shirt.

"All right, who's in fucking charge here!" Munchkin zeroed in on the maître d', standing by the slot car track, shaking in his boots. He rushed over and grabbed him by the collar, dragging him over, and said, "I want everything from the fucking register in that bag. Understood?"

Ed Sullivan nodded mutely, terrified.

"Every fucking thing—" Munchkin hissed. "Tips included. Dinner checks… the whole fucking lot. Now beat it!" He thrust him away and the maître d' crashed into the slot track and then picked himself up and walked on jelly legs to the bar to open the register.

"How are we doing Honey Buns?" Munchkin asked his partner-in-crime, making his way over to the Chrysler New Yorker where Lukas and Mikail sat. Honey Buns came over with her bag of goodies and Munchkin cockedhis gun at Mosley and Tia.

"Wallets out," he said, in a low-key voice.

Mosley Horace, never taking his eyes off Munchkin, slowly removed a thick, snake-skin wallet from his vest. His upper lip curled in a tight sneer as he handed it over.

"What about her? Where's her purse?" Munchkin motioned with his gun at Tia.

"She ain't got no motherfucking purse!" Mosley growled.

"I'm traveling light, bozo," said Tia.

"All right, back off," Munchkin snapped. Neither of them moved an inch. He looked down and saw Mikail snickering, covering his mouth with his hand to keep from laughing out loud. Lucas kicked him again under the table.

"Oi. What's so funny?" Tim Roth moved his aim at them. His pale green eyes sparkled with nervous intensity.

"Bitch be cool," said Mikail, repeating a line from the film. Lucas, unable to contain himself any longer exploded in laughter. He pounded the table, sending a salt shaker tumbling to the floor.

"What's going on?" Amanda Plummer called nervously, from the bar where she was collecting the night's proceeds.

"Nothing Honey Buns, just a pair of jokers," said Munchkin. "One more sound out of you and I'm going to unload in your fucking face," he hissed at Mikail. "Come on dipshits, wallets out."

Lukas reached in his pocket and handed his to Munchkin, who moved around the car booth to take it, when he spied the briefcase, sitting on the floor near Mikail's shins.

"What's that?"

"What's what?"

"The briefcase at your feet. Pull it out—"

Mikail lifted the case and placed it on the table. Mosley Horace's eyes fairly bugged out of their sockets at the sight of it, and veins stood out on his thick neck. He took a step forward.

"Hey! That's my motherfucking case!"

"Back off you!" Munchkin swirled around, thrusting the barrel of his revolver into Ving Rhames' rodinesque skull.

"You ain't leavin' with my motherfucking case," Rhames thundered. He turned to Uma Thurman, "These are the two thieves Vinz was telling me about... as for you Ringo fucking Starr—"

"Shut up!" Munchkin yelled.

"What is it?" Honey Buns hissed, her attention diverted from the loot to the increasing commotion.

"Looks like we got ourselves a vigilante here," Munchkin said. "Is that what you fucking are big boy?"

Honey Buns marched over, her orange mop of hair shining in the tacky neon light. She thrust her hammerless pistol into Rhames' mastiff mug.

"Any more trouble from you and I'll execute both you and your cracker bitch!"

Mikail seized this moment of inattention to fling out his own revolver. He cocked it at Munchkin. Honey Buns screamed and jumped up on the stage, brandishing her firearm at Mikail.

"DON'T YOU FUCKING HURT HIM!!!"

Following his brother's lead, Lucas whipped out his Spanish pistol and pointedit at Honey Buns.

"Shut the fuck up, Yolanda—"

She started trembling with fear and uncertainty, arcing her gun between Lucas and Mikail, while her boyfriend swung his around at Lucas.

"You shoot her, you die," he stated, matter-of-factly.

In a jiffy Mosley whipped out his own handgun. A tiny little sexy nub of a pocket pistol and thrust the barrel against Tim Roth's cheek.

"You shoot him—*you* die, motherfucker," he said.

"You brought a gun to the restaurant?" Tia asked in astonishment.

"Baby, you know I never leave home without it—"

"DON'T YOU FUCKING HURT HIM," Honey Buns screamed. "OR I'LL KILL EVERY LAST ONE OF YOU SONSOFBITCHES…"

"We've heard this before," Mikail was grinning from ear to ear. This was fun.

"Don't you clowns say another fucking word," Tim Roth snarled. "I'm warning you!"

"Tell that bitch be cool…" Lukas added to the confusion.

Amanda Plummer was shivering and screaming and stamping her feet. The entire diner was speechless at the turn of events. All eyes were riveted on the five criss-crossing firearms. It was quite unusual a predicament, even by L.A. standards.

"It seems like we got ourselves a bit of a situation, Honey Buns," reflected Munchkin, with false bravado. "A Guatemalan standoff."

"It's called a Mexican standoff—fool!" Mosley growled. "And your ass ain't walking its way out of here with my briefcase!"

"SHUT UP!" Honey Buns screamed. And her face was now as bright red as her hair. "SHUT UP! ALL YOU DICKLESS MOTHERFUCKING PRICKS!"

"Tell that bitch to chill!" Mosley barked. "She's getting on my nerves—"

"Chill Honey Buns," said Tim Roth

"Now tell her it's going to be all right."

"It's going to be all right. I love you."

"I love you too Munchkin," she said. Then after a brief silence, "I have to pee—"

Lucas and Mikail started laughing again, this really was a riot. Most of the customers were staring aghast at their nonchalant behavior in such a dire situation.

The Donna Reed waitress in the poofy skirt with the polka-dot apron now spoke up, "You've got the money—please, just leave," she implored them.

POW!

Amanda Plummer's nerves gave way and she inadvertently let loose a shot into the ceiling. The customers screamed. Plaster rained down. There was a moment of terrible silence and then all hell broke loose.

Mosley fired at Honey Buns—but missed. A bullet whizzed past her and smashed into the guitar-bearing Ricky Nelson impersonator, sending him flying back into a table full of yuppies. Honey Buns got off two rounds. A TV on the wall behind him exploded and Mosley crumpled to the floor with a manly grunt, as the other bullet tore into his left shoulder.

Steve Buscemi as Buddy Holly, shrieked like a girl and

dropped his platter.

"RAUS!" Mikail screamed, leaping from the car booth and grabbing the briefcase with him. Munchkin swung his gun around to fire at him, but Lucas beat him to it, letting loose a double-tap to his chest and Tim Roth flew back and crashed into Donna Reed who screeched, as the executives and doo-wop singers ran for their lives.

The brothers fled through the diner, shots being now fired at them from both Honey Buns and the injured Mosley Horace. As they ran through the hail of bullets, Bonnie-and-Clyde style, they saw parasols topple, clients struck by ricochets, Johnny the Midget cowering behind a palm frond, and stage-lights explode and fall like meteors.

Something struck Mikail in the thigh and he cried out as a sharp, searing pain seized him and his leg buckled under him. Lucas swirled around and fired at Honey Buns, catching her dead center in the chest and Amanda Plummer crumpled dead on the stage.

He hoisted his brother up and dragged him toward the exit, glancing over his shoulder seeing Mosley struggle to his feet, moving in a daze, his massive figure swaying from side to side (just like when he went after Bruce Willis in the movie) as he hollered at them—punctuating his demands with pistol shots.

"Get back here—motherfuckers! I ain't through with you yet!"

POP! POP! POP!

And they burst out of the diner and through the band

of motley bikers, Lucas dragging Mikail toward the Chevy, when he saw the red Malibu convertible parked alongside it and two terrifyingly recognizable figures standing beside it in grim black-and-white suits with pencil ties.

The hitmen Joel Winston and Vinz Vegas!

They reached for their weapons…

"DIE DIE DIE!" Lucas yelled out, unloading his firearm at them.

He emptied the whole clip, but nothing happened. John Travolta and Samuel L. Jackson looked at each other, then down to their miraculously unharmed bodies.

"Oh shit—" murmured Lucas.

And the last image he saw were their two barrels being simultaneously raised toward his face.

Lucas woke up in his dinky apartment in Duisburg, screaming. Beside him, Mikail leaped from the tattered couch, doing a mad Rumpelstiltskin dance… pounding his feet on the rug as if they were on fire. Both of the brothers gripped each other by the shoulders, hollering and jumping about wildly.

It took a few minutes for them to regain their senses. They were still in one piece, despite having received a few shells each to the face. The shock was so intense that they were reduced to blubbering wrecks.

"We're alive!" Mikail gasped.

"Totally epic!" His brother responded.

14

The bulls turned Janko loose after forty-eight hours, and a series of fruitless interrogations. They had nothing, and even worse the guy wasn't scared. The credit-card scam charge was for real, but it would be ages before the docket even went to court—if it ever got there. Both sides knew what the police really wanted. They wanted Janko to sellout someone in the higher circle of the trafficking ring. They wanted to know what was being sold and who was selling it. But even if Janko had told the truth, they might not have believed him anyway. It was that preposterous.

So they released him, and Janko returned to his hideout in Duisburg. He immediately tried to get in contact with Albino Toby, but received no reply. Toby wasn't in H-town, or in the city so far as he knew. Something was definitely up.

Janko went to Oberbilk next, and was stunned to find his cousin—Darko—at the internet and call shop. The fucking slimeball was sitting there with the girl who ran the shop, chatting away like he owned the place. Darko. Fucking Fukushima! Janko must have known he'd show up sooner or later, as soon as he got a whiff of the money they were raking in.

He put on his best commercial smile and greeted him. "Ciao Darko. What brings you here?"

Darko scowled at Janko as if he were almost annoyed

by his intrusion into the place that he owned. By the way he contemptuously responded Janko knew at once that he had moved in on his well-plotted turf. It was the same fucking story since the old country. If Janko liked a girl, Darko moved in on her. If Janko had a scam going, Darko showed up, wanting a piece of the action. He always pushed Janko to the sidelines. And Janko relented, partly because Darko was family, and partly because he was a dangerous man and he was afraid of him. And now Darko managed a smile... a horrible smile of false zlato-plated teeth, and his gold orthodox cross glinted from around his wiry neck, like a lighthouse beacon flashing over a sea of criminality.

"Mr. movie man," sang Darko, moving in now and pinching Janko's cheek, twisting the flesh between his fingers. "You weren't going to hold out on me again, were you?"

Janko sighed. "You know about the tapes then. Who told you?"

"It's my business to know things," said Darko, licking his lips. He opened the fridge behind the counter, where the cashier sat and helped himself to a Monster. "I know about Toby. I know about Nasr. I got your boy going to Nasr for me. Of course, not to be ungrateful for this wonderful business opportunity that you have presented me with, I'd like to keep you on as a runner."

Runner! A fucking runner! This was taking the piss. Janko was furious. He'd kill those traitors: Albino Toby and Dejan fucking Vidic. Two days in the pen and they had chewed up his entire operation.

As if reading his thoughts Darko now said, "It's not like you or anybody else has a choice in the matter. I got my runners in Venlo. I even got a foot in Amsterdam. Ha! You didn't know about Amsterdam-west, did you?"

He saw the look of consternation on Janko's face and he laughed.

"You think there's only one lab making these? There are five in Holland. Two are being set up in Germany: Berlin and Hamburg. Another in France. What? You didn't know that. You are so fucking ignorant."

"It was my deal," Janko said, miserably.

Darko's countenance softened and he threw his arm around Janko in a brotherly fashion. He smelt of amphetamines; of speed-sweat right through his unclean chetnik pores. Darko had always been a speed freak. The last thing he fucking needed was another energy boost to his metabolism. Still, he gulped a long swallow of Monster and smacked his lips and said "You need me—Janny—face it. This is big, too big for you to handle alone. With enough distributors, why we are going to be fucking millionaires!"

"You mean *you're* going to be a millionaire," grunted Janko, disengaging himself from Darko's slimy embrace.

"Don't be such a party-pooper. We're *all* going to be rich."

"Look—it's no joke this," Janko said. "You've got to keep a low profile. It's not like back home. Right off the bat they don't like guys like us. The cowboys are looking for any excuse to nail me."

"I don't care," snorted Darko. "I'm tired of all the old shit. The way I see it: these tapes are made of money. And the best part is: nobody's going to know what we're doing. There's nobody to see it. Everybody's back home."

"Darko, I got to tell you, I already got pinched twice for no reason. I really got to be careful. I'm running a licensed place here. Everything's legit—

"Quit fucking worrying. Leave it to me. I got your back now. Nobody's going to fuck with you."

And that was the end of the conversation and his complaint. Janko knew it was useless to argue further. He knew his cousin, he knew his methods. What was he going to do—muscle Darko? Darko *was* the muscle.

(TRIASSIC PARK TAPEWORLD)

Walking in the misty dawn, with Robert Muller leading the way, his virile, hunter's face swathed in the shadows of the slouch hat he was wearing, Matthias felt a genuine thrill at the possibilities the tapeworld offered. Muller carried a SPAS-12 shotgun, slung on a strap from his shoulder, the barrel pointed down near his bare knobby knees. Matthias found himself wondering, briefly, what brain-dead movie costume designer had outfitted him with those very gay shorts.

"I can't believe I'm listening to you," Muller muttered. "Ten years hunting in Nairobi… 5 years head game warden at Mr. Hammond's wildlife park in Kenya… and here I am taking advice from a bloody teenager… pardon my French."

"And I'm talking to a DVD, so we're quits," retorted Matthias.

"Huh?"

"Aw, never mind."

They were moving cautiously from the emergency bunker toward the adjacent raptor pen. Muller had given Matthias an M16 automatic rifle with a tactical flashlight mounted ahead of the front sight. He'd taken the weapons from the bunker, and although he was wary about putting such a deadly firearm into the hands of an inexperienced boy, he would still rather be prepared for a worst-case scenario.

"Don't fire that thing unless it's absolutely necessary," advised Muller. "If you have to shoot at a raptor, or any other bloody predator on this island, aim for the neck, or ribcage. Aim high, higher than you normally would, if shooting at close range, which I hope to God won't be necessary."

"This is so cool," marveled Matthias, cupping the charging handle. He raised the rifle and pointed the searchlight on the path leading to the fortified quarantine pen.

"Cool? It's bloody uncool!" snarled Muller. "This isn't a goddamn *Duke Nukem* MS-DOS video game! Do you have any inkling just how dangerous these creatures are? They're pack hunters—move at speeds of up to fifty miles an hour! Attack in groups..."

"Yeah, I know, I know," scoffed Matthias in his most blasé tone. "Velociraptor—ooh so scary. You know I wasn't even born when this movie came out. My girlfriend was like ooh you've got to see *Triassic Park*. I'm like, Spielberg, oh please. If I want to see a monster movie, I'll take John Carpenter over Steven the E.T. puppet-master anyday… wouldn't you agree?"

"What the devil are you blabbering on about?" Muller asked. "What movie? What the hell kind of dimwit talks about the cinema at a crucial time like this? Are you hallucinating? Did you eat any berries in the park? These are real life… hold it…"

He knelt down, inspecting a series of birdlike tracks that ran in the earth. Then he looked up at the raptor pen, which stood in a clearing, some fifty yards in front of them, with its concrete walls and guard tower glinting in the early morning light, like some foreboding, maximum-security prison. When they approached it his worst fears were confirmed. The electric wires on the top of the barricade had been chewed through in several places. The raptors were loose.

"I can see the power shed from here," said Matthias. "We can make it if we run."

"No we can't," said Muller quietly, removing his hat and placing it on a low-lying liana.

"Why? Because we're being hunted?"

He turned his steely blue gaze to Matthias. "Who made you so bloody clever? She's right there up ahead, through those ferns. It's OK. I've got her…"

He crouched low in the brush and unfolded the stock on his shotgun. Matthias took a few paces back and waited patiently for the *other* raptor to attack from the side, while the warden had all his attention on the decoy.

"I've got her—" Muller repeated, squinting into his sight.

There was a rustle in the ferns and suddenly to his left appeared the elongated snout and beady reptilian eyes of a second raptor. The predator was poised over Muller, prepared to strike. It opened its jaws and squealed.

"Clever girl," Muller whispered, and the ambushing raptor sprung at him and then its head exploded as a gunshot went off, blowing it to pieces, like a watermelon dropped from a great height. The raptor crashed on its side, and Robert Muller's face was covered slick with dripping bits of gore and itty bitty skull fragments and bloodied dino brain.

"Not so clever," said Matthias, clutching his smoking M16 and feeling every bit like Rambo.

Riding back along the tour trail, with Muller grim-faced and sulking behind the wheel of the Jeep, Matthias couldn't help making a few snide remarks.

"So how long were you hunting in Africa?"

"Shut up."

"What did you hunt? Squirrels?"

"I said cork it!" Muller was fuming! Over twenty years of big game field experience and here he had been out-maneuvered by a sniveling amateur punk kid! He felt his manhood draining away.

They passed through the main park gate. Behind its arched, torch-lit portal they could see the craggy peaks of volcanic mountains in the distance, obscured by a thick, steamy, jungle mist. To the right were the gently rolling plains that led down to the *Brachiosaurus* territory. He saw one of them now, its slender neck rising gracefully out of a lake, while a herd of crest-headed parasaurolophus scampered toward the border and dipped their bony snouts into the water. The ethereal beauty of the scene was flawed on only one account. There was no soaring musical score. It added to the haunting realism of the tape world.

They had reactivated the park systems manually at the maintenance shed, and now that *Triassic Park* was back online and the *Tyrannosaur* and female leader of the velociraptor pack were dead there really wasn't that much else to do. Through their actions, Matthias and Heike had brought the movie to a grinding halt. Of course it was great fun bothering the characters like the kooky Mr. Hammond, and socializing with the actors, but there was really only one thing Matthias was now after, and that was to find the bonus at the *Tyrannosaur* lagoon. The lagoon hadn't been mentioned in the movie, and so he reasoned this undoubtedly was an extra scene that had been put in by the programmers. Kind of like when you broke the code in *Tomb Raider* and got to see Lara Croft nude.

"I don't know how you did it—" Muller was muttering through clenched teeth. "These creatures are the most lethal, intelligent animals I've ever encountered…"

"Oh, don't beat yourself up over it," smirked Matthias. "Call it beginner's luck. Besides, I'm sure you managed to kill a few warthogs back in the day…"

Robert Muller gave him a murderous stare. A hissing

came over the Motorola radio on the dashboard. Matthias picked it up and switched it to channel two.

"Ja?"

"Robert, is the raptor pen still intact?" John Parker worriedly inquired.

"Oh, they got out," explained Matthias casually. "But we took care of them. I mean there are still two out there, roaming around, probably chewing up some of the herbivores… but the leader of the pack, she's gone Swayze…"

"Who is this? It better not be who I think it ish—" Parker roared.

"Give me that," Robert snarled, reaching for the handset. Matthias pulled it away, chiding him playfully.

"Ah-ah… you shouldn't use it while driving! It's dangerous…"

And now Richard Attenborough was virtually screaming into the radio. "If you harm another of my precious creations I'll festoon this island with your Heiney innuts!"

Robert snatched the handset away from Matthias. "John?"

"Yesh… what ish that juvenile punk horror doing with you? I thought I told you to lock him up."

"I'm going to pick up his girlfriend and bring the two of them to the east dock. They're taking the next boat back to San José."

"Why that's the first intelligent thing I've heard you say all week—bravo! Now don't bloody let that assassin out of your sight until he's off my island," Parker ordered. "Is that clear, you nincompoop?"

"Yes Sir," Muller gulped.

"Over and out." The transmission ended. They were driving past the *Dilophosaurus* enclosure, which was a region of densely populated cycads—the stumpy prehistoric predecessor of the palm tree—punctuated by mournful swamp cypresses. The air was thick with buzzing insects, and Matthias was busy slapping tapeworld mosquitoes off his neck and arms. The atmosphere had that pure, clean smell that comes after a hard rain. Most of the jungle fronds and foliage were glistening wet.

"Neri is out there somewhere—probably dead," Matthias mused. "Some people never learn… Did you know that they're going to make a *Triassic Park* part four? Crichton's dead obviously, but the studio will get a team of those unimaginative screenwriters to recycle something from the slush pile. Don't you just hate it when those greedy, money-grubbing Hollywood executives try and make a million sequels off a franchise that has clearly run out of steam?"

Muller abruptly slammed the brakes and the Jeep skidded in the mud. He turned to face Matthias and his face was livid.

"Why are we stopping?"

"Let's get one thing straight!" The masculine hunter stabbed a finger emphatically in Matthias' face. "Stop with the bloody gibberish. You go on and on about these movies… who the bloody hell is Spielberg anyway? I never heard of the name. Sounds like a Swiss watch. And why the devil do you keep on referring to Triassic Park as a goddamn movie! We never had a damn filming crew authorized on this island since its inception."

Matthias drew a deep breath and exhaled slowly. "How can I explain this... look... you're not real. You may think you are, but believe me you're not. You're really a figment of my imagination. I mean, that's the reason I know everything that's going on here. This whole island, everything around us, why it's just a neurochip that's playing in my head right now..."

The game warden blinked a few times, totally bewildered. The boy was clearly delusional—in the grip of a psychotic episode. Probably one of those video game junkies suffering from a variant of the Tetris effect.

"It's quite simple," Matthias said. "I'll prove it to you. You've been working here how many years?"

Muller stared at him blankly. "Five. What's the point?"

"OK, so think hard. What do you really know about the people you've been working with for all that time? Think of the engineers: Dr. Wu and Ray Arnold. Do you know anything about them, besides their names? Do you know anything about John Parker, other than the fact that he's an eccentric billionaire and creator of this place?"

"I really don't see where you're going with this—"

"You've spent five years living with these people and I'm betting you don't know the first thing about them. Now how do you explain that?"

Beads of sweat began to collect on the game warden's forehead. His lip quivered. His eyes were glassy.

"Everybody here has been programmed, like computer

generated imagery. It's really not that difficult to comprehend—"

There was a low rumble in the distance, and a tremor passed underneath them. The suspension of the Jeep creaked.

"Quiet!" said Muller, and his face was ghostly pale.

"CGI!" Matthias called out, and he began chanting it. "CGI... CGI!"

"I said QUIET!"

Another rumble, then a thunderclap. The fronds of the cycads shook, a wind swept through the banyan forest... the earth began to shake and roll. The reverse mirrors clinked and tingled.

"C-G-I!"

And Muller could contain himself no longer and sprung on Matthias, clasping his hands around his neck and choking him... and as he was gasping for air Matthias looked down and saw that the game warden's hands were severed from his forearms. In fact he no longer had any arms at all, just hollow sleeves—*blank spaces in the tapeworld.*

The warden saw it too—saw his arms missing—and he panicked, releasing his grip. His hands tumbled from Matthias neck and rolled onto his lap. Matthias picked them up. And when he moved them a white patch appeared through the windshield of the Jeep, all the way to the sky beyond—a white streak like a Tip-Ex smear.

"I believe these are yours—" Matthias said, dumping the hands in the warden's lap, and Muller opened his mouth and gave a sharp scream and leapt from the Jeep, running armless into the jungle, and he passed in-between two banyan trees and vanished.

Matthias climbed into the driver's seat, tossing Muller's hands out the side. "What did I tell you—CGI—" he said, and whistled as he took command of the Jeep.

BERGAMBACHT, SOUTH HOLLAND

"… I mean he had me, Micky Santino, his best friend, watching his ass… and he had Ginger, the woman he loved, on his arm… but in the end we fucked it all up…"

Joe Pesci's distinctive New Jersey twang rang through the lab, where the programming team was copying samples of the voice-over and integrating it into the Micky Santino persona file. A revolving volumetric display of Robert DeNiro in a flamboyant salmon-colored suit lit up the OLED monitors with style.

The order had come in for 20,000 copies of Martin Scorcese's 1995 epic Las Vegas mobster tale *Casino*, and the crew was working overtime in order to get it done before the weekend, when half of them would take a much-appreciated break.

The big question was exactly how much nociception to encode. Or in layman's terms just how much pain they were going to allow the taper to feel or endure in the film before the exit stimulant discharged and woke the user up. Part of the thrill of the tapeworlds resided in the sense of actual physical danger. You could get hurt, and you could feel pain, but moderately.

In *Casino*, the programming team was faced with a literal avalanche of brutal and bloody set pieces. There were stabbings, beatings, finger-hammerings, a stunning by a cattle prod, a baseball bat beating in a cornfield, mention of an icepick to the testicles and the infamous head-in-a-vice eye-popping scene. If they wanted to remain faithful to the atmosphere, this meant subjecting the taper to the mercy of Nicky Santino's psychotic outrages. In order to make sure that the violent episodes were tolerable for the user, Dr. Yin had asked for a volunteer to enter into a test scene from the tapeworld and provoke Nicky Santino. When no one volunteered, it was decided that they would pull straws. The shortest straw was picked by Johannes, and the other programmers applauded loudly.

"Goddamit! Hold on," Johannes protested. "What scene do I have to test?"

"We're going to stick you in the fountain pen scene," Rick explained cheerfully. "We want you to go up to De Niro and tell him to fuck himself. Then let Joe Pesci go hogwild on you."

"Are you crazy? You want me to take on that psychopath! He's going to kill me!"

"Relax," Dr. Yin said. "If your system floods with too much adrenaline, you'll wake up. We need to know whether or not Nicky Santino is too violent—and whether the pain he metes out is tolerable…"

"Of course he's too violent! He's a fucking mobster.

Why can't you guys do a nice movie, for once? What's wrong with *Notting Hill*, or something with Meg Ryan? I'd even take a shot at Robert Pattinson's bare chest in *Twilight*... anything but this!"

"Tapers don't want nice," said Dr. Yin. "They want action! Excitement!"

"Yes... but not being stabbed in the neck by a fountain pen!"

"Quit being such a pussy," Xander said, and the team exploded in laughter.

"Yeah," chirped Laeticia LeJeun, sarcastically. "Be a man."

Johannes looked desperately around the lab, like a mouse searching for a hole in the wall. He turned to Kim Nguyen. "This is unnecessary, Kimmy. Tell him!"

Kim shrugged, "Then don't do it..."

"Oh for crying out loud," Dr. Yin rolled his eyes in exasperation. "We'll stick you in the desert scene then. We'll put in a panic trigger, OK? Do this for me and maybe we make a special copy of *Brokeback Mountain*, just for you..."

He chuckled and Johannes went red in the face.

"Fine, I'll do it," he sulked. "But I want a good exit trigger. Something easy to remember..."

"How about *pussy*?" Dr. Yin suggested, and the whole lab went riot again.

(FATAL IMPULSE TAPEWORLD)

Dejan watched the couple, Michael Douglas and Jeanne Tripplehorn, or rather, Nicky Curry and Becky Garter, as they parked their cars at the base of the apartment block where her address had been listed in the white pages. It was one of those Mediterranean-style residences with a lot of flair: sandstone walls with ogee-arched portals and Moorish decorations around the windows. He had been waiting a half hour, on a bright sunny street, overlooking a drop to the waterfront, but the moment that Nicky Curry's Ford Mustang came bounding up the curb, the sky went dark and a wind blew, rain drizzled and the pavement shone suddenly wet in preparation for the scene.

He waited as they engaged in a bit of small talk, ambling toward the entrance. He could hear Nicky Curry ranting, obviously upset about something. He was complaining about an internal affairs investigator who was giving him a hard time.

"That Nilsen is such an asshole! I shoulda let him have it."

"You'd be playing his game then, that's exactly the kind of reaction he's expecting."

"Goddamit Beth, why do you have to always analyze everything?"

They entered the residence and Dejan let a minute go by, to ensure himself that they wouldn't notice they were being followed, and then he crossed the street, and slipped into the foyer.

There was a wrought-iron spiral staircase, leading to the upper floors of the complex. Dejan could hear Michael Douglas' whining nasal voice echoing through the corridors (still complaining), and their footsteps marching up the stairway. He waited at the foot of it until they were out of earshot, then he crept silently up the stairs.

He got off on the third-floor landing and heard a door click shut down the hall. He walked briskly toward it, and waited an additional minute until he could hear a certain commotion coming from inside the flat, accompanied by raspy breathing. This was it!

Carefully, Dejan opened the door, ever so slightly, and peered into the room.

Dr. Becky Garter was bent over the backrest of an armchair, in black stockings and a garter belt, her ass exposed, while Nicky Curry still wearing his blue work shirt and tie, but with his dress pants lowered around his ankles, was pumping her from behind.

He was really giving it to her.

Through the French windows leading to the balcony Dejan could see a ladies dance class being held in a studio in the opposite building. Becky was struggling, partly resisting, and partly submissive and Dejan was distracted momentarily from his mission by the somewhat less appetizing sight of Michael Douglas' clenching bum cakes.

"Verhoeven you crazy genius—" he said to himself, and then he grabbed the Bart Simpson keychain on the wooden dresser to his right.

He softly closed the door behind him, while they were still going at it like minks and he twiddled Beth's keys between his fingers as he made his way out.

Her car was a white 1980 Nissan Datsun with a sunroof and a cheap Sony cassette deck for a sound system. There was even a collection of vintage 1980s music tapes in the glove compartment: Paula Abdul. Cher. Olivia Newton John. Just reading the titles made Dejan glad that he was really in 2010. It was precisely the kind of middle-of-the-road crap you'd expect from a well-balanced shrink.

He drove away quickly from the scene, knowing that Becky was going to kick her ex out of the flat as soon as they'd finished humping and the last thing he needed was being chased by a cop for driving a stolen vehicle. He cruised through the neighborhood, looking for a sign, something to bring him to the Shoreline Highway, which led to Kathleen's place. Although Dejan had never murdered anyone in real life, and had no desire to do so even in a tapeworld, he was almost certain that by killing Kathleen he would destroy the primary tape which was stuck repeating itself over and over, like a broken record, and thereby free Milinka.

Only one thing disturbed him, and that was the nagging question: just how had Kathleen and Foxy managed to deceive his girlfriend into thinking that he had been kidnapped even before he entered the tapeworld? How was that possible? Unless the neurochip had used pieces of Milinka's memory to reconstitute an image of him. But that still didn't explain the phone call she had received from him in the Tosca café. She had insisted it was his voice she had heard, telling her to meet him at Ronnie Roz's club. But Dejan hadn't even been in the tapeworld at the time. In any case, once he found Kathleen, he'd put an end to the mystery.

He negotiated his way through a series of zig-zagging streets that rose and plummeted so many times he felt nauseated. It was daytime again and the traffic intensified as he drove down a wide, palm-lined boulevard along the eastern waterfront and passed a long, sky-blue ferry terminal—the minute hand on the clock tower moving counterclockwise at an accelerated pace. The two tapes were fusing, and things were starting to go haywire.

He accelerated, passing underneath a suspension bridge, and then through a short tunnel, the entrance to the bore marked by a stark painted rainbow, the interior a wash of gold lights and when he emerged out the other side he looked in the reverse mirror and saw that the whole city had vanished. Behind him was only a hilly landscape.

Ahead was a two-lane road that snaked its way up through a nest of steep, chaparral-cloaked hills. He had barely been on the winding road for a minute when he came up behind a Gray Line sightseeing bus. He saw a sleek black Lotus Espirit overtake a freight truck on the other lane with ease and speed past him in the opposite direction, and he caught a glimpse of a blonde figure through the tinted windshield.

Kathleen!

In front of him the tour bus honked loudly and Dejan slammed on his brakes as the bus nearly collided with a large brown Plymouth. The driver swerved back into his lane at the last second, avoiding a crash by centimeters, and when the car veered past him, in hot pursuit of the Lotus, Dejan saw Michael Douglas at the wheel, pale-faced and sweating behind oversize smoky sunglasses.

Kathleen had left her mansion to visit Hazel Hopkins—an old woman who had killed her own parents in a plotted boating accident in the 1950s.

He would find her house and wait patiently for her to return.

15

PUBLIC MENTAL HOSPITAL, NORTH ALSACE

The Centre Hospitalier Spécialisé is not one building, but a psychiatric compound composed of various separate units for the housing and treatment of the mentally ill. There are numerous minimum-security houses, named after tropical plants, of different sizes and colors and one maximum-security ward which is in a block well removed from the others, surrounded by a high wall topped by barbed-wire fencing.

There are no long, echoic corridors as these produce perceptual distortion and are aggravating to the inpatients. Furniture in the patient rooms is heavier than normal, to prevent patients from lifting or throwing it. The floors in the lobby and lounge are sheet vinyl. The walls are washable, for obvious reasons. All doors are equipped with vision panels.

Inside the high-security ward are two seclusion suites, which are used for the immediate emergency isolation and containment of particularly violent individuals. The room is a pastel pink (intended to reduce aggressive behavior), padded with sheet cushion vinyl, and contains nothing in the way of furniture but a soft-edged mattress with restraints attached to it, and a pillow. There is a tamper-proof smoke detector in the ceiling, and three secured overhead lights. There is also an anti-vandal toilet and recessed washbasin and hand wash unit.

Officers Perrin and Lambert were led to one of the seclusion suites by a massive black orderly. They were accompanied by Dr. Frederick Courbier—a slick, noxious character, who explained to them the reasons of Christopher's confinement in the ward.

"...On the afternoon of July the 5th he was taken to the MRI suite at the CHU for a comprehensive brain scan, at the request of Dr. Sameer. Somehow the exam woke the patient from his catatonic state, possibly due to the magnetic field—in any case he was highly agitated and the radiographer on duty removed him immediately from the machine, when she leaned over him to remove his head coil he did this to her—"

Dr. Courbier removed a photograph from his vest pocket and showed it to them saying, "The doctors managed to save one of her eyes... and reset her jaw... more or less. He never said a word, even after he ate her tongue. I keep him in here..."

They stopped outside the suite, and through the observation panel they could see an inoffensive-looking boy, with sandy hair and pale gray-green eyes, his hands bound behind his back, tethered by a harness attached to a metal bracket on the wall behind him by a thick leather strap.

"How long has he been contained here?" Officer Perrin asked.

"Two days. Ever since the attack," replied Dr. Courbier. "I'm going to have José let you in to speak with him. Do not approach him, do not touch him, you pass him nothing. No pens, paper, paper clips or other such writing materials... Do not accept anything he might offer you. Are we clear?"

The officers nodded. The orderly moved forward and unlocked the steel door and they stepped into the suite. The boy watched them impassively as they entered the room.

"Christopher Venet," said the first officer. "My name is Nicolas Perrin and this is Philip Lambert. May we speak with you?"

The boy took a step forward, as far as his restraints would allow, and then he spoke, and his speech was precise and measured. Not the nonsensical ramblings of a lunatic that they had expected.

"May I see your credentials?"

"Certainly—"

Perrin removed his Europol Investigators card and showed it to Christopher.

"Closer, please..."

He extended his arm.

"Clo—ser—" he repeated, in a sing-song voice.

"I'm afraid I can't do that—"

"May I ask what an inter-governmental law enforcement agency is doing in a psychiatric clinic?" Christopher inquired. "You have no official jurisdiction here," he winked at them.

"Do you know the reasons for your incarceration?" Officer Lambert countered.

The boy went silent. He stared straight past the men, as if they weren't even there. They waited for several long minutes before he spoke again.

"Do you like my room?" he asked them. "Some psychiatric pencil-pusher obviously reasoned that the use of this atrocious color would serve a physiological effect for the suppression of human aggression, but I beg to differ…"

"Why did you attack the nurse?" Officer Lambert asked.

Christopher's head recoiled and then his mouth opened ever so slightly, like a cobra.

"Don't try and quantify me, Agent Lambert," the boy warned them. "A Jehovah's Witness once tried my patience… I ate his kidneys with some garden peas and a nice Lambrusco…"

"It was only a simple question. You'll either answer it or you won't."

"Yes," Christopher hissed. "My guardian—the learned Dr. Courbier—won't even begrudge me the gift of a pen while I am bound in this cell like an animal—and here you come to me, free men begging for a handout. It won't do…" he tut-tutted.

The officers looked at each other, uncertain where this interview was going or how to continue it. The boy was acting so strangely; very out of character for a person of his age and upbringing. Officer Perrin decided to try something else.

"Do you know who Marie Venet is?" he asked him.

The boy's head turned a fraction.

"No."

"Can you tell us anything about yourself?"

"I won't waste your time or anybody else's with tedious

recollections of my childhood," said Christopher. "Perhaps—if you could arrange a transfer for me, to another institution, I might oblige you."

"I'm afraid we are not authorized to do that."

Christopher chuckled. "Your appeal is waning by the minute. Still, one aims to please. So I'll offer you a deal, non-negotiable. *Quid pro quo.* I tell you things, you tell me things. *Quid pro quo*, what will it be?"

Officer Perrin looked at his partner. Nicolas' brow was furrowed; he appeared to be thinking deeply.

"Who is Christopher Venet?" Nicolas now asked.

"I'm afraid I don't have the answer to that one," the boy said.

"Who are you then?"

"Have you read my case file? Everything you need to know is in those pages…"

"Tell me your name—"

"… All good things to those who wait. I've waited—I've been in this room for eight years now, and I know that they will never ever let me out while I am alive," said Christopher, rolling his eyes to the padded ceiling. "What I want is some place with a view, where I can see grass, or even water. I want to be in a private institution, far far away from here…"

"Tell me your name—"

The boy looked away, down at the floor. He retired into himself, and was absent again. They could not coax anything more out of him. He was obviously experiencing some kind of psychosis—he wasn't his own self. But what had triggered this maniacal episode? When he had ignored them so long that they were about to leave, Nicolas was seized by a sudden piercing flash of insight.

The attack on the nurse reminded him of something he had read, or watched on TV.

A hospital for the criminally insane.

Quid pro quo.

He ate her tongue...

Suddenly it struck him. He took a step forward, dangerously close to the bound criminal, and he spoke in a loud clear voice.

"Hannibal Lecter."

The boy looked up, and his eyes flashed in recognition. He smiled darkly.

"Close but not quite. It's Doctor Animal Dissecter, if you please."

(TRIASSIC PARK TAPEWORLD)

As Matthias arrived at the site of the carnage, he saw the pair of paleontologists and the lawyer and the mathematician and the grandchildren of John Parker all standing around Heike, listening to her talk.

He parked the Jeep near the smashed up outhouse, where the lawyer had been eaten in the original movie. Here in the tapeworld, he was still his bloodsucking, sniveling self, thanks to Heike.

"Matty!" Heike saw him arrive and ran to him. "I killed the T-rex."

"I know!" He gave her a high-five. "And I blew the head off a raptor. I got an M16 in the Jeep. What were you talking about?"

"I'm trying to bring them up to date on major world events."

"What?"

"Yeah, you know. Like 9/11 and the war in Iraq, and iPhones and Facebook. I told them about Michael Jackson's death, but nobody believes me. They're completely clueless—still stuck in 1993."

"Duh. Heike they're programmed bots. They won't understand what you're talking about…"

"Milestone sort of does. He says my logic is twisted but it's consistent with every inevitable cataclysm inherent with a complex system—"

"Who? That crazy mathematician prophet of doom." He looked over her shoulder at the group of characters who were gathered in a circle, talking among themselves and casting curious glances toward him and Heike.

"You best be careful what you tell a tapeworld character, Heike," Matthias whispered. "I tried to tell this one guy, from the control center, that he had been *programmed*. And he just like disappeared—I mean a piece of him went missing. And a piece of the sky too… look it's still there—"

He pointed upwards, where a white streak was visible, above the canopy of jungle trees.

"What's happening?"

"I think it's like a tear in the fabric," Matthias said. "Maybe a mini-transistor or electrode in the neurochip burnt out. Anyway we've got to go to the lagoon in the *Tyrannosaur* territory—"

"Why?"

"There's a bonus there—"

"How do you know?"

"I just do—"

"Well how do we get down there? It's a fifteen- to twenty-meter drop from this side."

"I brought a topographical map with me—from the bunker. It shows all the service roads and gates. If we go north there's a maintenance tunnel leading from the main road directly into the *Tyrannosaur* paddock. We'll cross the jungle all the way south to the lagoon."

The others ceased their murmuring and came over. They all looked muddled and quite anxious.

Dr. Graham removed his fedora and spoke first. "Now that you've brought this Jeep—we really should be getting back to home base. At least the kids."

"Take it," said Matthias, tossing him the keys. "We're going on."

"Going on where?"

"In there?" He pointed to the jungle.

"That's absurd!" Genco spoke up. "You can't simply go wandering around the park."

"Anyone want to come with us?" Matthias proposed.

The boy, Tim, the dinosaur enthusiast, took a step forward, but his older sister grabbed him by his shirtsleeve.

"Don't be an idiot—"

"Lemme go—"

Jeff Goldblum held up two forefingers and said, "Here we have another fine example of unpredictability."

"Oh shut up"all three adults chimed.

"You're really going to go into that jungle—after what you've just seen?" the paleobotonist—Ella—asked Heike, with concern.

"Sure," Heike shrugged. "Beats the hell out of a goddamn Sunday picnic," she winked at Genco. "Tchuss" she called out, as Matthias slung his arm around her shoulder and they went sauntering down the trail.

Dr. Graham looked at Ella—and mouthed. "T*chuss*?" she hunched her shoulders and shook her head.

"Is Michael Jackson really dead?" one of the kids called after them.

"Dead as disco!" Heike yelled back. "And Lady Gaga is the next Madonna."

A short while later and they were crossing the lush Mesozoic jungle, picking their way over the root mat of tiny palms and gingkoes and decomposing leaves that made up the forest floor, trying to orient themselves in the subdued light under the thick, overhead canopy, in which they saw nesting the forms of strange beakless birds with extraordinarily long tails and feathered legs.

Heike shrieked as a pair of giant red dragonflies whizzed past her head, batting their large, translucent wings.

"Ew, gross!"

Matthias noticed a strange effect. He was neither hungry nor thirsty. Although the air was full of dank, decaying smells, he wondered if he would be able to taste anything in a tapeworld. He wished he had dug into the buffet back at the cafeteria.

"How long do you think we've been in the movie?" Heike asked him.

"I'd say over an hour," he replied. Although it was very difficult to make sense of time, he had the impression at least a day had gone by. But this was possibly due to the differences in lighting between scenes.

"It's weird," said Heike. "But the more this goes on, the less I have the impression we're in a movie. I was talking with the kids back there—they were telling me about their school and their hobbies. It was so surreal. It may sound weird, but I'm actually going to miss them when we get out of here."

Matthias gave a sharp, mocking cackle. "Haven't you got enough online friends that you don't need to go poking around for more virtual ones?"

"But this is different," Heike sighed. "They're like— flesh and blood. And it got me thinking."

"Yeah?"

"What would happen if the tapeworld went on longer? Not just for hours, but say they found a way to make it last for years. Now imagine we were to live together—in the tapeworld. We'd get married and have kids. Our children would only exist in this alternate universe. Inside the tape. Do you think it could work?"

"You're crazy," he laughed, ducking underneath a low overhanging vine. "You want to raise children in a tapeworld?"

"It's just a thought. If a kid was born in a tapeworld, he wouldn't know he was cybernetic. He'd think he was just a normal kid."

"First off, you don't even know if you could get pregnant in here. That would have to be built into the chip, and I doubt they went that far. It's just a movie, Heike. It's for kicks. It's not a place to settle down, let alone raise a family. And even if you could, what would happen to the kid when you exited the tape world? He'd just disappear."

"But if we took turns? If one of us was always in the tapeworld, it would keep things alive, wouldn't it?"

"I don't know. But what would be the point?"

"We'd get away." Heike said.

"From where?"

"Earth."

16

WWII Bunkers, Duisburg

The tape-party was being held in secret, in an abandoned air-raid shelter on the southern outskirts of the industrial city. The shelter was a massive, square concrete block, what looked like a medieval fortress, with brown mold streaks and perennial vines growing up its walls. In front of the steel door leading to the interior of the bunker were a group of hoodies and junglists. There were a few Tobys in the lot.

The tapers came mostly on foot, after dark. Scores of them moving silently across the rutted path that led from the railway toward the tower. There were boys and girls of various ages and backgrounds—most of them upper middle-class kids, some as young as fifteen. A few in their late twenties. The gossip had gone round, and for many of them this would be their initiation into a tapeworld. They were all prepared to pay the €300 entrance fee.

Darko surveyed the new arrivals with a hawk's eye. Everyone from the schoolgirls, giddy and whispering excitedly, to the white hip-hoppers with their Karl Kani baggies, the Aüslanders elite, the scene kids with their extravagant dress codes, the emos, the rockers, the playboys and *huppelkutten*, the brainy gamers and cyber-maniacs, all joined together to partake of the next big thing.

They had all been warned that no cell phones or cameras, purses or handbags would be allowed, and they were each subject to a pat down at the door by the beefy and intimidating members of Darko's crew.

Once inside they made their way up the thick, concrete steps to the bunker master room, their voices echoing off the damp chilly walls, the corridors lit by portable indoor power packs. There were mattresses strewn around, in the master room and the separate niches that surrounded it. The tapers lay two to a makeshift bed, their arms folded over their chests, eyes wide shut or staring vacant at the ceiling. The newcomers gathered around the distributor, knelt before him as if he were a master of ceremony—while he removed stacks of petri dishes from an isotherm box.

They crowded eagerly around while he dished out the activated tapes, one by one, like a priest giving the wafers at a communion mass. They held out their tongues and one by one he posed the tapes onto them and directed the users to different niches.

They were entering into an interstellar voyage, the ticket being a gold-colored tape of *2001: A Space Odyssey*. But there were no *oohs* and *aahs*, no gasps of wonder and delight, cries of shock or heavy-handed applause. The niches were all ghostly silent, lending the bunker an eerie air as inside the tapeworld the post-millennium youth were gathering with the apes around the monolith, or finding themselves grouped together as stowaways aboard the Discovery One spaceship— in another world, another time.

(CASINO "TEST RUN")

Johannes was walking through the Mojave desert, outside Las Vegas, with the Spring Mountains blue-gray on the horizon, the desert sand pockmarked with stones and sage brush. He was kicking at the stones and cursing the programming team for using him as a guinea pig, all the while secretly thrilled at being allowed into a tapeworld. He saw a silvery, hardtop Cadillac slantback up ahead, with two sinister men in gray suits standing nearby it—one short and stocky, and the other tall, lean and well groomed, his eyes shielded by an enormous pair of Carrera sunglasses.

The short one was gesticulating wildly and yammering aggressively at the taller man who pinched the butt of a cigarette in-between his fingers, and countered him defensively.

As Johannes approached the pair he could hear them arguing:

"...anything goes wrong with the casino it's my ass—it's not yours—it's my ass!"

"Oh, I don't know if you know this or not, but you only have your fuckin' casino because I made that possible!" the short guy was screaming. "I'm what counts out here! Not your fuckin' country clubs or your fuckin' TV shows!" He paused, chest heaving, for breath, "And what the fuck are you doin' on TV anyhow?"

"Uh—good morning." Johannes interrupted them as

pleasantly as possible. "Do either of you know which direction to take to get to Vegas?"

The little mobster, his finger still pointed in the air at the taller one twisted his head around at Johannes. He did a double-take. And then he cocked his head, "Who da fuck are you?" He turned back to the casino manager. "Who's this dimple-cheeked motherfucker? What's goin' on? Are ya bringing your fuckin' crew to our meetings now, you Jew motherfucker you."

The other mobster—Sammy Goldstein aka Spade—scrunched his shoulders and gestured in that typical, pleading De Niro fashion. "Micky, what are you talking about? You're being paranoid—"

Micky Santino advanced toward Johannes, looking like he wanted to tear his head off. "What are ya—a fuckin' fed?" He was red-faced and boiling mad from his dispute and he channeled his rage now on the intruder. "Are ya a fuckin' snitch for the county commissioner? We're having a fuckin' private meeting here!"

Johannes was terrified. If he gave an unsatisfactory answer, Micky Santino was liable to shoot him dead on the spot, at the very best. He flustered, and stammered.

"I… I'm… I was just passing through." He glanced nervously at Robert DeNiro. "Hey Bobby—would you sign my T-shirt… I'm a huge fan. But I got to tell you *Little Fockers* was an epic fail…"

DeNiro flung his cigarette stub to the ground and stomped it out with his chic Italian loafers. "Are you talking to me? Are YOU talking to me!?"

"Who are you with?" Joe Pesci stabbed his finger aggressively in Johannes's face.

"N… no one! I'm w-with no one…"

"Then what da fuck are ya doin' here you stuttering prick you!"

"Nicky take it easy—" Sammy Goldstein put his hand carefully on Micky's shoulder.

"Back off—" He knocked it away. He glowered at Johannes, "You're goin' to tell me something tough guy—"

He went straight to his Seville and popped the trunk. He pulled out a baseball bat. Johannes fairly pissed his pants.

"Micky—what the fuck are you doing with that?" Spade tried to intervene.

"I'm gonna squash his motherfuckin' head!"

"We don't even know who he's with. The guy could be lost for crying out loud."

"OUT HERE!" Micky screamed. He advanced menacingly toward Johannes, tapping the slugger against his palm for effect. "I'm gonna ask ya this one time and one time only motherfucker! Who the fuck sent you here to spy on me?"

And Johannes panicked and said the trigger word to exit the tapeworld.

"Pussy!"

But nothing happened. He was still standing, face to face with Micky Santino.

Spade looked away. Joe Pesci recoiled, stupefied at the insult. "What did you just call me?"

"Pussy!" Johannes repeated. Then louder, frantically. "PUSSY! PUSSY!"

And then he realized the awful truth. There was no exit trigger. Dr. Yin had tricked him.

"You got some fuckin' balls, I'll tell ya that!" Micky bawled and he swung the bat at Johannes's knee. It struck home with a horrible popping sound and Johannes' legs buckled out from under him. And the bat came down again on his head with a sharp CRACK! And he cowered in the sand, his hands shielding his face, as the bat came down again and again, smashing against his ribcage, his arms and face… blood was gushing into the dirt…

His assailant was screaming in-between strikes, "Who's the big fuckin' tough guy now? What called me a pussy—huh? Answer me, ya fuckin' prick!"

And Sammy Goldstein was doing his best to calm him down, "C'mon Micky, he's had enough—come on let's get out of here…"

The bat came down one last time, striking Johannes in the temple, and he realized that despite his absolute terror, there wasn't really that much pain. In fact the swings hardly felt stronger than a slap. He should have at least a few cracked ribs, or a broken nose, but he felt fine… as he lay there, debating whether to play dead or make a run for it he could hear Micky still going on…

"… so what if he's dead? I'll dig the fuckin' hole. Won't be the first time I dug a fuckin' hole in this fuckin' desert!"

And Joe Pesci, sweating and panting from his efforts

with the slugger, now came over with a shovel from the trunk of his well-equipped ride, and he began to dig in the hard earth near Johannes's prone figure, Sammy Goldstein looked away, guiltily, as his gangster friend struck the tip of the shovel into the ground, cursing with the effort.

"… motherfucker dug his own fuckin' grave comin' out here—I'll tell ya that… so I'll bury the fucker… I don't give a fuck…"

A streak of white light flared in the sky above the mountains and the desert fell away and Johannes blinked and he was sitting in an armchair surrounded by the programming team who burst into rounds of scattered applause and giggles.

"You assholes!" Johannes stood up.

"How was it?" Rick, the computer engineer, asked. "Did I get the character right? I mean was he aggressive enough?"

"He was terrifying," said Johannes. "He came at me with a baseball bat—"

"He chose the bat?" asked Laeticia LeJeun. "That's interesting—"

"Why? What do you mean?"

"We popped a crowbar and a .45 in the trunk as well…" she explained. "To give him a bit of choice."

"And you didn't warn me!"

"Oh come on—it wasn't that terrible was it?"

"I was scared shitless—I almost pooped my tapeworld pants!"

"Yeah, but the pain?" inquired Dr. Yin. "Was it tolerable?"

"It didn't feel that bad—all things considered," Johannes admitted. "But that's not the point! You tricked me. You told me I had an exit trigger. And when I used it—nothing happened."

"You used it on Nicky?" Xander asked.

"Well, yeah."

"You called Micky Santino a pussy?" He chortled and the lab engineers choked up. They howled away, and Johannes stood there, arms folded grumpily as they took the piss out of him.

"It's not funny!"

"OK, that's enough—" Dr. Yin held up his hands. "The boy has demonstrated bravery going up against such a fearsome gangster. Xander—let's increase the nociception level… a hit from a baseball bat should feel like a hit from a baseball bat. Not a glove slap. OK—and then we'll try it again."

He clasped Johannes warmly on the shoulder.

"Huh?"

(FATAL IMPULSE TAPEWORLD)

Dejan pulled up in front of the stone wall surrounding Kathleen's beach mansion. He got out and peered over it and saw her white Lotus parked in the driveway. Kathleen was still away, probably being pursued through the streets of Petaluma by Michael Douglas. He parked the Nissan down the road, in the shade of a tall cypress tree and walked back to the property.

He entered through the wooden gate and made his way to the frosted-glass door leading to the foyer. He could hear the spray of the Pacific Ocean from behind the mansion. The air was very cool. His heart was racing as he turned the brass doorknob softly, hearing it click and then open.

He sucked in a breath and entered the house.

He crept across the polished tiled floor of the foyer, the ceiling skylight casting a web of shadows from the decorative plants that bordered the walls. He moved on, straight into Kathleen's study.

It was very modern (for 1991) and elegantly furnished. There was a bookshelf surrounding a TV cabinet to the left, and some strange designer frosted-glass panel to the right. In front of him was a desk with a lamp sitting atop it, and on the edge of the desk a folded newspaper.

Dejan picked it up and read the caption:

"Cop Cleared in Tourist Shooting
Grand Jury Says Shooting Accidental"

He unfolded the bottom half of the newspaper and there was a photo of a well-groomed Michael Douglas staring gloomily into space. Dejan peered closer at the article text, trying to decipher it. It was an illegible string of randomly assembled characters. tapeworld programmers were becoming a bit lazy. He put the paper down and moved on through the hallway. Her bedroom was down to the left, but he resisted the temptation to go sniffing through her wardrobe. He moved on to the right toward the rear of the house where there was another bureau with white laminate window shades, this one cluttered with her work materials, all in a palette of white. White fax machine. White telephone. White lamp. More newspaper clippings of a shifty-looking Michael Douglas in a trench-coat. Additional headlines that read:

"Killer Cop to Face Police Review
Tourists Killed by Cop"

Dejan moved toward the glass double doors and peeked out at the cliffside deck and stairs that ran from the back of the house down to the beach. He half-expected Kathleen to be sitting there on the deck, like in the beginning of the picture when the cops first come to question her, but the long-chair was vacant. He climbed the main stairway up to the great room with its vaulted ceiling and art-deco furnishings and he poured himself a drink from the white liquor cabinet near the long window overlooking the bluff. Jack Daniels, straight up. There was an ice pick in the stainless-steel sink and he picked it up, weighing it in his palm.

A voice behind him caught him by surprise.

"Looking for something?"

Dejan spun around, guiltily, and found he was staring straight into the barrel of a .38. The gun was in the hands of a grim-face siren in black jeans, a black tank top and Cuban heel boots.

"Foxy!" gasped Dejan.

And the girl—Leilani Sarelle—seemed momentarily startled at hearing her name being said. She glared at Dejan contemptuously.

"How do you know my name?"

"Kathleen's watchdog," said Dejan. "Isn't that your designated role?"

"Put that down," she said, gesturing at the ice pick.

"Or what," said Dejan. "You'll shoot me to death in her home? I doubt it. You know as well as I do that would be a foolish thing to do, especially in light of the murder of Ronnie Roz."

"Who are you?" Foxy demanded. "What's your connection to Kathleen?"

"I'm here to see that justice is meted out," said Dejan. "She killed him, and you know it. The police will be here any minute—you'd best clear out, unless you want to be charged as an accessory to murder."

Foxy licked her lips and her hand trembled, but she steadied herself. "Nice bluff," she said. "Now be a good boy and drop it."

Dejan looked at the ice pick clenched in his hand. He wasn't here for Foxy. If he could back out of the situation, he could wait until the tape replayed and try the scene again, knowing this time that she was in the house.

"Fair enough," he said, placing the instrument on the edge of the sink. "What do we do now?"

Foxy smiled. A sneering vamp smile that reminded him of Saskia. And that was the last image Dejan saw before she smashed the butt of the gun into his face and he blacked out.

…A blur of female voices around him. Dejan groaned, his head throbbing. His eyelids fluttered and opened and he found himself face-to-face with Sharon Stone. She was staring at him with her mysterious blue eyes, so close that he could smell her delicious breath and her enticing perfume (Hypnotic). She was stunning in a body-hugging taupe gown and a gold long-sleeve open cardigan. She had a green matte and gold necklace around her slender neck, and when he came to she smiled, flashing a row of perfectly gleaming choppers.

And just when Dejan felt himself getting aroused (2.3 seconds considering this was a 30 year old Sharon) her smile vanished and she slapped him across the face. He winced and bolted upwards, straining, suddenly aware that he could not move. He was stripped down to his underpants and tied, hand and leg to the corners of a four-poster bed in a small bedroom. Tied with a white silk Hermes scarf! His clothes lay in a messy pile on the floor.

Foxy appeared beside the bed.

"What's your name?" Kathleen Kastel asked Dejan. "What are you doing in my home?"

Sensing it was useless to lie, he gave her the truth.

"My name is Dejan Vidic. I'm here because that girl you framed for Ronnie Roz's murder—Milinka Trajkovic—she's my girlfriend."

The two women looked at each other, confused. "What are you talking about?" Kathleen snapped. And Dejan realized that they had no idea Milinka was being charged for the murder of the retired rock star.

Kathleen surveyed him coldly, and then she got up, from the edge of the bed and walked over to Foxy.

"What do we do with him?"

"I say kill him," said Foxy flatly. "Whoever he is—he knows too much."

Kathleen Kastel walked over to a dresser, near the door and picked up an ice pick. The same one Dejan had menaced Foxy with. She strode back toward his bound figure, her icy gaze piercing him. She caressed the sharp tip of the instrument across his bare torso.

"You hear that—she wants me to kill you. And right now, I'm inclined to follow her idea."

Dejan struggled against his bindings, in a panic. His thoughts were racing. "No!"

Kathleen cocked her head. "And why shouldn't I? You come here with all these nasty stories about me. Spreading lies. Fucking poisonous lies. Give me a reason why I shouldn't stab you through the fucking heart right now…"

"The police! They'll be here any minute…"

"He's lying," said Foxy. "Do it!"

Kathleen fiddled the ice pick.

"I talked to Detective Curry," Dejan yelled out. "You're his prime suspect."

Kathleen paused… her eyes flickered indecisively.

"Who the hell are you? You're too young to be a cop! How do you know Shooter?"

"I'm telling you!" Dejan pleaded. "If you let me go—"

"You'll run straight to the police." Kathleen finished his sentence. "No. I'm afraid it's sweet dreams for you darling."

And she raised the ice pick high again and Dejan squeezed his eyes shut and screamed out his girlfriend's name.

"MILINKA!"

"Wait!" Foxy interrupted. Dejan grimaced and opened his eyes slowly. His heart was hammering in his chest.

"Don't do it." Foxy said.

"Why not?" Kathleen inquired.

"Because I've got a better idea," she said. "Let me get the phone, from the other room."

Kathleen eyed her lover, almost suspiciously. "What for?"

"Trust me, baby," Foxy said and leaned forward and kissed her softly on the lips.

Foxy came back into the room with a white telephone and placed it on the dresser near the bed.

"This girl—Milinka—where is she?" Foxy asked.

Dejan licked his lips. What should he say. County jail? They wouldn't understand.

"She's in the city," he said.

"What's her number? Where can she be reached?"

"I don't know."

"This is a waste of time," said Kathleen. "Let's kill him now and dump the body in the water."

Dejan's mind was racing. His heart was pounding hard. Beads of sweat formed on his temples. He was thinking fast, thinking hard, trying to find a way out of his predicament. In this tapeworld Milinka wasn't in county jail. So where could she be—think! He cursed himself. She enters the primary tapeworld where is she? Where's the first place she goes?

I'm standing on the sidewalk on this street corner, and I don't know where I am. It's pouring rain, and it's cold and windy. I don't recognize any of the buildings...

...Right across the street is this glowing café sign... so I go to it, thinking maybe I can find somebody who can explain me where this is...

"The Tosca Café!" Dejan hurriedly exclaimed.. "She's at the Tosca Café... she's waiting for me there."

Kathleen glanced at Foxy. "What are you thinking?"

Foxy bit her lip. "I'm thinking we're going to have you make a little call," she said to Dejan.

She dialed the number given to her by the operator, and held the receiver to his ear as he read from a card that Sharon Stone held in her hands. A text written in clear block print:

"Meet me at the Ronnie Roz nightclub in the Fillmore district."

Noise on the other end. Clink of glasses. Hiss of a coffee machine. Lots of people talking and laughing. Some other ruckus in the background.

A bartender's busy but affable voice: "Good evening, Tosca Café, how may I help you?"

"Hello. My name is Dejan Vidic. I'd like to speak with Milinka Trajkovic if she is available…"

"Milinka, you say… Hold on one sec…"

He heard the bartender calling out her name, and then a rustle and then his girlfriend was on the phone.

"Hallo? Wer ist da?"

"Milinka…"

"Yes?"

"Milinka, its Dejan…"

"Dejan! Was ist los?"

"Please. I need you to listen very carefully. You must meet me at Ronnie Roz's nightclub. It's in the Fillmore district. Go to the main bar near the vestibule, and ask for a martini. I'll explain everything when you get there…"

"Dede, I… I don't understand. What's going on? Where are you?"

"Just do it…" he said, and then after a pause added, "I love you."

Foxy snatched the receiver away and hung up, slapping him on the head.

"Ow!"

"Stick to the script." She picked up a sock from the dresser drawer and stuffed it in his mouth and taped over it.

Dejan fought the gag, breathing hard through his nostrils.

"Time for your close up, darling," Kathleen said. She twiddled the ice pick and held it over him, in a menacing pose while Foxy stood behind her and snapped a shot with a Polaroid. The print rolled out and Foxy shook it.

"Nice one," she said.

The doorbell rang. Downstairs. And rang again.

"Wait here!" Kathleen said. "Keep an eye on him!"

She flurried off, barefoot, down the hallway. Foxy went over and listened at the door.

They heard her descend the stairs, followed by some muffled conversation, then footsteps climbing back up the stairs, and Michael Douglas' familiar nasal whine, intermingled with Kathleen's sensual and throaty voice.

"…no, thanks."

"Oh, that's right. You're off the Jack Daniels too, aren't you?"

"…I've got a uh… few more questions to ask you…"

Nicky Curry was in the great room, just down the hall! Dejan strained to listen. Foxy had shut the bedroom door, and he could only catch fragments of the conversation. But they were enough for him to understand that a scene from the original movie was playing. He could hear Kathleen chipping up a block of ice from the cooler with the pick, and Dejan knew that in a few seconds Kathleen would be taunting Nick about the tourists he had accidentally shot to death while pursuing a suspect high on cocaine. Then she was taunting him about his wife who had committed suicide.

Dejan mumbled something through his gag. Foxy hissed, "quiet, you!" And then she exited the bedroom and Dejan heard her boots clicking through the corridor and then Sharon Stone's sultry voice.

"Hi, hon… you two have met, haven't you?"

And the sound of Michael Douglas walking away, defeated, and Sharon's mocking voice calling after him.

"You're gonna make a terrific character Nick!"

They came back into the bedroom, laughing, giddy as schoolgirls, and Kathleen said to Dejan, "well, there goes your great white hope!"

Foxy broke into heaves of laughter. She flapped the photograph in Dejan's face. "Thanks for being so cooperative."

And then she left and Dejan was alone with Sharon Stone, aka Kathleen Kastel, utterly at her mercy. And he knew now that by some bizarre tapeworld logic he had set off the chain of events that would lead to Milinka's bogus confession and to her subsequent imprisonment, and that he himself was somewhere out there, at the beginning of the tape, trying to find Milinka—chasing after himself!

What the fucking hell is going on? Dejan thought. He knew he must get out of here. He must intercept Milinka, before Foxy found her and coerced her into turning herself in to free him. If he could do that, then maybe he could get Milinka out of the tapeworld. But he was bound and gagged and couldn't move an inch or scream for help.

Kathleen stared at him, amused. Her beautiful face broke into a cruel grin. "You really think you're off the hook?"

She broke into a peal of icy laughter and clasped her hands together. "So naive. You made the mistake of your life, boy, coming here." And then she moved to the bed and Dejan twisted his body hard, struggling against the binds, pulling them as taut as possible and she laughed and said, "Don't you think I know how to tie a body?" (Programmer reference to Neil Jordan's *The Crying Game*?) She leaped atop him and straddled him, her lithe body clenching him between her thighs. She picked up the ice pick and twiddled it in her hands, and despite his rage, despite his fear, certain that he was about to die, Dejan experienced a certain ironic epiphany—namely that there were worse ways to meet one's death than being mounted by a young and very beautiful Sharon Stone.

He closed his eyes, savoring the final insult.

17

STATE MENTAL HOSPITAL, PROXIMITY OF STRASBOURG

The two security aides—beefy bull-necked men, smelling of sweat and aftershave—came to Christopher's seclusion suite, in the early evening. One of the aides looked through the observation panel and saw the young boy in the padded cell, sitting on the edge of the bed, sketching on a sheet of butcher paper with a dark crayon. A small plastic table and some art supplies had been provided by the distinguished Dr. Frederick Courbier in the interest of scientific observation, and Christopher had proved a very productive patient. The padded walls of his small suite were full of his impressive artwork. There was a quite astounding reproduction of the Duomo, as seen from the Belvedere in Florence; and another of a doe-eyed, long-haired woman cradling a lamb in her arms.

An mp3 player was also on the table where Christopher was working, playing a Glen Gould interpretation of an Aria from Bach's Goldberg Variations—the melancholy and wistful notes of piano haunting the air.

The bigger of the guards—Agent Bouyer—rapped his guard stick against the steel door and slid back the panel in order to speak to the patient.

"OK, Christopher. You know the drill. Stand up and back against the wall. Don't move from there. We're coming in…"

Christopher Venet paused for a second, his crayon held suspended in mid-air. Then he placed it down gently and stood up, slowly, and spoke in a suave, cultivated voice.

"Certainly."

He backed up against the wall and stood there, erect as a dancer, while the two men cautiously entered the cell. The other guard—Agent Pembroke, an English intern—held a canteen serving tray in his hands. He had a taser in a holster around his waist. It was for use only on particularly aggressive individuals. They had been warned that Christopher had savagely attacked a nurse after an MRI scan, but to their experience he had proved an incredibly lucid and docile patient. Still, it was the calm ones you had to watch out for.

"The sonofabitch demanded a second dinner," he said, incredulously to his colleague. "Lamb chops, extra rare."

"All right… put that down there," Agent Bouyer said, keeping his eyes on Christopher.

Agent Pembroke grunted accordingly and moved to set the serving tray down on the table.

"Mind the drawings, please," Christopher whispered, ever so politely.

Pembroke grimaced and set the tray on the floor. He looked over at Christopher's latest artwork: a tinfoil reproduction of a half-naked woman and an old man with a long tousled beard. Urizen by William Blake. The foil was glued to a piece of cardboard. He pushed it to the side, and then he picked up the tray again and put it on the table.

He shook his head at the artwork.

"Kind of a kinky drawing, wouldn't you say?"

"It's an etching," Christopher calmly corrected him.

"A what?"

"Tinfoil glued to cardboard and covered with acrylic paint. You see that Popsicle stick over there? I use it to scrape off the paint, producing the design you see before you…"

"An etching," Agent Pembroke repeated dumbly. "Sounds like a bloody kindergarten trick to me."

Christopher Venet closed his eyes, savoring the closing aria. He hummed along to the music and time seemed to slow down and spread out, as it always did when he went into action. If Agent Bouyer had looked closely, he might have noticed a certain stiffness to Christopher's torso. For beneath his pale blue patient pajamas the cardboard and tin foil had been used for an entirely different purpose from the art of etching.

To create a stun gun shield.

But Agent Bouyer had his eyes locked to Christopher's—which were maroon with tiny flecks of red in them, and seemed to bore into his very soul. He felt uneasy, and dare he say, a little frightened of the boy.

Ridiculous notion. A skinny, seventeen-year-old boy.

And yet there was something uncanny and all-too-knowing in that piercing regard.

"I suppose you'll want to know what I did with the body," Christopher said suddenly, and the two men looked up in surprise.

Agent Bouyer stepped closer. "What was that?"

The music ended and suddenly Christopher's hand shot out and seized Bouyer's guard stick, gripping it tight with a surprising amount of wiry strength.

Bouyer called out.

"Pembroke!"

And Pembroke fumbled for his taser, his fingers trembling with nervous excitement as Christopher's free hand gripped Bouyer by the neck and he sunk his teeth into his cheek, shaking his head like a terrier shakes a rat, gnawing it to the bone. He spit a wet flap of flesh into Bouyer's face—into his screaming bloodied face—and Bouyer crumpled to the floor in shock and horror.

Groaning now.

"Pembroke! My face! He ate my face!"

And Officer Pembroke let loose a shot from the stun gun, but the probes struck on the foil-wrapped cardboard shield taped to Christopher's chest and shorted out. There was a terrifying moment of realization that the assailant was not incapacitated, and then Christopher strode forward, slowly, decisively, calmly and he raised Bouyer's guard stick high in the air and Pembroke screamed in horror—screamed for all he was worth as Christopher brought it crashing down onto his head, again and again, in hard, deliberate strokes, repeating "Ready—when—you—are—Agent—Pembroke!"

After the police, Marie Venet was the first to be informed that her son had escaped from the state hospital ward for the criminally insane. He had killed two orderlies and a night watchman and then driven out in a service ambulance and abandoned it at a highway rest stop outside the city. He had also killed a tourist and made off with his clothes and money.

"He could be anywhere by now," the police inspector informed her by telephone. He could hear her sobbing on the other end.

"I know this is difficult, but should he try and contact or visit you, you must inform us, so that we can bring him in."

Marie Venet hung up, and cowered against the wall of her living room, still weeping.

Five-hundred and twenty kilometers away, in the inner sanctums of his offices at The Hague, First Officer Perrin received an identical call, notifying him of the details of Christopher's escape.

All the events in the report matched up to what he had expected, and afterward he thanked his interlocutor and hung up and turned his eyes back to the portable DVD player where he was watching a similar portrayal of Christopher Venet's flawlessly executed escape from the mental asylum as portrayed by Anthony Hopkins in Jonathan Demme's 1991 cinematic masterpiece: *The Silence of the Lambs.*

18

GLEN NEVIS, SCOTTISH HIGHLANDS, 1295 A.D.

Lukas was panting with effort as he trekked up yet another steep and rocky Munro of the Grampian Mountains range, for the umpteenth time—totally oblivious to the wondrous natural scenery surrounding him. He was sweating profusely through his Dolce and Gabbana tank-top and had tied his Jack and Jones vest around his waist, and his feet were aching from the thistles that had sneaked into his trainers, the muddy and wet grass of the mountainside soaking into his socks, and his nose dripping from the morning chill and the fog. He was listening to a new club track by the Black Eyed Peas on his iPod, humming along with the frisky music, and intermittently cursing Scotland's rugged terrain for all it was worth.

He stopped at the summit of the Munro, removed his earphones, cupped his hands together around his mouth and called out, "MICKEY!," his voice echoing through the dreary hills and deep corries, all the way down to the shimmering blue lochs below. But there was no response.

"Fucking hell!" Lukas cursed. He narrowed his eyes down at the treacherous trail that led to the glen, barely distinguishing what appeared to be a small collection of stone huts with sod rooftops overlooked by a crude wooden stockade.

The entire scene was strangely empty, as if the settlement had been suddenly and rudely deserted.

He made his way down the rutted path from the Munro, slipping on a maze of briars and thistles, stopping every once in a while to scour the glen and call out his brother's name. He was nowhere to be found.

He passed through a dense thicket of beech trees, and then waded across a shallow river lined by blossoming alders, before reaching the village in a sunlit, grassy clearing on the other side of the riverbank.

Smoke plumes rose from the embers of charcoal fires, now smothered. The fort overlooking Lanark was abandoned, the flags rising from the wooden buttresses torn to shreds and the guard tower burnt down. A few black chickens zigzagged past him, squawking brainlessly, and Lukas spotted a bright garment lying on the ground near one of the huts and when he came closer he saw that it was an orange soldier's tunic with a lion's motif across the front. It was torn and bloodstained. A few feet away there was a kettle hat helmet that had been bashed in by a heavy mace, or some other blunt weapon.

He bent down and picked the helmet up, feeling the jagged indents of the crumpled metal. He turned it over and saw dark bloodstains and clumps of matted hair glued to the inside.

"Ew!" He shivered and dropped the helmet in the mud, and a noise behind him caught him off guard and Lukas whirled around and found he was face-to-face with an old woman wearing a dirty woolen kirtle. Her face was very white and wrinkled, and she wore a wimple over her graying hair, and she bobbed her head from side to side, as if searching for something, and called out,

"Halo! Who is it? Hamish? Is that you?"

As she held out one of her frail hands, Lukas saw that her eyes were clouded over by cataracts and he understood that she could not see him—although she sensed his presence.

He cleared his throat and the old woman jumped. Lukas spoke softly so as not to frighten her.

"Keine Angst! Um… I mean—don't be afraid!"

"Who are you?" the old woman asked, stepping closer. "Your voice is unfamiliar to me. Are you Irish?"

"Hell no! I'm German."

"Chan eil mi 'tuigsinn," the peasant said, and clucked her tongue. Then, somewhat suspiciously, "That sounds very odd indeed. What's your business here? Have you come to help us fight the English?"

Lukas rolled his eyes, "Not really. I'm looking for my brother, see. He's somewhere around here, and I've got to find him. His name is Mikail…"

"Ha?"

"Black hair, green eyes. Six foot tall… he's got a lip piercing and… oh, forget it," Lukas said dismissively. "Where is everybody? Why are you all alone?"

The old woman smiled, revealing a half-row of blackened rotting teeth, and a perfect example of 13th century oral hygiene. Lukas recoiled in disgust.

"They've gone to Stirling!" she proclaimed

triumphantly. "To fight the bloody English bastards and put an end to their tyranny! My boy Hamish and my husband are with the lot."

"Stirling," Lukas repeated thoughtfully. "So they're on the battlefield with William Wallace I suppose…"

The old hag's face lit up at the mention of this name. "You know William! The Great William!"

"The alcoholic Mel Gibson, more like it…Yeah… uh kinda. Look, I think my bro might be with the lot, you see. And I've really got to find him, and like my cell phone doesn't work here because there's no bloody connection in this country—I mean this is like medieval times and all—so no damn satellites—but it would be really nice of you if you could just like, point me the way to Stirling, you know…"

The hag raised her bushy white eyebrows, trying to make sense of Lukas' babble. Then she said, "Holy Mother of Christ and all the blessed saints! What manner of bleedin' fools have we got galumphin' through our highlands these days!" And she dismissed him with a contemptuous wave and strutted off toward one of the gloomy huts.

Lukas watched her bent figure striding away and made a mental note to try and keep his future conversation on the level of medieval peasantry. He popped back his earphones and scrolled to another tune, following the peat path that led through the clearing and into the woods beyond.

"…*baby I just wanna dance… I don't really care…*" Rihanna's moany voice, backed by a funky electro-disco David

Guetta soundtrack drowned out the noise of heavy cavalry and marching foot-soldiers lining up for battle, so that Lukas was hardly aware of them until he was halfway into the battlefield—a wide open plain of grassland and heath where he could see the two armies gathering together in preparation for war. On the one side the Scottish rebels—an unruly, mismatched and feeble bunch of clan warriors, dressed in Buchanan tartans, wielding tiny wooden targs, clumsy halberds and homemade axes. And across the meadow upon a gentle rolling hilltop the English army: a frightening buildup of lance-wielding heavy cavalry in mail hauberks, accompanied by hundreds of leather clad archers and thousands of infantry, their steely plate-armor gleaming in the warm sun.

Lukas could see the English nobles calmly discussing strategy atop the hill, and the Scots milling about, uncertainly, with the lairds struggling to bring a sense of order to the lot and to calm their nervous troops.

He crossed the field toward the Scots, and as they became aware of his figure striding to them, two of the nobles on horseback rode to him.

They brought their steeds to a halt a few feet away, and one of the lairds—a gray-haired old man with a sorrowful countenance—scrutinzed Lukas, trying to make sense of the odd garments he was wearing, and figure out if he was English or Welsh… or possibly Irish.

"I'm Lochlan, and this is Mornay," the man said. "We are the captains of this army, and we speak on behalf of its men."

Lukas popped out his earphones. "What was that?"

The other laird cleared his throat, spat on the grass and said, "Well... has Longshanks accepted our proposal for a truce?"

"Huh?"

"How many acres of brown land does he promise?" Lochlan inquired.

"And the titles? What about the titles?" Mornay piped.

Lukas threw up his hands in surrender. "Whoa! Guys. Lordships... Hold on—you've got it all mixed up. I'm no messenger."

The lairds stared at each other doubtfully—wondering if Longshanks was pulling another of his sly, dirty tricks on them. The hard-faced clan Captain with the braids, the one named Mornay, drew closer to Lukas and unsheathed a heavy two-handed broadsword and pointed the tip of it at Lukas throat, in the direction of the jugular.

"If you're not with the bloody English... then what the devil are you doing on this field?" he growled.

Lukas gulped, discreetly sidestepping away from the point of the blade. "I'm uh... looking for someone. A boy... er... a *lad*, as you might say. I believe he's with one of your clans."

Mornay's fierce eyes narrowed suspiciously. "Sounds like a mischievous errand to me."

"No I swear it's true. By St. Andrew's Cross! By the thorn and the thistle! He's my brother, see. His name's Mikail... but I call him Mickey. Like Mickey Blue Eyes. He's a big fan of *Braveheart*—"

"Braveheart?" Lochlan furrowed his brow.

"Er... William Wallace."

The two captains regarded one another and then Mornay sheathed his sword and said, "So you've come to join us."

"Er... yes. That's it." Lukas wisely agreed.

"Splendid. We're quite short on warriors—and any brave man willing to die for us is most welcome."

"Come on—" Lochlan gestured at Lukas. "I doubt there's any spare armor, but I'm sure one of the lads can begrudge you a club or a mace. You'll want something nice and heavy to bash an enemy's face in."

"Huh? But wait..." Lukas protested as they flanked him with their horses, leading him to the garrison of rebels. "What about the negotiations? Let's not be too hasty, right? I mean... look at the odds... it's like 50 to 1... and all those archers and knights... it would be a shame to die today, what with such lovely weather and all."

"Every man dies. But not every man really lives!" Mornay said, pithily, and Lochlan nodded solemnly.

They escorted him back to the rebels, and all eyes were on Lukas as he walked shakily between the two lairds. The men were grumbling among themselves; a collection of ruddy, desperate farmers and young highland boys wielding rusty scythes and clubs. They glowered at him, in a hostile mood, while Lukas scanned the lineup for a sign of his brother.

He spotted him standing in the center of the front row,

near a young highlander sporting a 1980s "mullet" haircut, looking something like Rudi Voller in the 1986 World Cup—holding a pike and muttering to his neighbor—a rugged veteran wearing a blue headscarf.

"Mickey—" Lukas called out, and his brother looked up as he approached him. He was wearing a clumsily tied tartan, his face was painted with blue streaks, and he wielded a flanged mace in one hand.

He seemed astonished at seeing Lukas.

"Lukas. Was gibt's? What are you doing here?"

"I should be asking you that. What the fuck are you doing at Stirling?"

Mikail shook his mace. "I'm gonna help Wallace fight the English. What do you think?"

"You've got to come home."

"Huh?"

"Mom's worried about you. She says you don't go to the gym anymore. You've stopped going to school. You lock yourself in your room and lie around all day sleeping. This can't go on—you've got to come back."

"Back where? To Lanark?"

Lukas grabbed Mikail by the shoulders and shook him, hard. "Not Lanark, you idiot! Home! Jesus, to fucking Duisburg. You're not a fucking highlander, for Chrissakes!

A horseman came galloping across the plains, from the direction of the English army. He drew his steed to a halt in front of the nobles Lochlan, Mornay, and Craig.

"Well, what news?" Mornay asked.

"We're outnumbered. At least 3 to 1," the horseman said.

"How many horse, then?"

"Three hundred. Maybe more."

"Three hundred heavy horse!" Mornay gasped.

Lochlan grimaced. "We must try to negotiate."

The peasant boy standing next to Mikail turned to the veteran and asked, "What are they talking about?"

"I can't hear, but it doesn't look good," the man said. "The nobles will negotiate. If they do a deal, then we go home. If not, we charge."

Lukas gripped his brother by the arm. "Come on—let's go."

"Hey! Lemme go!"

"You can take as many *Bravehearts* as you want on the weekend! But you've got to go to school. You can't just leave the real world behind. You've got obligations to fulfill!"

"Why not? I like it here," Mikail grumbled. "At Lanark, when we charged the garrison, I threw an English soldier from the walls of the fort. And I Macy Grayed another in the face. It was a helluva lot more exciting than playing pool at a fucking bar or going to the disco! And besides, I've got a good life here. I'm set to marry Hamish's sister. See this—" Mikail withdrew from the pocket of his Rocawear jeans, a piece of cloth embroidered with a purple thistle. "I'm part of the Stewart family now. I've got a tract of land to plow, and seven sheep!"

Lukas jaw hung slack. "Listen to yourself Mickey! If you want to herd sheep and play bagpipes all day—that's fine with me. But you can't stay forever in a tapeworld!"

"Why not?"

"It's… not natural!"

"You said this was better than life… you told me so."

"I know what I said but."

They were distracted by a heavy rumble in the distance, as over the crest of the hill across the field appeared the upraised points of hundreds of sharp lances, and the sound of many horses stomping. More English troops were arriving to join the already impressive army. Knights in full battle armor rode in, while the woefully outnumbered Scots watched in dismay. And behind them, more marching infantry! They advanced, covering the entire expanse of land—thousands of them.

The highlanders bowed their heads and swallowed hard. A ripple of fear swept through the ranks. Even Lukas, who knew that this was only a tape, could not help but feel alarmed. Tapeworld or not, he had no desire to be trampled or bludgeoned to death on a muddy field for a cause he didn't even care about.

The young boy next to him seemed to share his opinion. "There are so many!" he muttered. "I didn't come here to fight so they could own more lands! Then I'll have to work for them."

And the man standing next to him spoke up. "Nor me. All right lads. I'm not dying for these bastards. Let's go home!"

"He's right," Lukas said. "Words of wisdom from the village idiot. Come on, Mickey."

"But I wanna fight the English!"

The clans began to break up, many of the men turning heel and lowering their weapons. Lochlan rode up to the ranks, gesticulating wildly in desperation.

"Stop men! Do not flee! Wait until we've negotiated!"

They continued to walk away, heedless of his pleas. Then they stopped, as a small band of fearsome-looking riders wielding a war banner and sporting blue warpaint across their faces rode from in behind them, to join in the fight. The men stared at the newcomers curiously.

"Braveheart!" Mikail clapped his hands together excitedly.

"Oh shit, here he comes," Moaned Lukas. "And here comes that speech."

Leading the pack was Mel Gibson, gripping the reins of his stallion and surveying the fleeing warriors. His face was stern and determined. He looked very heroic with his broadsword slung across his back and his hair flowing in long, handsome curly locks. Behind him were the other members of the cast. The rugged, red-bearded thug of a giant, Hamish. And the crazy Irishman Stephen. And Hamish's father, the Elder Stewart.

Mel Gibson led his crew down through the despairing army, looking very noble and brave atop his horse, his nostrils flaring.

"It's William Wallace!" the boy said.

"Can't be. Not tall enough!" another commented.

Behind him, a group of footmen carried bundles of wooden spears between the ranks, intending to use them to block the charge of the English cavalry. He rode up to the nobles.

Lochlan looked Mel Gibson up and down. "Where is thy salute?"

"For presenting yourself on this battlefield, I give you thanks," Wallace said.

"This is our army! To join it you pay homage," Lochlan insisted.

"I give homage to Scotland!" Wallace shouted. And then he turned to the ranks. "And if this is your army. Why does it go?"

"We didn't come here to fight for them!" a veteran shouted back. And the other highlanders roared in approval.

"Home! The English are too many!" the boy yelled.

"You heard him!" Lukas agreed, pinching Mikail by the cheek.

"Ow!"

"We're leaving this field right now!"

"No! This is my favorite part."

Mel Gibson rode forward and spoke to the multitude. "Sons of Scotland! I am William Wallace!"

"William Wallace is seven feet tall!" the boy cried.

"Yes. And if he were here he'd consume the English with fireballs from his eyes and bolts of lightning from his arse!" Mel Gibson remarked wittily. And the troops broke into scattered laughter and Mikail elbowed his brother in the ribs. Then his face became very grave and he spoke in a gravelly, belting voice.

"I *am* William Wallace. And I see a whole army of my countrymen gathered here in defiance of tyranny! You've come here to fight as free men. And free men you are! What will you do without freedom? Will you fight?"

"Bloody hell yes!" Mikail raised his club. Lukas slapped him across the head.

"Don't listen to Mr. Hairy Legs. Get a grip on reality!"

"No!" the rebels chorused and thrust their swords forward for emphasis. "Against that? No. We will run... and we will live!"

"Aye," William said calmly. "Fight and you may die. Run and you'll live... at least a while... and..."

"AYE!" Mikail broke free from his brother's grip and ran forward, waving at the crowd and shouting. "Aye! And dying in your beds many years from now, would you be willing to trade all the days from this day to that for one chance, just one fucking chance to come back here and tell our enemies that they may take our lives... but they will never take our freedom!"

And he let out a war-whoop and thrust his mace heavenward, expecting the crowd to burst into cheers and applause. But there was nothing. The men stared at him dumbly. A vacant, windy silence swept through the plains. Mel Gibson gulped in confusion and turned to Hamish who scrunched his huge shoulders.

"Come on—freedom!" Mikail sang.

The crowd suddenly burst into a ruckus of wild, mocking laughter. The highlanders doubled over, choking with merriment. The men whistled and booed.

"Aye. Listen to the lad. He's off his rocker."

"Taken one too many a fall from a horse!"

"Been kicked in the head, pullin' on a cow's teat!"

William Wallace glowered at Mikail, as the ranks of rebels scorned and took the piss out of him. He rode along the lines of sneering highlanders, trying to restore courage and dignity to the lot, but it was no good. Mikail's interruption into his carefully plotted speech had thrown the whole dynamic off kilter. Instead of filling them with a sense of pride and valor, he had taken the wind out of the entire rebellion. The clansmen were now walking off, abandoning the ranks in droves. Some of them were raising white banners of truce. Others sat down lazily in the long grass and chewed honeysuckle.

"Well," sighed Lochlan. "The men won't fight, William. There's nothin' left to do but negotiate with the English."

Mel Gibson's eyes flickered with disappointment at this betrayal of his countrymen. His entire strategy had just been demolished. He took a last, despairing look at the imposing English army and at the departing clans and then he snorted in exasperation and spurred his horse and rode off, followed by the rest of his men.

They watched him ride away and Lukas laughed and said to Mikail, "So much for Braveheart... you just fucked up the Scots' chance at freedom. Now how great is it here? And I don't think I have to remind you what's going to happen to your bride-to-be as soon as the first English lord comes back to claim the right to *prima nocte!*"

"Ew!" said Mikail, shivering at the thought. "The lovely Hectorina is going to become tainted goods!"

"Hectorina?" Lukas sneered. "You're going to marry a girl named Hectorina..."

"Shut up."

"Man, and I thought I had bad taste in girls..."

"I said shut up."

"Does she shave in the morning? Can she throw a boulder with one hand?"

"Cut it out—" Mikail shoved him off as Lukas followed him, still taunting, trailing the broken and retreating army back to the highlands.

The tape ended and Mikail woke up in the Duisburg Park Nord—a decommissioned metalworks that had been reconverted into numerous recreational facilities as part of the city's beautification plan to merge industry and nature. Mikail was lying in the grass near the bicycle path that ran around the factory grounds, just a stone's throw from the panoramic tower that had been developed from a blast furnance, and Lukas was sitting up beside him, hugging his knees.

Mikail rubbed his eyes. "What are you doing here?"

"I came to get you," Lukas said. "You can't keep disappearing like this. Going off and *taping* whenever you feel like it. Do you realize you've been gone for two days straight?"

"So. It's the weekend—"

"I had to lie and tell mom you were with me," said

Lukas. "She was going to go to the police and file a missing persons report—and she says you've stopped going to school. What's that all about?"

"I only skipped a couple of classes," shrugged Mikail defensively. "How did you find me?"

"Toby said he'd seen you here last."

"Oh," Mikail said and sat up. "I didn't mean to be gone so long… it's just… I started to like living in *Braveheart*. I met Princess Isabelle. I fought the battle of York. I even saved Wallace's life by warning him of the trap in Edinburgh… you wouldn't believe it Lukas. I was really there, you know. I wasn't just me anymore. I was *somebody*. I was part of the rebellion. I was a real Scot—"

Lukas shook his head. "Mickey, you've got to keep a lid on things. You have to draw the line between reality and fiction. How many tapes did you take?"

"Five or six—I forget. Not at the same time, of course…"

"What?" Lukas exclaimed in astonishment. "Where did you get the money for all that?"

"I got them for free," said Mikail. "For helping Toby."

"You're dealing tapes now?"

Mikail stood up, rubbing his knees. "Kind of—"

"You can't be serious."

"Why not?"

Lukas got up as well and jabbed his finger emphatically at his brother. "Using is one thing… selling tapes is another. You've seen how secretive Toby is. Do you think he'd be that way if these were legal."

"You said no one knew about their existence."

"I'm not so sure anymore. I read an article in the *Rheinische Post* this week. It talked about police investigating a possible new designer drug circulating between Germany and Holland. They said the drug may be responsible for an alarming number of medically inexplicable comas..."

"What the fuck are you talking about? That's totally unrelated. This isn't a drug."

"They're blotters, Mickey. We can't be sure what secondary effects they may have... all I'm saying is..."

"Oh shut up," Mikail snapped impatiently, cutting him off. "You're the one who got me *taping* in the first place. And you know what... I like it. I like *taping*... I'm happy being a *taper!* If you don't want to tape anymore that's fine with me but that won't stop me from taping. And if I've got to be a tape runner to keep on taping, why that's just what I'm going to do, weisst Du?"

And he marched off angrily down the bicycle path leaving his older brother standing there speechless in the park.

19

MÖNCHENGLADBACH, GERMANY

Albino Toby was pacing back and forth in Dejan's tiny apartment, his keen red eyes keeping vigil on the sleeping couple in the bedroom. Both bodies were immobile, their breathing slowed to a near inaudible whisper. It had now been over fifty minutes since Dejan had entered *Fatal Impulse*, in order to retrieve Milinka, and he gave no signs of returning to consciousness yet. Toby was just minutes away from calling the EMS and getting the fuck out of MG with the rest of the tapes when he heard Dejan's handy buzz with an incoming text.

He picked it up and flipped the screen. The sender was marked "Darko," the message beneath very clear:

"Bring's nach hochfeld. Schnell. D."

Toby snapped the handy shut and bit his lip, thinking. If he ignored the message and Dejan didn't come out of *Fatal Impulse*, then Darko would come looking for him. And if he found him and his girlfriend in this state, who knows what he might do to them to keep the police and medical services from intervening, or questioning them if they recovered. Dejan was Toby's one genuine friend in a world of crooks and sharks. He had to protect him. He grabbed the canister containing the ninety-eight remaining copies of the *Fatal Impulse* tape and pocketed them in his motorcycle jacket, and then exited Dejan's flat, running down the stairs...

...bursting out the front door... mounting his Kawasaki Ninja ZX 14... kicking up the sidestand... twist of the throttle... powerful whine of the ram air and fuel-injected engine...

Flash along the A52...

Zipping past Audi, Mercedes, VW...

Flashing golden/orange lights of tunnel...

Acceleration under highway overpass... vibration of rumble strip...

Honk of truck horn!... Roadwork... Traffic cones... Accident... Pause...

Blue lights... Cop wave... OK... Long bridge over black water shimmering golden flecks in the night...

Cut to:

10
Kreuz Moers
Venlo

A40
Essen
Duisburg
Moers

Enter Duisburg–Hochfeld

20

(Triassic Park Tapeworld)

Heike and Matthias pushed through the giant Cypresses and ferns at the edge of the forest and gasped as they arrived at the *Tyrannosaur* lagoon—a stagnant, inland body of sparkling turquoise water bordered by lush wetland plants and a stony coral reef. They climbed atop a giant granite boulder, overlooking a fifteen-foot drop to the water and they stood there, scanning the scene for signs of the bonus. There was nothing out of the ordinary, except the ethereal haunting beauty of the scene. It looked like a lost paradise with its white crescent beach and sparklingwaters.

"Isn't this romantic?" Heike observed, clinging to Matthias. "It reminds me of that old movie—*The Blue Lagoon*."

"Never heard of it," said Matthias.

"That's because your idea of a romantic film is an X-rated one," Heike moped, releasing her grip. "What do we do now?"

"I have no idea," Matthias shrugged noncommittally. "All I know is that we're supposed to come here."

"Do you think there's something to find in the water?"

"Maybe. I can't see any other possibility."

"But how do we get down there?"

"Easy," he said and sat down on the rocks and began

removing his shoes and socks. "We dive in."

"Are you crazy?" said Heike, watching him strip down to his underpants. "You don't know how deep the water is. It could be shallow. You might end up injuring yourself."

Matthias shook his head and laughed.

"What?"

"Come on baby. It's just a tapeworld. There's no risk of anything bad happening… don't you want to find the bonus?"

Heike bit her lip. "Not if it involves breaking a leg."

He stood up and gave her a kiss. "Wish me luck," he said, and before she could fathom it he pinched his nose shut and leaped from the boulder and Heike gasped and watched him plummet downward and hit the water with an icy splash and disappear under.

"Matty!"

She scanned the surface of the lagoon, worriedly, expecting him to resurface. But he didn't. Seconds elapsed, and then long minutes went by but there was no sign of him. Heike felt her heart skip a beat. What had happened? Why didn't he break water? Matthias was a powerful swimmer—there must be something wrong. Was he hurt?

"Come back, Matty, please…" she whispered, to no avail. The surface of the lagoon was flat and undisturbed. She glanced around at the coastal hinterland in a panic. There was nothing but the dense canopy of jungle-clad mountains. Whatever was in that lagoon was now with Matthias. She would have to go in as well. She kicked off her slip-on Vans and stripped down to her bra and thong and approached the brink, the granite slick and cool beneath her bare feet.

Drawing a deep breath she mustered up all her nerves—and jumped in after him.

She hit the water with a cold splash and sank rapidly, as if sucked under by a powerful vortex. She struggled against it, arms and legs flailing wildly, thrashing about, trying to break the surface, losing all sense of direction in the inky blackness. This was no lagoon. The water was dark, dense and oily. Her breath escaped her in a flurry of iridescent bubbles as her heart pounded fiercely against her ribcage. *What the fuck was happening? Was she drowning?*

Panic seized her.

I can't die like this! Heike thought. *I'm not going to die in a fucking tapeworld!*

And just when she thought she had no force left she saw a thin filter of light above her and she swam toward it, rising faster and faster, as if pulled by some unseen force.

She gasped for air as her head shot above the water, her eyes and nose streaming. Coughing and spitting against the waves. Where was she? All around was water, as far as the eye could see, with no sign of dry land.

She treaded the water, lungs heaving, shouting out, "Matty!"

Her voice drowned out by the high-pitched whine of an approaching engine. An airplane maybe! The sound grew louder and louder until Heike realized it was coming from directly behind her. She craned her neck and saw a grungy, olive-green Jet Ski racing toward her, belching oily gray crud. Sitting atop the Jet Ski was a man in a shredded leather outfit, his face blackened by soot, eyes covered by goggles, head mashed into a hockey helmet. He was wielding a three-barrel pistol and firing shots in her direction!

Heike screamed and ducked underwater, just as the slimy, algae-covered hull of the Jet Ski rushed over her, barely avoiding decapitation. She stayed under for as long as she could manage, and when she broke water again the Jet Ski was gone and she was looking at the hull of an eighteen-meter-long trimaran with its sails down, and a vertical axis wind turbine spinning lazily around the mid-center of the mast.

Her boyfriend was floating in the gentle waves, hanging on to the port side sponson of the trimaran, just beneath a wiry metal folding chair fixed to the outrigger hull.

"Matty, where are we?"

He held a finger to his lips and whispered, "Quiet!" and then pointed to the helm of the vessel, where they could see a navigator in a raggedy, pieced-together yachting jacket and slick mahimahi-skin and Spandex trousers—standing at the stanchion of the vessel and aiming a powerful harpoon at a sailboat drifting alongside it. The drifter was speaking a bizarre combination of English and some other, unidentifiable language.

"What is this? The free bonus?" Heike whispered to him.

They heard the navigator call out to the man.

"Nothing's free in Hydroworld!" And they both looked at each other.

"Holy shit. Kevin Costner!"

He turned around and spied them clinging to his raft.

"Hey! Hey what are you doing to my boat!" and he ran across the center hull, grabbing a spear-pistol propped against the mast and aiming it directly at Matthias' head.

"You've got two seconds to let go—both of you," Costner growled.

"Ew!" Heike shrieked. "Matty, he's got webbed feet!"

The navigator's eyes flashed angrily and he aimed the spear-pistol at her. A shark's tooth glinted from the tip of the harpoon. Heike gulped.

"If you want to keep that pretty face of yours waterproof, then you better stop talking," he grunted menacingly.

"She didn't mean anything by it," Matthias said, in her defense. "She's not used to seeing mutan... uh er... drifters..."

The navigator's steely countenance did not soften, but he removed his finger from the trigger of the spear pistol.

"Where are you from?" he asked, unable to camouflage the curiosity creeping into his voice. "You speak strangely. You seem afraid of the water. Very unnatural. I haven't seen the likes of you at any atoll..."

Matthias thought back quickly to his recollection of the film. "We've come from Dryland..." he said.

The idiot drifter on the other sailboat (wearing a hat reminiscent of Marlon Brando in *The Island of Dr. Moreau*) clapped his hands together and cackled like a lunatic, running around his stern and chanting, "Dryland! Dryland! The boy's mad he is… says he's seen dryland… too long at sea he's been… so he has…"

"Quiet, you!" Costner barked, and the fool slapped two hands over his mouth, whining like a baby.

"Dryland's a myth," Costner said simply.

Matthias suppressed a burp of laughter. His girlfriend looked at him, her eyes pleading for him to be quiet. She couldn't understand. She hadn't seen the film.

"Let go of my boat—" he said.

"Please, can't you at least take us to the next atoll? Matthias begged. "She can't swim well… she'll drown out here if you leave us…"

"That's not my concern," the navigator said. "You haven't got anything to trade—nothing that could interest me…"

Matthias turned his head slowly toward his girlfriend, whose eyes widened, and she hissed under her breath, "*Don't—even—think—about it!*"

The other drifter gave an excited yelp, interrupting them. He was jumping up and down and pointing to two black flecks on the horizon.

"Marauders!" he yelled. He spoke tauntingly to the navigator. "You'll never make it with your sails down—good luck! Haha!"

And he began sailing away, laughing maniacally to himself, as the ambushing pirates accelerated on their jet skis, rapidly advancing toward the immobile trimaran.

"Don't leave us here!" Heike pleaded.

The navigator grimaced, his gaze flashing indecisively between the young couple and the approaching marauders. He swept briny strands of hair out of his face and he said, "You owe me. Understand? Next atoll... you find a way to repay..."

They nodded in agreement and he set down the spear pistol and offered his hand to Heike. She grabbed it and he hoisted her from the water and pulled her onto his raft, carrying her easily in his arms and setting her down on the center deck.

"Ooh that was just like in *The Bodyguard*," she cooed.

"Shut up!" Matthias snapped, climbing onto the boat. "He's old enough to be your dad..."

The navigator rushed to the mast of his craft, slamming down a lever, which folded in the eggbeater blades surrounding it. There was the crunch of a gearbox, as an old recycled Ford transmission pulled at a cable, and then a hidden boom rose out of the hull as a heavy counterweight bag fell down, pulling a patchy mainsail up the mast. It billowed in the wind... then a jib unfurled, catching the breeze as he jumped to the grinder at the helm and steered the vessel away from the raiding marauders.

"Faster, alter!" yelped Matthias excitedly, egging him on. "They're gaining on us..."

"Why do you have those gills behind your ears?" Heike gently inquired.

"Come on... lose the bastards!"

"What was it like working with Whitney Houston?"

"Can I fire the harpoon at them?"

"Is it true Madonna was supposed to play in *The Bodyguard*… but she had to be replaced because of you?"

"Heike, this is Water… hem… Hydroworld," Matthias corrected her.

The navigator just snapped. He let go of the grinder and wheeled around, his face bright red.

"STOP YOUR GODDAMN RACKET! FOR THE LOVE OF POSEIDON! I can't even hear myself think with you two yammering on and on and…"

A shot whistled through the air and a flare tore a hole in the center of the mainsail. The marauders hooted and gunned their jet skis. They were just a few hundred feet behind and gaining—it seemed there was no possible way to outrun them.

"I'm going to have to jettison one of you…" the navigator said, quickly assessing the situation. "The boat's too heavy!"

"Huh?"

"One of you is going overboard!"

"Bullshit!" Matthias objected. "Just dump some of this junk." And he picked up a jar covered with a distressed rope harness and casually tossed it over the side.

The navigator's eyes fairly shot out of his head. "WHAT HAVE YOU DONE?"

"It's nothing special—just a bunch of dirt."

"Just dirt!" Costner screamed. "JUST DIRT!!… Are

you insane? Do you know how many chits that was worth? I swear to Poseidon I'm gonna..." He lunged for his spear pistol but Matthias beat him to it, grabbing the hefty weapon and tossing it overboard as well. Kevin Costner jumped at Matthias and head-butted him in the face and Matthias went sprawling on the deck. He straddled him, grabbing him by his ruined Tokio Hotel hairdo, his face twisted and furious, "I'll give you dirt!" he yelled, livid, and raised his fist to strike him.

"Don't you hurt him!" Heike screeched, rushing forward and grabbing a potted lime tree and hurling it at him. It struck Costner in the small of his back and he bellowed as limes went rolling everywhere, and he scrambled on his knees, trying to salvage what he could, growling, "*I'm gonna sell you piecemeal to the first slavers I come across.*"

The marauders—three of them—circled the trimaran from both sides while the navigator tried to collect his limes. He froze as they drew up to the amas. One wielded a sawed-off double-barrel shotgun, the other an MP5. Matthias picked up a grappling hook, intending to use it to defend himself.

"Leave it. It ain't worth it," Costner said to Matthias. He wore a grim and weary expression, as if he'd been confronted with this gang on more than one occasion.

One of the marauders flipped up the goggles he wore over his soot-blackened face, laughed and said, "You heard the mutant—drop that thing and put your hands in the air. We're comin' aboard..."

And he hopped off the back of the jet ski and climbed onto the trampoline fitted between the hulls and strode cockily up to Kevin Costner, his MP5 gripped in his fish-leather gloved hands and said, "We'll be takin' command of this here… well, I guess you could call it a boat… Hope you don't mind."

The other smoker pilot yee-hawed. "Well look-e here. Seems like we got us a good catch to take back to the 'Deez…"

"Yessir!" his colleague hooted. His leering gaze turned to Heike, who stood frozen to the spot, whimpering in fright. "C'mon, girl. Nothin' to be afraid of—" he jeered, caressing her cheek with the cold barrel of his machine-pistol. "Today is your lucky day. All of you. You're all gonna meet the bishop!"

The marauders brought their captives to the *Exxon Valdez*—a behemoth, derelict oil tanker that looked like hell on oars. They ran their jetskis to its barnacle-encrusted base surrounded by floating debris, and made their captives them climb a rusting gangway ladder, over ninety feet up, to the main deck of the barge, which was littered with more debris; among them the burnt-out carcasses of old automobiles, a scout plane, scrap metal and heaps of junk tires and literally thousands of empty cigarette packages and cans of smeat surrounding a maze of pressure valves and oil tank hatches. A thorny crown of wide-flange beams jutted out from the perimeter of the deck.

Their captors led them to the wheelhouse, which rose an additional sixty feet from the tanker's massive stern and all the way up the rusted steel ladder that led to the bridge. Heike cursed her boyfriend for inciting her to jump into the lagoon back in *Triassic Park*.

"…how could I know it would take us to Hydroworld?

I don't know how these bloody chips work," Matthias objected.

"This is such a guy's film," snapped Heike. "Look where we are, Matty... look how ugly this thing is. We could be dancing in the ballroom at the *Titanic* right now. We could be standing on the bow."

"Oh give it a rest," Matthias shot back. "At least this ship's not gonna sink to a premature and watery grave... at least I don't have to endure the sight of Leo waving his fist and shouting 'I'm the King of the World'..."

"You are such a jerk."

"Hey!" one of the marauders nudged the barrel of his shotgun against Heike's bare thigh. "I told you to cork it!"

Heike grimaced, gripping the railing, an automatic weapon aimed at her rear and the unsightly spectacle of Kevin Costner's webbed feet marching in front of her. This was one escapade she wasn't ready to forget.

21

PARIS, 8TH ARRONDISSEMENT

Johannes sat with his date, Kim Nguyen, in a swanky nightclub on the tourist-filled Rue de Ponthieu, just off the Champs-Elysées. The nightclub was called "A Touch of Class," and had a very retro late 70s to early 80s feel to it. It felt as though they had stepped back in time, directly into the disco era. There were the U-shaped tacky sofas surrounding low, circular metal tables, and warped, mirrored ceilings from which spun flashy disco balls. In the center was a translucent dancefloor with the image of a black panther mosaicked across it. The clientele was not what Johannes might have expected. They looked like a bunch of squares. Mustached and square-jawed American expatriates sat at the booths, with their dates wearing sparkling cocktail gowns and furs, heavy on the gems, heavy on the makeup, their hair done in kitsch perms. The women chain-smoked and fingered their pearl necklaces. Some of the women even wore suits with shoulder-pads. Everything looked gaudy and tacky, and Johannes wondered if all of Paris was really this old fashioned. The people were all older than him, and though they appeared wealthy, consuming bottle after bottle of Chandon and Cristal champagne, they seemed to have very outdated tastes.

But maybe that was just the theme of the club. Maybe

it was all just for kicks. After all, this was the old Paris that the tourists flocked to—they didn't come for hardstyle and underground electro. The music was bizarre too, especially the particular number the DJ was now playing: it sounded like an Argentinian tango set to a reggae beat with some electronica undertones. Johannes almost thought he recognized the number, as a warm female voice sang an ode to Parisian nightlife:

> *Strange, I've seen that face before,*
> *Seen him hanging 'round my door,*
> *Like a hawk stealing for the prey,*
> *Like the night waiting for the day,*
>
> *Strange, he shadows me back home,*
> *Footsteps echo on the stones,*
> *Rainy nights, on Hausmann Boulevard,*
> *Parisian music, drifting from the bars,*

Johannes turned his attention from a group of boisterous businessmen in pricy tweed suits and gold rings on their fingers, and back over to Kim. There was something so odd about the place, but he couldn't quite get his finger on it. Everybody just seemed so bizarre, but maybe that was due to his being in a foreign country. Or maybe that was just how it was in France. He'd pictured it very differently.

"It's funny," he said, sipping his club soda.

"What is?" Kim asked, stirring a long drink.

"I never figured you for these kind of places…"

"What do you mean by that?"

"Just… I had this idea of you as a very modern girl. Avant-garde, you know. But now I see that I was mistaken. You must be the only girl I know who actually likes this oldie goldie stuff."

Kim smiled at him, amused. "Are you enjoying yourself?"

Johannes shrugged, "I've never been to Paris before. I didn't think Parisians were so… backwards… no offence."

His gaze wandered across the crowded club to the edge of the dancefloor, where a stocky, Middle-Eastern man stood, arms crossed, watching the night owls. The singer was now speaking seductively in French.

"Do you want to dance?" Kim suddenly proposed.

"To this?" Johannes responded, incredulously. He had never been one for moody romantic tunes.

Kim shrugged prettily. "Why not? Just one dance… then we can leave, if you don't like it here…"

"That's not what I meant—" he apologized, but she stood up and took him by the hand and led him onto the dancefloor, between the women with the perms and sequined gowns and their male partners—every other one of which looked like Omar Sharif.

They began dancing—Johannes making a desperate effort not to look silly, because he felt so out of place, so much like a fish out of water, and everybody around him was old and graying, and the place smelt musty, and was full of smoke, and there were these old, art nouveau cabaret paintings hanging on the walls—like this one of a black cat with brilliant yellow eyes that kept grabbing his attention, until he pointed it out to Kim.

"That's a reproduction of *Le Chat Noir*... a painting which was commissioned for a famous cabaret here in Paris, during the late 1900s," she explained. "It was owned by an entrepreneur named Rodolphe Salis, who had this wonderful idea he could blend art and alcohol into the thing of the future."

"You seem to know a lot about a lot of things," Johannes said, struggling to keep time to the odd music.

"I have my moments," Kim said, and as they danced Johannes became increasingly aware of another couple on the dancefloor next to them. A middle-aged man in a formal gray suit was standing awkwardly in place, barely moving, while a young and beautiful blonde girl, with dark eyes and wearing a bold and very snug red dress that highlighted her delicious forms, slinked seductively around him.

Kim caught Johannes gawking and whispered in his ear, "It's rude to stare."

"I wasn't—" Johannes started, then laughed, knowing he had been caught. "She looks familiar, that's all," he explained.

"You're talking about her face, I assume," Kim teased. She saw Johannes go bright red. He was really easy to wind up. This trip to Paris was going to be great fun. "Don't worry," she told him. "She's used to being watched."

"What are you talking about?"

"Don't you know who that is?"

Johannes shook his head. Kim said, "That's Emmanuelle Seigner. She's one of the most famous actresses in France."

"Oh," said Johannes, thinking, "Isn't she the wife of Roman Polanski?"

"Yes," Kim said. "She even played in one of his films—*The Ninth Door*—you know, with Johnny Depp."

In the dim light of the club, the man in the gray suit dancing absently with the sexy French movie star was now turning to face them. The girl twirled around him, draping her supple body sensually against his awkward stiffness.

"She looks so young…" Johannes mumbled, feeling uneasy. All around the smoky club, mustached, Middle-Eastern men were standing sentry. He realized they were keeping an eye on the dancing couple. *What was going on? Were they celebrity bodyguards? Were French film stars really worth all that much attention?* And the man dancing with her now turned to face him, and his slicked back hair and clean-shaven face was obscured by the smoke and by the halo of lights that surroundedhim, and Johannes' mind was racing as the Jamaican beat rumbled on and the brassy sensual music filled his ears, the distorted reflections of the dancers assailed him from the mirrored walls and ceilings—thinking to himself *this couldn't possibly be 2010, not with these curious people, this decadent room, this strange music—not with an over-forty actress who looked only 18 or 20 years old… and that man dancing with her…who was he?*

Roman Polanski's wife. What's she doing with that man. That's not Polanski.

And then it hit him—hit him hard and he felt a rush of shock. He wasn't in Paris. Not really. He was in a tapeworld. He was in Roman Polanski's classic 1988 thriller *Frenetic*—a movie about an American cardiologist investigating the mysterious disappearance of his wife while in Paris for a medical conference.

A younger Harrison Ford pushed past them, followed by Emmanuelle Seigner. His face was a tableau of mixed emotions. He looked confused and desperate. Johannes looked at Kim, bewildered.

"What are we doing in *Frenetic*?"

"Surprise!" Kim clapped her hands together. "I didn't think you'd piece it together so quickly…"

"But… I don't get it. How can we be in a tapeworld? Our trip to Paris was real… I'm sure of it—we took the train to Rotterdam… we were at The Hague airport. We checked-in… I had my boarding pass in my hand…"

"So you did," smiled Kim mysteriously. "Only our flight was delayed… so…"

"You spiked my coffee!" Johannes gasped, his memory returning. "Where are we now? Really…"

"Catnapping in the waiting room at the airport… I didn't plan it like this… honest, I wanted to surprise you with these when we got to Paris for real, but the wait was too long… I hope you're not upset."

They saw Harrison Ford sit back down at a table with

the girl, and one of the Arabs converse with him.

"...we take American Express... and Visa... and MasterCard... and checks," the Arab said, in a voice that sounded almost dubbed over..

"I've got something else too," Ford said, handing the man a leather wallet.

"Where is he now?"

"Dead..."

The man opened it and Johannes eased closer to listen.

"We still have your wife, doctor," the man said.

"And I still have what you want," Ford countered. "I got the stuff that you want, I got the thing that you need... I got more than enough to make you drop to your knees..."

Johannes shook his head and whispered to Kim incredulously, "Am I hallucinating or did he just quote Whitney Houston?"

She giggled, "A little tribute to my favorite singer... I slipped it in there—"

They continued eavesdropping.

"Then I propose another exchange," the man said, coolly.

Ford pointed a finger at him and gritted his teeth in that stiff, unchanging Fordian manner of his. "And this time, I decide how it's gonna be done! You'll hear from me—"

And having finished his righteous speech he got up, taking the girl with him and exiting the club as the Arab picked up his drink.

"Come on—let's see where they're going," Kim said,

taking Johannes by the hand.

They tailed Harrison Ford and Emmanuelle Seigner out of the nightclub, but were interrupted by one of the waiters who ran after them, insisting they pay their bill before leaving. When they had done so (Kim having wisely filled her purse with French francs beforehand for this purpose) they left "A Touch Of Class," but the couple was nowhere to be seen. Across the street they could see the dark, swirling waters of the Seine, where a brightly lit riverboat was passing underneath the pont de Grenelle, and behind it the towering replica of the Statue of Liberty on the Ile aux Cygnes—its giant bronze arm raised high against the dark velvety backdrop of the night.

"Merde," cursed Kim. "We just missed them—okay let's go down to the riverbank across the water. There's another scene there—it comes near the end of the movie... they're going to exchange his kidnapped wife for the nuclear weapons trigger... hurry!"

Johannes gulped. "I'm not sure—Kim—I'd just like... prefer it if we went to a sidewalk café and had some croissants... I'm not in the mood for this cloak-and-dagger shit... and besides... what if our flight comes up, and we're still asleep in the waiting room, won't we miss it? And won't the airport security find it odd that we're zonked out? Won't people steal our belongings?"

"You worry too much..." Kim said, gripping him by the arm and pulling him along. "You need to enjoy life..."

"That's the whole point," Johannes grumbled. "And it

begins with not being shot to death by terrorists!"

Kim giggled as she led him across the steel bridge to the other side of the river and they descended a flight of concrete steps leading to the Rive Droite.

"There they are!" exclaimed Kim excitedly, gesturing to the movie couple who were running along the right bank, down to the waterfront. The girl now had a shiny black leather jacket with metal studs over her slutty red dress. The pair of them ran under a shadowy bridge, watching a white motorboat draw up to the banks.

"Hold it there!" the skipper of the boat called out.

Johannes and Kim crept closer, being careful to stay in the shadows of the bridge's arch.

"Let's see it," the skipper ordered, and Harrison Ford reached into his jacket and drew out a tiny object—the krytron—an electronic switch tube capable of handling high-current, high-voltage pulses, used as a trigger for slapper detonators in nuclear devices. He held the macguffin in the air so it was visible to the kidnappers.

One of the Palestinians held up a pair of binoculars to verify that it was genuinely the krytron, without having to bring the motorboat closer.

"Give it to the girl!" he ordered. "She comes alone."

"My wife first!" Ford insisted, pointing again in that very authoritative and Fordian manner of his.

"Jesus Maria, what a boring and mannered actor," Johannes commented.

The kidnappers seemed to agree, because they ushered

another woman, also wearing a red dress, from the back of the motorboat and up the docking ladder of the riverbank. The drug-smuggling prostitute moved forward, holding the krytron, while Harrison Ford's wife walked shakily toward her. The exchange was being made!

"God isn't Polanski such a great filmmaker!" exclaimed Kimmy.

"This is boring," mumbled Johannes and walked away, back up the steps to the bridge. Kim was so absorbed by the movie climax playing right in front of her eyes that she didn't see him go.

Harrison Ford's wife crumbled into his arms, whimpering. The smuggler, Michelle, stood on the riverbank, clenching the krytron in her hand. One of the Arabs on the boat held out his palm.

"Give me my money or I'll throw the fucking thing in the river," she told the abductors.

"Money? What money?" the crooked Arab said, feigning miscomprehension.

"I still wasn't paid," she said.

"I... I don't have any money," her interlocutor mumbled, fishing in his suit pockets and drawing out a few skimpy bills.

"Oh really," she scoffed and she made as if to throw the krytron into the water, and the man panicked.

"Hold it!" the man yelled. "How much?"

"Ten-thousand francs," she said.

Above her, Johannes walked by the railing of the

overpass, peered down at the scene briefly and walked away. *(Watch the scene and you'll see Johannes.)*

"Quick," she urged and the Arab nodded. He spoke a few words to his partner in the motorboat and then he climbed on the bank, his feet crunching on the gravel. He abruptly flung himself at her, seizing her by the leg, and she dropped the kryton on the gravel and went toppling to the ground, her arm outstretched, trying to recover it while the Arab pulled her back.

"Freeze!" two men suddenly called from the top of the bridge. They were pointing pistols down at the motorboat. "Nobody move! Nobody fucking move! The girl brings it up here!"

Emmanuelle Seigner's deep, mascara-lined eyes looked up at the secret Israeli agents, debating what to do—and Harrison Ford as Dr. Richard Walker, clung to his wife, looking very tired and frightened.

Kim walked up to the pair of them, "Excuse me—"

Harrison Ford spun around, thrusting himself protectively between her and his wife.

"What do you want? Who are you?"

"I just want to tell you that *Indiana Jones 4* was a mistake—Steven should have never let you near a whip again!"

He stared at her, tense, his eyes flickering; still in bewilderment and shock over the recent events... the abduction of his wife... and what was this Asian girl talking about? Indiana? Was that a code word for something? Were additional Mossad agents and Palestinian terrorists going to storm the scene?

"Honey—what's she talking about?" his wife asked in a shaky voice.

"I… I don't know…"

"Now!" the man on the bridge yelled, and Michelle picked herself up, slowly.

A flash of shots rang out from the second man in the boat. He fired his automatic weapon up at the Israeli agents atop the bridge. The bullets whistled through the air and sparked against the guard rail. The agents fired back. The Arab grabbed the smuggler girl by her hair and pulled her up.

"Aie!"

Harrison Ford flung himself and his wife against the concrete pillar underneath the overpass, shielding her body with his.

Kim backed up against the wall beside the terrified couple as more shots rang out.

"You're really better looking in person," she said to Ford. His wife narrowed her eyes at Kim, who held up her hands defensively, "Hey, this is all just a movie—"

The other Arab remaining on the boat fired his weapon and then jumped onto the riverbank, seizing the krytron and running away with it, hot on the heels of his partner, who was forcefully dragging the girl with him.

The agents on the bridge fired down at him, and he zigzagged, miraculously dodging the first few shots until one caught him in the chest and he fell backwards, onto the white gravel, his hand unclenching to reveal the battery-size nuclear trigger. Harrison Ford made to go after it, but his wife pulled him back.

"No…"

"I'll get it—" Kim offered, rushing in front of Ford and stooped down near the prone figure, deftly picking up the krytron from the dead Arab's palm.

She made off with it, dashing up the steps… in the opposite direction…

"Hey! Hey you! Bring that back!" Harrison Ford shouted angrily, and ran after her. Who was this fucking magpie snatching the trigger right out from under his nose—after all he had gone through to bring it here! He was furious.

Kim ran up the concrete steps, with Harrison Ford chasing after her (boy could he run!), and the two Mossad agents on top of the bridge spotted her and they aimed their guns at her and yelled out, "Don't fucking move!"

And Kim sprinted off, like a gazelle, away from them and the fatter of the two agents, the one wearing dark sunglasses and a white shirt fired at her and a shot ricocheted off the railing, and another whizzed past her.

"No!" Johannes bellowed, rushing forward and tackling the man to the ground. He wrenched his gun from his hand. The other agent spun around to fire—Johannes kicked him in the crotch and the fat man doubled over choking.

"Get her!" the fat agent coughed, and Johannes belted him in the face, splintering his sunglasses and knocking him unconscious.

The other Mossad agent limped off after Kim, who had

darted across the street, slaloming through a line of joggers. Johannes ran after him, the gun clenched now in his hand, yelling, "Kimmy!"

And the injured Mossad agent in the brown trench coat raised his handgun to fire at her, but Johannes aimed his pistol at the man and fired first. Pow! Sending him sprawling to the ground.

"Kimmy!" he repeated, pursuing her as she dodged through the zany Parisian traffic, bowling over scooters and pedestrians, and Johannes, despite the adrenaline rush and the fright, could not help but feel slightly ridiculous, running through such a serious movie, being chased by Mossad secret agents, Palestinian terrorists, a sultry French model, not to mention Captain Han Solo aka Indiana Jones aka Doctor Walker… there running behind him, wheezing and gasping for breath, shouting out between gasps, "GET—BACK—HERE—YOU! I'm an AMERICAN!!! And I'm pissed off!"

22

LE MARAIS, PARIS

It was shortly after 1 A.M., and the Inox was crowded with the usual mid-week nightlife. The house music thumped from the bar and into the street, where the regulars hung out, smoking and socializing. There were the tough cruisers with their snakeskin motorcycle jackets and Kozo jeans; the older sugars in cashmere sweaters and Prada knockoffs; the young, waifish trendy twinks in tight and colorful D&G and Guess tops—hair spiked and gelled—smiles bright and gleaming.

The American had a few drinks, chatted with the buff server at the bar, then headed out to his car, to move elsewhere. He was alone, mid-forties, with a mild potbelly. He had short cropped blond hair, slim black glasses with cateye frames, and an elegant silk-and-wool V-neck jumper. A tasteful Maurice LaCroix watch glinted from around his wrist.

The boy was arguing with another kid, what sounded like a lovers spat. The two exchanged heated words, and the boy went back to the bar at the club entrance. The American headed to asheltered parking lotand a few moments later the boy emerged from the club and followed him down a narrow, crooked street, lined with private couture salons and art shops with rainbow flags projecting from the beige and pink brick façades of the limestone buildings.

He accosted him before he got to the parking lot. He knew the American drove a silvery Z8 roadster, but he didn't want him to think he was after his money. He knew a few things about this man—he'd been observing him since he arrived.

"Monsieur, attends... tu as oublié quelque chose." the boy called out, and the American stopped walking. The boy had a small men's purse slung over a pink polo shirt and balanced on his left hip. Tight jeans and an easy smile. He was dangling a silk scarf from one hand. "You left this," he said, in English, with only the slightest traces of a French accent.

"That isn't mine—" said the American.

"Oh," the boy looked questioningly at the scarf, then to him. "My apologies... somebody left it where you were sitting. I'll take it back to Jean-Marc."

"You know Jean-Marc?" the American said, sounding mildly interested. The club owner was a good friend of his.

"Sure," the boy shrugged. "I model for him—on occasion."

The American knew his friend was an avid photographer. He even used some of his portraits to adorn the velvet walls and dark backrooms of his club. Possibly one of those gorgeous Adonis bodies belonged to this boy. He was quite a catch: dark eyes, soft brown hair, and a full and smooth complexion. He shifted his shoulder strap.

"You're leaving early," the boy now said, seeming eager to engage in conversation. "You should know the Inox doesn't heat up until after two..."

"You speak very good English," said the American, sounding pleased at the attention he was getting. "But you are French, no?"

The boy smiled. His mouth opened and his head recoiled just slightly, almost like a cobra. "No," he said, slowly. Then, "I hate to be this direct—but I couldn't help but noticing... you have a very pleasant way about you. The way you are dressed. How you carry yourself. Are you involved in any way with fashion?"

"No. I'm an art dealer—" said the American, the flattery crackling at his ears. "Listen... would you like to join me for a drink? I know this great little dive just around the corner..."

"Why don't we go to your place?" the boy cut him off. "Just for a nightcap, of course."

The American hesitated. He was tempted, and the boy looked nice enough. He had a mysterious aura about him that attracted and intrigued him.

"Or perhaps that is not a good idea? Perhaps you are living with somebody?" the boy suggested.

"N...no," said the American. "I live alone. I live in the Marais, actually... only a few blocks from here. And you?"

He crossed the street to the car park, and the boy walked alongside him. "I live with Louie... that's my friend. But we had a fight, so I don't think I will be going home tonight."

"Oh... well I'm sorry to hear that. This is my car," said the American, pointing his keys at the BMW. There was a light chirp as the doors unlocked. The boy started laughing.

"What is it?"

"Pardon me—it is just—one would think you Americans did not have legs to carry you around. You are so close to home."

The American chuckled and got in his roadster, gesturing for the boy to do the same. The nappa leather smelt cool and fresh. The control knobs were smooth and shiny. The doctor found the elegant contours of the cockpit most delightfully European.

"What did you say your name was?" the American asked, turning the ignition on the dash above the wheel. The 5 liter V-8 revved with the appropriate combination of power and smoothness.

The boy turned his face to the window. A few errant drops of summer rain splashed down from the sky. His reflection, in the clear glass of the passenger window, was leached very white—as if he had not been exposed to the sun in a long time.

"Animal," he said finally.

The American raised his eyebrows, doubtfully. "Odd name. And your accent... what is that... east European?"

"It's Lithuanian," said the boy. "That's where I was born. But I lived in France, with my Aunt, when I was very young."

The American took him to a modern, two-floor penthouse, near Les Halles. It had a beautiful kitchen on the first floor, trendily furnished, with blonde wood cabinets, a whole range of high-end appliances, and a glass-ceramic stove. The living room was a dialogue of contrast, with walls of Persian murals and laquered panels. A spiral stairway of perforated metallic treads led to the upstairs bedrooms and second bathroom. From there, a small skylight portal offered access to the rooftop deck.

The American tossed his keys onto a long and sleek art deco table, in the center of the living room and pointed to a sofa adorned with ornamented Morrocan pillows. A gray-schist Buddha near it seemed to serve as the decorative centerpiece of the room.

"Is that Ghandaran?" asked the boy, pointing out the statue.

"Yes," his host answered, seeming pleasantly surprised. "It's uh… from a monastery in the Swat Valley. 2nd century AD. Do you know about sculptures?"

"I collect the occasional piece myself," the boy said. His host seemed dazzled and intrigued. This boy was not the usual vapid sugar hustler that you got hooked with down at the Inox.

"Are you an artist? I mean… are you in the beaux-arts?"

"No," the boy named Animal turned his deep, maroon-colored eyes on his host. "Perhaps you would care for a drink?"

"Oh right, excuse me," his host coughed apologetically. He made for the espresso-colored liquor cabinet which divided the living room and kitchen, drawing out two tumblers, but the boy rose swiftly and intercepted him.

"Why don't you put on some music?" he suggested.

"Let me pour the drinks. I've got a special cocktail in mind which I'm sure you're going to love—"

He took the glasses playfully and his host relented. The boy whistled a showtuneas he slid open the drawers, drawing out a vintage rye whiskey and a bottle of sweet vermouth. Also, a small bottle of Angostura bitters.

"What do you like... jazz... opera? Maybe some Gershwin or Debussey? Or perhaps something a little more out-there... some Eotvos?"

"I have what you might call classic taste," said Animal, mixing the drinks. He selected cubes from the ice-maker with a sleek aluminum shovel. "I think something baroque would suit the moment just fine, wouldn't you agree?"

His host searched through his collection, and found an album of Henry VIII compositions, as performed by an ensemble from Heidelberg. He put it on, and the airy notes of a flute trio surrounded them. The boy handed him a tumbler, the short drink was pale-amber.

"What is it?" the American took the glass. The cubes rattled against it.

"It's like a Manhattan," said Animal. "With an added twist."

They clinked their glasses and both drank. The American sucked his cheeks. "There's something there," he said. "But it's not the whiskey... not the vermouth either... could it be a touch of Campari? No, that's not it—"

"I may have put just a tad too much Angostura," confessed Animal. "Oh bother—at any rate it should do the trick—"

His host returned to the sofa. He had exchanged his shoes for a pair of soft Moreschi slippers. He swished his drink around, sipping it further. He was suddenly all coy. "So... Animal. What do you do?"

"I'm a psychiatrist."

"Really," his host regarded him appraisingly. "You seem very young—oh, I'm sorry —you mean to say, you are a student in psychology?"

"No," replied the boy, setting down his drink on the low table. The flute recital came to an end, and was followed by a viola and harpsichord bit. "I received my M.D. from Johns Hopkins years ago. I run a small private practice in Baltimore—"

What is he talking about? What practice? He's so young... so clever...

"Ha," laughed the American. He leaned heavy into the sofa. "You could have had me fooled... how old are you anyway?"

The room slanted. Trick of the light. The American felt an overwhelming sense of calm—as if the shutters had opened on his mind—and a warm, serene light spilled in. Everything was clear and beautiful, but he couldn't remember...

His hand fell to the side. The glass slipped from his grasp, and with lightning speed the boy caught it, before it shattered. Animal was suddenly right beside him, very close-but there was no fear. He felt well, remarkably well.

"Would you like another?" The boy sitting beside him

and his voice light-years away, but clear as a bell in his head.

"Wha…"

"Midazolam. I picked it up from the ambulance. They give it to you to keep you calm before an operation. It's a sedative with wonderfully hypnotic properties…"

Hypnotic. What is he talking about? Who is this boy?

"Who are you?"

"Don't worry," the boy smiled. "You won't remember any of this."

He drew a small object from his pocket. The American looked down. The boy's hand was close to his thigh. Tiniest sting of the faintest needle.

"Ow, that hurts," he slurred.

"Sorry—but it's got a short half-life. And we can't have you coming out too quickly now, can we?"

The man relaxed further—his breathing was shallow but stable. The room was all bright colors and the boy so close to him… but *who is this?*

"This is really happening," said the man.

Then the boy had disappeared, and his head lolled back against the sofa. He shut his eyes and swirls of orange danced around. When he opened them the boy was sitting across from him again. He had a computer on his lap, hooked to a laser printer on the coffee table.

"Are you real?"

"Of course I am," the boy checked through the browser history. "We're going to do a little online banking… all right? Mr. John Ableman." He read the name off a business card.

"Hey—that's my wallet…" No accusation. Just stating a simple fact.

"Mr. Ableman," the boy said, his tone officious. "Have you got a money transfer account?"

"Wha… Western…"

"Western Union, thank you," the boy clicked a key. "I'll need your user name and password please…"

"Password…"

"Yes, just spell it out."

The man was talking now, about everything under the sun. He talked about his clients, and some woman named Gillian, then his password, then the PIN number of his Platinum MasterCard and AmEx.

"Daily withdrawal limit?"

"3,000… as I was saying…"

"Spending limit?"

"9,000… but you see here's my point…"

The boy booked a last-minute flight, using a special site. There was a plane scheduled at 7:15 from Charles DeGaulle airport to Miami, Florida. From there, he could catch a correspondence to the Biminis, where he would track down the smarmy hospital director who had tormented him for eight long years. He printed out the invoice. Then he closed the computer. He took Ableman's passport and studied the photo. It was much the same as he was now. He fought to look young, but even the best probiotics and skin treatments didn't erase the wrinkles around his neck and his crow's feet.

Animal gave him a last shot while he was rambling on

about Sothebys and some auction. He went into the bathroom, which was sleek, and modern—all blue-glass countertops and large, charcoal-colored porcelain tiling.

Earlier that afternoon, he had purchased a crème developer and a blend of hair dyes and powders at a cosmetics shop in the district. He selected a bleaching powder and mixed it with the developer in a small bowl, and let it sit. He then parted his hair in sections, and added the mixture, wearing white latex cooking gloves, being careful not to apply too much at the roots. Then he put a plastic grocery bag over his head and tied it.

He listened to music for an hour, keeping an eye always on his host, who was dozing comfortably.

When the time was up, he rinsed his hair and washed it with a special shampoo to neutralize the PH. He had a selection of various colored contact lenses in his kit, and he chose the pale green to match the eyes on the photo.

He opened his purse and withdrew a bottle of skin-colored liquid latex, a makeup brush and highlighter. He washed his face and dried it, applied a foundation, then worked on shading in the areas under his eyes and jowls. He took a deep breath and puffed up his face, until it was as bloated as possible, and he coated the latex on, and then dried it with a hair-dryer. When he relaxed his facial muscles, the skin wrinkled.

He put on John Ableman's glasses. Then he packed a suitcase with his clothes, perfume, accessories. He took his driver's license, passport, ID, all his papers. He took his calfskin strap loafers and tried them on for size. They were slightly too large. He would wear additional layers of socks, and then buy new ones. He took his cell phone and removed the SIM card and flushed it. He would leave in the early morning, before anyone was awake—calls would go unanswered during the day.

The man stirred on the sofa, and mumbled something. He was coming around.

Christopher rinsed out the glasses and put them away. John Ableman blinked his eyes, and when he opened them he stared up, confused, at the spectre of himself.

"W… who are you?" he gasped—his memories evaporated, like gas escaping a tank. He tried to sit up, but weakened by the last shot of Verser mixed with the skeletal relaxant Lorazepam, he was unable to.

"I'm afraid I'm out of needles," was the last thing he heard and then the plastic bag came over his head, as the boy smothered him with a pillow, kneeling hard on his chest and bearing his full weight down on him.

Even without mental awareness, the body fights on its own to live. John Ableman blacked out within thirty seconds, but he thrashed his arms and legs for long minutes. The boy pressed down harder, blocking his arms, careful that a blow did not accidentally strike him and cause a bruise. Once his victim's foot struck out and knocked into the leg of the coffee table. Only once.

When at last his victim stopped moving, he waited an additional ten minutes, with his fingers on the pulse of the wrist. At last, satisfied, he removed the pillow. John Ableman stared up at him, with open, unseeing eyes.

He carried his body upstairs, to the guest bedroom. He lifted it with surprising ease. Size for size, Animal was as strong as an ant.

He put him under the bed and shut and locked the guest room.

Then he went back downstairs washed the glasses and put away all the evidence of his visit. He went to the kitchen and ate from a platter of amuse-bouches in the fridge, feasting on Scottish salmon, foie gras and brioche, Osciétre Royal caviar and a fine tart of scallops with Perigord truffles, courtesy of the luxury caterer Fauchon. The man might be unlucky in love, but he certainly had gourmet taste, Christopher mused.

Exhilerated after his killing, and his fine meal, he went into the salon and turned off the lights, picked up a remote and switched on the wood-toned aluminum flatscreen TV.

There was a late night crime film playing on TF1, the national channel, and the boy decided to watch it, to test his command of the French language. He could speak seven languages.

On the screen, a young female FBI intern was sitting in the cluttered office of her section chief, being assigned an "interesting errand." Her boss explained how the bureau was interviewing all the serial killers in custody in order to establish a psychobehavorial profile, to aid them in unsolved cases. He asked her if she spooked easily.

"Not yet, Sir…" Jodie Foster replied.

Her eyes wandered to the pinboard behind his desk,

where there were various newspaper clippings depicting the corpses of flayed women dragged from muddy rivers in the midwest. "Bill Skins Fifth," ran one headline.

"The one we want most refuses to cooperate," continued Scott Glenn. "I want you to go after him again today, in the asylum."

"Who's the subject?"

"The psychiatrist—Hannibal Lecter," said the FBI chief.

"Hannibal the Cannibal," whispered the FBI trainee, softly.

Christopher laid down the remote control and smiled at the screen. *Hannibal,* he whispered back, into the darkness of the room. *Just like me... remarkable.*

23

INDUSTRIAL BOROUGH, SOUTHWEST DUISBURG

Toby parked his Kawasaki outside the neon-lit entrance to the Club Eva Dance and Disco—a tacky table-dance dive in Hochfeld, owned by Darko and his associates (which he had been graciously introduced to at the barrel of a Skorpion machine-pistol). The joint had all the flair of a typical east European mobster hangout, with its decadent furnishings, silicon base podium with removable pole, red velvet curtains, pushy girls, indifferent barmen, an annoying emcee, Vin Diesel-esque bouncers, and the regulars tanned, wearing flip-flops, and belting out karaoke tunes over Radler and shots of Absolut.

Toby spotted Darko in the VIP area—a small raised stage near the curtained entrance, separated from the main room by a velvet rope barrier. He was sitting at a round table, with four of his thugs, one of whom was the bald, muscular goon that served as Darko's chauffeur. Toby didn't know his name, and he didn't really care to ask. If he had to call him something, it would be "Inkman," owing to the charming tattoo of a butterfly knife wrapped by barb wire that decorated his thick neck.

There was also a skinny, pouty Asian bimbo, sitting between Darko and Inkman, looking like Nicole Scherzinger of the Pussycat Dolls—on crack.

He walked slowly up to the group, who were all smoking and drinking and howling with laughter, except for the bimbo who sat very still and composed, her hands folded daintily in her lap, resting on a sleek designer purse. When they saw him standing there, the laughs petered out and Darko motioned for Toby to come closer.

Toby drew up to the table, standing just short of the VIP barrier.

"What are you doing here?" Darko asked him. "Run out of tapes already?"

"I came to bring you this—" Toby said, reaching into his motorcycle jacket and withdrawing the *Fatal Impulse* canister. He set it on the table, and Darko's cronies leaned in and looked at the small plastic cylinder with something akin to awe.

Darko drummed his fingers on the tablecloth and pursed his lips. His lazy eye glinted in the hazy light of the club.

"And where is your friend?" he asked quietly. The entire table was suddenly very still. A dance ended, to scattered applause, and a bad-ass Jentina-style (before she was slagged off by Lady Sovereign) Romanian stripper wearing a chain bra and white silk stockings, descended the stage and strode over to the bar and began chatting up a tourist.

"Dejan apologizes for not bringing it himself, but he is having some family trouble—he asked me to deliver this for you," Toby said, trying to keep as neutral an expression as possible.

Darko sucked his teeth and smacked his lips. He picked up the canister and opened it, checking the reel. He replaced it and closed the lid.

"Two copies are missing," he said, without missing a beat.

"I had to make a sale on the way," Toby replied. His heart was thumping hard. "The *Fatal Impulse* tape is one of our hottest sellers, as you know well…"

"Je to tako…" Darko agreed, scratching his cheek with a sharp fingernail. "Personally, I am quite tired of this tape. Personally I am weary of the wiles of Sharon Stone as this Kathleen character…" he chuckled, "although we seem to have a lot in common… And yes, she is 'the fuck of the century' as this American detective so candidly puts it… a fact I have had occasion to verify for myself while in the tapeworld, but I do not see the purpose for this fat nonsensical policeman with the cowboy hat, or this doctor with the rabbit teeth and all these endless charades of cat-and-hamster."

"You mean to say cat and mouse?"

"Yes, whatever," Darko waved him off, irritably. "But all of this is beside the point. What I mean to say is—what I want to make abundantly clear…" and he stared hard at Toby, his light wit abruptly leaving him, his face becoming a lean and shrunken scowl, "You boys better not be running anything on the side," he warned them. "Remember who is Papi Chulo."

Toby swallowed what felt like a cancerous growth in his throat. "You're Papi Chulo," he agreed.

The Asian chick sitting beside Darko mumbled

something, stirring in her seat, her head nodding and her eyelids fluttering as if she were in a trance. She looked blitzed. Suddenly she spoke up:

"…Sie kleiden Mich wie eine Puppe an! You even make my hair like a doll… why?"

Toby could not contain his curiosity. "What's wrong with her?" he asked Darko.

The mobster shrugged. "Mia likes tapes… too much for her own good. I keep telling her she shouldn't take so many… but I cannot make her listen. Now she is no good for anything, not the fucking and not even the dancing. Only for reciting movie dialogue and sleeping. But what can I do? She is my girl… I want her to be happy…"

The girl stood up abruptly and sleepwalked toward Toby, her hips swaying sensually. Her lush lips pouted and her soft face was flushed and carnal.

"You want me to be a doll forever?" she asked him.

While he was trying to make sense of her statement, the girl opened the black Fendi purse she was carrying, and withdrew a pair of hairdresser's scissors. She began to clip her hair, to the astonishment of Darko and his crew.

"Mia, what are you doing? Stop your foolishness. Sit down," Darko ordered, but she paid no attention to him. She kept cutting, letting strands of her long bleached hair fall onto the table and carpet.

Darko stood up. "Mia—ich warne Sie!"

The girl paused, turning slowly around and caught her reflection in a rococo mirror hanging on the wall behind the

VIP booth. She pulled at her remaining hair, letting out a horrible piercing scream that brought the whole club to a dead standstill. Even the metrosexual DJ trancing out in the tiny glass box near the chrome bar brought the mix to a screeching halt.

She whirled around angrily, pointing an accusatory finger at Toby.

"Which of you did it? Which of you made me the way I am?"

"Huh?"

"It wasn't always so!" the girl snapped, and her eyes were black expressionless saucers. "I had a mother once! And Louie—he had a wife! He was mortal the same as she. And so was I…"

"Stop talking nonsense!" Darko scolded her. "Sit down and quit making a scene. You've had too much to drink—"

And he pulled at her arm but she wrenched herself free and turned on Toby, her eyes blazing with coals of spite. "You made us what we are didn't you?"

"Stop her, Darko!" Toby said, frightened.

Mia screamed: "DID YOU DO IT TO ME?"

And she lunged at him, scoring his face with the scissors. Toby yelped in pain and fright, as dark droplets of blood ran down his cheeks and dripped onto the carpet.

The mobsters all jumped back, astonished by the outrageous lunacy of this assault. Darko seized Mia by the wrist and twisted it, hard—the scissors fell from her fingers and clattered on the table. She tottered on her long, slender legs and then she fell back against him, and shuddered, as if her whole body were collapsing. She rolled her eyes up at him and spoke in a scant whisper:

"I hate him. But I cannot bear to lose you. You're the only companion I have, forever. You taught me everything I know. Please tell me Louie. Tell me how it came to be that I am this... thing..."

"Sie ist total verrückt!" Toby hissed angrily, dabbing at his wounded cheek with a paper napkin. "What the fucking hell is going on? What's the matter with her?"

"She's stuck... in between worlds," said Darko, delicately stroking the girl's ruined hair. She closed her eyes and her lip movements were now almost imperceptible. "Sometimes she is with us... other times she is not herself." He gestured to Toby's face, "It's just a flesh wound," he said. "Don't make a big fucking deal of it—Albino Boy. Come on—sit down... Don't be afraid. She didn't mean you any harm. See how she sleeps? So peacefully... like an infant..." He pushed the girl to the side and her body toppled over against the suede leather sofa. He patted the space left in her wake... "Take a seat."

Toby reluctantly did as told, keeping a careful eye on the sleeping girl. The scratch was a minor one, and the bleeding soon stopped. But he was amazed at how fast she had moved. Almost inhumanly fast.

"I've got an errand for you, now that you're here..." explained Darko, his spidery fingers caressing the gold orthodox cross that hung from his wiry neck. He opened Mia's purse and took out a sheet of colored paper and handed it to Toby. On the paper was a printed the cover poster to Neil Jordan's film adaptation of Anne Rice's *Rendezvous With The Bloodsucker*. The grainy, chromatic tone of the image of Tom Cruise's reptilian gaze hovering over Brad Pitt's wounded and brooding vampire, and the child vampire Chloe standing nearby, wrapped in a dark cloak, made everything clear to Toby. Darko's nammer girl had been acting out a scene from *Rendezvous*—he held the paper closer and saw that it was composed of hundreds of tiny blotters. So this was a sheet of tapes—only they didn't look anything like the tapes he picked up in Venlo. They weren't put together on a strip, and they had previously been fabricated in monochromatic series, not as these puzzle-like pieces. He wondered if this was another laboratory's production.

"You take this to Hamburg," Darko instructed him. "Go to the Rote Flora. Ask for a girl named Maja Jung and deliver them to her. Tell her that this is for the platform."

"What platform? Where do these come from?" Toby ventured.

"Hey! Ruhe!" Darko snarled. "Too many fucking questions. Don't go getting ahead of yourself. I want you there tonight, OK?"

Toby nodded, picking up the sheet of blotters. "Can I fold this?" he asked. "For safekeeping…"

Darko dipped a finger in a cocktail glass, swirled his vodka-caramel, "As many times as you like." He licked it. "But just remember who is Papi Chulo."

Toby left the Club Eva with 500 copies of *Rendezvous With The Bloodsucker* in the cargo pocket of his lined motocross pants. He decided to try and contact Dejan, to see if he had been able to successfully retrieve Milinka from the *Fatal Impulse* tapeworld. If he was still stuck there, then Toby would have no option but to call the EMS and give them Dejan's home address. It had now been close to two hours since Dejan had entered the tapeworld, and he knew that if he hadn't re-surfaced by now, it was a hopeless case.

He scrolled Dejan's number, pressed the call key and waited…

His handy buzzed for fifteen long seconds, and Toby was about to cut the connection when someone picked up.

"Hello?"

"Dede, is that you?"

"Who is this—" the person asked. It was a female voice on the phone, with a sort of rough and raspy edge to it.

"Sind Sie der Milinka?" Toby inquired.

There was a long pause and then the person replied, "Yes. I'm Milinka—"

Toby breathed a heavy sigh of relief. "I'm glad to hear it… how's Dejan? How are you both—I thought you would never get out!"

"Who are you?" Milinka asked, and Toby realized that she could not know his identity. They'd never met.

"I'm a friend of Dejan's," he said. "Is he there?"

"… he's gone out," she informed him blandly. "Should

I tell him that you called when he returns?"

"Yes. Just tell him that I got the stuff with me… I took care of it… tell him Toby took care of everything."

"So your name is Toby?"

"Ja."

"Nice to meet you, so to speak," she laughed dryly. "Maybe you'd like to come by the house sometime? I'd like to put a face to that sweet voice of yours…"

What the hell kind of skank is Dejan coupled with, Toby thought. He could have sworn by the sensual tone of voice that Dejan's girlfriend was giving him the come-on.

"I'll come by when Dejan is back," he said. Then, "Do you know where he went?"

"Too bad," the girl said, ignoring his question. "I had a feeling we'd hit it off…" she exhaled softly. "Well, I'd love to talk more with you, but I've got some things to care of first— if you change your mind you can always drop on by…"

"Milinka—" Toby started but the connection went dead. He uttered a mild curse and then he tucked his iPhone away. *What was going on with Dejan? Where could he have gone? And why did Milinka have his handy?* He had a queer feeling that their problems were far from over.

He climbed onto his Kawasaki and kicked up the stand. It was beginning to rain, and the asphalt was slick. He put on his crash helmet decorated with a cartoon caption of UK grimster queen Lady Sov—shoving her revolted fist at the viewer. He had a good three-hour ride to Hamburg and he was hungry, so he decided to find a drive-in KFC, accosting two

Bandidos bikers who were entering the stripclub to ask for directions.

When he throttled the engine and took off, with a long screeching burn, he passed by a silvery Audi 6 parked on the corner of the street, opposite an Indian night shop.

A few seconds after he had zipped by, the headlights of the Audi illuminated and the car rolled onto the street and accelerated on his trail.

24

(FATAL IMPULSE TAPEWORLD)

The stab never came! The doorbell rang—again—and Sharon Stone paused, her arms still raised high and the ice pick clenched in her neatly manicured and deadly fingers. She cocked her head and listened as the visitor insisted. Then she looked down at Dejan's bound figure, stared right into his eyes which were wide with fright, and she gave him an icy look and said, "We'll have to finish this later, darling."

She climbed lithely off him and exited the guest bedroom, taking care to shut the door behind her. The minute she was gone Dejan began to pull at his bindings, thrashing wildly about, pulling as far as his restraints would allow... the bed creaked, and his muscles ached and cramped, his entire body was soon slick with perspiration, but he simply could not break free.

Frustrated and anguished beyond belief, he started to swear at her absence. The gag muffled his indignant yelps, but the translated version went like this:

"Bloody whore! You fucking Buddhist cunt! I hate this fucking movie! I hate Paul Verhoeven. I hate the 90s! I hate *Last Dance* and *Sliver* and that god-awful *Catwoman*! I hate every goddamn movie you were in with the exception of *Last Action Hero*... and you were only in that as a CAMEO!!!"

He ranted and raved for several interminable minutes, and then he stopped as he heard a man's voice in the foyer downstairs. He listened carefully. It sounded like Detective Curry speaking... like he had returned with a Colombo-like insistence on one last wheedle! Or was this another original movie scene playing?

He contorted his body with renewed vigor, flopping up and down, trying to shake the whole bed and create a racket... he Linda Blaired the bed until it rumbled against the floorboards. He screamed against his gag, the sock drowning out his cries for help until only a low muffled groan escaped. This wasn't going to work! He'd have to get rid of the gag if he wanted the man downstairs to have a chance of hearing him... but how?

Swallow the sock.

I can't... I'll choke to death.

It's a tapeworld... you can't die... at the very worst you'll wake up...

But I'm afraid to... what if I can't breathe?

Trust the programmers. They wouldn't let someone asphyxiate in a tapeworld. It's bad for business. Swallow the sock...

He tried it. Steadying his nerves he twisted his tongue and sucked the twisted bundle deep into the back of his throat... it stuck against his tonsils, and his gag reflex kicked in and Dejan bolted upwards like a fish on a line, his eyes bugging out of their sockets, he was choking!

Don't spit it out! Swallow the goddamn sock! It's a tapeworld... you can't die here... it's only a programmed trick...

And he fought the gag reflex, sucking even harder, gulping down the sock, taking it all the way to the back of his throat… sure he would never be able to breathe… that he had made a fatal mistake.

But it vanished. The sock disappeared! Dejan sucked in air greedily through his nostrils, the lump in his throat had gone. His mouth was empty! There was only the tape over his lips and he licked at it to moisten it so that it would unstick.

His voice came through easily now:

"HELP ME! I'M UP HERE! GODDAMIT! CAN ANYBODY HEAR ME? HELP ME!!!"

There was a moment's silence and then he heard footsteps bolting up the main stairway, and he heard Kathleen's chilly voice, "Nicky! Wait! What are you doing? I told you I was alone…"

"I'M IN HERE!" Dejan yelled. "LET ME OUT!!"

He heard some commotion, doors being opened and shut down the hall, footsteps zig-zagging this way and that, and then the door to the bedroom flew open and Michael Douglas stared straight at him, his beady, intense eyes quickly assessing the situation. He was bedecked in his Nino Cerruti wool suit, the one he had been wearing down at the station, and Dejan knew that this was the Nicky Curry from the secondary tapeworld… the one who he had spoken to upon his arrival, planting a seed of doubt concerning Kathleen Kastel. He recognized Dejan instantly.

"It's you!" he said. Then gave him his typical Michael Douglas white-male paranoia act: "What the hell's going on here?"

"She did it!" Dejan gasped, "Untie me, please!"

Michael Douglas nodded and rushed forwards; undoing the knots at Dejan's wrists... he was leaned over him, so close that Dejan could see his laser-whitened teeth and his immaculately groomed hair slightly graying at the temples. He'd just freed Dejan's hands when he said, "Will you tell me what the hell is happening?"

"Look out!" Dejan screamed, as Sharon Stone appeared behind him. The detective spun around, but it was too late— she drove the ice pick directly into his throat! Arterial blood spurted from his wound, splattering her pretty face. He chortled as she drove the pick in again and again, stabbing him repeatedly in his throat, face, chest... echoes of *Psycho*—he crumpled to the floor in a low whimper and Kathleen Kastel gnashed her teeth and sprang at Dejan.

He blocked her attack, seizing her by the wrist, crunching her pricy Kieselstein-Cord alligator bracelet. She threw her entire weight on him, struggling to drive the pick into his throat. His arms shook as he held the point of the weapon just an inch above the jugular... straining against her, then he twisted her wrist violently and she shrieked as he diverted the point of the pick away and head-butted her in the face, sending her reeling backwards.

He grabbed her by her silky blonde hair and pounded his fist into her face, feeling the bones in her nose mash as her blood dripped onto the silk bed sheets. She slumped over, groaning. He leaned forward, quickly undoing the bindings at his ankles.

He got off the bed, moving in a daze, picking up his clothes, unsure of what to do. He dressed quickly, putting on his pants and shoes. He rushed for the door... she cried out and threw herself at him, her face an angry mask of blood, grabbing him around the leg with one arm, her right hand groping for the fallen ice pick....

"I'm going to kill you!" she shrieked, as her fingers wrapped around it.

Dejan pivoted around and hit her twice with his fists and slammed his knee with bone-crushing force into her jaw. Left, right, Thai kick! This time the hit was a home run. Sharon grunted and toppled over and plopped dead on the carpet, right on top of Michael Douglas' prone figure; the two lay there together, hero and villain, sandwiched in a manner of near poetic irony.

"How's that for the *Quick and the Dead*?" Dejan smirked.

He searched quickly through Detective Curry's clothes, taking his badge, his wallet and his gun. He also took the keys to his Ford Mustang GT and ran away—hoping to get to the nightclub before Foxy approached his girlfriend...

NORTH BIMINI ISLAND, BAHAMAS

Christopher Venet sat on the terrace of a small outdoor café shack, opposite a seaplane ramp, just off a busy street in the heart of Alice Town—a settlement of shanty houses painted in tropical hues of lime, peach, turquoise and sunset pink, accented by white windows and screen doors. The street was heavily congested with colorfully dressed locals and tourists strolling by in thongs and Bermuda shorts, heading to the restaurants and shops at the water's edge, or to the Bimini straw market to pick up souvenirs.

He had returned from the open-air market where he had purchased an elegant Panama hat that now rested on his lap. He wore a clean and spanking-new linen suit, shades over his eyes, and his widow's peak was obscured by a crafty blond wig.

He picked up the pay phone receiver and dialed an international number.

The phone rang only once before his mother picked up, some 7,500 kilometers away…

"Hello. Who is this?"

"Well Marie, have the sheep stopped bleating?" he whispered.

"Christopher!" she gasped, frantically. "What's going on? Where are you? What have you done! I can't believe what they're saying about you… you didn't kill all those people, tell me you didn't!"

"Don't bother with a trace," he replied calmly. "I won't be on long enough…"

"Where are you, Christopher?"

"I have no plans to call on you, Marie," he said. "The world's more interesting with you in it. So you take care now to extend me the same courtesy…"

"What… What do you mean? I don't understand?" she stammered.

"I do wish we could chat longer," he told her, watching an incoming seaplane taxi on the ramp. "But… I'm having an old friend for dinner. Bye."

He hung up, as his mother called out his name. His fingers poised on the receiver for a moment as he watched passengers dismount the plane. He was searching among them for a very particular and smarmy individual in a checkered suit. He could not hear his mother blindly repeating his name on the other end:

"Christopher… Christopher… Christopher… CHRISTOPHER!"

He stood up slowly and put on his straw hat, and then he stepped out from under the shade of the terrace, leaving his piña colada untouched, and adjusted his brim as he made his way tranquilly down the crowded, palm-lined street—in search of a man named Dr. Chilton whom he would never find.

The call ended and the Europol agents and Marie all stared mutely at the Caller ID number displayed on the LCD screen on her digital house phone: 242–347–35012.

"He said don't bother with a trace," said Officer Perrin. "Why would he think a house phone can't track a landline number?"

"Because his thinking is twenty years outdated," explained Officer Lambert. "In his mind, if his call were to last under one minute, it cannot be traced. It's standard movie fare."

"I'll look up the number… find where he is," said Perrin, typing on his laptop.

"Go ahead and check, but I believe I already know where he is…"

Marie Venet chewed her fingernails, and stared at the Europol agent in anticipation.

"He's in the Bahamas, I suspect," said Officer Lambert.

"The Bahamas?" Marie gasped. "What would my boy be doing there?"

"You're right," Perrin confirmed, after running his search. "He's somewhere in a place called Alice Town."

"He's looking for Dr. Chilton," said Lambert, stroking his chin thoughtfully. "Contact the local authorities through our home office, put out a bulletin for Christopher. Warn them that he is most likely armed and highly dangerous."

Marie slumped onto the sofa in shock. Her hands felt clammy and cold. How, in the course of just a few short weeks could her son have transformed from a sweet and innocent seventeen-year-old boy into a ruthless and lethal fugitive with the cunning of a mature killer? And what was all this business with the movies? Christopher had always been a film fanatic, but certainly his obsession could not have taken him so far that he was now actually acting out scenes from films.

"I don't believe he will return here," said Officer Lambert. "Not to France, in any case. And I doubt he will stay in the Bahamas for long. He's going to leave the island as soon as he finds out that Dr. Chilton is nowhere to be found."

"Who is Dr. Chilton?" Marie asked, feeling faint and confused. The whole situation was so alarmingly surreal, she had to pinch herself.

"He's a fictional character in a film called *The Silence of the Lambs*," said Perrin. "A movie Christopher appears to be imitating…"

"Christopher wants to kill him," explained Lambert. "But he won't be able to, because Dr. Chilton does not exist in the real world, and so he will leave the island and go to the city where he has always dreamed of living…"

"Where? Where is he going?" Marie whispered.

"Florence," Lambert said. "With maybe a brief stopover in South America for some plastic surgery… I don't know if that's mentioned in the book or the film… but we'll contact the authorities in Rio as well. But he is most definitely going to wind up in Florence… unless they can arrest him in the Bimini Islands. But I'm not sure they will succeed…"

"Why not?" Marie inquired nervously. "Surely they should be able to bring him in. He's just a boy… he's not insane… he's just…" she exhaled softly. "So you mean to say… you really believe he thinks he is this movie character? This Hannibal Lecter?" Marie questioned Officer Lambert. She gave a short dry and nervous laugh. "That's ridiculous…" But she did not sound convinced.

That's the trouble, thought Officer Lambert quietly to himself. *I don't know if the boy simply believes he is Hannibal, or if he actually is Hannibal.*

(*HYDROWORLD* TAPEWORLD)

"I thought we were in for a nice romantic weekend," Heike nagged Matthias, as they reached the skydeck of the supertanker's weathered wheelhouse. She looked over at Kevin Costner who was standing tall, stoically squinting at the entrance to the cabin, his seashell earring glinting in the hot sun.

"Oh like *Triassic Park* is a walk in the park, no pun intended," Matthias shot back. He bumped the navigator on the shoulder. "Honestly… off the record. Were you on ecstasy when you got involved in that *Postman* project?"

Costner glared at him. "What are you talking about?"

"Just checking," Matthias patted him on the back. "Hey is that a Rolex on your arm?"

"Touch me again and I'll kill you," the navigator said, in a low-key sort of way.

"Mensch!"

Matthias took a wide step back, raised his eyebrows at Heike and leaned against the skydeck railing.

One of their captors pushed past them and entered the wheelhouse. The other one pulled out a pack of Black Death cigarettes and began to smoke vigorously, while propping the scratched barrel of his shotgun against the rubber shoulder pads tacked to his carp-skin vest.

From inside the cabin they could hear two men having

a dispute:

"They ain't gonna row forever—it don't matter how many of those speeches you give… we're nearly out of the black stuff."

"Don't you think I know that! Now I promised them results and I'm gonna get 'em. I swear by Saint Joe…"a man snarled. And then his voice softened, and took on a false friendliness as he addressed himself to someone else.

"Now you were saying that Chinesey thing on your back… is actually a map?"

"It shows the way to dryland," a little girl said.

They heard the man inside respond with excitement, "So it *is* a map! Now we're making progress… how about we make a deal and I'll give you some of these crayons… I know you like to draw…" Then some interruptive whispering and the man snapped, "Hell… what is it now? Can't you see I'm busy talking to my friend here?"

Some more whispering and then clunky footsteps like boots on a plank floor. "Well don't leave 'em standing out there, it ain't polite. Bring 'em in to your bishop-ship."

The smoker came back out, an impish grin on his tarred face. "Get in here, all of you!" he ordered.

They marched Heike and Matthias and the nameless navigator into the pilot room which was an apocalyptic hovel made of metal, cardboard and plastic flotsam, that had been rudely fitted together into a crude lounge.

A small girl sat on a makeshift sofa that had been fashioned from a salvaged car seat covered by a plastic tarp. She wore a raggedy silk dress colorfully decorated with felt-tip marker drawings of plants and waterfalls. Beside her was a tall, able-bodied Nordic man, brandishing a kludged-together futuristic weapon that looked like a blend between a rifle and a whale-bone.

And then there was the leader of the marauders, the Bishop himself!

He stood before them, looking like a strange cross between a pirate and a priest. He wore a biker's leather jacket with spring-laden epaulets, and dried blowfish attached to the shoulders. On top of his thuggish head was a bishop's miter. He had a long shawl draped around him, to which were attached bits of junk: bottle caps and radio parts, Band-Aid boxes and squashed dolls heads. He looked very crazy. Heike clutched her boyfriend tightly around the arm.

"Matty, who is he?" she whispered.

"Dennis Hopper," Matty whispered back. "But he's dead in real life."

"So sorry to disappoint," the Bishop said, extending his arms to them benevolently. "But I'm very much alive and kicking!"

"I was talking about you as an actor... I mean a real person..." Matthias tried to explain, his voice trailing off as he realized that both Dennis Hopper and his chief lieutenant had no idea what he was on about.

The Bishop stepped toward them, his salvaged Adidas golf shoes making the cabin floor planks creak. He regarded Matthias and Heike curiously and then his gaze turned to

Kevin Costner, who stood unflinching, looking ready to kill the first person that touched him, as he had warned Matthias.

"My, my... what do we have here!" the Bishop exclaimed. He looked Costner up and down, spotting his webbed feet, and then he grabbed him by the chin, and Costner's jaws clenched and his muscles bunched as Dennis Hopper twisted his head to the side and pulled back his ears, checking his gills.

"An icky freak! A mute-O!" he jested. "A human-fish for the organo sludge tank!"

"You shouldn't make fun of him," the girl said. "Just because he's different..."

The Bishop whirled around, beserk. "I'll get to you in a minute! I'm gonna find out what's on that goddamn map if I have to cut it from your back." Then he turned his attention back to Matthias and Heike.

"Where do you come from?"

"Duisburg," replied Matthias. "That's a city in West Germany—"

The Bishop stared baffled at the smoker guards who were standing behind them. "Where did you pick these two up?"

"On his boat," said one of the jet-ski pilots, pointing to the navigator. "They said they came from Dryland!"

"Holy Saint Joe Almighty! I knew it!" Dennis Hopper cackled triumphantly. "I knew my visions were the Gospel truth... and now these two come from the promised land and into my fortress! Here look at this!" He grabbed the atoller girl by the arm and dragged her from the sofa. She squealed as he turned her around, revealing the ideogrammed map on her back. "Do you know what this is?"

"That's Tina Majorino," said Heike. "She's Napoleon Dynamite's girlfriend..."

"Ew! I don't have a boyfriend," the girl objected.

"Shut up, granola!" The viking-looking chief lieutenant snapped.

"It's Enola—" the girl shot back. "And Helen and Gregor are going to come looking for me..."

"Ooh... I'm so scared," he taunted her.

Dennis Hopper removed his miter and ran a grubby hand over his lumpy, bald scalp. He came so close to Heike that she could feel his hot breath in her face. He smelled unpleasantly of leather, oil and dead fish.

"Decipher the map for me, and I'll let you live—hell, I'll even give you a job on the 'Deez! You can go down to the baffle and row with the crew! Your boyfriend can work in the refinery..."

"Thanks, but we'll pass," said Matthias. "We're eco-friendly... you know... going green and all that? You heard about Greenpeace? No? Save the whales..."

The Bishop's pudding face twitched at this statement. "Boy you must be gone plum crazy from drinking saltwater! Save the whales... I hate whales! If I ever catch one I'm going to cut open it's big fat head and I'm gonna eat its brains! Now if you neither of you will talk, we're gonna make you useful..." He motioned to the smoker guards standing beside them.

"Take the boy and the freak below... put 'em in the galley with the oarsmen. As for you—" he tickled Heike's chin, "you're stayin' right here with me! You're gonna be the 'Deez's hood ornament..."

The guards grabbed Matthias and the Navigator, brutally separating them from Heike and Enola.

"Matty!" his girlfriend squealed.

"Quiet!" the norseman cuffed her across the head.

"You're making a big mistake," Matthias said bravely to the Bishop. He elbowed the navigator. "Tell them... huh, Kevin..."

"That's not my name," the navigator said.

"Ha! He doesn't even have a name!" Dennis Hopper scoffed.

"That's so death can't find him," said Matthias ominously. The norseman and the Bishop burst out laughing.

"He doesn't have a home, or people to care for," Matthias continued, as their laughter died out in the face of his sincerity. "He's not afraid of anything, men least of all. He's fast and strong like Jackie Chan on steroids. He can hear for a hundred miles and see a hundred miles underwater. He can whip up an omelette with his bare fingers! He can hide in the shadow of a midnightsun. He could be right behind you and you wouldn't even know it 'til you're dead!"

For a moment it seemed that his dramatic speech had actually frightened them, and then the spell was broken by the sound of Kevin Costner clearing his throat.

"Uh... that's not true," said the navigator, glancing

oddly at Matthias. "I'm just your average drifter… trying to get by."

"Jeez! Why do you have to destroy the myth?" Matthias groaned. "I was trying to make you look like a hero—not a grungy survivalist who drinks his piss from a pyrex beaker!"

"All right you, that's enough! Take 'em below," the Bishop ordered.

The guards pushed and shoved Matthias and Costner through the segmented belly of the tanker—taking a series of ladderways down to the undersection—hot drafts of sunlight entering in through jagged holes in the steel ceilings, where the metal had been stripped for the marauders to fabricate bullets and weapons. Oil fires burned in trash barrels, around which scores of the tanker's hyperactive crew were gathered, hooting and acting rowdy, descending sliding poles and chain ladders from the deck and scurrying into the bowels of the ship. Welding sparks rained down from the forge on one of the upper levels, where munitions were being fabricated in preparation for an assault on the nearest atoll.

"Come on, react goddamit!" Matthias harangued the navigator, as they reached the oar room, where the marauders were shoving massive, ironclad paddles through rusted oarholes, churning the water in a fanatical frenzy as the great vessel slowly gained momentum…

"I thought you were supposed to be a kickass antihero—don't take no shit from nobody! Every damn movie you play in you're the hero: *Robin Hood*, *Wyatt Earp*, *The*

Bodyguard… Field of Dreams… You're the most self-serving actor in Hollywood. Do something for chrissakes!"

"Don't you ever shut up?" Costner wailed. "You're the damn reason I'm here in the first place! I should have never taken you on my boat… I…"

"Oi! Get rowing you two!"a grimy, soot-faced galley captain, in rawhide trousers, his torso slick with oil and sweat, growled at them. He had a Black Death cigarette stuck between a gap in his upper teeth, and a stupid tire-brim cap atop his head. He pointed behind him to the gung-ho crew who were heaving it out Ben Hur-style.

The captain watched them as they were forced to pick up one of the insanely heavy oars and struggle to keep up with the infernal rhythm.

"Row!" The galley captain screamed to his crew of psychos. "Row! Row! Row!"

"I'm rowing! I'm rowing! For shit's sake" Matthias whimpered. "Jesus, what's this obsession with getting to Dryland…"

Beside him, Kevin Costner gritted his teeth as he strained at the oar handle. "Dryland… doesn't… exist…" he grunted between strokes.

"How can you be sure?"

"Because I haven't seen it, and I've sailed further than most men have dreamed!"

Matthias cracked a grin. "Haha, I knew you would say that. But for real, it does exist. It's basically the top of Mount Everest," He replied, noting that despite the effort he was not feeling in the least bit fatigued. It seemed that there was little in the tapeworld in the way of actual physical discomfort.

"We've got to get out of here!" Costner whispered, looking around him at the galley crew who were grunting and groaning with effort, yo-yoing back and forth as they dragged the massive oars, their textured carp-skin boots clunking on the oil pipes underneath their feet. "I saw a scout plane on the upper deck. If we can make it there, we can fly away from here."

"What about my girlfriend? And Enola?"

"You want to stay on this goddamn barge and play hide and seek with that crazy Bishop, that's your problem," Costner barked. "As for me, I'm getting the hell out!"

"And the oil tank?"

The navigator cocked his head. "What about it?"

"Say we dropped a flare down the hatch and into the reservoir... in Hydroworld... uh I mean *here*... that's the way you blew the 'Deez to smithereens... it's worth a try..."

He could see Costner thinking carefully about this. "Now you're talking sense," he said. "See that big ugly goon there," he hinted at the galley captain who was striding up and down the ranks, puffing his cigarette and yelling out obscenities. "I'm gonna lure him over here and snatch his crossbow... and you neutralize the other guard... grab one of those chains and choke the nicotine-addicted bastard!"

"How do you want to bring him over here—"

Pow! Kevin Costner belted Matthias a left hook to the face. He sprawled on the steel floor, and some members of the crew were distracted from their labors by the commotion.

"You hit me!" Matthias bellowed, rubbing his jaw where Costner had socked it! "I'm gonna show you who's untouchable!"

He scrambled to his feet and swiped at Kevin Costner, who deflected his blow, enraging him even further. Matthias swung at the movie star, going in with an old combination Ali shuffle. He got a jab in just under Costner's cheekbone.

The galley captain came running over, his fishbone crossbow clenched in his oily hands. "Oi! What's going on here? Break it up you two!"

The rowing marauders were chanting in excitement. "Fight! Fight! Fight!"

"Come on, that's enough," the captain grabbed ahold of Kevin Costner who instantly Zidaned him one to the face, squashing his tire-brim cap and busting his nose, which spurted blood. The captain yowled and lifted his crossbow and Costner drove his knee into his groin, and he doubled over, choking.

The other smoker guard ran at them, hollering and brandishing a sawfish rostrum. The navigator wrenched the crossbow from the captain's hand and fired a bolt at him—it pierced him straight through the sternum and he slumped to the floor, his weapon slipping from his grip.

The whole galley stared dumbstruck at the dead guard and then they dropped their oars and charged Matthias and the navigator.

Matthias grabbed the sawfish axe from the dead guards' hands and swung it into the face of the nearest smoker, gouging out his eye. Costner smashed the heavy stock of the crossbow into another's gut before letting loose a bolt into the throat of a third.

Two of the marauders whipped heavy chains at Matthias, who deflected them with his axe, while Kevin Costner delivered a powerful roundhouse kick to another, smacking his webbed foot so hard into the marauder's face that he swallowed his cigarette.

"Let's get out of here!" Costner yelled.

They ran from the oar room, and through a hole in the bulkhead, being chased by the rabid crew, Matthias struggling to keep up with the Navigator, as he darted this way and that, through the dense maze of perforated ballast tanks, the shouts and excited cries of their adversaries gaining in intensity, as more marauders joined in the pursuit, and some of them began firing automatic weapons, harpoons and bows at them. Bullets and arrows ricocheted off the steel walls and ladders and hydraulic pumps—whizzing past them as they climbed through the stratifications toward the upper deck.

All around them were flames, sparks, chains and metal—it was like being in an Alice Cooper music video!

"I can see the plane!" Matthias exclaimed, as they moved through a wing tank and up another corrugated hold ladder, toward a wide hole in the deck where they could see the Bishop's single-engine Helio Courier seaplane—lounging on the aftcastle of the tanker.

They darted across the open deck and toward it, crouching behind a giant metal shipping container, listening to the armed marauders searching the galleries below them.

Costner rummaged through the heaps of debris scattered around the container, among the nets and buoys and plastic flotsam, and he found a crude leather helmet and two pairs of goggles.

"Put these on," he said to Matthias. "And this—" He punched a hole in a plastic tarp so Matthias could wear it like a raincoat. "Now you look like one of them," he said. "Except for that underwear—why aren't you wearing any pants?"

"I left them in *Triassic Park*," said Matthias.

Costner's eyebrows lifted just a fraction. "Please don't go into detail," he said.

They moved out from behind the container and toward the seaplane when a voice called out to them loudly over a speaker system.

"Hey you!"

Kevin Costner and Matthias froze and looked up, where they could see the Bishop and his consorts standing on the rust-stained railed balcony jutting out from the bridge. The norseman was holding Tina Majorino, who was kicking away and biting at his hands, and two other goons were pawing their grease-stained grubby hands over his girlfriend.

"Why aren't you two rowing?" the Bishop called out, not recognizing either of them.

"Oh shit," Matthias groaned. "They've spotted us!"

Kevin Costner shrugged and continued toward the seaplane. Matthias grabbed him by the arm.

"What are you doing?"

"I'm getting off this damn ship!"

"But my girlfriend—and Enola… this is the part where you burn the whole shizit down and save the day!"

"I don't know what you're talking about—" the navigator said. "I'm not here to save anybody…"

"Get back down with the others!" the Bishop ordered.

Matthias realized it was up to him to do what chickenshit Costner wouldn't. He took a step forward and removed his goggles, revealing himself to the pirates.

"Well I'll be damned," said the Bishop. "It's the gentleman yuppie and the gentlemen guppy." He took a draw off his cigarette and looked around at his henchmen. "You know you're both like a couple of turds that just won't flush."

Matthias pointed his finger up at Heike.

"I want the girl," he said. "Actually I want both girls…"

Heike cried out, "Matty!" And she tried to pull away from her captors. The chief lieutenant cocked his whale-bone shotgun. Enola kicked him in the shin and he howled in pain and slapped her across the head.

"You know, I thought you were stupid, friend," said Dennis Hopper, puffing on his cigarette. "But I underestimated you. You're a total freakin' retard!"

"I want the girl," Matthias repeated. "That's all…"

The Bishop cackled villainously. "Well what on this screwed up earth makes you think you're going to get her?"

Matthias looked at the mouth of the open tank hatch which led down to the fuel reservoir. It was then that he realized he didn't have a flare or a torch with him. He nudged Kevin Costner in the ribs.

"What do you want?"

"A light! Give me the flare!"

"I don't have one," Costner mumbled. "And thanks for blowing our cover."

"Jesus, you're totally useless," sighed Matthias in exasperation. "No wonder your career is in the shitter…"

Dennis Hopper began laughing like a maniac. "Golly gee! I don't know which of you is the bigger freak!" He turned to his viking lieutenant. "Kill 'em both."

The norseman aimed his hybrid shotgun down at them…

"No!" Heike cried out.

"Later," said the very unheroic tapeworld Kevin Costner, and he sprinted off toward the seaplane and Matthias ran the other way as the norseman and the other guards on the bridge fired at them. A line of machine-gun shells spattered along the runway. Matthias dove for cover behind the carcass of an old automobile, as a spray of bullets pocked into its corroded shell. Costner jumped in the Helio and throttled it— as the plane began to roll down the deck gathering speed the Bishop's men fired at it.

Costner made it to a tentative lift-off just before his right wing exploded and the plane tilted and came crashing down again on the runway, its fuselage bursting into flames. A moment later he ran, hollering, out of the wreckage with his hair and clothes on fire, and sprinted like a human torch to the edge of the tanker and dove off it into the water.

Up on the balcony the Bishop and his goons were

laughing heartily. Then they spotted a flying machine breaking through the clouds over the horizon and descending to the tanker.

"What the hell is that?" Dennis Hopper's voice echoed over the loudspeakers.

"It's Helen! I told you she'd come," Enola said. "You guys are in so much trouble—"

Matthias craned his neck and saw a creaky-looking dirigible of stitched-together old rags, breaking through the clouds, with two people aboard it, waving their arms and shouting.

He popped his head from behind the car's frame. "JUMP!" he yelled up at Heike. He ducked down as the norseman fired a spray of lead and a side window shattered.

"WHAT?" Heike yelled back.

Matthias stood up again. "I SAID JUMP! IT'S A TAPEWORLD! YOU WON'T GET HURT!"

A flame-lit crossbow bolt whizzed past his ear. Matthias crouched down low.

The Bishop pointed to the zeppelin flying in over the forecastle. "Shoot it down!" he ordered his men. "We're having ourselves a hot-air balloon barbecue!"

The marauders hooted and turned their attention to the incoming aircraft—bolts and bullets whistled through the air, some of them striking against the wicker basket. Inside it a woman cried out, "Bring us in closer!"

"I can't, it's too dangerous—"a man in the pilot chair called back.

Matthias took advantage of the distracting apparatus to stand up again.

"JUMP!" Matthias instructed his girlfriend. "LIKE IN *THE MATRIX*! YOU HAVE TO LET IT ALL GO! FEAR, DOUBT... DISBELIEF... FREE YOUR MIND AND JUMP!"

Up on the bridge his girlfriend nodded. She grabbed Enola and said, "Do you trust me?"

"No," Enola replied.

"Well you're going to have to! Climb on my back... and hold on tight, spider-monkey..."And she picked up Tina Majorino and swung her onto her back. She bit her lip and said a prayer before climbing up on the railing, overlooking a sixty-foot drop to the tanker deck.

"What the hell do you think you're doing! Get back here—" Dennis Hopper grabbed at her, but Heike leaped from the balustrade, falling through the air with Tina Majorino shrieking in her ear, the ground rushing up to strike her in the face.

She landed with a loud metallic thud on her bare feet, the shock of the impact sent her toppling over and Enola fell beside her. There was a slight jolt of pain in her ankles, but other than that she was miraculously unharmed.

Up on the bridge Dennis Hopper's cigarette fell from his lips. "Well... I'll be damned..."

"Are you all right?" Heike asked the girl. She nodded. "Come on—let's get out of here!"

They sprinted across the deck, dodging fire, and

Matthias ran to join them. The flying machine was now hovering above the smouldering wreckage to the Bishop's plane, its tail propeller spinning, and Helen (Jeanne Tripplehorn—again) threw them down a rope from the balloon basket.

"Grab onto this!" she called down.

Matthias seized the rope in his hands and began to shimmy up it, while Heike did the same with Enola on her back, clutching her around the neck.

"You—can—hang—on… a little… less tight spider-monkey," Heike coughed.

Up in the aircraft, Helen pulled at the rope with all her strength. Matthias reached the basket and climbed inside.

"Hi. How's it going? How come all the stars from the 90s end up in television serials?"

Jeanne Tripplehorn stared at him vacantly.

"Ah, nevermind… hot bodice by the way…"

"Take us away, Gregor," Helen said to the pilot. He tipped his windmill-hat and flipped a lever in his control box.

Suddenly there was a heavy tug on the rope, and it stuck as she and Matthias struggled to bring it up.

"What was that?" Helen said. She looked down the length of cord, where Heike was still climbing up, about midway, with Tina Majorino clinging on to her. At the bottom of the rope was Dennis Hopper, climbing after them, and gnashing his teeth as he reached for Enola's leg.

"I ain't finished with you yet!"

The dirigible swung out, over the water. Enola kicked

at the Bishop and then shrieked as he caught hold of her leg. His hand slipped and one of her shoes came off and fell down into the waves. He seized her by the ankle.

"Haha! Gotcha now!" Hopper cackled. "I'm gonna rip your cute little lungs out! They can have what's left of you in a goddamn jar!"

Helen grabbed a bottle of Hydro from inside the basket and threw it down at the Bishop, striking him in his forehead. He slipped from the rope and fell gracelessly into the cold water, with a loud splash, resurfacing and shaking his fist up at them.

"I'll get you for this!"

"Nice shot," Matthias complimented Helen.

"Thanks—" she grimaced, pulling at the rope. Heike reached the brim of the basket and toppled inside with Enola, who threw herself into her surrogate-mother's arms.

Jeanne Tripplehorn regarded them curiously. "Thanks for helping us… whoever you are… you don't know how much she means to me…"

"Sure we do," said Matthias. "She's the key to Dryland."

The old mechanical wizard of a pilot sitting in the kludged up patio chair above them looked down in surprise and said, "My friend, it seems you are privy to our biggest secret—"

"How do you know…" Helen looked at Enola. "Did you tell them about the map?"

"No."

"Who are you?" Helen asked them.

Heike bit her lip. "It's a long story," she grinned.

They reached the atoll after several hours of flight, during which Heike related to them their various adventures, beginning with their arrival in a place called *Triassic Park*. Her tale of a lush tropical jungle island filled with strange fantastical creatures seemed to Helen to be the usual *Hydroworld* lore (or pipe dreams), but then the girl's account grew slightly more surreal and confusing when she went into stories of actual Dryland cities, in which lived millions of people, and how these people went to places called cinemas where they watched other people acting out various fantasies. Sometimes these fantasies were recorded on little discs. It was on one of these discs that the boy claimed he had seen a recreation of *Hydroworld* in its entirety.

"Anyway… that's how we know so much…" Heike concluded. "Things nobody else knows."

"Yeah," Matthias cut in. "For instance that the polar caps have reversed… so that map on your daughter's back is basically upside-down."

The old pilot literally fell out of his seat. His hands trembled on the rudder's controls. "Helen! They have solved the mystery…"

"I told you," Heike grinned. "We know *everything.*"

"We're like gods, more or less," Matthias added, already envisioning a life for him and Heike on an atoll surrounded by subservient and worshipful tribes, kowtowing to their every wish.

"Here we are!" said Gregor, pointing to the sea below.

They flew over the atoll—with Matthias and Heike scrambling to the side of the dirigible basket, to admire it, as their altitude decreased and the floating Verne-esque city revealed itself to them as a circular collection of boats that had been weaved together with other salvaged plastic debris, into a stockade, complete with guard towers and metal parapets and a great metal spherical desalination tank for obtaining drinking water. An eigty-foot tall canvassed windmill supplied the atoll with electricity for a sprinkling of lights. The atollers stood on the catwalks, and cotton net trampoline-floors that strung out over the water. They were brandishing crude bows and lances and looking up at the descending dirigible.

A group of the elders, strange looking people wearing jellyfish-shaped hats, their morose faces obscured by netlike veils, were gathered atop an ancient wooden Chinese junk, waving their arms at Gregor's craft.

Helen tossed the cable out again and they anchored it to one of the barges near an organo rice paddy. She then threw a rope ladder down the other side of the hovering aircraft.

The entire population of the atoll gathered around as Helen and Gregor, Matthias and Heike and Enola came down from the dirigible.

The atoll's law enforcer—a severe, wolf-eyed man in a fish-leather tunic—strode up to them, clutching a sawfish bill as a sword. He glared at Heike and Matthias coldly. Then he turned to Helen.

"What is the meaning of this? You know that all

strangers to our city must check in at the gates."

Behind him, on the desalination sphere, Matthias saw a glowing green sign:

"Tapeworld Bonus Ending"

"We won't be staying long," Matthias said to the enforcer.

"They helped us retrieve her," Helen explained, her arms wrapped around Enola. "They were prisoners on the marauder's citadel."

"Yes," said Matthias, addressing the crowd of raggedy, grim-faced onlookers—most of whom looked as if they hadn't had a freshwater bath, or eaten anything containing vitamin C, in years. "And the marauders are heading this way—they're planning a raid!" he added.

"Matty!" Heike whispered. "There's no need to scare them."

"You can stay a half hour!" the enforcer said. "Anything you want to trade, you can do so at the assay office. After that, you must leave our atoll. "

And as he spoke, Matthias noticed that various bits and pieces of the scaffolding around the inner walls of the city were missing. He saw too, that a guard on the parapet had vanished, leaving only his boots. The blinking sign on the side of the desalination tank grew more luminous. He grabbed Heike by the hand, leading her across a catwalk and toward the massive, bifolding gates.

"Wait!" Enola called out, disengaging herself from Helen's grip. She ran at them.

Heike stopped and turned around, "What is it?"

Behind her, Gregor's flying machine had disappeared, leaving only the rope-ladder suspended from thin air. All around them parts of the set were vanishing. Trawlers and nets vaporized, cogs and gears shrunk. The armory disintegrated. Headstones went missing from the cemetery above the organo barge. Sails flew off the junk.

"I want you to have this," Enola said to Heike, opening her hand. In her palm was a smooth pink crayon. "It's so you remember me…"

"Thank you," Heike said, taking the crayon. Tina Majorino's face was frozen in a statue-like expression, her arm still extended, offering the tapeworld gift. Heike looked down and saw water rising up at her knees, and then it was all around her! And she was sinking!

"Matty what's happening!"

"We're leaving the tapeworld," he said, as the boundless blue ocean came rushing in, engulfing them, and Heike clenched the crayon in her hand and held to him tightly—and the world was drowned out by a mighty tapeworld tidal wave.

There was the sound of knocking on the door. And then her mom's worried voice.

"Are you guys all right in there?"

Heike woke up in her bedroom, with Matthias clinging to her. They were both lying on the bed fully dressed. It was 12:30 on a Saturday afternoon; a half hour after they had taken the tape.

"We're fine, mom," Heike called back.

"Oh… well lunch will be ready soon," her mother informed her. Matthias rubbed his eyes and licked his dry lips.

"Hey, baby… who was that?"

"Just my mom," said Heike. "I think we might have been making some noise in our sleep."

Outside the bedroom door, Heike's mother turned away, shaking her head. *Kids today. She could have sworn she'd heard the sound of an engine—like a propeller—coming from inside that room. And a man speaking in Hindi. What were they up to?*

As she descended the stairs to the kitchen she did not notice the slight imprints that the moist soles of her shoes left on the linoleum floor.

Inside the bedroom Matthias sat up and asked, "So how did you like it?"

"It was great," Heike smiled at him. "Best birthday present anybody's given me…"

"That's not all," said Matthias. "I got something else for you."

"Oh really…"

"Yeah, but I've got to piss like a racehorse first… must be a psychological effect from seeing all that water" he said, jumping off the bed and moving into the hallway. Heike laughed.

"You're so romantic," she called out, and flopped back down on her pillow. She could hear him whistling as he peed.

Then she looked down at her arm, noticing that her right hand was clenched into a fist. She could feel something small and round in her grasp. She jolted up, leaning forward.

Her heart throbbed as she turned her hand over slowly and opened it.

There, in the middle of her palm, was a pink crayon.

Un-fucking-believable! Heike gasped. *That can't be possible…*

Matthias reentered the room, still whistling, and he stopped and looked at Heike who was sitting on the bed, staring at her open palm, transfixed.

"What are you looking at?" he asked her.

Heike flexed her fingers, blinked and glanced down at her hand—it was empty.

"Uh… nothing," she said.

"Happy Birthday, darling," he beamed at her—an engagement ring around his pinky finger.

25

SCHANZE QUARTER
(One of those formerly seedy neighborhoods turned into a yuppie hotspot thanks to urban gentrification)

Toby arrived in Hamburg shortly after 3 A.M., entering the Schanzenviertel, the center of much of the city's alternative culture and nightlife. All the bars, restaurants and clubs in the area were rife with activity, owing to the recent gentrification of a previously rundown borough, home to an eclectic blend of immigrants, punks and artists. Hamburg, like Berlin, prided itself on its anarchist and liberal culture.

He asked for directions and followed a group of first-generation ravers to the Rota Flora—a notorious left-wing social center set in an old theater building which had been, among other things, a cinema, department store and squatter's paradise. On this evening there was some progressive-techno party being held in the venue, and a sizable collection of hedonists and technomanes, dubsteppers and skankers were all gathered around, drifting in and out of the graffiti-and-poster tagged building, huddling in small groups of parachute vests and fatcapped silhouettes, skinny speed-freak bodies wrapped in oldskool rave shirts, hip-hop baggys, neon tees, prolls sporting burberry visors and scarfs, rastawear, trinkets—

Inside the pitch-black of the smoke-filled room, he

wandered through flashes of blue and green laser-light, the slinky two-step rhythm WOOOM WA WA WA—offset by insanely loud subwoofers that kinked his hair and made his trousers flap, and the music crazily and eerily atmospheric, abstract, brash, and at the same time laid-back. Beyond rave. A fucking mix-match of styles that brought together hip-hop, techno, electro and grime into one big fusion: sound of the future.

He moved through the human forest, past the lost goa girls trancing out underneath the venue banners, with their bead necklaces and psychedelic garb and strange, shuffling gait, past the somber hardcore fanatiks armed with their spiked caps and paramilitary outfits, and past the student fuck-ups, toxic wasters (dreads and WWII gas mask combined, need I say more?), the ex-nu-metalers and ex-emos all moving on to the next thing.

The DJ cut to a track of Britney Spears' "Toxic," remixed Dubstep-style and the sound came so low and dirty the whole room went riot.

As the squelches and shrill piano notes gave way to the tremendously wobbly bass, eliciting screams of delight from the crowd, Toby moved toward the chillout area, near the twisted metallic LED-illuminated stairway that led to the upper loft and he worked his way over to the side bar where he saw a fit girl in a white-and-pink Adidas halter top, her hair done in giant blue and white beaded braids and her eyelashes abnormally long and highlighted in fluorescent blue. She was chatting away with a couple of black dubsteppers and popping out cans of Effect and bottles of Jagermeister and after watching her for a bit he drew up to the bar and accosted her.

"Hi—"

She moved straight past him to the other end of the bar and leaned over it as some scene girl threw her arm around her and whispered something in her ear, and then she nodded and the girl stepped back and whispered something to a jungliststanding next to her, his face obscured by his hoodie, and he nodded in turn and skipped off toward the sound.

Flashes of light so hard they hurt his sensitive eyes and the deep and dirty bass shook.

WA WA WA WA WA WOOOMMMMM...

Miss Adidas was back again. She just stared at him like some owl. "Yes?"

"Do you know Maja?" Toby said.

"What?"

"M-A-J-A!" he shouted, his voice all but drowned out by the subwoofers.

"Wait—" she flounced off again, this time toward a flock of huppelkutten looking chic and hyped, gleaming wide eyes and slinky forms, metal-plated designer jeans—tugging at their neon wristbands, and they asked her something and she nodded and replied.

She was back again, and Toby was beginning to wonder if this yo-yo trip was going to go on all evening when she said,

"I'm Maja. What do you want?"

"Oh... well... I've got something for you—" Toby said. He reached into his trouser flap and pulled out the

Rendezvous With The Bloodsucker tape-sheet. He held it up to the strobe light, then placed it on the bar in front of her. She slid it directly back to him.

"What?"

"Not here," she said, shaking her head.

"But Darko sent me... he said this is for the platform?"

She leaned over the counter toward him, close, until her lips were almost against his ear; her breath hot against his cheek. "In twenty minutes you go out back... that way, through the service door. Behind the center there is a skate park. OK? Wait for me there..."

He nodded and she smiled and moved back to juggling bottles of Astra beer from the plastic crates stacked behind the bar.

Outside in the park, Toby sat on a wooden bench and watched as two young and rowdy skateboarders performed backside tailslides and 360 board flips in the illuminated skating bowl below him. He heard them hooting and chattering away as their boards grinded the concrete ramps. A band of dubsteppers came around and burnt some grass, arguing about a possible after-party.

While Toby was watching them, a guy drew up to him, walking on the brink of the skating bowl like a funambulist. This was no dubstepper. He looked pure electro. He had blond bangs, like minimal DJ Sven Väth, and was attired in a red jumpsuit tucked into black boots. He wore black suspenders over the jumpsuit.

He stood a few feet away from the bench, his head bowed at the grass littered with candy wrappers, used condoms and splintery shards of broken beer bottles. His eyelids drooped, like he'd dropped an E too many—or was just strung out from the vibes.

"What the fuck are you staring at me for, man?" Toby snapped at him irritably.

"Just chillin'," the blond held up his hands peaceably. "Epic party... wouldn't you agree?"

Toby ignored him, but the guy pressed on. "You looking for an after party?"

"No," Toby replied curtly, hoping to deflate the guy's interest in any further conversation.

"That's OK," the blond said. "Where do you come from?"

"What's it to you?"

"You know Maja?"

Toby's ears pricked at the mention of her name. He regarded the specimen cautiously. "Not really..."

"You came to see her," the blond said and hooked his thumbs behind his suspenders—looking uncannily like Alex from *A Clockwork Orange*. "Everybody comes to see Maja. She knows how to get the right stuff to party—"

"I don't know what you mean..."

"Come on," the metrosexual said. "We both want the same thing..."

"And what is that?" Toby asked, wondering if this was a Hamburg taper.

"The connection," said the metrosexual. "Everybody's talking about it. They say the Flora is the place to find it. That's why I come here tonight. I'm going to buy myself the baddest trip in town… I want what she's got… but she won't talk to me… she's pissed off at me…"

"Why?"

He laughed, revealing a row of twinkles. "It's an old story. We used to work together, back in Frankfurt. Worked at the U60311… this is a techno club in a subway stop."

"I know the U," said Toby, cutting him off.

"Anyway," continued the metrosexual, undeterred. "We also partnered in this sound system and record label: AudioWave. We were rad, man. Signed the Geist and Frantik… Aces of Hardtechno. We ran sets at the Nature One… Elek'tronik Noize, etc. Then we split because of artistic differences… Maja… she wanted to expand. She was bringing in the grime scene from the UK, right, and she starts siding with this grimester used to run with Skepta and his crew. Fucked up the gig. He was pure gangsta, man, too much of a rudeboy… and me, I was just minimal (minimal minimal minimal minimal minimal…)"

Listening to this diatribe, or excuse for a beef, Toby realized with no small irony that ten years earlier he would have thought the guy was a total wasteman, talking out of his rear. But it was 2010, and alarmingly his little explanation made perfect sense.

"So… can you sort me out?" the minimalist asked.

"Sorry buddy," Toby said. "But I don't know what you

want. I only came here for the sound. If it's drugs you're after—
"

The minimalist cackled again and the twinkles glued to his upper teeth shone fluorescent in the dark. He laughed so hard that his entire body shook, and he covered his mouth with his hand, tears running from his eyes as he bent over, coughing.

"What's so funny?" Toby snapped. He thought the guy was one of those wasters bombed out of his head. Too much speed. Too much sound. He was getting fairly annoyed with him, when the minimalist straightened up, shaking his head.

"I'm sorry; I'm not laughing at you," he apologized. He took a step back and danced on the brink of the skating bowl, supporting his weight on the toes of his boots. "It's just the game that gets to me," he said.

"I don't understand—"

The metrosexual suddenly lost his footing and slipped, teetering precariously on the brink of the bowl.

"Hey! Watch out!" Toby grabbed at him, to keep him from falling off the edge, and the minimalist clutched him by the arm, gripping tight, as he regained his balance. The guy breathed hard, and then he did a queer thing, he placed both hands on the sides of Toby's head, like a monk giving a blessing and said, "Thanks, friend..."

He stared intensely at Dejan for several long seconds, and then he mumbled, "Ich gehe Weg." And he ran off quickly into the park, disappearing like a thief in the night.

Toby scanned the perimeter, trying to gather where the weirdo had run off to when he heard someone whistle and he spotted Miss Adidas waving at him, standing near the grill fence that ran behind the grounds.

He approached her and she smiled warmly at him and zipped up a snug white windbreaker. All Day I Dream About Sex.

"Come on," she said. "I'll take you to the real party."

She led him down a cracked and narrow back alley; the walls they passed tagged and covered by posters, with the ubiquitous bent-and-beaten bicycles propped against them.

They came out onto another street, where two young Turkish boys, both dressed identical in sporty vests with baggy sweatpants, were playing the accordion in front of an internet and call shop. They walked past a Doner Kebab shop, a Greek Imbiss, and a red-brick mini-mall—a group of left-wing punks squatting in front of it, playing fetch with a squashed plastic bottle of Mezzo Mix and a ratty German shepherd dog.

"How do you know Darko?" Toby asked, unable to contain his curiosity any longer.

"Does it matter?" she shot back. Then, after a moment's silence skipped streets, turning onto a side lane, past a row of Bohemian clothes shops—the commercial vans parked in front decorated with stencil graffiti. Che Guevara and Betty Boop.

"So you used to live in Frankfurt," Toby asked her, trying to find some neutral ground for conversation. Maja gave him a queer look.

"Who told you that?"

"I met somebody—at the steil. He said he used to work with you at the U—that you were in the music business together… but you broke up… because of artistic differences…"

"You were talking with Manni?"

"Is that the creep's name?"

Maja laughed and spun a beaded braid around one of her fingers. "Manni was never a part of my project. The guy's a drifter, basically. He moves from scene to scene, weisst Du?… When I left Frankfurt he followed me here, to St. Pauli. He knows everybody everywhere… and nobody can stand to be around him for long…"

"That's the impression I got."

"But he's always *there*," Maja said. "Sometimes he'll disappear… for months on end, he'll squat in Copenhagen, build some shack in Christiania, with his own-goddamn two hands… or he'll move with a band of travelers to the East… to Bulgaria, or to Hungary. He'll be following some sound or another. And then he's back, like time never went by. He prides himself on what he calls 'the connection'. He says he's plugged in, and that his biggest fear on this planet is being 'unplugged.' He's basically a philosophical jerk."

"Is he a taper?"

Maja stopped in the street, standing under the pale yellow glow of an iron-wrought street-lamp. "No," she said. "Here in Hamburg, we try to keep the tapes a secret… Manni's no good at keeping secrets, see. And that sixth 'connection' sense of his tells him that there's a new toy in town. He's sniffing at it like a pig on truffles. Sooner or later he's gonna find out—but it won't be because of me. We got enough problems with the state in this town as it is. If they ever found out about the tapes, it would be one more reason to raid our squats… you didn't tell him, did you?"

"Of course not."

"Good," she said.

They came to the end of the alley, where it opened into a wide, cobblestone courtyard surrounded by red-brick Hanseatic houses with gabled roofs and vines climbing up the outer walls. At the far side of the courtyard was a more modern-looking building , composed of gold-glazed clinker bricks arranged in an expressionist style—sometimes recessed, sometimes protruding from the façade in a variety of geometrical forms. The entrance boasted square double doors offset by an irregular arch portal.

The movie posters on the illuminated glass display cases were all bizarre indie films with strange titles. Emocore comedy. Latin American erotica. Arthouse docudramas… But the marquee above the entrance proposed a more conventional film playing tonight.

Kino Klaus presents:
Interview With The Vampire "Drink from me and you will live forever."

"Clever," said Toby. "You're using the kino to sell the tapes?"

"It's a bit more imaginative than that—" Maja smiled. She opened the door and they entered the theater lobby which was small, warm and carpeted, with a row of circular steps leading to the ticket booth, where a Danish girl sat, flipping through a Shôjo booklet. She set it down as they entered and flashed them a warm smile.

"Hey doll… I was getting worried you wouldn't come—"

"One of our runners got stopped by a highway patrol outside of Bremen," Maja explained. "So I called in some refuel from the network. This is Toby—he's here to help us out."

The girl exited the ticket booth and came around. She couldn't have been more than twenty-five years old, but she walked with a cane and a slight limp. Her eyes were fierce and energetic, despite her apparent fragility. She had a printed silk tunic—Bohemian—over lambskin trousers that molded beautifully shaped legs. A chiffon scarf was wrapped around her slender neck. Toby was smitten by her charm.

"I'm Kirsten," she said, kissing him lightly on both cheeks. "Come on… we'll go to the theater."

She led them through a soundproof door and into a curtained auditorium, which was a very classic art deco picture palace, all in lush gold tones, with scallop-shell wall lights and a fiber-optic starry ceiling.

The entire theater was filled, each of the twenty rows of thick velvet seats were occupied. Toby guessed there must have been somewhere between two- to three-hundred moviegoers in the theater. They seemed quite riveted by the film, as the auditorium was extraordinarily quiet for a place so full. No giggles and whispering, no cries of shock or squeals of delight. No clapping. No beeping cell phones or pagers. No arguing, no snogging, no crunching of popcorn. They all sat, their eyes riveted to the silver screen, where F.W. Murnau's classic silent expressionist horror-film *Nosferatu* was playing, the flickering black-and-white images on screen captivating the audience.

Maja and Kirsten led Toby down the aisle, toward the silver screen.

"But this is an old movie," Toby was saying.

"It's a cover," Kirsten elucidated. "We don't have the original Interview With the Vampire in stock. This is an indie theater, you know."

"So where are the tapers?" Toby asked, as they came to the end of the aisle.

"You're looking at them," said Maja, and Toby gasped in shock, because he could now see that the entire auditorium—every single person present—was staring with their eyes wide shut, arms reposed sphinx-like on the armrests of the bonded leather seats. They were looking straight at him, their faces and bodies frozen in a catatonic pose. No one moved, and not an eye blinked. Two-hundred and forty human statues were gathered together in that indie movie theater.

"How much longer until the session ends?" Maja asked Kirsten.

Kirsten checked her D&G wristwatch. "About twenty minutes." She reached for the lambskin belt around her waist and unclipped what looked like a sleek, oval-shaped smartphone. She scrolled the screen and entered in a text message:

"NEWS FLASH FOR ALL TAPERS:

For those of you who wish to prolong the platform… give me your seat number, please and a new tape will be administered to you. Otherwise the session will end in nineteen minutes. Anybody wishing to exit the tapeworld immediately, please use one of the scene-exits provided for you by the programmers."

Toby watched as she flipped a key and sent the message. A few seconds went by and then the first incoming response came and he gasped in shock:

TAPER ROW NUMBER 5, SEAT 9

"How's life back in the real world?

"I'm in Paris, and a Paris-vampire must be clever… haha. You get the joke. I met Armani. He's a really nice vampire. He took me on a tour of the catacombs… he says he was going to drink my blood but that I fascinate him too much now for him to hurt me… it helps to have read Anne Rice. Oh, by the way, where is the scene exit? Is it the well prop on the stage in the Théâtre des Morts-Vivants?

"Oh, nevermind, I'll find it, I'm sure."

And another text message:

TAPER ROW 15, SEAT 6
"I just came to say, Hello… hello hello hello… lol
"Sorry for the Martin Solveig reference… couldn't help myself. Having a great time in Louisiana on the plantation. Love to prolong the session… I'm thinking about settling down here.
"Peace out."

"What the hell is this?" Toby wondered aloud. "Tapers can't send messages…"

"Next-generation tapes allow it," said Kirsten. "This is a tachyon communicator. Everybody sitting in this room is equipped with one. They've got it with them in the tapeworld. If they have a problem, or are lost somewhere in the film, or they can't come out for some reason… or need some information… they can contact the tape-moderator. Some of them want to live in the tapeworld… so we set up a platform. What this means is that, say they find work, or start to create themselves a life in the tapeworld… well, in order to keep the session from disappearing once it ends, they group together, so that the tapeworld is kept active by the other tapers. Some of them come out and others go back in… in turns…"

"How long have they been in *Rendezvous With The Bloodsucker*?"

"For weeks," said Maja. "Some of them, in any case. Most of them come to the tapeworld in the evenings, or on the weekends. But there are always a certain fixed number of users in this room… so the tapeworld is sustained. We don't end it unless we get a majority vote that they want it to end. In that case we move on to another tape. But Rendezvous seems to be working well so far. Both with the couples and the singles. I think it's because this is another time period… and so many people wish they could live in a different century."

Toby stared at the rows of people-statues, their mouths hanging open in dumb wonder.

"So, users are living in the tapeworlds now," he said.

"Uh-huh… that's the idea," Kirsten affirmed.

Suddenly Kirsten's communicator beeped, and they heard someone in the audience cough, the sound so unexpected that it startled Toby. A taper cleared his throat and stood up, near the rear of the auditorium. The effect was that of a mannequin coming to life. It was slightly creepy. He saw the three of them at the far end of the theater, gave them two thumbs up and said, "Hey everybody… amazing tape, really great. I wish I could stay longer, but I got to go to work the graveyard shift. I'll be back tomorrow evening, nice and early."

"So you found the exit," Kirsten called out.

"Yeah, no hustle. It was a green arrow above the well, like you said. Oh, can you send a message to my girlfriend? She's right next to me… Row 5, Seat 10. Tell her to tell Armani that I've got some business to attend to, but I will most definitely return to Paris to see him ASAP. Thanks."

And the guy walked out of the theater like a regular moviegoer leaving a show during the commercial break, not some taper who'd been prancing around Paris with Antonio Banderas in the late 1800s.

"Holy shit, this is crazy…" Toby said, stunned. "And are they all together? I mean can everybody see each other?"

"Well, technically yes," said Kirsten. "But the movie spans two continents. So some of them are in America, and others in Europe. But they can meet-n'-greet, sure. I know that some of the tapers even have a favorite tavern in New Orleans where they like to meet up and hang out—enjoy the local Cajun nightlife. They say that they see Brad Pitt and Tom Cruise cruising for fresh blood there almost every night."

"I… I didn't think that was possible," stammered Toby, flabbergasted.

"Next-generation tapes," said Maja. "The show must go on. Iit's a great film. You should try it."

"I'm not into horror—"

"Don't be silly," Kirstin smirked. "It's practically a documentary. Rumor has it Tom Cruise didn't even know they were filming him half the time. The fangs are for real. Brad Pitt delivers his usual moody performance with all the intensity of a toilet seat. But it works quite well, I must admit."

Toby smiled and turned to Kirsten, "I guess you want the copies then," he said. "Darko says €25,000."

Kirsten giggled. "Darko doesn't fix the price. Bremen does. Oh, well. I guess we can indulge that Serbian prick this once."

Suddenly they heard a noise, and the taper who had exited the platform moments earlier came rushing back into the theater. He ran straight toward them, gesticulating wildly and yelling, "Polizei! The cops are coming!"

Kirsten turned to Maja, her eyes widening in shock. "What the fuck—"

Maja questioned the taper, her face dead-serious. "Which police?"

"State and special intervention forces... There are at least three transport vans, blocking the alley," gasped the taper, breathless from his sprint. They didn't see me, but I saw them. They're gearing up to move in on the theater... it's a raid... I'm sure of it!"

"How could they know..." Kirsten started, her voice trailing off. She was looking at Toby curiously.

He shifted, uncomfortable. "What? Don't look at me like that... I'm no rat..."

She leaned in closer. "What's this?"

"What?"

"Don't move—" she cautioned.

And she reached forward carefully and pinched two fingers at the corner of his eye, as if she were about to rub sleep from it... and she jerked them back, and Toby winced, thinking she had pulled out an eyelash.

"Hey, what's the idea?!"

"Ssssh!" She held up her forefinger, where balanced on the tip of it was a tiny black dot. Like a beauty spot.

"A tracer—" Maja gasped.

"Hitachi mu-chip," whispered Kirsten. "I used to work for the company. Somebody planted it on you... probably not long ago. It's got a short lifespan. Quick, Maja… you take this!" She handed the communicator to her. "Contact the tapers, tell everybody to exit the tapeworld immediately! I'll go up front and see if I can stall them."

"What about the tapes?" Toby asked, patting his pockets. "I've got 500 copies of *Rendezvous* on me."

"Down there to the left," Kirsten pointed. "Go to the mensroom and flush them. They'll dissolve in the drain pipes. Don't throw them anywhere else! You got it!"

He nodded and ran off to the toilets. Kirsten and the user walked as fast as her disability would allow, back up the aisle, past the rows of immobile heads and waxwork bodies. When she opened the soundproof door to the theater they could hear police officers calling gruffly from the foyer.

"Shit!" Maja cursed, fumbling with the communicator. She entered in a general text Message:

"WARNING!!!

"Police officers are entering the theater. All tapers must head IMMEDIATELY for the nearest scene-exit. Look for the green arrow. I repeat, look for the GREEN ARROW. This is not a drill.

"GET OUT NOW!!!"

Across the entire expanse of the movie theater, bodies stirred and came to life—blinking, coughing, scratching their noses and wiggling in their seats, as the tapers' senses re-adjusted to the physical world. They started popping up, all over the room, while others sat frozen, still lost in the tapeworld, searching for the exits, like mice seeking their way through a labyrinth.

"What's going on?" One of the newly woken tapers asked. He was an emo, with the nose-ring and mascara to prove it.

Beside him an emo girl shifted in her seat, her eyelids fluttering. She shivered and stood up, blinking. "Who called the police?"

The tapers were reanimating in scores—standing up, looking around, and ambling through the aisles like confused cattle. Maja spoke to the group of roused tapers, most of who were grumbling and griping about having been yanked prematurely from the tapeworld.

"The platform's going to collapse!" one of them called out accusingly.

"It's a raid—" Maja shot back. "We must evacuate!"

More incoming messages on her communicator:

TAPER ROW NUMBER 2, SEAT 4
"I can't find the exit! Help! I'm in the Lafayette Cemetery in New Orleans! Is it in a tomb? Help me, please!!!"

TAPER ROW NUMBER 15, SEAT 3
"I'm on Market Street, but I'm staying in San Francisco! Chop up my damn body and use it for firewood—but I refuse to exit the tapeworld!

"—Proud to be punk!"

More shouting from the foyer as the raid advanced and suddenly the theater doors burst open and a squadron of armed Bereitschaftspolizei—the special rapid reaction and support unit of the state police —swarmed into the room, in full gray-green protective gear, with white storm trooper helmets and clocking 9 mm Parabellum pistols and MP5s at the tapers.

Police leutnants and oberleutnants were moving through the crowd, shouting out instructions:

"BePo! Everybody line up against the wall... this side here. A police officer will search you. Do not resist inspection! I repeat... do not attempt to resist inspection!"

The tapers hooted and booed as the police officers rounded them up, separating the crowd into smaller, more manageable units. Those tapers still seated were roughly shaken by the shoulder and yanked to their feet. Those still stuck in the tapeworld toppled to the floor between the rows... and some of them screamed as they woke up to find riot police in full battle gear staring down at them.

Some of the punks shouted insults and tossed plastic water bottles at the invaders, while the more intelligent students filmed the raid with their cell phones to upload onto YouTube. A BePo officer snatched one such handy away and stomped on it with his boots, eliciting a chorus of boos and threats from the anarchists. A few emos wept actual tears as they were lined up against the walls and frisked. A young hooliganresisted arrest, and stupidly socked one of the intervening officers on his helmet. The officer responded by tasering him nine times, which caused the left-wing activists in the room to holler in condemnation, before they were silenced by additional clubbing and tasering.

The oberleutnants continued issuing instructions to their men (partially to demonstrate to anyone recording that they were conducting the raid in a civilized manner):

"Have them empty their pockets! Search their shoes and socks! Have them open their mouths!… Issue a full-body pat. You may ask them to remove their outer layers of clothing but not their underwear…Confiscate their handys and any electronic device. When you are done bring them to the lobby… two at a time!"

In the restrooms, Toby had barricaded himself in the toilet stall, and he could hear the shouts and tension that the raid was provoking, as the tapers were being searched. His hands trembling, he reached into his cargo pockets and unfolded the sheet of blotters. He looked at it despairingly—at the €25,000 image of Tom Cruise in fangs—and then he crumpled the sheet up and dumped it in the porcelain toilet bowl.

He hit the flush lever and the tank emptied, water swirling around in the bowl. But the sheet didn't go under! It floated like a turd.

"Scheisse!" Toby cursed. He waited, heart thumping hard as the water-reservoir refilled. The shouts from the theater were becoming louder. Some of the raiding officers were nearby! He flushed a second time, and the water swirled around again, but the sheet still did not go under! Tom Cruise stared up at him, from the toilet bowl.

"Go down! Goddamn you…" Toby snapped. He froze in terror as the outer door to the restroom flew open and an officer shouted out:

"Come out of there immediately!"

There was a heavy banging on his locked stall. More clanking footsteps—stomp of heavy boots.

"Just a sec, please—I'm almost finished…" Toby said, trying to camouflage the shakiness in his voice. The banging on the door grew louder—the door trembled as somebody kicked at it.

"Raus! KOMM JETZT RAUS!!!" the order came.

Toby hit the flush again, agitatedly, but the tank was nearly empty and only a slight trickle of water ran into the bowl. The sheet of tapes was still afloat! It wouldn't dissolve… and it wouldn't flush. The cubicle door shook and the bolt-lock threatened to snap under the repeated assaults of the BePo's boots.

"OK! OK! I'm coming!" he informed them, his mind racing, as he struggled desperately to find a way out of his predicament. Then his panic gave way to a strange calm as he realized what he must do—he reached in the toilet bowl and grabbed the sheet of soggy tapes, and he shook off the excess water and closed his eyes.

"This is your last chance—" the police lieutenant threatened.

Toby crumpled the tape-sheet into a ball and stuffed it

in his mouth, chewing on it ferociously, as if it were bubblegum. Then he swallowed the incriminating evidence—right down his throat, ingesting 500 copies of *Rendezvous With The Bloodsucker* in one go!

He steadied himself and undid the bolt—a hand grabbed him by the shoulder and flung him violently out, projecting him against the restroom sinks, and he banged his head on a hand-dryer. A leutnant grabbed him roughly by the shoulder and yanked him around, while Toby held up his hands, defensively, "Whoa! Take it easy Serpico! I didn't do anything…"

The BePo leutnant scrutinized him carefully, looking into his albino-red eyes for signs of deception and substance abuse. Toby felt his heart doing a drum n' bass shuffle against his ribcage. Another officer turned him around and spread his legs, then submitted him to a full-body pat. He searched his pockets, made him open his wallet, made him turn his socks inside-out and confiscated his handy.

"Hey! That's personal"

"Shut up!" the officer issued him a slap on the head.

"Ow!"

"All right you, go with them—" the leutnant ordered, as two of his men gripped Toby by each arm, escorting him out of the mensroom.

They dragged him back through the movie theater, which was being progressively emptied, as those searched were being taken to the lobby, for additional inspection, and to decide which of them would be carted off to the police stations for further questioning.

As the policemen walked him up the steps of the aisle, past the now-empty recliners, Toby felt a queer sense of nausea building up in his stomach, accompanied by ants in his limbs… as if his legs had fallen asleep. In the gold light of the cinema he saw the blue uniformed police marching the last, protesting arrestees off toward the lobby.

A flash of light—or was it a flame? —flicked from one of the decorative seashell lamps on the walls.

Toby blinked, feeling the numbness spread through from his limbs to spine, the ants creeping up his back.

His legs felt weak.

"Come on, smartass! Get a move on, will you," he heard one of the escorting officers say. The man was right beside him, clutching his arm, but his voice seemed to come from very far away.

Another flash of light—this one even stronger.

On the upper-row of seats, in the far corner, Toby saw her—a small, pretty girl with a reddish-blond curly coif, wearing a silky blue Victorian-style bustle gown, with a ruched train. She stared straight at him, her skin pale, her lips dark red. She had a preternatural glow to her.

"*Do you want me to be a doll forever?*" she whispered.

Toby stumbled against one of the steps, fell on his knees. The officers were shouting out, ordering him up, but their voices were warped—as if his ears were plugged, or he had his head immersed in a bath. The light intensified, from all corners of the theater, until every seat seemed to come alive and glow with an inner radiance.

On the projection screen behind him Tom Cruise appeared, as the Vampire Leech deScientolocourt, bedecked in his finest ruffled silk shirt, with a velvet jacket and silver cane. He smiled, baring his lustrous fangs and walked right off the screen, materializing in the theater, pointing the cane at the girl.

"Chloe, Chloe…" he chided, in a mock-reproving tone. "Will you never learn? Who will we get now to finish your dress?"

Toby screamed as a piano teacher flopped down dead on the carpet beside him, his yardstick clenched in his stiff fingers. The police officers had vanished. He scrambled to his feet in terror, running toward the exit—the steps soft as marshmallows sinking beneath him.

There was a loud clang and a rumble. Flames spewed from the wall-lights. The cinema's ceiling and walls contracted and expanded, as if they were alive and breathing. Toby ran in place, ran like *Alice in Wonderland*, treading the carpet as the room revolved and the décor broke into pieces, and the projection screen shattered like glass. The ceiling flew away and a draft of cold and misty air rushed in, chilling him to the bone.

The sky overhead was dark and starry—and all at once he was standing in the open air, no longer in the movie theater, but outdoors, on a wide road lined by magnificent live-oak trees, draped in Spanish moss, their gnarled branches hanging over the path, nearly criss-crossing, creating a tunnel effect.

A few hundred meters ahead of him was a large antebellum mansion surrounded by a wide porch and marble balcony supported by stately, plastered doric columns; the mansion was topped by a gabled, slate roof, with wide French windows flaunting blue-green louvered shutters. Lights shone in the upper windows.

He ran toward the mansion, and he heard a horse galloping behind him, and a rider with long blond hair passed him.

When Toby saw his face he shouted at him.

"Hey! Brad! Brad Pitt! Wait up…"

But both rider and horse vanished into the mist and Toby found himself standing on the veranda in front of the main entrance of the mansion—a heavy cypress portal topped by a fanlight. Far off, in the fields behind the house he could hear the beating of drums and chanting—and saw in the distance the faint glow of a campfire.

He pushed open the heavy double-doors and peered down the central hall. He could hear two men arguing, in one of the opulent side rooms. Toby crept down the hall toward the noise, and peered around an open doorway where he saw Brad Pitt and Tom Cruise, both dressed like poofs, and seated at either end of a long and sumptuous dining table with mahogany veneers and decorative pedestals. The table was laden with crystal decanters, candelabra, silver platters of uneaten food and crystal wine glasses.

"…but you must know something about the meaning of it all," Brad Pitt complained, in his annoying, atonal voice.

Tom Cruise slammed his fist down hard on the table, sending grapes and cutlery flying. "Why?! Why should I know these things! Do you know them!?" He got up and paced around the luxurious dining room, giving vent to his wrathful pontifications.

"That noise!" Tom Cruise bellowed, pointing to the French windows. "That noise, it's driving me mad! We've been in the country for weeks with nothing but that noise!"

"Yes, they know about us!" Brad Pitt taunted him, rubbing his pale and cold hands together. "They watch us dine on empty plates and drink from empty glasses…"

Cruise waved his hands in a foppish manner. "Come to New Orleans—" he exhaled wearily. He strode over and leaned close to Brad, "The Paris Opera's in town we can try some French cuisine…"

He stopped as his reptilian gaze fell on Toby standing in the doorway. He stood up straight, surprised that he had been taken off guard—and by a mortal no less!

"W… What are you doing here? Why aren't you beating the drums with those other voodoo savages?"

Brad Pitt's mournful eyes regarded Toby, oscillating between pity and blood-hunger. He looked weak, as if he hadn't fed in days. "Leave this place at once!" he warned Toby. "Your master is the devil!"

"How dare you come into this house, slave!" Leech roared. "Or have you come to taste death?"

"Whoa! Hold it!" Toby flipped. "I'm no fucking slave! I'm a homeboy… from H-town…"

Brad Pitt as the Vampire Louie de Pont du Big Mac looked like he had sucked in a lemon rind. "Who are you?"

"The name's Toby... well, actually Alioune Kebe. I'm a tape runner... I'm also an MC for this rap crew in Duisburg... not like you would know or care about hip-hop..."

"A what?" Pitt gulped. "Hip-hop?"

"Enough!" Leech slammed his hand again on the table. A wineglass shattered on the marble floor. The boy seemed to have absolutely no fear of him, something he had never encountered before in a mortal. He was more than a bit disconcerted. He bared his fangs and rushed at Toby who crossed his fingers into the shape of a crucifix.

Leech froze and began howling with laughter, like it was the funniest thing he'd seen all week.

"I believe the boy is a vaudeville buffoon! Come Louie—take him and feast!"

Brad Pitt rolled his soulful eyes at Leech. "Forgive me if I have a lingering respect for life—"

"Does he always complain like this?" Toby asked.

Leech clapped his hands together, all of his rage leaving him. He choked with laughter. "That's what I keep telling him... Merciful Death, I call him..."

Toby relaxed and walked straight up to Leech, like it was the most natural thing in the world. He didn't look the least bit terrified. He grabbed a bunch of grapes from one of the dishes on the table and a piece of roast Cajun chicken and began tearing into it, chewing avidly and lecturing the pair of them between mouthfuls.

"Honestly Brad... or whatever your name is... I saw the state of those chickens in the garden aviary, and I really think you should drop the Ozzy Osbourne diet—if it's not making you happy, why bother? And Tom... give it up with those *Mission Impossible* films. We've seen about enough of you as an action hero—weisst Du?"

The two vampires' faces went even whiter, if that was possible. They'd never seen the likes of this before. The boy was clearly a lunatic. And he was dressed so bizarrely, and he had the strangest air to him, like he didn't belong in this time period.

"Where's Kirsten Dunst... I mean Chloe?"

The two vampires looked at each-other. *Chloe?*

"Oh look—what a beautiful sunrise," Toby pointed a chicken drumstick at the windows.

Both vampires freaked. Leech screamed and dove under the table, while Brad Pitt turned to face the sun, his arms spread open, intending to meet death in as melodramatic a fashion as possible.

"Uh... that was a joke—" Toby chuckled, watching Leech crawl out from underneath the walnut table, his monstrous ego deflated. "I really got you didn't I... hehe..."

Leech flew at him, his fangs bared and Toby tossed his drumstick in his face and sprinted from the room and he ran down the great hall, with the vampire flying behind him, and he burst back out of the mansion and ran into an angry mob of plantation slaves in long cotton shirts, wielding flaming torches and sickles, intending to burn down the property.

The whole mob stopped dead in their tracks when Toby came out the door.

"Your suspicions are correct. They're vampires," he assured them. "So that should put an end to the mystery…"

The slaves stared at him dumbly. Then they recoiled as Brad Pitt came storming through the entrance, the corpse of a freshly slaughtered creole female servant in his arms. His face had a renewed vigor to it and there were bloodstains on his lips. His eyes flashed iridescent in the night.

"Hear me now!" he cried out to the mob. "This place is cursed! Damned! And yes your master is the devil!"

"So over-the-top… so melodramatic… it's a wonder Leech can stand to live with you at all—" Toby commented. He looked at the hesitant slaves, "Well… what are you waiting for? Have you run out of steam already? Go on—torch the place!"

Brad Pitt was so stunned at this statement that he dropped the dead maid and she landed on the porch with a dull thud. The slaves gnashed their teeth and rushed past him, into the hall, and spread from room to room, setting fire to the curtains, to the oil paintings hanging from the walls, to the rugs and carpets… within minutes the whole house was ablaze, with smoke and flames spewing from every window…

The vampire Leech came running out, his face livid. His gorgeous blue frock coat and blond wig were singed.

"Aargh… perfect! Just burn the place… burn everything we own!" he yelled. "Have us living in a field… like cattle!"

"You thought you could have it all," Brad Pitt droned.

"Oh, shut up, Louie!" Cruise and Toby chimed in unison.

Toby ran back down the alley, as the slaves dancing around the burning mansion waved their torches and chanted. As he ran, another Brad Pitt rode by on his steed, turning up from the direction of the river. Toby started to worry.

Just how many of these fucking tapes are playing?

He exited the property, turning onto the river road where more cotton-shirted creole slaves were dragging dead bodies from the muddy waters, and wailing.

A black carriage rushed at him, and Toby yelped and dove out of the road, landing in a murky swamp from which protruded the knotted, moss-covered stumps of rotting cypresses. The air was thick with the sweet, putrid scent of azaleas. An alligator slinked into the water, from the banks on the other side of the marsh. As his eyes re-adjusted to the dark, Toby could distinguish a floating form—what looked like a log.

He screamed again as Tom Cruise's withered corpse bobbed past him, wrapped in a bloodstained coverlet.

Kirsten Dunst stood on the banks of the swamp with her child's body bundled in a cloak, surveying the scene solemnly while Brad Pitt kneeled beside her, looking remorseful and tragic.

"He belongs with those reptiles Louie," she said. "He deserved to die!"

"Then perhaps so do we!" Brad Pitt retorted.

"Holy shit!" Toby cursed, dragging himself out of the

dank swamp. "You guys are everywhere!"

He stood up and was no longer in the bayou but standing on an ancient cobblestone street, his clothes mud-stained and dripping wet; the air was cold—a river flowed beside the street, its waters dark. Ahead of him loomed the archway of an old stone bridge, and in the shadows underneath he saw the silhouette of a young blond vampire with top hat and cape, his white-gloved hands folded daintily together; he stared upwards with amusement as an identically attired vampire swirled and danced upside-down from the archway above him—defying gravity.

In the city above the riverbanks, a church bell rang, adding to the Gothic atmosphere of the scene.

The dancing vampire dropped down behind the spectator and knocked his top hat off—Brad Pitt whirled around and the vampire issued him two glove-slaps to the face. Pitt lost his composure and reacted by grabbing him by his waistcoat and hoisting him in the air.

"Buffoon!"

The fool of a vampire floated in the air, rising higher, like an angel on his way to heaven.

Antonio Banderas materialized beside Toby, his chiseled Latino face leachedwhite, his hair long and silky black. He leaned on a cane.

"Santana!" Banderas called out, and the dancing vampire vanished.

Brad Pitt strode over, angrily. "I've searched the world

for an immortal... and this is what I find!"

Antonio Banderas moved silently toward him, reached into his waistcoat and drew out an engraved invitation. He offered it to Brad Pitt.

"Bring the petite beauty with you, no one will harm you—I won't allow it. Remember my name... Armani."

The well prop in the Théâtre des Morts-Vivants! Toby thought to himself, with a sudden flash of insight. *That's where the scene-exit is located. I need that invitation card!*

Armani backed off and bumped into him and when they made contact the four-hundred-year-old vampire was suddenly aware of Toby's presence as two of the hundreds of playing tapeworlds fused. His bloodshot eyes sparkled and he bared his fangs and sprung at Toby.

Toby dodged Armani's eager canines and jumped at Brad Pitt, swiping the invitation card from between his fingers— "*Pardon, Monsieur!*" He dove straight into the Seine, past the boundaries of the movie scene, so Armani couldn't follow him.

He sank underwater, carried by the current, kicking his arms and legs wildly, resurfacing in the sea. The sky was dark and cloudy. A port was visible on the horizon above the waves, its lighthouse beacon shining bright yellow like a cat's eyes. In the water ahead of him was a 177-foot-long Portugese barquentine—the *Gazela*—its eleven Egyptian cream-colored sails swelling in the wind.

Toby swam toward the coast, as the ship sailed past and the crew gathered on the deck and dumped a sheet-wrapped corpse into the water.

It landed with a splash right beside him.

"Ew!" He swam faster. The sky above him thundered, and Brad Pitt's monotonous voice-over echoed through the straits of Gibraltar.

"*...we reached the Mediterranean. I wanted those waters to be blue—but they were black, nighttime waters...*"

"Give it a rest already!" Toby shouted, swimming frantically for the shore. He was beginning to get the impression he would never find a way out of this tapeworld. There were too many scenes playing for him to keep a sense of orientation. He was bouncing from Louisiana to Paris to California, as though in a pinball machine, with absolutely no boundary from scene to scene.

He hit the coast and the scenery revolved, the sky suddenly below him and he was free-falling through the empty space, flailing about in a panic, and then striking the ground with a hard *thump*!

Darkness all around—

Toby breathed hard and stood up. He was alone in a vast, must-smelling subterranean chamber—a crypt of sorts. He looked around, taking note of the porous limestone walls, into which had been carved endless rows of rectangular niches, many of them holding flickering candles. Minute carvings of angels and demons decorated the loculi. In the center of the crypt stood a railed passageway, the stone slab pulled back to reveal a flight of narrow stone steps leading to the underground galleries. And to his left another musty, railed stairway rose upward to a vaulted ceiling. The dank floor was decorated with religious mosaics and statuettes of demons. Beside him was a row of ornate and lustrous wooden coffins, illuminated by silver candelabra.

Where the hell am I? he thought. *The catacombs! I must be somewhere in Paris.*

He took the stairway that led upwards, noting that all the loculi were empty—except for the flickering candles and resident cobwebs—there were no ossuary remains. They had been cleaned out by somebody.

They must live here! Toby realized, with no small horror. He'd only seen *Rendezvous With The Bloodsucker* once, and he was struggling to recall the film, but he couldn't remember much, except that he knew there was a scene-exit on the stage in the Theatre des Morts-Vivants. Maybe that was on the upper-floor.

At the top of the stairway he came to an iron-clad wooden door with a rusted iron clasp. He pulled at the clasp but the door would not budge—locked! He was trapped in the catacomb. And all those coffins—in a vampire movie they could only mean one thing:

A BUNCH OF CREEPY GHOULISH SLEEPING VAMPIRES!!!

He pulled at the creaky clasp again, with all his strength, but the door was tightly sealed into the wall and he gave up, figuring he'd have to wait it out in this dungeon.

He descended the stairwell once again and looked

around the crypt. There were no other exits—except for the dromos in the center of the room.

Grabbing a candlestick from one of the burial niches he moved toward it, peering into its somber interior, the cracked sandstone steps scarcely visible in the faint candlelight leading into inky blackness. He had no wish to bury himself further underground, but maybe those steps led to some other subterranean passageway—and he could find an exit that way.

Down he went—advancing cautiously, holding the flame before him, his whole body tense, ready to bolt at the first noise. The air was even thicker here. It smelled dry and decayed. He felt along the walls, the bumps and tiny fissures and grottos, trying to convince himself that it was all just fantasy. But how did the goddamn programmers manage to weave so much detail onto one neurochip? Surely they hadn't programmed the Paris catacombs in their entirety.

I wish Buffy was here, Toby thought with a chuckle. *She's fit and she'd know what to do! And why the hell can't the labs give us one goddamn tape that doesn't involve bloodshed and creepy villains! What the hell was wrong with programming a romantic comedy? Or something with Danny DeVito or Michael J. Fox. Hell, right now I'd even settle for one of those overblown and boring Merchant-Ivory productions.*

He felt his way through the underground passage, sensing the ceiling becoming lower and the walls narrowing as he advanced through the tunnel.

Suddenly the walls on both sides gave out and Toby gasped as his hands groped at emptiness. He stood frozen to the spot, his heart thumping wildly, as he held out the candlestick into the darkness before him. The flame from the candle flickered and grew tall, but it revealed nothing. He stretched out his other hand, tentatively, and felt only air. He backed off a pace and crouched low on the tuffaceous floor. Then he held out the candle again, carefully, and ran his fingers over the stone, advancing them slowly inch by inch—barely two feet in front of him the passageway gave out into empty space. What lurked in the recesses of the tapeworld catacomb? Some hidden horror? Or was this a programming flaw?

He felt around in his pockets and found a Zippo. He flicked it and the flame jumped in the dark. Now he could sacrifice the candle. He lifted it up and tossed it into the void.

The candle fell, spinning around and around, its light diminishing as it was sucked into the great, seething emptiness. He watched as it became a mere pinpoint before blacking out.

I'll have to go back, Toby thought, with dismay. *There's nothing for me that way.* He turned around and stood up, holding the Zippo in front of him. He had barely taken a step forward when he heard a dull thunk behind him.

What was that?

Chills rose up his spine. Toby forced himself to turn around. "Who's there?" he called out, his voice shaky. "Answer me!"

There was nothing—he moved his Zippo around, squinting in the gloom, and then he froze as he felt his feet crunch on some round object. He knelt down again, very carefully and touched it—feeling its unmistakably smooth and tallow surface.

The candle!

What the hell? He'd tossed it into a bottomless tapeworld pit, and like a boomerang the candle had returned right at his feet. Just to be sure, Toby tried something else. He unzipped one of his low-cut biker boots and pulled it off. He threw it in the hole—and down it fell.

He waited, breathing hard and counting… 1 – 2 – 3…

Wham! The boot ricocheted off the wall and landed in his lap!

What's going on here? Toby thought. He called out into the darkness—into the abyss.

"Hello."

And exactly three seconds went by before he heard the call returned to him—in his exact voice. "*Hello.*"

"Who are you?" he called out. And three seconds went by before he heard a reply.

"*Who are you?*"

This was no echo! The voice was too close—too real to be a sound reflection. It had to be somebody mimicking him—

He stepped up to the brink and reached his arm into the void, abandoning all conventional wisdom, overcome by a strange, strangling curiosity. He had to know what was out there. He reached as far as he could, his fingers piercing the somber hole, feeling cold emptiness.

And then he touched something!

Toby let out a yelp and recoiled. He waited for a moment, listening, breathing hard. Then he reached out his arm again, and again his fingers made contact—with the fingers of another hand! Slowly he splayed them out, and flattened his palm. And he let loose a gasp of wonder as the palm of his hand made contact with another palm! He pocketed the Zippo and reached out his other hand, moving it to equal length. It too touched another hand! He wiggled his fingers and the fingers in the grotto wiggled back. He clenched them, and the other pair of hands grasped his.

Toby moved his face now forwards, and he pulled at the hands and felt them tug with equal strength… drawing him in one direction, as he pulled in the other… and he tensed his arms and tugged the hands up to his chest in one wild jerking motion and he flew forwards, into the cavernous recess.

And SCREAMED as he came face-to-face with himself!

It was like looking into a mirror—only this was a three-dimensional flesh-and-blood replica of himself. Or maybe it was the real Toby, and he was the surrogate. Toby faced himself, all sorts of strange and frightening sensations coursing through him, and his other self seemed just as bewildered and afraid as he was, for no matter how identical they were, Toby could not ignore the uncanny feeling that they were two separate and autonomous beings.

It's me in another tapeworld! I've come to the same place… and the two tapeworlds have met. He's mirroring my behavior because he is me, and because he is thinking the same thing that I am thinking!

Toby looked at himself—pondering the image, the

flesh replica of himself. *Let's join together and see what happens,* he thought. *Let us fuse both tapeworlds… you shall become me and I shall become you!*

He took a few paces back, and so did his surrogate—the two Tobys regarded each other reverently. And then they rushed at each other, leaping into the open space, into the no-man's land that separated them.

WHAM!!! They collided with stunning impact. The cavern exploded in a shimmering burst of light. A kaleidoscope of color and sound and motion swept furiously around him, and Toby felt a searing pain as his flesh seemed to consume itself, to melt and merge with his other self—and as he entered his surrogate he was overwhelmed by a stunning vision.

The dark was suddenly inhabited by a forest of strange, plant-like growths. Bluish-gray filaments extended from gray bulbous masses, pulsating over a hexagonal lattice. Flashes and sparks coursed the length of each tendril, culminating at the epicenter. The organic network surrounded him, undulating and pulsing with electrical activity.

It's my brain! Toby thought, with exhilaration. *I'm seeing the neurochip as represented to me by my mind!*

The neural network spread out, snaking in every direction at once, and Toby felt himself plummeting, spinning around as on a carousel, as the web receded and the circuitry began to take form—it was at first opaque and indiscernible, but slowly the outlines of an image became apparent.

He was at the bottom of a dry stone well, which rose

some twenty feet above him—the mouth of it covered by an iron grill, with moonlight filtering through the criss-crossing bars and illuminating the dusty ground in square patches. Across from him Toby saw an unforgettable spectacle—two carbonized figures, a woman and a small girl were interlaced, hugging each other protectively. They had been, in all appearances, burned alive, their ashen faces contorted into grotesque grimaces of pain. Toby drew closer to the smoldering ruin, reached out his hand to touch the burnt girl's doll-like face, but the moment his fingers poked at the charcoaled bodies, they crumbled and disintegrated into a heap of ashen flakes.

Toby wiped his soot-smeared hands off on his trousers and as he did so a door carved into the well was pushed open, and Brad Pitt entered the welllooking a mess with his pretty-boy face streaked with dirt, and his silk vest and breeches smeared with fresh mortar. He was having a bad hair day, for a Hollywood movie star—his normally lustrous mane framed his pouty face in disheveled clumps.

"W… what are you doing here?" the vampire Louie addressed Toby, his luminous eyes swiftly scanning the pit. "Where's Chloe? and Madeleine?"

"I don't know what you mean—" Toby feigned ignorance, reasoning it might be better not to inform Brad the vampire that his beloved undead-daughter-surrogate had been burned alive by the sun.

"Who put you in here?" the vampire demanded.

Toby rolled his eyes. This was going to be hell to

explain.

"I'm a part of the coven," he lied, thinking back to the Latino vampire that he had seen on the Parisian riverbank. "Armani. I work for Armani! You know… the salsa dude. The fanged desperado."

Brad Pitt seemed stunned that this sassy mortal was on familiar terms with the oldest living vampire in the world.

"What happened to Chloe?" he narrowed his eyes and pointed a sharp index fingernail at Toby. "Where is she?"

"How the hell should I know?" Toby snapped back. Brad Pitt did a double-take and stumbled back against the wall. No mortal had snapped at him in over a hundred years. His eyes popped wide.

"I'm no goddamn babysitter," Toby continued, giving vent to his frustration. "And besides, I've had it with this fucking night-crawler lifestyle. I'm sick of tombs and catacombs and running around in the dark playing patty-cake with a bunch of bloodsucking goons! And what's more—as far as I'm concerned you need to revamp your wardrobe, because you all dress like Liberace! Andthis whole gothic trip and all these ruffled shirts have been out of style since like…the 80s!"

"But you…"

"I'm not finished!" Toby snarled at Brad, shocking him into silence. "Furthermore, in my opinion, you make about the most unconvincing vampire since Edward Cullen! So, lose the Manson makeup, get yourself a tan, and for heaven's sakes, stop with the GODDAMN WHINING! Because when I get out of here I'll probably be in jail for trafficking, whereas you, *mon ami*, get to go home and bang Angelina Jolie every fucking night of the week—pardon my French… "

And feeling thoroughly vindicated he walked out of the cell, leaving a much dumfounded Brad Pitt to make sense of his speech.

He ducked out of the sun well, finding himself in a dim and chilly catacomb corridor. To his right was Antonio Banderas, as the vampire Armani, sitting on a stone stairway brooding, his handsome, chiseled face swathed in moonlit shadows. He looked up as Toby waltzed out of the chamber, his mouth dropping open.

"What is the meaning of this?" Banderas sprung to his feet.

Brad Pitt followed hot on Toby's heels. He looked at Armani questioningly. Grouped up and down the length of the corridor was Armani's coven: a troupe of Grand Guignol vampire-actors in showy stage costumes. They looked like the most satanic bunch of folk since the coven in *Rosemary's Baby*. The leader of the pack—a slack-jawed, saturnine vampire named "Santana" (as played by Irish actor Stephen Rea)—had ordained the imprisonment of Chloe and Madeleine in the sun well, in order to execute them for having killed the vampire Leech. He looked equally confused when Toby came wandering out of the cell.

"Where's Chloe!" Brad Pitt asked Santana.

Stephen Rea's mug dropped. This was not the reaction he had been expecting. The other vampires exchanged glances.

Santana turned to a redhead female vampire lounging in one of the loculi carved into the wall of the catacomb.

"Babette. Who is this boy?"

"I… d… don't know, Santana!"

"It's witchcraft! She's a shapeshifter!…" cried out one of the more imaginative members of the coven. The other vampires hissed and mocked him.

"How did you find us, mortal!" Santana advanced with a predator's gait toward Toby.

Behind him Antonio Banderas and Brad Pitt argued:

"…if this is a joke it's in bad taste! Now tell me where she is or I'll kill the whole lot of you!"

"…Louie you must believe me, I am at a loss… I do not know what happened…"

"You sir, are a liar!… You mean to tell me you have no idea who this mortal is? He called you by name… He said he worked for Armani… that's what he said—Armani…"

"Louie, this is not true… I've never seen the boy before…"

And all of a sudden everybody was interrogating everybody else, and the whole catacomb was rife with dispute. The vampires argued and gesticulated theatrically, baring their fangs, hissing and flicking their snake-like tongues, pointing their sharpfingernails at Toby, before turning on each other, every one of them blaming the other for the mix-up.

"How could you have let her escape?"

"He was walled in!"

"We locked the door—"

"Not even the almighty Dracula could have survived the sun well!"

"Dracula shmacula… you've been feeding off the absinthe-drinkers again…"

"She's a shape-shifter, I tell you! That boy is her! Just look at his pale skin!"

"Go eat some aioli, buffoon!"

The cacophony grew in intensity until Toby could bear it no longer.

"GUYS! VAMPIRES! CREATURES OF THE NIGHT!!!" he yelled at the top of his lungs. The catacomb fell silent, and the entire coven, Armani and Louie included, stopped their bickering and stared at him.

"Er… what I mean to say is… SO LONG SUCKERS!"

He bolted for the stairway and for an instant the two dozen or so Paris vampires watched him flee, and then the whole coven flew after him—their glabrous faces and luminous eyes glowing with malice as they pursued him, like a camp of bats out of hell.

26

MARXLOH, DUISBURG
(Rundown working-class neighborhood, also known as "Little Turkey" due to its majority of foreign residents)

It was Lukas' mom who called him that afternoon, when he got home from work. She sounded tense and hysterical on the phone. She said to come to her house immediately—his brother had snapped!

He drove over in his economy Twingo (favored by students and pot-marauders everywhere) and got to the cul-de-sac where she lived. His loathsome stepfather was standing in the driveway, next to his bulky four-wheeler, hairy arms crossed over his sagging beer-belly, his shirt un-tucked, his gross feet squashed into a pair of cheap sandals and his bald cranium shining as red as his face.

"Oh shit," Lukas groaned, reluctantly getting out of the car.

"What have you done to him!" Hans Erfort growled. He was a German–Croatian truck driver with a fuse as short as Danny DeVito.

"What are you talking about?" Lukas scowled at his stepfather.

His mother came running out of the house, hurrying across the lawn, nearly tripping over a garden hose in her haste.

She was having a Bonnie Tyler hair day (which generally meant bad news). Lukas wondered if she was drinking again.

"Lukas!" she shrieked, oblivious to the stares they were gathering from the neighbors. "Lukas what did you do to your brother!"

"Whoa! Peace!" Lukas exclaimed. "I don't have a clue what you're on about! What's wrong with him?"

"What's wrong with him?" Hans blustered. His jaw muscles bunched and his trucker's biceps flexed. "Ha! I should be asking you that. Ever since he's been hanging out with you again… he's gone completely mad! He barricades himself in his room all day—acting out his fantasies and hallucinations… yesterday he was a pirate. Today, he thinks he's a bumblebee!"

"A bumblebee?"

"He's an insect!" Lukas' mom added, her face shining with anxiety. "He flies… he skips… he crawls from room to room! What did you do to him?"

"I didn't do anything!" Lukas shouted back—exasperated. "Where is he?"

"He's upstairs," Hans bluntly informed him. "You're going to go up there, and you're going to fix this. Or I'm going to call the cops and have them search that hovel of yours for the drugs you're giving him… oh yes… I know all about your kind—you goddamn sorry excuse for a punk! You mad raver, you… or whatever it is you kids are calling yourselves these days…"

Lukas pushed past them and went on into the house, his mother running after him, calling for him to be careful…

she handed him a rolled newspaper.

"What's that for?"

"If he tries to bite you, swat him!" she advised. Lukas shook his head and climbed the stairs to the top floor, where he could see the door to his brother's room slightly ajar. A trail of shiny, multicolored candy wrappers led from the hallway to the interior.

"Mikail," he called out, approaching his room stealthily, with his mother cowering behind him, clenching the newspaper as if she were heading to the bathroom to tackle a spider that had crawled out of the drain. "Mikail, answer me!" Lukas insisted.

He pushed open the door to his brother's room and gasped in shock. His mother covered her mouth with her hand.

It was absolute pandemonium in there. The bed was upturned, the mattress and curtains torn to shreds, and the duvet from his quilt strewn everywhere. All the drawers to his dresser had been tossed around, and the clothes and belongings in them scattered in a garbage heap. The room stank of filth and organic decay—there were rotting piles of half-eaten food everywhere: candy bars and packets of gummi bears, marshmallows, syrup stains on the bedsheets and carpet, open packets of sweets and toffees, a broken jar of honey, powdery piles of white and brown sugar cubes, peanut butter smears, nutella, strawberry jam and marmalade—

"Where is he?" Lukas scanned the empty room. He looked up, and screamed at the sight of his brother, hanging upside-down from a ceiling beam, his face sticky with the mess of countless devoured candies, observing them with a nervous intensity.

"Mikail!" Lukas called out to him, advancing cautiously into the room. "What are you doing up there? Come down at once!"

Mikail's head jerked from side to side. He licked a rivulet of dark caramel off his bare arm. He was wearing only underwear, and his body was stained with the traces of his gluttony. He let go of the ceiling beam and plopped down in the center of the room, landing gracelessly on his back in a pile of junk. His arms and legs twitchedas he rolled over. He didn't stand up, but crouched low, halfway upright, moving toward Lukas and his horrified mother with a skittering gait. His eyes twitched in their sockets—going in ten different directions at once. He licked his lips and rubbed his hands together.

"He likes the sugar," his mom said stupidly.

"I can see that!" Lukas gasped. "Mickey what's gotten into you? Are you crazy?"

"It wants to… turn me into something else…" Mikail explained, his face twitching as his limbs jerked spasmodically. "That's not too… terrible is it? Most people would give anything to be turned into something else…"

"Turned into what, dear?" their mother inquired worriedly. Her fingers clenched the newspaper roll so hard they were white. "What are you evolving into?"

"Whadda you think, a gnat?" Mikail hissed. "Am I becoming a hundred and eighty-five pound gnat?"

Holy fucking shit almighty!" Lukas stammered. "He's

copying that DavidCronenberg movie... this is bad! Almost as bad as watching the real thing!"

"You can say that again," his stepfather thundered from behind them. "It's like living with Franz Kafka..."

"You read the *Metamorphosis*?" Lukas eyebrows shot up. Hans' little pigged eyes glared harshly at him.

"Does it astound you that I'm literate?"

"No... I just meant... well, yes it does as a matter of fact!"

"Why you little—" Hans lurched at Lukas and his mom stepped between them, defending her son.

"I'm going to get the goddamn bug spray—this has gone on long enough," his stepfather grumbled...

"Wait—I have an idea," Lukas said.

"It better be good..."

In *The Gnat*, by David Cronenberg, an eccentric scientist designs a teleportation device which he tests on himself, unaware that a mycetophilidae is in the telepod with him. The machine merges him with the gnat at the molecular–genetic level and thus begins his hideous transformation. This was the tape that Mikail was imitating.

"Mickey," Lukas spoke gently now to his brother, who was on all fours, spitting onto a box of chocolate donuts, trying to get his enzymes to dissolve the pastries. "I think we can stop the transformation! I'm going to reset the telepod in reverse—we'll separate the mutating cells from your body..."

"Do... you think it will work?" Mikail looked up, a glimmer of lucidity lighting up his face. "The gene splicing program has never been set in reverse…"

"Jesus God!" Hans grumbled at Lukas. "You're even crazier than he is."

"I think it's your only chance," said Lukas, and he winked at his terrified mother. "Come with me… you have to trust me…"

He led him to the bathroom, with Mikail creeping along on all fours, sometimes stopping to rub his hands together. Lukas got him inside, on the tile floor, and then he said, "I'm going to close the airlock to the telepod, and re-program the cycle…"

He shut the door to the bathroom and called out, "INITIATING REVERSE DNA SPLICE. I'm going to activate the molecular transformer…"

And he flicked a switch on the wall off and on a few times.

"That's no molecular transformer! That's a light switch, you moron," his stepfather gnarled.

"Let him try it," his wife said. She watched as Lukas flipped the bathroom lights off and on, faster and faster, and then he stopped, and he spoke in a pristine, mechanical voice.

"REVERSE   DNA   SPLICE   SEQUENCE TERMINATED…"

Hans slapped a hand to his head. "I need a beer… No, actually I need my goddamn shotgun…"

Lukas opened the door and the three of them stared in apprehension.

"Mickey?"

His brother stood up, blinking slowly… he flexed his limbs, rolled his neck, and looked down at his body—then to Lukas.

"You did it!" he marveled. "You separated me from the gnat. You're my goddamn hero—"

"There," said Lukas to his stepfather, wiping beads of sweat from his brow. "Problem solved!"

Downstairs in the kitchen, with Mikail wrapped in a blanket and drinking hot chocolate, his mother and stepfather conversed in low, urgent tones with Lukas in the hallway.

"What if he regresses? What then?"

"I don't know what's gotten into him," Lukas said.

"Bullshit!" Hans objected. "This has your stamp all over it. If he starts acting that way again… I'm sending him to goddamn military school. You hear?" he threatened. "Next time it's the cops…"

"There won't be a next time," Lukas said, unconvincingly.

Hans regarded him somberly. "There'd better not be!"

It was this incident that convinced Lukas that their little forays into the tapeworlds were not as innocent and harmless as they might appear. And if there were labs producing such dark films as *The Gnat*, then what was to be next? Would he see his brother doing the crabwalk down the stairs *à la façon* of *The Exorcist*? Would he wake up one morning to find that Mikail was John Doe from *Se7en*?

Sloth—Envy—Gluttony—Wrath… *What's in the box?*

No, he'd have to put an end to the madness right now! Things were already spiraling way out of control. He'd have to follow his stepfather's advice, for once.

He would go to the police.

27

(FATAL IMPULSE TAPEWORLD)

Dejan rode back along the Shoreline Highway, but this time the road through the hills was empty. He saw the Golden Gate Bridge, glowing a rusty-red over the ocean to his right. It was dark when he entered San Francisco (two minutes and thirty-two seconds later), driving along Howard Street, heading west, with the city skyscrapers scintillating in the distance. He came to a roadworks, the flashing yellow road-signs and traffic cones indicating some construction in progress up ahead.

Suddenly and without warning, an identical car as the one he was driving came tearing up the street to his right, burning a stoplight, and swerving in front of him, its tires screeching as the car fishtailed on the wet road.

"What the hell?" Dejan watched the car speed through the intersection, nearly slamming into a row of red-and-white striped isolation barriers, overlooking a drop to a large concrete pit. Dejan followed the Ford, watching it veer right and left, cutting across the hosed-down lanes, nearly plowing into a parked bulldozer.

And then he saw the source of the driver's folly. Racing toward it, in the opposite direction, was a sleek black Lotus Espirit, its driver sideswiping across all lanes of the street, speeding directly toward the Ford, seeming intent on a head-on collision.

"Holy cow!" Dejan slammed on his brakes as the Lotus swerved left, at the last second, and the driver lost control and the car smashed into the roadside barriers, and flew through the air in a magnificent arc before crashing onto its roof some sixty feet below, landing near an air compressor.

The driver of the other Mustang stopped his car in the middle of the street and got out. He was wearing blue jeans and a black leather jacket. Even in the dark Dejan could recognize his stocky form and slicked back hair. It was Michael Douglas. He hurdled a concrete barrier and slid swiftly down a tarp-covered ramp, to the bottom of the pit and Dejan ran to the brink of it, peering over the edge.

Suddenly there were lights all around him. Police vehicles and fire department trucks appeared out of nowhere. The whole pit was alive and teeming with SFPD officers and members of the fire brigade. They ambled about the crash site, underneath the construction tower lights, and around the wreck. Dejan saw them load a body bag onto a metal gurney which was hoisted by a motorized cable through the air, toward an ambulance parked right next to him.

He spied dimple-chin Douglas, down near the smashed up Lotus, being questioned by plainclothes police inspectors. They were shouting at him and he was shouting back at them:

"Fuck you!" one inspector in a Bogart raincoat was yelling. "I told you to stay away from Kastel!"

"You didn't tell me to stay away from the car!" Douglas shot back, shoving away a pesky internal affairs officer.

"Hey, what are you doing?" A fireman caught Dejan staring at the accident scene and waved at him.

"N... nothing, I was just wondering what happened," Dejan said.

"Well there's nothing to see here—move on," the man instructed him.

As he returned to his ride, Dejan paused midway and asked the fireman the way to the Fillmore.

The Sergeant tugged at his hard hat, pointed to the Mustang, which had its doors open and its headlights on, and he said, "Is that your car?"

"Uh... yes."

"You'd best turn back the other way," he said. "You've been driving against traffic."

"Oh," said Dejan, feeling sheepish, "Thanks."

"Just follow the lights of the city, straight on up ahead," the fireman told him. "And you'll find the club on Geary Boulevard... it's big, you can't miss it."

He stroked his mustache and winked at Dejan. "Follow your instinct, Mr. Vidic," he said and walked back to his truck.

"Hey!" Dejan called after him, but the man had vanished. And in a flash he realized that this nameless fireman was also the desk sergeant who had checked his ID at the SFPD station. He wondered how many background characters were doubles. And the guy even remembered his last name.

He made a U-turn and headed in the opposite direction, toward the twinkling battery of skyline lights, where somewhere out there, were two copies of his girlfriend Milinka.

One was sitting in the county jail awaiting prosecution for murder in the first degree, and the other was sitting in an acid-house nightclub, stirring a martini and waiting for him to show up.

Milinka, hold on, I'm coming…

He floored the accelerator and the 5.0 L, V-8 engine roared in response, and Dejan felt his pulse quicken, hoping that his plan would work—hoping that by intercepting Milinka before Foxy did, she wouldn't fall into their trap.

He spotted the strobe-lights cutting through the sky, and drove toward them, finding an old episcopal church that had been reconverted into a discotheque at the end of a long avenue of designer boutiques and upscale stores. Even from the corner of the street Dejan could tell that this venue was the city's hotspot. There was a queue of clubbers gathered for a quarter mile around the block, some of them arriving in sports cars, others by fat yellow Taxis pulling up on the curb. They were all in glitter, face paint, hot pants and some of them in real old-school neon ravewear—stuff that could only have fit the 90s: colored arm and legwarmers, Lycra leggings, neon socks. He parked Nicky Curry's Mustang illegally on the sidewalk across the street and he flipped open his wallet and looked through it quickly.

There was an AmEx card, about a hundred dollars in cash, and—Dejan chuckled as he found a photograph of Michael Douglas and Catherine Zeta-Jones in it. Tape programmers had a sense of humor, after all.

He got out of the car and crossed the street, drivers honking at him as he dashed through traffic. The rain had stopped but the pavement was still wet. He clutched Nick's police badge in one hand and elbowed his way through the crowd of acid-house club kids, gathering stares and grunts of disapproval as he did so.

"LAPD... uh... I mean SFPD, move aside," Dejan pushed his way through the gathering. A towering blonde transsexual in a magenta sequined cocktail dress, with magenta-stained fox fur around the neck puckered her bloated red lips at him.

"Wait your turn, darling..."

"Hey—you're that bimbo from the Tiga clip—"

Amanda LePore winked at him. "I wear my sunglasses at night."

He moved to the portal where a handful of leather-clad bouncers were surveying the lineup. They stopped him as he approached the red-painted double doors.

"Whoa buddy... this party's on invitation only."

"SFPD!" Dejan flashed the badge in the bouncer's mug. "I'm pursuing a suspect. How's that for an invitation?"

The bouncer gulped and ushered him in. He passed through the coat room decorated in red leather panels and onyx crosses, where he saw a very dismal looking and coked out Harvey Keitel harassing one of the cloakroom girls.

"Holy cow! What the hell is *Bad Lieutenant* doing here?"

Harvey Keitel stumbled by him, moving toward the

interior of the club, his grim face obscured by three-day beard stubble. He got as far as the metal detector crew and began arguing with the indoor bouncers, who seemed intent on kicking him to the curb. Dejan drew up to them and showed his badge to one of the security. He scrutinized it, while his colleagues harangued Harvey.

"I'm here on official police business," Dejan told one massive obsidian slab of a bouncer. Behind him he could hear Harvey Keitel as Abel Ferrara's *Bad Lieutenant* using the same sorry excuse to bring his firearm into the club.

The black bouncer handed him back his badge. "OK, Mr. Curry, we can let you in… but you've got to leave the gun with me. We have a no-weapons policy."

"Fine," Dejan said, thinking that if there was any trouble, he'd have to wing it. He handed the bouncer his .38 and the man pushed back a navy velvet curtain and Dejan moved on into the club.

He came to the ground floor reception bar, separated from the main room by old church colonnades. A bunch of wasted clubbers were chatting in high spirits in front of a neon-lit Plexiglas aquarium with fish swimming around inside. They cast him curious glances, wondering where he was from.

He pushed on into the nave of the church where the main dancefloor was—it was packed out with mad ravers grooving to 90s classic breakbeat. The sound was loud and sharp, the strobes so brilliant they hurt his eyes. Above him, hanging from the vaulted ceiling was a cross-shaped truss—bordered by blue neons. An iron staircase led to a metal catwalk overlooking the dancefloor, the whole catwalk crowded with clubbers in Buffalo boots and mirror jackets, trancing out underneath the mirror balls. Metal cages were suspended over the dancefloor, in each of them a scantily clad girl, or boy, or sometimes both, were flaunting the junk at the dancers below.

"*Milinka—where are you?*" Dejan whispered. He moved through the crowd of E'd out dancers, all shuffling and grooving sensually around him, and he saw the DJ in a cage of chain-link fencing, at the other end of the floor, waving his arms over the ecstatic crowd. A crew of bouncers, all dressed in black were standing near the box, muscular arms crossed.

The DJ cut to a track of "Rave the Rhythm" by Channel X and the crowd went wild. He spotted Harvey Keitel, stumbling through the dancefloor, having somehow wormed his way in, and he was being hooked by Amanda LePore who led him off toward a black velvet curtained section, near one of the side colonnades.

The music pumped louder and the room was spinning—Dejan hurriedly scanning the crowd, trying to locate Milinka—

A draft of clubbers were fighting for space up at the main bar—a slick, pink marble-topped station on carved white oak pedestals. Four barmen, all dressed like priests, were struggling to keep up with the wave of demands. Dejan moved toward the bar and a group of kittens split and he saw Milinka standing at the other end, a martini in front of her, looking anxiously around the club.

Feeling a rush of relief, he moved toward her, when he

spotted Leilani Sarelle, also working her way across the dancefloor toward his girlfriend.

He shoved his way through, knocking the party-goers aside, oblivious to their insults and curses, bowling over a transvestite, who responded by tossing her drink at him. Foxy was closing in on his girlfriend, her vamp's face cut in a cruel sneer.

Milinka turned around to the approaching girl and Dejan cut in just as Foxy was about to speak—

"Let me buy that drink for you!" he said, tossing a $20 bill to the barman.

"Dejan!" Milinka jumped in surprise. She threw her arms around him, hugging him close. "I was getting worried you wouldn't come... what is this place? What are we doing here?"

Dejan held her in his arms, and he looked over her shoulder and saw Foxy change direction, wandering off to the main floor—without looking back.

"I'm so glad you're here," Milinka whispered to him as he stroked her back.

The DJ cut to a more sensual, ambient tune—an electro remix of "Blue," by LaTour.

"Where are we?" Milinka asked again.

Dejan held her tighter, and as he scanned the dancefloor he saw Sharon Stone in a sparkly gold backless cocktail dress, rubbing up against a very naff-looking Michael Douglas in an appalling green V-neck sweater. Foxy was executing some godawful dance moves (looking like she was trying to hit somebody) and she was eyeing the pair of them jealously.

Dejan smiled. The scene was back to normal. The secondary tapeworld had imploded with Kathleen's death! Only the original remained, playing itself over one last time.

"We're in a movie, schatzi," he whispered to her. "That's all this is—a movie."

He took her hand, "Come on—let's go…"

"Where?"

"Home," he said, casting a last glance at the dancing detective and killer. "We're going home."

They woke up together in bed, their bodies interlaced. Dejan stroked Milinka's hair gently and she rolled over. He kissed her on the lips.

"I'm so glad you're back," he said. "I thought you would be stuck in the tapeworld forever…"

Milinka groaned, her eyelids fluttering as the room around them slowly became clear. She squinted at the cheap IKEA furniture, looked down at her body, looked at the alarm clock on the night table.

It spelled 00:31 in red digital letters. What a strange clock! A pair of scissors lay next to it, underneath a hideously lackluster nightlight.

Dejan breathed in her perfume, wrapping her silky hair around his fingers. "Don't ever go into a tapeworld again without telling me," he said. "You're lucky I managed to find you—"

Milinka stretched like a kitten, feeling a soft breeze filter in through the half-open bedroom window. She sat up and shivered, then she said to him, "Would you get me my cardigan… the one in taupe with the shawl neck…"

"I'll… see what I can find," Dejan said, "Are you cold?"

Milinka smiled at him warmly. "Just a little—"

"OK. But I'm getting something to drink first," Dejan said, getting up from the bed. His head was throbbing, and his throat was dry. Milinka watched him leave the room and then her eyes fell back on the night table.

In their tiny apartment kitchen, Dejan had opened the fridge, noting that the *Fatal Impulse* canister was gone. He found his cell phone and saw that there was a missed message from Darko, asking him to bring the tapes to Hamburg. He realized suddenly that Toby was gone.

Dejan flipped the handy shut and scratched his head. He filled a tall glass with orange juice from the fridge and when he closed it he jumped—

Milinka stood in the doorway to the kitchen, barefoot, her arms behind her back. She looked very coy.

"Want something to drink?" he asked her.

"Sure," she said. He poured her a glass and put the carton back in the fridge. "Toby's gone—" he told her. "So I guess he must have taken the tapes with him… I'm going to call him and find out…"

"Toby," Milinka repeated softly as Dejan removed an ice tray from the freezer. He went over to the sink and began pounding it against the side to knock out the cubes. He shook the tray but nothing came out.

"Let me help you with that," Milinka said, and she moved lithely toward him.

Dejan smiled, "Thanks... I'll go look for your cardigan..."

Milinka raised a hand and swept errant strands of hair from her face. She felt her gold alligator bracelet cold against her cheek.

"Time for your closeup, darling," she whispered, and Dejan's body went very still, before he turned around.

28

THE HAGUE AIRPORT, ROTTERDAM

Johannes came to his senses in the KLM airport lounge, with Kim sitting in an eggshell chair beside him, sipping a latté from a Styrofoam cup and checking her e-mails on her laptop. He stretched and exhaled, wiggling his fingers, which had gone numb. A vague impression of being pursued by an edgy Harisson Ford through the streets of Paris resonated in his mind. He looked through the panoramic observation glass at the airplanes taxiing on the runaway, and he turned to Kim.

"Hey Kimmy—"

"Oh hi," she smiled at him. "How do you feel?"

"A bit groggy," he confessed. "I hope our holiday in Paris will go more smoothly. Nothing against Polanski, but if you have to spring a tape on me by surprise, particularly one set in France, how about something more along the lines of *Amélie*…"

"You sissy boy," she smacked him playfully on the arm.

"By the way—when's our flight due?"

"In half an hour," she said. "I've called my aunt, she's going to put us up at her place in Montmartre. We might be staying a little longer than expected…"

"Oh… how come?"

"I got a message from Dr. Yin. He said not to return to

Bergambacht, but to wait in Paris until further notice…"

"What do you think is going on?"

"I don't know. I have a feeling we're not going back to Holland anytime soon. But I've brought something to keep us company—" She reached into her purse and withdrew a small canister surrounded by a coolant gel pack. She popped the top—inside was an unmarked, transparent reel of film.

"What is that? Another movie?" Johannes asked.

"Not really… you'll see," Kim gave him a Mona Lisa smile. She tucked the canister away. "It's our own little corner of paradise—you can help me build it."

"A blank tape," Johannes guessed. "You're building your own tapeworld…"

"You catch on quick," Kim said praisingly. "You're going to like what you find—I'm sure of it. The others are all waiting to meet you—they're very excited…"

"The others! Who? What others—"

Kim sipped her latté then got up and said, "I'm going to the ladies room. Keep an eye on my bag, will you… our future life is in there…" She set it down on the plastic lounge table in front of them.

She headed toward the restrooms, and Johannes looked at her purse with a mixture of apprehension and awe, wondering just how many people were living in that twenty-micron-thick film. It was no longer a question of scenario or movie nostalgia, of meeting actors and cinema characters in person—no, this was the next step in the adventure—the key to a new world being built entirely from scratch. What sort of creatures would inhabit it? Would the user-built tapeworld follow the laws of motion and gravity, of time and thermodynamics—or would it allow for an entirely new set of rules—or maybe none at all.

Oh well, thought Johannes. *I guess I can give it a try. After all, we've come to the end of this planet. What's left to explore? Whatever is out there—waiting for us—whatever universe is being constructed, it can only be a chance at something better. At least a 50/50 chance.*

He was willing to take that risk.

He got up and stretched, and as he did so his gaze fell on Kim's vacant seat, where he saw a small glass vacuum tube—like an odd-shaped lightbulb.

"What the hell is that?" Johannes wondered. The cathode tube looked alarmingly similar to the krytron that Emmanuelle Seigner had been holding on the banks of the Seine in the *Frenetic* tapeworld... the one that Kim had pried from the dead terrorists' fingers...

It can't be.

Johannes leaned over to pick it up, but as soon as his fingers touched the glass bulb it disintegrated into a wash of sparkles and then thin air.

(*FRENETIC*, REVISITED)

In February of 1988, in the Intercontinental Le Grand hotel in Paris, a prominent American cardiologist named Dr.

Richard Walker was telephoning his children from his hotel room, while his wife unpacked their luggage.

"Walker's residence—"

"Hi, buddy…"

"Hi Dad."

"How are you doing?"

"I'm all right…"

The doctor checked his watch. "It's eleven o'clock at night, what are you doing up?"

"You woke me up," the boy sighed.

"I know… just testing," said his father.

His wife popped open her suitcase, stood up and said, "Honey, do you want to go out to eat, or should we order room service?"

"Yeah, just one minute," Harisson Ford said. He turned his attention back to his son. "Have there been any calls for us?"

"No," The boy said. "None at all."

29

(RENDEZVOUS WITH THE BLOODSUCKER TAPEWORLD)

Toby ran, with all the legions of hell at his heels, through the underground quarries of the vampires' lair, the walls of which were piled with human bones and skulls arranged into crosses or heart-shaped patterns. He could hear the coven of vampires gaining on him, and he spurred himself onwards, taking no heed of direction, just running in a sheer panic through the catacombs, until he came to a spiral stone stairwell leading from one of the crypts upward, where behind the mortared walls he could hear the gurgling sound of water— an underground aquifer. The vampires' chorus of bloodthirsty howls echoed in his ears as he bounded up the stairwell, toward what looked to be an opening.

He emerged in a white limestone mausoleum surrounded by cast-iron fencing. He was in the middle of an ancient cemetery of columned, mossy tombs, Greek chapels and cracked marble monuments. There was a full moon out, and the air was very cool. At first Toby ran quickly through the garden cemetery, expecting the horde of vampires to burst out of the mausoleum, but they did not, and when he was convinced that they had been trapped in one of the tapeworld boundaries, he relaxed his pace, and searched for the cemetery gates.

He found them at the end of a long cobblestone path lined by leafless ash and acacia trees. Beyond the gates was a bustling Parisian street, lit by gas lamps, and peopled by night strollers in fashionable evening attire. Ahead of him was a gentleman with long golden-brown hair spilling over his suit. He was accompanied by a young girl with an unmistakable reddish-blonde coif and a shimmering blue bustle gown. The girl moved with a grace and assurance beyond her years.

That's Chloe, Dejan thought, as he slinked out of the cemetery and followed the couple toward the entrance of the Théâtre des Morts-Vivants, which was housed in the belly of an old gothic church with gargoyles projecting from the façade.

Brad Pitt was lecturing her as they approached the theater.

"Now remember what I told you... they have different powers. They'll read your thoughts..."

Toby presented his invitation card to the usher at the entrance and entered the auditorium which was filling up with the social elite of the city. The sound of a church organ filled the domed theater as the velvet stage curtain was pulled back to reveal the set and painted backdrop. He moved down the raked theater pews, toward the stage, where the vampire Santana was costumed like the Grim Reaper, complete with scythe, and performing a macabre act as he slashed with his scythe prop at a young couple sitting on a park bench in a rose garden:

Two lovers, wandering down their violet way

Whose passionate embraces each to each
Permit no meditations on decay
Until they find themselves within my reach!

"Tapeworld vampires who pretend to be real vampires who pretend to be humans pretending to be vampires!" Toby commented. "How avant-garde!"

The crowd applauded and the scenery was exchanged for that of a stone well in a monastery courtyard. An actor in a monk's habit advanced toward the well, a wooden pail in his hand.

The vampire Santana continued his performance:

"The monk whose soul with heaven doth commune… and spends his days in pious contemplation… finds he will meet his maker all too soon…

Santana booted the monk into the well, as he was leaning over it to draw water, eliciting scattered laughter from the crowd.

Toby scanned the scene and saw a flashing green arrow, suspended in the air, pointed downwards from the proscenium arch, directly over the well.

The tapeworld exit!

He made his way hastily down between the pews, with some of the theater goers diverting their attention from the spectacle and to him as he advanced toward the stage mumbling vague apologies.

Stephen Rea continued his monologue,

The lesson endeth here, and it is this,
Each one of you my clammy hands must touch…

The theater sat spellbound as the grim reaper delivered his macabre lines. Behind him the red velvet curtain to the stage was being drawn for the changing of the décor.

"NO!" Toby cried out, running to the stage. The entire theater gasped in shock at his interruption to the play. The vampire Santana settled his mantis gaze on Toby, swishing back the silky black cloak he was wearing.

"Methinks a mortal doth approach," he said.

Toby jumped up onto the elevated apron, to the astonishment of the onlookers.

"You wait your turn!" Stephen Rea hissed. "Or are you so eager to meet death you cannot wait?" His powdered face loomed ghost white and his eyes flashed with menace.

"Sorry for the nuisance…" Toby apologized. "I've just got to get to that well prop… don't mind me… just carry on like I'm not here… excellent play by the way… beats *Twilight* any day of the week…"

The vampire Santana, in all his centuries at the Théatre des Vampires, had never encountered a spectator so casually offhand in his manners. Few were bold enough to speak aloud during his morbid theatrics, not to mention actually climb onto the stage.

Toby pushed back the stage curtain, revealing the still unremoved set, and the vampire called out loudly and ominously:

"That way leads to death!"

"Yeah, I know, I know... Just give me a minute," Toby called back.

The theater exploded in laughter, most of the audience thinking that this was a planned interruption for the purposes of comic relief. The vampire Santana glided across the stage and picked up his scythe.

"Let me assist you with what you seek," he whispered, moving up behind Toby.

"LOOK OUT!" a more sensitive member of the audience cried out.

Toby heard the warning and ducked on instinct, as the blade swished over his head and the audience gasped in fright. He picked up the empty pail that the actor playing the monk had left behind him and he tossed it at Santana, who deflected it with his scythe, sending the prop rebounding with a clatter into the auditorium. There were cheers and scattered applause.

"That's the spirit!"

"The boy defies even death!"

Santana, enraged, but struggling to maintain his dignity, now swiped his blade at Toby's legs, intending to lop them off. Toby jumped up onto the brim of the well as the stroke missed him by inches, and the audience let loose cries of terror and exclamations of praise. He stood there, feeling like Errol Flynn in *Robin Hood*—he saw Santana utterly losing his composure, his devilish face filled with an unspeakable fury.

"GET HIM!" Stephen Rea yelled, completely

abandoning all sense of posture, and from the wings of the stage emerged a fair dozen vampire-actors in black hooded capes —the same coven that had pursued him through the catacombs.

"Not you guys again!" Toby lamented.

"DRAIN HIM!" Santana bellowed, and sparks flew from his black, malicious eyes. "DRAIN EVERY LAST DROP OF HIS VULGAR STINKING PEASANT BLOOD!"

The vampires flew at him, their capes swishing in the air, and the whole house held their breath as Toby looked up at the flashing green arrow hovering over the well, to assure him that this was indeed the exit; although to them it appeared he was looking to heaven, as though preparing to meet his maker.

And then he dived, headlong into the well, to the utmost astonishment of Santana and the vampire-actors, who stood in a semi-circle around the prop, peering inside and wondering how he could have vanished.

The bourgeois audience sat motionless, not sure whether to applaud or to wait for the next act.

Up in the balcony box, Brad Pitt turned to Kirsten Dunst.

"What an odd second act!"

"Amateurish," Kirsten Dunst nodded. "We should have gone to the opera."

Down Toby fell, through an inky blackness without form and void, and as he plummeted into the depths of the tapeworld he was assailed by myriad subliminal images…

Do you know how few vampires have the stamina for immortality?

A flash of a flame-lit medieval room—Antonio Banderas seated in a high-back renaissance chair, cupping his chin thoughtfully

I've come to answer your prayers...

Tom Cruise in a blond wig, seductively stroking the curtains to Louie' bed

Do you still want death? Or have you tasted it enough?

Cruise (again) his mouth gushing with blood, taunting Louie de Pont du Big Mac as he spirited him in the air, over the docks—

And as soon as I smelled the air, I knew I was home. It was rich... almost sweet... like the fragrance of jasmine and roses around our old courtyard. I walked the streets savoring that long-lost perfume...

A shot of Brad Pitt exiting an old-fashioned cinema and walking down a New Orleans street lined by flat-fronted rectangular shotgun houses—

Toby fell through the cold, black air—the images from the movie flashing around him by the hundreds, then the thousands. Relentless. Scene after scene. Still after still. Every bit of dialogue, every nuance, every costume and décor and backdrop swirling around him like a tornado, gaining in strength and intensity as he surrendered himself body and soul to the movie, and the last image he saw was a gaunt, yet still energetic Tom Cruise springing on him by surprise from the backseat of a car, sinking his fangs into his neck and draining his blood—speaking to him softly:

Don't be afraid... I'm going to give you the choice... I never had.

The police kommissar flicked his fingers at Toby, as he was coming to. He blinked a few times, the contours of the interrogation room becoming visible; a burly police captain in silvery blue uniform bearing a silver star, with a deeply creased face and a stern air, sat at a plywood desk in front of him. To his right, standing upright and leaning against a metal closet was a hauptmeister, or detective lieutenant, thin and balding, wearing plainclothes and flicking a ballpoint pen in and out. The room had nothing else in the way of furniture. It was illuminated by neon lighting. Behind the desk was a radiator, and above it a window with the shutters and curtains drawn. Toby could hear cars passing on the street below. He realized he was on the upper floor of a building somewhere.

"Glad to see you're with us Mr. Kebe," the husky-looking kommissar said. "Do you know why you're here?"

Toby looked down at his hands which were manacled by steel, nickel-plated Clejuso handcuffs. He then looked at the two interrogators, back and forth.

"Why were you at the Kino Klaus?" the svelte lieutenant leaning against the closet asked him.

"We know that Darko 'The Dog' Karadzic sent you to Hamburg. What were you transporting?" the kommissar asked.

"I regret that I do not understand you," Toby said,

tilting back in his seat.

The burly kommissar leaned forward, his weathered face tense. A vein stood out and throbbed on his thick neck. "Where did you come from? Duisburg? Or was it Venlo?"

"I come from Paris," said Toby.

The two men looked at each other.

"Paris?" the lieutenant asked. "You came from Paris?"

"As did the one who made me," sighed Toby. "But that's all ancient history now…"

"Don't mock us—Mr. Kebe. We know you didn't ride three-hundred kilometers in the dead of the night to watch an old horror flick in an artsy-fartsy movie theater… We've got reason to believe that you're a high-scale operator in the Zemun trafficking ring… maybe this will help you put things in perspective…"

The interrogating kommissar reached into his coat and pulled out the smooth, oval-shaped communicator that they had confiscated from Maja at the cinema. He laid it down gently on the table in front of Toby.

"Can you explain what this is?"

Toby regarded the gleaming object curiously. His fingers crawled forward and delicately stroked the smooth polycarbonate surface of the black screen.

"… strange, is it not," he said, "How few of our kind have the stamina for this gift… for this immortality. The world changes, but we do not… and therein lies the irony that finally kills us…"

"What the hell is the matter with you, kid?" the

lieutenant asked, twiddling his ballpoint pen. "Don't you know how to answer a goddamn question?"

The heavyset kommissar glowered at Toby. "Who makes this technology? Is it a hacking device? A codebreaker? What?... answer me... answer me or by god you'll never leave this room..."

The lieutenant came over and placed his hand on Toby's shoulder. He was so close that Toby could feel his pulse. He felt a delicious nausea overtake him.

"We can do this the easy way, or the hard way," the bald lieutenant said. Toby could hardly hear him. His head was spinning with the sweet, coppery scent emanating from the man's pores—from the rich blood running through his veins.

"All we ask is that you cooperate," the detective said, standing up and twiddling his pen. It flew from his fingers and landed at the far side of the interrogation room, near the door.

"Let me get that for you," Toby said helpfully. He raised his shackled hands, holding the pen niftily between two fingers, like a magician materializing a card from thin air. Both men recoiled, flabbergasted.

"H... how did you do that?" the lieutenant stammered.

"The same as you," Toby said calmly, laying the pen on the table. "A series of simple gestures. Only I moved too fast for you to see..."

He could feel the pulses racing of his two interrogators. He could smell the fear that sweated through their pores as they regarded him in a whole new light.

"I'm flesh and blood," Toby said, "But not human. I

haven't been human for two-hundred years…"

He smiled at them, revealing gleaming white teeth with elongated canines, and the kommissar pushed back his chair. "Ach, mein Gott! Was haben wir den hier? What are you?"

"Isn't it obvious?" Toby asked. And suddenly he sprang from his seat with the speed of a jaguar, and he had his arms around the lieutenant's slender frame, and he was garotting him with his cuffs, while the Kommissar kicked back his chair and reached for his gun.

Toby sank his teeth into the struggling lieutenant's neck, feeling his warm blood gush into his mouth as the kommissar shouted at him, "Stop it! Let him go! I'm warning you…" His eyes were wild and panicked as he fumbled for the handgun in his holster.

Toby released his victim and the lean detective slumped to the floor in a whimper, blacking out from shock and blood loss. His superior drew his gun to fire at Toby, but in a flash Toby was behind him, and he sunk his teeth into his massive throat, piercing through the layers of muscle and fat, directly into his artery—and his prey jerked the trigger of his handgun and let loose a round into the room, which ricocheted harmlessly off the wall. He got off one more round, which shattered the neon light, immersing the room in darkness, before Toby violently twisted his neck and broke it. The kommissar's body sagged heavily in his arms, as Toby eased him onto the floor, and then he searched his pockets in the darkened room for the handcuff key, his eyes adjusting perfectly to the shadows.

He looked up, his nostrils flaring, as the sound of other humans approaching filled him with a delicious sense of exaltation. It was time to flee.

He sprang for the window, and pulled back the shades just as the door to the interrogation room flew open and three armed cops entered the room, their weapons drawn.

"Holy mother of god!" one of the cops cried out in shock and horror. The interrogation room was splattered with the blood of the dead detective and police captain, while Toby stood before the open window, shrieking at the sunlight, his albino-eyes smoldering like red coals in a whitened sepulcher of a face—he dove on the floor as they fired, his hands blackened and his hair smouldering.

"Hilfe!" a female officer screamed as Toby materialized behind her, using her body to shield him from the ghastly sunlight.

The other officers spun around, their hands trembling, unable to fire with Toby exiting the room and dragging their colleague with him, his face unnaturally pale, his bloodstained lips quivering as he snarled like a wild animal.

"Oh god… oh god!" one of the intervening officers was repeating over and over.

Toby bit hard into the female officer's neck and her gun fell clumsily to the hallway floor as he drank from her.

"Let her go!" one of her braver partners cried out shakily.

"As you wish," Toby sneered, tossing the woman's drained corpse at them. They recoiled in horror as she landed in a pitiful heap at their feet, and then they chased after him into the police station hallway, just in time to see him disappear around the corner.

"Call for backup!" one of them shouted excitedly. The other fumbled for the radio clipped to his duty belt. Far off they could hear the shrieking of a female secretary, and then a desk sergeant crying out, before their cries gave way to an eerie silence.

"What the hell was that?" the officer with the radio said, after he had launched a request for assistance.

"I think... it was some kind of vampire," said the other.

30

Powerhouse Fitness Club, Mönchengladbach

Milinka Trajkovic had been working out at the gym when Horst Hellmann and Lonnie Oberfeld dropped in on her. She was at the bar, nursing a vitamin-fitness drink and relaxing inbetween exercise sets.

"Ms. Trajkovic?" Hellmann asked, stepping up to the barstool where she was sitting.

Milinka turned slowly around. She was wearing a Lycra top and gym shorts, exposing a slim, well-toned body with sheen of clean perspiration.

"I'm Hauptmei…"

"I know who you are," Milinka replied coolly, cutting the police lieutenant off. She stared at her reflection in the large polished mirror behind the bar. Her newly cut hair had been bleached blonde.

"How did he die?" she asked the detectives.

"He was murdered," said Oberfeld.

"Obviously," she said, "Or you wouldn't be here. How did it happen?"

"He was found in a Holiday Inn hotel room, just outside the city, tied to a bed with an H&M scarf and stabbed through the throat with some sharp object… When did you hear about this?"

"I saw it on the news this morning," Milinka replied flatly.

"How long were you dating him?" Hellmann asked her.

Milinka's lips curled in a slight smile. "I wasn't dating him—I was fucking him," she stated flatly.

The two detectives glanced at each other, a bit taken back.

"How long were you having sex with him, then?" Hellmann continued.

"About a year and a half…"

"Were you with him last night?"

"No… look if you're going to question me any further, read me my rights and take me down to the station. If not— please fuck off," Milinka said dismissively.

"Very well," retorted Oberfeld curtly. "You're coming with us."

"Isn't that a surprise," said Milinka sarcastically. "You mind if I shower and change into something more appropriate first? It'll just take a minute…"

"Go ahead, we'll be waiting," said Hellmann.

"I'm sure you will be," she licked her lips and pushed her vitamin shake away and headed off in the direction of the locker room.

The two detectives were standing outside the building when Milinka emerged, wearing a short sleeveless dress in winter white wool crepe. The dress had high cut armholes and a roll neck. She also had on a white shawl wrap overcoat, diamond stud earrings and beige stilettos with tall wooden heels. She held a thin, aluminum Tsubota pearl cigarette case in one hand.

Hellmann opened the backdoor to the police-issue Mazdaspeed6, motioning for her to get inside. Oberfeld got in the driver's seat and Hellmann went up front beside him. As they drove away from the gym, Milinka turned to Hellmann.

"Do you have a cigarette?"

"Ich rauche nicht…"

"Yes you do," she smirked.

"I quit," he informed her.

She flipped open her fancy cigarette case and pulled one out. Hellmann watched her light up and then he said, "I thought you were out of cigarettes…"

"I found one in my purse… would you like one?"

"I told you, I quit," said Hellmann, turning away and staring out the window.

"It won't last," Milinka smirked, and blew a thin line of smoke to the car roof.

They took her to the station and down to a large, antiseptic interview room with soundproof walls and fluorescent lighting, set in the department basement. There were two other men present in the room, and a female stenographer in one corner.

"Ms. Trajkovic, I'm district attorney Boris Becker… I have to inform you this session is being taped…" a slick, gray-haired gentleman addressed her. He moved like a weasel. "Can we get you anything? A cup of coffee, perhaps?"

"No, thank you," Milinka said, moving forward to the center of the interview room where there was a metal folding chair set up in front of a lineup wall.

The station polizeirat, or captain—a fat, grandiloquent man named Jürgen Rommel—held up his hands and said, "Will your attorney be joining us?"

"Ms. Trajkovic has waived her right to an attorney," Hellmann informed the room. The police captain and district attorney seemed quite surprised at this information.

"Why have you waived your right to an attorney?" Boris Becker asked her.

"I have nothing to hide," Milinka said confidently.

She sat down on the interrogation chair and the police inspectors and district attorney sat at two folding desks across from her. They shuffled their papers and twiddled their pens as she flipped her cigarette case open and removed a cigarette.

"It's forbidden to smoke in this building," Polizeirat Rommel informed her.

"What are you going to do? Charge me with smoking," Milinka shot back, and the district attorney cracked a smile.

"Would you tell us the nature of your relationship with Mr. Dejan Vidic?" the police Captain asked her.

Milinka blew a cloud of smoke at her interrogators. She stared straight into the camera on the tripod that was filming the interview.

"I had sex with him for about a year and a half… I liked having sex with Dejan. He knew how to give me pleasure…"

The district attorney gulped and smoothed out his tie. "Did you ever engage in any particular sexual activities together?"

"Such as…?"

"Sadomasochistic activity… any bondage?"

Milinka smiled coyly at the prosecutor. "No, Dede liked to use his hands too much…"

Polizeikommissar Oberfeld interrupted them. "So you weren't living with Dejan Vidic in the weeks prior to his murder?"

Milinka looked straight at him. "No."

"May I ask where your current address is?"

"I live with a friend. She runs a café downtown—the Tante Maja…"

"Ah yes… Ms. Roxanne Saril," said Hellmann, flipping through his notes. "So she's your alibi?"

"If you want to call it that—"

"Did you kill Dejan Vidic!" Polizeirat Rommel questioned her suddenly.

"No." Milinka replied, without missing a beat.

"We uh… found a manuscript in Mr. Vidic's apartment… on his home computer… a novel penned by you, in which you describe the murder of a Serbian drug trafficker in a luxury hotel room by a female escort."

"I like to write," admitted Milinka, removing her shawl and readjusting her hair pin. "But I'd have to be pretty stupid to write a book about killing somebody and then kill that person in the exact same way I described it in my book. I'd be announcing myself as the killer—I'm not stupid, Mr. Rommel."

"We know you're not stupid," DA Muller assured her.

"Do you ever use drugs," Lieutenant Oberfeld asked her.

"Sometimes."

"Did you ever use drugs with Mr. Vidic?"

"Yes."

"Can you be more specific?"

"A little X. Sometimes cocaine… have you ever fucked on cocaine, Captain? It's intense."

The interview room went silent—all four men stared at Milinka as she leaned back in her chair and slowly uncrossed her long, smooth legs, revealing an absence of underwear beneath her short skirt. They caught a tantalizing glimpse of her nakedness before she crossed her legs again

Polizeirat Rommel gulped and reached for his coffee mug.

"Would you like me to take a lie detector test?" Milinka asked them.

A short while later, as they were taking a break, Hauptmeister Hellmann and Kommissar Oberfeld watched Milinka as she smoked and preened behind the two-way mirror.

"She's hiding something," said Hellmann, shaking his head. "She's too confident—"

"It doesn't add up," Oberfeld agreed. "An uneducated

refugee with the IQ and mannerisms of a university graduate… and did you see what she's wearing? Where does she get the money for clothes like that? And that jewelry."

"If she's an escort," said Hellmann, "she must be damn good at it… but what would she be doing with a lowlife like Vidic?"

"Maybe she knows who killed him."

Behind them Polizeirat Rommel was on the phone with the Dutch KLPD. He covered the receiver with his hand and snapped at the pair of them to be quiet. They looked around, wondering what was up…

"Uh-huh… ja, moment bitte…"

Rommel glared at them. "What was the name of the book she was writing?"

Hellmann squinted, "Love… something…"

"Liebe-schmerz," said Oberfeld helpfully.

"Yes, that's it," Hellmann flicked his fingers. "Love Hurts."

The police captain relayed this to the KLPD and then he hung up the phone.

"The Hague is on their way," he informed the detectives. "They say to be very careful with her—she's an ice-cold murderer and a pathological liar… manipulative and highly intelligent… we'll keep her in custody until they get here."

"What's their interest in the case?" Hellmann asked, but his boss ignored him. He had flung on his jacket and now he moved past them to a side-door and reentered the interview room, going face-to-face with the slender Albanian girl named Milinka Trajkovic.

She looked up as he came in, her stenciled eyebrows and bleached hair seeming a grotesque caricature of a Hollywood femme fatale.

"How much longer is this going to take?" she asked Rommel.

"As long as necessary… until you start telling us the truth… Ms. Trammel," he said to her.

Milinka paused, smoke curling up from the cylindrical ash of her cigarette. Then she batted her eyelashes at him and said, "It's Kastel. But you can call me Kathleen."

31

GAMBLING SALON, OBERBILK, DÜSSELDORF

The bulls picked up Janko Konjovic at his Düsseldorf-based Spielothek, where he'd been idling around, selling the occasional tape, and feeding cash into the slot machines all afternoon. He seemed exasperated at their insistence on pursuing him, and he was rude to the inspectors in the car and all the way to the station, threatening them with legal retaliation for their harassment of an innocent and law-abiding citizen, until they took him to a private office and presented officers Perrin and Lambert to him—who confronted him with a statement signed by an anonymous Duisburg resident, explaining, in detail, the existence of the neurochips being marketed under the street name "tapes."

Janko was so stunned at this news that he almost fell off his chair. It was the first time the word had been uttered to him by a member of law enforcement. He tugged nervously at his Pantelic football jersey.

"Who makes the tapes?" Officer Lambert questioned him. Janko looked around the small bureau which was crowded way too close for comfort, with members of the German Kripo, the Europol agents, and some other *Men In Black* lookalikes who didn't seem to belong to the police, but introduced themselves cryptically as being with "a global intelligence network." It was a budding young mobster's worst nightmare.

"I... d... don't know who makes them!" Janko pleaded. "I know very little..."

"Start with what you do know," said Officer Perrin bluntly. "Tell us about Toby..."

"Toby is just a name," Janko explained. "A name for anyone who sells the tapes."

"You mean a tape runner," said of the MIB types. He looked as grim as Tommy Lee Jones. Only this was no actor. Janko could feel the man's penetrating gaze from behind his sunglasses, which he wore even indoors.

"Yes... that's it! A tape runner," affirmed Janko. "Toby is an alias used for any dealer."

"Who else do you deal with?" Officer Lambert asked. "Who is in the ring?"

Janko thought hard about this. If he gave them Darko's name, he might as well throw himself in front of a roller-compactor. He had to give them the name of somebody less dangerous. He settled on his guy in Venlo.

"Nasr," said Janko. "He lives in Venlo. I don't know his last name—he's called 'The Turk', but I believe he's of Algerian descendance. He sells the tapes... that's all I know, really..."

The inspectors noted this. "And this device here? Do you know what this is?" one of the intelligence agents showed him the silvery communicator that had been shipped to them from Hamburg. Janko stared at it dumbly. He shook his head.

"Is that a yes, or a no?"

"I've never seen this before—" Janko responded, and

the intelligence agents, well versed in the art of interrogation, knew that he was telling the truth.

"Do you know a person by the name of Alioune Kebe?" Officer Lambert asked him. "He lives in Duisburg. A white albino."

Janko nodded slowly. Yes. "He's a tape runner."

"Who recruited him?"

"I did."

"And who recruited you?"

"A guy I met in Willich prison told me about the tapes... he put me in contact with Nasr."

"What about Dejan Vidic?"

"He's a runner too," Janko said. "We met on holiday in Belgrade, a year ago. He's been working for me ever since,"

"And Milinka Trajkovic?"

"Who?"

"Milinka Trajkovic" Officer Lambert repeated.

"I don't know who she is," said Janko. "I've told you everything I know... please... you must believe me."

The MIB-types and the Europol agents conversed in low, hush-hush tones, and then one of them opened an attaché case and presented him with a stack of documents to sign. They were sworn statements, and included an oath of secrecy. They explained to him that if he spoke to anybody about the tapes, or about anything else that he had confessed, he would be in violation of his oath and prosecuted to the full extent of the law. The "intelligence" operatives then left, and Janko watched the Europol officers as they were gathering up their things and preparing to leave.

"Well?" he asked one of them.

"Yes?"

"What happens now?"

"Now," said Officer Lambert, checking his watch. "You're free to go—"

Janko stared at them, stupefied. "I'm not being charged with anything?"

"Not to my knowledge," said the man. "It's not our business to prosecute. And as far as the German government is concerned, the tapes don't exist. However, I must advise you, for your future activities, to stick to a more legitimate line of work."

He held out his hand and Janko reluctantly shook it—feeling numb and confused. The Europol agents left the office, and then a sergeant escorted him down to the lobby of the police station and out the front door.

"Would you like us to call you a taxi to take you home?" the cop asked him.

"No," mumbled Janko, still reeling from his encounter. "I'll walk."

"Have a pleasant evening," the cop said, and returned, whistling, into the headquarters.

Janko ambled down the street, walking from Unterbilk all the way back to his borough, while he tried to decide his next move. The Netherlands was dead. After ratting on Nasr, he couldn't possibly expect to do business there again. But Darko had mentioned alternate labs being set up in Germany:

specifically Hamburg and Berlin—he'd have to go to his cousin, inform him that the mystery of the tapes was out. He hoped Darko would interpret his warning as a sign of fidelity. He needed Darko on his side, in case Nasr's boys or anybody up the ladder in The Netherlands came after him.

It was getting dark when he arrived at the Spielothek where his convertible was parked, just a block away from his internet and call shop, and the apartment where he lived.

The night air was cool and fresh, and as he neared his car he overheard a pair of young Kurd hip-hoppers argue in the doorway of a kebab shop.

"...I'm telling you I was in Tony Montana's mansion! I swam in the pool with Michelle Pfeiffer... what a fox!"

"...get out of here! You've been smoking too much zetla again..."

"...it's a once-in-a-lifetime experience! You've got to try it..."

And as Janko passed them by they turned furtively away and started speaking in Kurdish. He rounded the corner and jumped into his convertible, gunning the engine. He fiddled with the radio and settled on a news station.

As he was crossing the cable-suspended bridge over the Rhine River, heading toward the highway that would take him to Duisburg, he heard a report that pricked his interest...

"...in a bizarre case of life imitating fiction... a cinema enthusiast, being questioned for his alleged involvement in a drug-trafficking ring at an underground movie theater, escaped from custody earlier this morning after killing two male officers and one

female officer by drinking their blood… the moviegoer had been
watching a film about vampires at the time of his arrest…"

"What the fuck—" Janko started.

A hand shot out of the backseat shadows, seizing Janko
by his neck—Toby sprung up behind him, sinking his teeth
into his throat, as Janko lost control of the wheel and the car
grated into the bridge's safety barrier, sending sparks flying.

Toby glanced up, his bloodstained mouth and
luminous eyes set in a grimace. He tossed the half-dead Janko
to the side and moved into his seat, taking control of the
vehicle. His clothes were ragged and his ghostly face smeared
with dirt, after having spent a day hiding in the subway and
sewers of Hamburg. He looked over at Janko, who was
moaning from his wounds, eyelids fluttering, staring up at him
half conscious.

"Ah! I feel better already," said Toby, licking his lips
with relish. He reached for the radio and switched stations,
saying, "You don't mind if I look for something a little more…
engaging…"

He settled on a Guns N' Roses cover of "Sympathy for
the Devil," with Axl Rose's raw voice-over set to syncopated
Latin percussions…

> *Please allow me to introduce myself*
> *I'm a man of wealth and taste…*

"Don't be afraid," Toby said, gesturing with sharpened
fingernails to Janko, as he lay there in a limbo between life and

death. "I'm going to give you the choice... I... never had."

He started laughing and drumming his fingers on the wheel as the guitars and drums kicked in and he accelerated Janko's convertible along the bridge where the lights of the city twinkled across the inky black water, and a whole world of possibilities offered themselves to his predatory senses.

32

Bergambacht, South Holland

Still the land of the Reefer, Home of the Weed
Still DJ Isis, Ferry Corsten, Tiësto, n' Erick-E
Still the champagne hustle, hoes doin' their thang
Since I left ain't too much changed… still…

—Soundtrack by Dr. Dre

On a warm and sunny afternoon, two armored transport vans moved up the winding dirt road to the remote farmhouse, carrying with them a platoon of DSI officers—the Special Forces section of the KLPD. The vans crashed through the gate and stopped brusquely in the courtyard, deploying the intervening officers who stacked up in front of the screen door, before smashing it in with a battering ram and tossing in a flashbang to facilitate their intervention.

A second unit used a tactical assault ramp to enter through the mullion windows above the heavy barn door, breaking them in and breaching the upper floor.

The DSI moved quickly through the house, clearing the rooms one by one, the team leader shouting directions to his men as they scoured the vast interior, their tactical rifles slicing and covering all angles.

The house was empty.

When both units had reunited on the ground floor the paramilitary officers lifted the visors on their helmets and looked at their leaders questioningly.

"There's nobody here, sir," one of the men said to the team captain in charge of the operation—Dirk De Bont.

"Either they knew we were coming," said De Bont. "Or we have received some fraudulent information…"

He radioed the mobile crime lab, informing them that it was safe to enter the premises. They arrived ten minutes later, moving in from the nearby village. A crew of six forensic technicians in blue jumpsuits immediately sealed off the property with a line of flexible barrier tape. They then went to work photographing and searching the scene for trace evidence. They ran over the bare and empty rooms with a forensics vacuum. They taped for prints on all possible surfaces. They combed the empty barn, noting the presence of spray adhesives on the walls, where the acoustic soundproofing foam had been fixed. They also found traces of mastic residue on the concrete floor, which led them to believe that the room had been previously tiled.

A blue light search revealed their first piece of tangible evidence. One of the specialists discovered a tiny sliver of transparent film stuck to a bit of the resin. He removed it delicately with a pair of blunt nose tweezers and examined it under a portable CSI magnifier.

"It looks like a bit of tape," the specialist said. Through the powerful lens of his magnifier he could see that the tape was dotted with a galaxy of tiny black specks. He put the find gently into an evidence bag and sealed and labeled it to send to the lab for further inspection.

"Was there a name, or a serial number printed on it?" his superior asked.

"No," said the specialist. "It appears to be a completely blank tape."

EPILOGUE

"This is it," Trinity said to Neo, as they came to room number 1313 of the Lafayette Hotel. "Let me give you one piece of advice—be honest. He knows more than you can imagine."

She pushed open the doors to an antique, mothy suite, where a tall, broad-shouldered black man, his stately figure covered by a shiny, black leather trenchcoat, stood beside the decaying curtains of a French window, looking out somberly at the pouring rain.

Lightning flashed behind him as he turned slowly around to face them.

"At last," he said, his thick, veal-colored lips stretching into an enigmatic smile. His eyes were hidden behind dark round sunglasses with armless frames. He strode toward them, his hands folded behind his back.

"Welcome Neo—as you no doubt have guessed I am Morpheus…"

Keanu Reeves held out his hand to Lawrence Fishburne. "It's an honor to meet you…"

"No—the honor is mine," Morpheus said. "Please, come… sit." He guided Neo to a tufted leather wingback chair, with carved lion's heads on the armrests. An identical chair was set opposite to it. A mahogany round table stood between them, on which reposed a glass of water.

Neo sat down halfway, tense, as Morpheus strode over and shut the hotel room door. He began pacing, his hands folded in front of him.

"I imagine that right now you're feeling a bit like Alice… tumbling down the rabbit hole… hum?" he smiled at Neo.

"You could say that," admitted Keanu Reeves.

"I can see it in your eyes," Lawrence Fishburne affirmed. "You have the look of a man who accepts what he sees because he is expecting to wake up. Ironically—this is not far from the truth… Do you believe in fate, Neo?"

Keanu Reeves looked up. "No."

"Why not?"

"Because I don't like the idea that I'm not in control of my life," Reeves explained.

Morpheus bent over him, "I know exactly what you feel." He sat down on the other wingback and crossed his legs. He fidgeted with a slender silvery box. "Let me tell you why you're here. You're here because you know something. What you know you can't explain…"

Keanu Reeves leaned forward, intrigued.

"But you feel it," Morpheus continued, spinning the box around in his hands. "You've felt it your entire life. There's something wrong with the world. You don't know what it is… but it's there. Like a splinter in your mind—driving you mad. It is this feeling that's brought you to me…" He paused, to allow his words to sink in—then asked, "Do you know what

I'm talking about?"

"The Matrix?" Keanu Reeves questioned.

"Do you want to know what it is?" Morpheus inquired. Reeves nodded affirmatively.

"The Matrix is everywhere. It is all around us. Even now in this very room. You can see it when you look out your window. Or when you turn on your television. You can feel it when you go to work... when you go to chuch... when you pay your taxes. It is the world that has been pulled over your eyes to blind you from the truth."

Keanu Reeves sat forward. "What truth?"

Morpheus bent his imposing figure close to him. "That you are a slave, Neo. Like everyone else you were born into bondage... born into a prison that you cannot smell or taste or touch. A prison for your mind."

He leaned back and exhaled thoughtfully. "Unfortunately no one can be told what the Matrix is," he said, flipping open the box. "You have to see it for yourself."

He set the box down on the table saying, "This is your last chance. After this there can be no turning back."

He unclenched his left hand, revealing a blue cachton. "You take the blue pill, the story ends. You wake up in your bed... and believe whatever you want to believe. You take the red pill... you stay in Wonderland, and I show you how deep the rabbit hole goes."

Keanu Reeves hesitated momentarily and then he reached for Morpheus' right palm. For the red pill.

"Remember," Morpheus cautioned him. "All I'm

offering is the truth. Nothing more."

Reeves took the red pill and put it in his mouth. He reached for the glass of water. Lightning flashed through the window pane as Morpheus smiled at him and he swallowed the pill.

"Follow me," said Morpheus getting up from his seat and moving toward the door.

He led Neo into a room across the hall which was filled with hi-tech computer equipment and steampunk electronic gizmos.

"Apoc are we online?" Morpheus asked the cyber-wizard in charge of running the tracing equipment.

"Almost," Apoc replied.

"Time is always against us," said Morpheus, gesturing to a chair as Apoc removed Neo's coat. "Please take a seat there."

As he sat down, the girl named Trinity began fixing white electrode pads to his arms and neck, wired to a headphone attached to his ear. The others hardwired the modules and drives. Morpheus picked up a telephone receiver and placed it onto a switchboard saying, "The pill you took is part of a trace program. It's designed to disrupt your input–output carrier signal so we can pinpoint your location."

"What does that mean?" Keanu Reeves asked in concern.

"It means buckle your seatbelt Dorothy," said Cypher (Joe Pantoliano of *Memento*), looking up from a futuristic binocular-like apparatus. "Because Kansas… is going bye-bye."

Keanu's eyes darted nervously around the room, as he

breathed deeply. Then he caught his reflection in an old, broken, oval-shaped rococo mirror next to him, and watched as the glass began to repair itself, the cracks running together and reforming into a smooth shimmering surface.

"Did you—" Neo began, looking around him. He reached over and touched his fingers to the mirror and they sank into it, sending concentric ripples outwards—he pulled his fingers back out and the mirror stretched like elastic.

Morpheus came up behind him. "Have you ever had a dream Neo, that you were so sure was real?"

Reeves unplugged his fingers and the liquid glass of the mirror expanded and contracted.

"What if you were unable to wake from that dream," Morpheus continued. "How would you know the difference between the dream world and the real world?"

Keanu Reeves stared at his hand, as the mercury-colored liquid of the mirror began to melt like candlewax around his fingers.

"This can't be…"

"Be what—be real?" Morpheus asked.

The mirror wax crawled up his arm, as he squirmed in his seat.

"It's going into replication," said Trinity.

"Apoc?" Morpheus asked the techie at the computer monitors. He was an Italian–German with moussed blonde hair, a scruffy goatee and thin mustache that did little to disguise his slightly feminine features.

"Still nothing…" Apoc replied.

"It's cold! It's cold…" Keanu gasped, shivering, as the liquid worked its way up his body, surrounding his neck and climbing higher.

Morpheus pulled out a sleek cell phone and dialed a number saying, "Tank—we're going to need a signal soon."

"We've got a fibrillation," said Trinity, watching a bunch of phosphorous lines shoot across Neo's vital signs monitor.

"Apoc, location…" insisted Morpheus.

"Targeting, almost there," Apoc responded, clenching a joystick control as a bright green geometrical pattern bloomed on his monitor.

Keanu Reeves was shaking, his body contorted, and his mouth wide open and tetanized as the mirror-wax crawled up the sides of his head.

"He's going into arrest!" Trinity warned them.

"Lock! I've got him!" exclaimed Apoc.

"Now, Tank… now!" Morpheus instructed the person listening in on the cell.

Keanu Reeves bent his head back and screamed as the mercury-liquid poured into his mouth, covering all of his inner cavities with a glossy silver sheen, and his voice blended with a grating electronic signal like a fax machine.

His eyes shot open and he was no longer in the Matrix, but in a large, brightly-lit workshop in a Parisian warehouse, with Leonardo DiCaprio, aka Dominic Cobb, and Joseph Gordon-Levitt. He was breathing hard, and Arthur (Gordon-

Levitt) came over to him and unplugged a tube from his arm—the tube was connected to a titanium-alloy briefcase filled with wires and nanocomposite cylinders. A LED timer display glowed next to an injection activation trigger for Somnacin release. Additional vials of the dream-inducing product were stored in the case.

"It's OK—" Arthur said, pushing on a spool which collected the unplugged IV.

"Why couldn't I wake?" Keanu asked him.

"The only way to wake from inside the dream is to die," Arthur bluntly informed him.

Leonardo DiCaprio woke up, sprawled in a lawn chair across the room. He unplugged his own IV tube, stood up and said, "He's going to need a totem."

"...A what?" Keanu Reeves blinked.

"Some kind of personal item—a small object that you can always carry with you. That nobody but you knows... kinda like this..."

He took a pewter spinning top from the pocket of his tan linen shirt. He spun it across the floor and said, "No one else can touch it. Only you must know its exact size and weight—"

Keanu Reeves watched as the spinning top began to wobble. "Why?"

"So you'll know you're in your own dream and not someone else's," explained DiCaprio. He stopped the spinning totem just before it toppled over and he put it back in his pocket.

"That hotel we were in… where you met this man named Morpheus—was it a memory, or imagined?" DiCaprio asked him.

"It was a reconstruction of a Warner Brothers movie set," said Keanu. "For a science-fiction film I starred in… back in 1999. *The Matrix*… Morpheus was my co-star."

DiCaprio shook his head seriously. "Never recreate places from your memory. Always build something new."

"How come?"

"Because building dreams out of your own memories is the surest way to lose your grip on what's real and what's a dream…"

"Did that happen to you?"

DiCaprio cast him a sharp look. "We're talking about you… not me."

A shrill beeping sound interrupted them. Joseph Gordon-Levitt opened the extractor -briefcase and pulled out a silvery, oval-shaped device.

"Is that the communicator?" Keanu asked him.

Gordon-Levitt nodded and checked the incoming message on the LED screen. He passed it to Keanu saying, "It's for you—"

Keanu Reeves took the communicator and read the blinking message:

"TAPEWORLD TRIAL ENDING…"

"Damn," he said, "And I was just starting to enjoy

this... sorry Cobb."

He looked up and Leonardo DiCaprio was frozen in front of him, his goateed mouth hanging half-open as if he were about to speak. There was a loud CRACK! And the entire studio splintered in half and the colonnades supporting the warehouse ceiling collapsed into dust. A plastic model of the Penrose stairs paradox, set on a workshop table, shattered into a thousand tiny flakes.

The décor revolved 360 degrees, spinning faster and faster, like Cobb's totem, Keanu Reeves closed his eyes as a nauseating dizziness overtook him and the entire tapeworld building imploded with a deafening roar.

Keanu Reeves woke up on a bamboo lounge chair, in front of the swimming pool outside his Hollywood Hills mansion. He blinked, accustoming himself to the dazzling LA sunlight. His head was reeling after a trip down memory lane and into the Matrix. Then that had led to the summer blockbuster *Inception*—he still couldn't believe what he had seen and experienced.

"How do you feel?" Darko asked him, smiling mischievously.

"Whoa, dude!" stammered Keanu, trying to steady himself. "Let me get this straight... I came out of the virtual reality generated by the Matrix... which was in fact a dream engineered by me and Dominic Cobb in *Inception*, which was actually a tapeworld version of *Inception*."

"And here you are," beamed Darko. "From one reality

to another. So what do you think about the tape?"

"Excellent… slightly overwhelming, but genius!"

"Worth the price tag?"

"Every penny of it…"

"Just remember, we are having them tailor-made now… well, for those who can afford it," Darko chuckled. "So anything you want… you tell us, and we'll design it for you. Like in *Inception*. You get to be the architect of your dreams."

Keanu shook his head, still struggling to fathom the tapeworld. "It was so werid. In *The Matrix*, I had no idea that it was a movie I had starred in. I thought I was really Neo."

"You just send us a message—for whatever you want… anytime," said Darko, handing Keanu a communicator. He shook hands with the Hollywood star and said, "Have a great afternoon… and thanks for the autograph… Mia will be pleased."

"Don't mention it," said Keanu. "I should be thanking you."

Darko laughed and patted him on the shoulder. His pager beeped and he checked it and said, "Oops, I really got to run. Tinseltown is going to be the end of me! I cannot get a moment's peace. Oh well, business is business and one mustn't complain. Maybe I see you at Ashton Kutcher's party."

"Yeah, dude, maybe." said Keanu, his fingers already opening the petri case on his lap, where two more thousand-dollar copies of *The Matrix/Inception* tape were floating in the saline fluid. He debated taking one right away, or saving them both until after dinner. He didn't want to get too addicted—

he knew how quickly the tapes were eating up the savings of some of his Hollywood confreres. *Hadn't Stephen Baldwin just filed for bankruptcy and been forced to auction his Rockland County home?*

The man's got no self-control, Keanu reassured himself, picking up one of the floating tapes. *I can control myself... and besides... one little tape won't hurt.*

He stuck the full *Matrix/Inception* tape on his tongue, lay back in his lounge chair and relaxed, looking up at the lazy clouds drifting by in a stark blue sky.

And watched as the clouds turned from white to a phosphorous green, and began to drift and merge together to form a blinking cursor. And then the familiar block print on a computer screen:

Wake up, Neo...

Also Available From Spore Press

LYKAIA
by Sharon Van Orman

"I'm afraid I won't be able to properly express my fascination with *LYKAIA*. It was such an awesome read I would definitely recommend it to all who'd love to spend some quality time with a really well-written book.

The main character, forensic pathologist Sophia Katsaros gets a phone call from Greece and finds out that her brothers have been missing for two months. She goes there to start an investigation of her own that might not end well for her."

- Amazon Review

WAITING IN THE SILENCE
by Rosalyn W. Berne

"Praise is due for this debut novel set in post-apocalyptic Nantucket in the USA, The complexity is dynamic between nano-enhanced humans who have access to universal knowledge and the independents whose access is limited. Oriana, our heroine, dangles between them, sometimes condemned and sometimes praised. The virtual mysterious intelligence, which rules the community, must control Oriana for she is the source of fertility for many barren women. Suspense. Drama. And the ending is a delightful surprise."

- Louise Meriwether, author, "Daddy

Was A Number Runner"

SEASON OF THE DEAD
by Lucia Adams, Paul Freeman,
Gerald Johnston, & Sharon Van Orman

"It is said that unto everything there is a season...these are the stories of a group of survivors during the season of the dead."

Four individuals fight to survive as the zombie apocalypse crashes over the world in a wave of terror and destruction. Color, creed, and social standing mean nothing as the virus infects millions across the planet.

Sharon: a zoologist from Nebraska, USA, has worked with the virus, and has seen the effects on the human mind. She knows more about the virus than nearly anybody alive, and far more than she wants to. Gerry: from Ontario, Canada, he gets his first taste of the virus from inside a prison cell. Locked up after an anti-government riot, his prison guard transforms before his eyes into a flesh craving zombie. Lucia: a chemist from Pittsburgh, USA, flees from a furry convention dressed as a giant squirrel, and escapes from the city in a Fed-Ex van. She's a girl who knows when to run and when to fight. Paul: thinks he can sit out the apocalypse in his apartment block in Dublin, Ireland, until the virus comes to visit, bursting his bubble and leaving him with no choice but to face reality or perish.

All four begin perilous journeys in mind and body as they face daily trials to survive: Four threads, four different parts of the world, one apocalypse!

www.ingramcontent.com/pod-product-compliance
Lightning Source LLC
Chambersburg PA
CBHW020823030726

47496CB00001B/67